Praise for *Ma*
Herdsfol

"Imaginative, funny, and smartly crafted, *Mailaise* is a can't put down read. If you thought the FBI had solved the Amerithrax investigation, think again!"

—Greg Jacobs
Producer of the major motion picture *Contagion* (2011)

"Original and compelling, from an expert who was in the forefront of responding to the real anthrax attacks. Weiss belongs to that rarest of species who can write a smart narrative with a rich cast of characters and ingenious plot twists -- and the authenticity that can come only from someone who has really been there."

—Stephen S. Morse, PhD
Professor, Columbia University Mailman
School of Public Health & author of *Emerging Viruses*

"A chillingly realistic techo-thriller page-turner."

—Allen Wyler, Vice President of Awards,
International Thriller Writers &
Author of *CHOP SHOP* (April, 2012)

"Don Weiss is a public health insider who knows the workings of bioterror investigations inside and out. *Mailaise* offers a compelling mix of suspense, wit, and authentic detective work."

—Neal L. Cohen, MD
New York City Commissioner of Health, 1998-2002

"Finally, a plain thinking, straight talking disease detective with a Colombo-like ease and a Berton Roueche knack for solving medical mysteries. Dr. Weiss has created a medical mystery crime genre for readers of the likes of Robert Ludlum and Robert Parker. We can only hope this is the first of many potboilers to come."

—Sandra Mullin
Former Director of Communications,
New York City Department of Health

"Although fictional, Weiss' intrepid epidemiologist-detective Mackey's resolution to the mystery of the anthrax mailings in 2001 raises a plausible alternative to anyone dissatisfied with the conclusion of the real-life investigation. This engaging page-turner is a must for epidemiologists, detectives and anyone interested in the anthrax story or criminal investigation."

—Jim Hadler, MD, MPH
Former Connecticut State Epidemiologist
& member of the 2001 Anthrax Investigation Team

MAILAISE

A novel

Don Weiss

To Lindsey,
With thanks for
the inspiration &
perspiration.

Don

Grateful acknowledgement for permission to reprint lyrics from the following:
"The World Spins Madly on," written by Deb Talan and Steve Tannen; published by Steve Tannen Music/Deb Talan Music © 2005.
"Absence of Your Company," written by Kim Richey; published by Red Equals Luck/Chrysalis Music Limited © 2007.
"Ghost," Written by Peter Bradley Adams; published by PLOV Music © 2003.

First edition October 2011

Cover illustration by Tim Sinclair

ISBN-13: 978-1466471450
ISBN-10: 146647145X

For Irma and Jules,
without whom I would not have arrived here

Mailaise

.| Prologue |.

Two punctuation marks appeared on the hill overlooking the reflecting pool of the Lincoln Memorial. The exclamation point wore a wool coat over silk pajamas, exposing gnocchi calves sunk into pesto boots. On his head sat a fedora adorned with a red feather. Beside him, hunched and pawing at the light snow, shivered a question mark. His baseball cap, worn leather jacket and blue jeans impotent against the chill. Almost two score earlier the Reverend Dr. Martin Luther King shared his vision for America mere steps from where they stood.

On this Inauguration Day morning such dreams were far from their minds. The question mark shifted from one foot to the other, his attention alternating between the footpath and the dawn shadows. His curriculum vitae read more like a curriculum muerte, including stints with the Air Force Special Operations Command and the CIA. Had he a W-2 it would list Cheyenne Global Security as his employer.

Exclamation point watched the sun elbow its way into an overcast sky. "The Russians made tons of anthrax in the 1970s and 1980s, where did it all go?"

"Don't know," question mark said.

"Find it before someone else does."

Question mark nodded assent, but exclamation point was already sliding down the hill to an idling car. He turned eastward his gaze falling upon the Washington Monument. The granite obelisk resembled a broadsword thrust triumphantly at the heavens. Combat was his livelihood but against whom this call to arms was he could not fathom.

.| 1 |.

The only thing worse would be to be seated between an insomniac name-dropper and a latter-day Elvis impersonator. Wedged between the window and a long-limbed neighbor, Mackey Dunn considered asking to switch seats, but the woman occupying the aisle seat was busy passing a crying toddler to her husband in the middle section. Mackey's claustrophobia and acrophobia would have to take a back seat to a growing elbow-a-phobia.

The plane banked left in its climb to cruising altitude. The lakes of Minnesota came into view and the skyline of Minneapolis grew smaller. He closed his eyes and swallowed hard to adjust the pressure in his ears. The Carl Hiaasen paperback he bought at the airport would remain nestled in the seat pocket undisturbed. He knew better than to think his journey would be tranquil. The words of Dan Fogelberg's "Once Upon a Time," were the first to pop into his head[1]. She was never far from his mind.

The seatbelt sign chimed off. Elbows-and-knees guy yawed dangerously toward sleep while the flight attendant loitered several minutes away with the service cart. Mackey's palms grew moist as his cerebral jukebox spun but got stuck on a scratch, repeating a line from "Your Bright Baby Blues," by Jackson Browne[2]. It was time to leave Alaska but Mackey could no more outrun his sorrow than forget his past.

Mackey checked for the attendant. She was reciting

the beverage menu for a blue-haired woman two rows ahead. Noting an increase in pulse and respiratory rate, he dug into the fob pocket of his jeans for a football-shaped blue pill. It began to dissolve in his palm, so he popped the Xanax into his mouth and waited.

"Ginger ale, little ice," he told the attendant before she could hand him a napkin. He gulped the pill like a pelican swallowing a beakful of anchovies with seawater. Mackey leaned back and took several deep breaths.

Mackey dozed fitfully. A cold shiver roused him so he checked the overhead fan. It was off. He was thrilled to be leaving Alaska though it filled him with anxiety, remorse, fear and apprehension. But could he tally happiness on the positive side of the ledger? Happiness was as fleeting as the adrenaline rush from hitting a home run and as fickle as finding a ripe, juicy peach in a bushel of mealy ones. And try as he might to savor a happy moment, it always passed too quickly. While benzodiazepine molecules serenely stroked the wrist of his anxiety, in another part of Mackey's brain a sparring match was entering round nine. Guilt had relentlessly pounded his heart against the ropes. But desire had been busy strategizing and now attempted escape. What would be the collateral damage?

The job awaiting Dr. MacPherson Alistair Dunn—Mackey to everyone who knew him— was with the New York City Department of Health. He was to join a team of epidemiologists nicknamed "disease detectives." Mackey distracted his ruminative mind with the challenges that lay ahead. An international economic and cultural hub, New York City had no shortage of disease outbreaks and fascinating cases. From hundreds of cases of imported malaria and typhoid fever to annual epidemics of norovirus and iatrogenic outbreaks of hepatitis, disease arrived by plane, boat, and hand. The disease detectives investigated cases of brucellosis, tularemia, Q fever, bubonic plague and botulism as a matter of routine. With so many diseases you might think the Big Apple was rotting to the core, but despite a population of more than 8 million the work of the disease detectives went mostly unnoticed. His future boss, Dr. Marci Layton, told Mackey during his interview that the one thing she had learned in her ten-plus years on the job was to expect the unexpected.

The day he was slated to begin his new job was the fifth anniversary of the destruction of the World Trade Center towers. But Mackey was too preoccupied with his past and in awe of the adventure that lay before him to allow that fact to invade his thoughts.

Mackey had rented a three-room railroad flat in Morningside Heights, the only part of New York he knew. Leaning against a pillar in the LaGuardia baggage terminal, he waited until the only bag left circling the carousel was his. He hailed a cab to Harlem where he met his new landlord who handed him a formidable set of keys, explained the tenement rules and when garbage pick-up was. What meager possessions Mackey owned were sitting in a warehouse in Canada awaiting a truck for the next leg of their journey east. Having returned his CDC-issued cell phone he set out to explore his new neighborhood while searching for a working payphone.

"Marci? It's Mackey. I'm calling to let you know I've arrived in New York. I'm looking forward to reporting to work tomorrow."

"Oh, hi, Mackey. Something has come up. The Mayor has requested an all-agency PEG."

The way Marci said PEG made it sound like something deliberately placed to impede one's way and not an expertly hurled baseball. Whatever it was, it didn't sound encouraging. He missed the next thing she said, something about decreased revenue projections and budget cuts.

"It stands for Plan to Eliminate the Gap. The bottom line is we are in a hiring freeze and your paperwork is stuck downtown."

"Is there anything I can do?" Mackey inquired, a twinge of panic constricting his throat. He was on the CDC's payroll until his vacation time ran out, but the move had taken a bite out of his measly savings and there was an unrelenting siphon draining his cash flow.

"I'll make some calls. See if I can get you prioritized. With the meningococcal outbreak we are dealing with I should be able to wield a little clout. Sit tight. See New York City. Enjoy the spectacular fall weather. In all my years here I've never seen this take more than a couple months to resolve. Except that one time." Marci hung up.

Mackey dropped the phone in its cradle and slumped against the kiosk wall. "A couple of months," he mumbled. Sitting tight was not something Mackey Dunn was good at doing.

.| 2 |.

Despite his disdain for tourist activities, Mackey succumbed. He climbed the 1,860 steps up to the Empire State building's observation deck but stood clear of the railing. He threw a salute to the Statue of Liberty, whose torch was closed still for security reasons, as he ferried to Ellis Island where he searched the exhibits for the names of his Scottish ancestors. He perused every museum on Museum Mile and several that weren't. He took the D subway train to Coney Island, the ferry to Governor's Island, the tram to Roosevelt Island, and the bus to City Island. He walked the Bronx and Central Park Zoos and saw *Zoo Story* on Broadway. He rented a bike and rode to Prospect Park, watched people fish in Pelham Bay Park, took in the dizzying array of performers in Washington Square Park, and played pick-up softball in Central Park with a group of old-timers who called themselves Softball for the Love of It. He fielded grounders on the dirt infield and discussed baseball as a metaphor with a seventy-five-year-old first basemen despite the man being a devout Yankee fan.

Mackey drew the line at the Circle Line cruise. But he did learn why the Bronx was up and the Battery was down. Where in Staten Island all of the city's trash went. Which hole in the ground took him to the Cloisters and which led to Little Italy. What the blue *C* on the cliffs of the Bronx stands for. That Brooklyn is the most populous borough, and that there are three Chinatowns in New York City: a sprawling multinational one in Queens, another in Brooklyn, and the famous one near his hopefully soon-to-be office in downtown Manhattan.

New York was a helluva town, but he was sure as hell bored. He stopped calling Marci daily for updates; his dialing fingers numb from the hiring freeze.

On rainy days when he was a kid and trapped indoors, Mackey's restlessness found trouble. Much to his father's consternation, Mackey enjoyed taking things apart. It started small with watches. As he got older he graduated to power tools and appliances. Failing to put them back together he'd claim that they had already broken before he tinkered with them. But since his father never used them all that much no one knew for sure. Using the parts he couldn't fit back into the disassembled gadgets, he built Frankenstein-like hybrids. The first transformers he boasted to unimpressed friends.

In what would become a recurring dream, sixth-grader Mackey wins first prize at the science fair for a robot capable of human emotion. After receiving the prize, the robot goes unexpectedly missing. He tries searching for it but his legs move as if they are stuck in thigh-deep, quick-setting cement. To make matters worse, all the doors are locked and he can't remember in which room he had last left his robot. The fair closes, the lights shut off, and buses pull out of the drive leaving him all alone.

For three days Mackey didn't leave his apartment. It was a peculiar thing, his fits of immobility. Some species of sharks are unable to circulate water through their gills and need to swim in order to avoid suffocation. Mackey too needed to remain in motion to breathe. This inertial mood began like all the others—with an invasion of self-doubt no larger than a pinprick. It could be triggered by a random sight, sound, or scent that dredged up some briny memory. The hole, enlarging behind the force of compressed guilt, would rip a gash into his life raft. If he could rationalize a patch he'd spin roughly into a panic attack. If not, he'd sink ever deeper, becoming part of the coral reef.

The physician in him tried to understand this catatonia in terms of brain physiology. As a medical student he once came across a man trying to cross the street to a post office. The man stood stiffly with his car door open. He was bent slightly at the waist with arms trembling and a face filling with confusion. Mackey recognized the symptoms from his tour in the neurology clinic; it was Parkinson's disease. He crossed the street, grabbing a 2 x 4 from a construction dumpster. He laid the stud before the man's feet to the alarm of passersby who must have thought him the vilest of muggers. The man stepped over it and shuffled across the street bobbing his head as he went. While the disease had robbed him of the neurotransmitter to initiate locomotion, the act of stepping over an obstruction was curiously left intact.

Not even a 2-by-4 to the head could knock him from an inertial mood. In the darkness of his still empty apartment, while staring at its walls for hours, another panic attack squeezed the air from the very last alveolar sac. He flashbacked to a recurring scene: slipping home in the early morning hours after a night of poker with his buddies. She had waited up for him but had fallen asleep on the sofa. Self-loathing plunged Mackey into the cul-de-sac of the abyss until, unable to sink any farther, he tossed and turned his way back to the surface.

The next morning, Mackey popped out of bed like toaster pastry. It was the day he was supposed to begin his new job and Marci was giving a lecture at the New York Academy of Medicine on emergency response. He hoped she might have an update on the hiring freeze.

He walked across Central Park to the Academy's 5th Avenue headquarters and slid silently into a seat in the last row of the auditorium. The lights were already dim.

On the screen was a bar chart showing the number of terrorism attacks across the world over the last twenty years. After declining during the 1990s, the number of events increased in 2000 and again in 2001. Marci next showed the exoskeleton remains of the World Trade Center towers and explained how the attacks had provoked in public officials concerns over a multi-pronged attack with the next wave including a biologic agent

Six agents were on the category A list of bioweapons: anthrax, botulism, plague, smallpox, tularemia, and viral hemorrhagic fever viruses like Ebola. Though anthrax was naturally found in soil it didn't normally pose much of a threat to human health. That is unless weaponized. The Russians had converted many of the category A list agents into bioweapons and amassed immense stockpiles. The political and economic instability of the former republics of the Soviet Union cast doubt on their safekeeping. The proximity of Muslim extremists to Soviet bioweaponry brought to mind an unattended candy store a mere ball toss away from a playground.

"An aerosol release of weaponized anthrax could infect hundreds of thousands of New Yorkers," Marci continued. "Anthrax spores are quite resistant to heat, ultraviolet radiation, and many disinfectants. A single spore or small cluster is the perfect size to penetrate deep into the lungs."

Mackey was with the CDC's Arctic Investigations Program in Alaska when the anthrax outbreak happened. He was given the ten-pound *Textbook of Military Medicine* and told to "familiarize" himself with its contents. It was definitely more entertaining to listen to Marci. The audience, seemingly unfazed by the implications, nevertheless remained sutured to their seats.

"Once spores reach the small airways of the lungs they are taken up by macrophages, the beat cops of the immune system. While some spores are destroyed, others survive, multiply, and produce toxins."

Mackey envisioned a sequel to the movie *Outbreak.* He pictured Dustin Hoffman behind a desk in a sea of research papers taking a frantic call from Morgan Freeman who is now retired from the military and the newly elected mayor of New York City. Drug and vaccine resistant anthrax is loose in the city.

"Initial symptoms are nonspecific and are often confused with influenza. Fever, malaise, fatigue, and muscle aches may be followed by a brief period of improvement. Shortness of breath, chest pain, and respiratory distress soon follow. Once the second phase begins there is little that can be done," Marci said.

Mayor Ford, the Morgan Freeman character, calls in the National Guard to lock down the city. Although anthrax cannot be transmitted from person to person no one is allowed to enter or leave the city in order to contain the chaos. Mobs roam the streets in search of antibiotics. Drug stores are raided and pharmacists are shot dead behind their counters. A black market for cipro emerges with pills going for $500 a piece.

"The toxins produce bleeding in the chest cavity. The anthrax bacteria invade the blood stream and seed the brain and distant organs. Death due to cardiopulmonary collapse occurs in nearly 100 percent of victims," Marci continued.

The morgue is overwhelmed. Bodies lie where they've fallen in the streets, in subway cars, and on abandoned buses. Through the death shroud a helicopter lands on the roof of the United Nations building, the last remaining bastion of civilization in the lawless city. Hoffman steps off and he's carrying a cooler. Inside is an antidote and new vaccine with enough supplies to curtail the outbreak and save the city. Mackey didn't buy into fairy-tale endings.

A woman near the front raised her hand. "Did surveillance systems detect the anthrax outbreak?"

"No, they didn't. We were looking for the more-serious lung infection, not the skin variety. That's a good segue to the next part of my talk."

New York had eight of the twenty-two cases of anthrax that occurred in the fall of 2001, all but one was the less-serious skin variety. The pattern of cases indicated that letters containing anthrax spores were mailed to American Media Inc., NBC, CBS, ABC, and the *New York Post*. Health Department teams were dispatched to each site. Mackey didn't see how the disease detectives and CDC conducted all the investigations; it was tantamount to one team playing four simultaneous baseball games or Bobby Fischer playing a chess simul.

"The massive effort included testing the subway system for spores. The results were announced in a news conference by the heath commissioner who quipped, 'We didn't find any anthrax, but conclude that the NYC subway system is not a sterile environment.'"

Marci paused to catch her breath and to allow the laughter in the auditorium to subside. "All told, five people died. The FBI considers this a case of mass murder and has not yet made an arrest."

A small crowd encircled Marci at the podium. Mackey waited until the last graduate student looking for an internship had dispersed. She waved him down and they exited to the street together.

"What did you think?"

"I think I need to start working," Mackey replied.

"I meant about the talk."

"Curious."

"How so?"

"That all the anthrax cases had in common the prodrome of malaise."

"Yes, I guess that's right. Could be toxin induced. Sorry, about the hiring mess. I tried to move things along but it is beyond the agency. All hiring packages in the city are being held, Mayor's orders. Are you okay financially?"

"Technically I am still on leave from the CDC. I think I have another three weeks of vacation time left." He thought better of telling Marci that his meager savings were shouldering a debt. "The boredom on the other hand … hey, do you know where the FBI anthrax investigation stands? There was that one guy who was in the papers several years back, the one who went to medical school in Zimbabwe. He doesn't seem to be a suspect anymore."

"When it comes to the FBI, I don't know any more than the average citizen. Probably less, with how rarely I read the paper or watch the news."

"Oh. I thought you mentioned a good working relationship with one of the agents involved in the New York investigation?"

"You mean Henry Karros. Sure, we go way back. Great guy. If not for him, I don't know how I would have made it through that fall. We happen to be meeting tonight to reminisce over margaritas if you'd like to meet him."

"Think he'll tell me the status of the investigation?"

"Probably not. He might not know himself. Hank retired a couple of years ago. But you should come. We'll be at Tres Bocas, Una Voz at eight o'clock. It's on Greenwich St. near Warren."

. . .

The crowd at Tres Bocas, Una Voz swarmed like a rugby scrum and surpassed the decibel level of West Broadway traffic. The patrons were a mix of Gordon Gekko wannabees and plunging v-necked, overly perfumed city hall aides. Mackey didn't see Marci when he entered and was about to take his chances at the bar when a meaty hand waved to him from a table in the back. A short, barrel-chested man with pure white hair extended a hand across the table to greet him.

"Dr. Dunn, I presume? I'm Henry Karros, call me Hank."

"How did you know who I was?"

"I used to be in the FBI. And Marci emailed that you might be joining us." He motioned toward the gauntlet Mackey had navigated. "You weren't hard to pick out. Grab a seat. Have a margarita. I took the liberty of ordering some appetizers."

An empty margarita glass, a bowl of greasy chips, and a half-filled stone vessel of guacamole formed a triangle around the ex-agent. He seemed content.

"Pleased to meet you Hank, call me Mackey and I'll have a beer." Hank waved to a frazzled-looking waitress.

"Marci tells me you've been living in Alaska?"

"Yes, Anchorage."

"I was up that way years ago. I went fishing with a buddy of mine at a place called Brooks Camp on Naknek Lake. Know where that is?"

"Sure do. A hop, skip, and a jump south of Anchorage on the Katmai Peninsula. Superb place to see grizzly bears."

"What were you doing way up there?" Hank asked.

"I was with the CDC's Arctic Investigations Program. We worked with indigenous populations to reduce infectious diseases within their communities. They have a lot of problems with encapsulated organisms and antibiotic resistance." A ditty he often recited when working long hours above the Arctic Circle popped into his head.

When your fingers are numb,
and there's no sun,
how do you conduct
an epidemiologic investigation?

Hank's eyes glazed over.

"The CDC offered me medical school loan repayment in exchange for a two-year commitment. It was hard to refuse. I stayed a few more years."

"Uh-huh." They were getting low on guacamole, so Hank hoisted the bowl to get the attention of the waitress.

"Need another beer?"

"No thanks, still working on this one. Do you do much fishing?"

"Nah, since I retired from the bureau I've been too busy. Go figure."

"Marci told me you were a key player in the anthrax investigation."

"She's too kind. I did my job. Those were certainly crazy times."

"Hey, what do you hear about the current status of the Amerithrax investigation?"

Mackey's question was met with a narrowed-eyed glare. "I'd have to be a lot more drunk to tell you if I knew."

Marci and Dr. Joel Ackelsberg, another disease detective, arrived. Hugs were exchanged and more margaritas ordered. Ackelsberg was the bureau's bioterrorism readiness coordinator and had been through 9/11 and the anthrax attacks with Marci and Hank. He wore a tweed jacket, a brioche too small for his frame, and a mustache in dire need of a trim. They first met when Mackey had come to New York to interview for the job.

"Cheers, Dr. Dunn, you've arrived! What have you been doing with yourself?" Ackelsberg asked.

"You are aware of the hiring freeze?"

Ackelsberg nodded over the top of a menu.

"I've been sightseeing."

"Have you been to the Bronx Zoo? My kids love it there." Without waiting for a reply, he turned to Hank, "You old coyote, what the hell have you been up to?"

"Mostly trying to stay out of my wife's way. She swore that if I took early retirement she'd kill me if I hung around the house and was underfoot. So, I've been busy taking inventory."

"Huh?" Marci said.

"Flowers, shrubs, mulch, that kind of stuff. I took a part time job at a home and garden center; now I'm practically running the place."

Marci, Ackelsberg, and Hank began chatting about the friends they knew and updated transitions. Mackey leaned out of the crossfire and into the faux wood paneling. When the conversation wound around to the events of 2001, Mackey reinserted an ear. Hank and Marci were recalling a white-knuckle ride they took to investigate a white powder incident on October 8, 2001.

"Turned out to be another hoax," Marci said, "but it was later that night that the first NBC case called me to say that she was concerned she had anthrax. I never did figure out how she got my cell number." Marci smiled accusingly at Hank who had a mouthful of chips and guacamole.

"I gave it to her," Hank said after a swig of margarita. "She had my number from when we tested the envelope and called me that night quoting all this medical stuff she read on the Internet. You know that medical stuff puts me to sleep. I couldn't answer her questions and told her she'd be better off speaking with the expert."

"It turned out two threat envelopes arrived at NBC," Ackelsberg said for Mackey's benefit. "The first envelope was negative for *Bacillus anthracis* spores."

"We learned that NBC got lots of crazy letters, some with powder or other things inside," Marci added. "The one the patient recalled was from September 25th. It was the first one tested but the second to arrive."

"Then all hell broke loose. The Postal Service was paralyzed and the US economy stalled," Ackelsberg said.

"October was crazy for both us and the CDC, especially the 12th," Marci said. "Not only did we mobilize to investigate the situation at NBC, including providing prophylaxis, but we heard about the cases at ABC, CBS and the *New York Post* as well as a hoax letter at *The New York Times*."

"It was the day the world changed," Ackelsberg said.

"One positive thing came of it," Marci said, "We got federal funding to be better prepared and able to handle emergencies. It is how we are able to hire you, Mackey."

"That remains to be seen," Mackey said sounding more edgy than he intended.

More tequila, guacamole and salsa flowed, mostly into Hank's mouth. They talked about upcoming drills and mock scenarios that Mackey couldn't get into having no role and more importantly no job yet. At nine-thirty, Ackelsberg was reaching for his coat.

"Gotta catch the train, see if the little ones are in bed." Marci followed suit.

They tossed twenties onto the table.

"Doesn't it bother you that the FBI has not apprehended the perpetrator and doesn't even have a prime suspect after five years?" Mackey said to no one in particular.

Ackelsberg shrugged. "Of course it does. But I'm more concerned about what our enemies abroad have in store for us. They'll catch this domestic wacko," he said.

Hank cleared his throat and placed a fatherly arm on Mackey's shoulder. "Rumor is that there's a suspect. The bureau is being careful this time. No more of that 'person of interest' crap. You likely won't hear anything until there is sufficient evidence to bring charges."

Marci rolled her eyes. Hank reached into the pocket of his suit jacket, withdrew a pen, and an old business card. He scribbled on the back and handed it to Mackey.

"Here's the main number for the NYC field office. Special Agent Chen was a rookie back in 2001. You could try asking her about the current status of the investigation."

.| 3 |.

With pomp in his step and disregard for his circumstances, Mackey trekked the next morning to Bryant Park toting his laptop to avail himself of the free Wi-Fi. He searched for anthrax news posts, websites devoted to the investigation, and medical journal articles. While in Alaska he had followed the investigation with keen interest and even volunteered for deployment. But this was different. Alaska seemed like another country then and now, in the city that had the largest outbreak, he wanted to believe that somewhere among the millions of words amassed on the outbreak hid clues overlooked at the time. A tedious and time-consuming task, but then time was a commodity he had in abundance. When his laptop power ran low he ducked into the New York Public Library Humanities and Social Sciences branch, nodding to the lions as he bounded up the stairs for a power charge and a library card.

He picked up the evidence trail of the first anthrax case, a sixty-three-year-old South Florida photo editor for the *Sun*, a tabloid of the American Media, Inc (AMI); the parent company of *The National Enquirer*. A natural exposure while hiking was initially considered. However, when two mailroom workers from AMI showed evidence of anthrax, one quite ill and the other with only spores in her nose, bioterrorism was undeniable.

September in New York City featured temperatures in the seventies and blue marble skies. Living again on the East Coast stirred bittersweet memories. Back when he played in every recreation baseball league he could find or was working five twelve-hour emergency-department shifts in a row, Mackey felt invulnerable. That all changed ten years ago. He had both feet firmly on the lid of the trunk restraining *those* memories.

The sun filtering through the trees created shadows of leaves and stems on the pad in his lap. His grip relaxed and the pad fell, jolting him awake. Bryant Park had filled with tourists, but no one noticed Mackey's gaffe. The crowds would take some getting used to. In Alaska, Mackey could run, dance, hop, skip, or triple jump in a straight or a crooked line and not collide with another soul. He'd already found himself impatient with people congregating mid-block, strolling at paces at odds with his own, or stopping to gawk at some New York oddity.

Interviews of AMI staff turned up two suspicious mailings. The first arrived around September 19, and it was a package addressed to Jennifer Lopez. He found amusing that tabloids often received mail addressed to celebrities. As if their publicists had desks next to the writers. In it was found a cigar, a Star of David, and powder. One of the mailroom workers recalled handling the package, but the other was away on vacation.

The second suspicious letter arrived around September 25th. This fit the illnesses timeline of the two Florida cases. Witnesses said that the letter released a puff of powder when it was opened, but both the envelope and letter were tossed in the mailroom trash without a glance. Had the letter been turned over to the authorities, the course of the outbreak might have been different.

Mackey felt the presence of watchful eyes. A squirrel on its hind legs peered at him. Mackey tore off a crust from his sandwich and tossed it to his guest. The squirrel sniffed at the bread and scurried away. Spoiled little fella, a winter or two in Alaska would make him appreciate the bounty of New York.

Eyewitness interviews published on the Web were scarce, so Mackey switched to the scientific literature. He found maps of environmental testing results at AMI. There were sixty-six hits for *B. anthracis* spores on the first floor with the most around the mailroom. Fewer hits were found on the second and third floors and the pattern resembled Gretel's crumb trail in the woods. The photo editor's third floor cubicle and keyboard were also hot, but the letter had been discarded on the first floor.

Some anthrax Web sleuths and keystroke gumshoes, a group to which Mackey grudgingly acknowledged he now belonged, believed the anthrax spores were aerosolized by the cleaning crew's vacuuming. Since none of the three-person cleaning crew took ill or tested positive, Mackey zeroed in on the mailroom. One clerk recalled opening the second powder-containing letter upon her return from vacation. So why did two of her AMI co-workers become ill, but not she?

Mackey considered this at length while listening to sparrows chirping at the base of a nearby bush. Though similar, their songs differed. The same was true for individuals exposed to infectious agents. People don't respond in the exact same manner. The immune system's integrity and the circumstances of the exposure determine the outcome. The two men who became ill were over sixty, the woman who opened the letter was in her thirties.

Mackey stood and stretched. His eyes landed on a voluptuous young woman in a tank top sunning and reading a Stephen King novel. The peaks of New York City were quite unlike those in Alaska, but no less alluring. In the midst of tracing a sultry crevice she met his gaze with a glacial glare, shifting the book such that her middle finger stood upright against the cover. Mackey flashed a toothy grin and moved to a spot on the lawn that was a respectful distance from anyone else and laid down on his back.

Closing his eyes his thoughts began to wander; neither at random, nor of his volition. A scene emerged from a blue fog like a message from a Magic 8 Ball. It was ninth grade biology class. On the bench at the front of the classroom was a large tank filled with wriggling frogs. Mackey's lab partner nominated him to get their frog. Mr. Lassiter, wearing a smirk just short of seductive but long on smug, grabbed a frog and placed it in a jar with ether until it became torpid. He then handed it to young Mackey who laid the incapacitated creature on a dissecting tray. Holes in the tarry surface marked the crucifixion of previous martyrs to science.

When all student pairs had their anesthetized frogs before them, Lassiter instructed the proper technique to pith a frog. Mackey's lab partner, Marianne, a pony-tailed cheerleader in a Cling-Wrap sweater and an abundance of powder blue eyeliner, insisted he do this. If he hesitated there'd be no rounding her bases. Not that he was of the mind to anyway, the girl who had harpooned Mackey's heart would not be impressed by barbaric chivalry. The object of Mackey's teen obsession was the lone conscientious objector who sat in the far corner of the room with her hoodie pulled up over her head and a botany book in her lap. She straddled the Brainiac and the Grunge clans while Mackey oscillated between the Brainiacs and the Jocks. The nexus of their disparate universes was biology class.

The frog's slick skin was cool and moist beneath his touch. With the confidence of a tightrope walker Mackey flexed the head forward and searched with one finger for where the skull joined the spinal column. With a long, pointed probe he punctured the skin and advanced forward. The probe struck bone. He moved it in a circular motion until it slipped through the opening into the skull. He scrambled the frog's brain. The legs went limp. He turned the frog over on the tacky surface. With two pins he fixed the frog's arms to the tray. For the first part of the experiment they took a live wire and demonstrated muscular contraction. They would go on to dissect the frog, inspect its internal organs, and inject a dye into its circulatory system.

Anatomy wasn't the message in the memory. The enduring image, the one that often invaded his thoughts, was not of a frog tacked numbly to the mat of the dissecting tray mindlessly jerking its leg. It was of himself, a probe carelessly piercing stomach, liver and pancreas. Although his heart could accelerate at the sight of a woman, he was incapable of leaping from his pinioned state.

Something more proximate nagged at Mackey's consciousness. If the letter that arrived at AMI was part of the first series of anthrax mailings, which only resulted in cutaneous anthrax cases in New York City, why were there inhalation cases in Florida? Did the various letters contain different grades of spores? Was this intentional or a result of the manufacturing process? Was this a clue to the mailer's identity? Silica was found in one analysis of the spore powder. Was it deliberately added, and if so, why?

Mackey removed from his wallet the business card Hank had given him with the FBI number on it. Did Hank have an unspoken motive for giving him Agent Chen's name? He played the scene at the bar over again in his mind. Unsolicited, Hank gave him the name and number of Agent Chen. That alone seemed unusual. But didn't a smile creep ever so subtly across Hank's face?

He hoped to convince Agent Chen to share the cloistered details of the FBI investigation. It was five years later and the investigation appeared stalled. He told himself the FBI was ready for a fresh set of eyes, specifically those belonging to an epidemiologist. He dialed the NYC FBI office on his new cell phone and was greeted by a woman's pleasant voice.

"Special Agent Chen, please." After a minute, it sounded like the same woman came back to the line. "I'm on hold for Agent Chen."

"This is Agent Chen." Her voice was firm, the feeling of undercooked pasta between his incisors.

"Hello, uh, my name is Mackey Dunn. Dr. Dunn. I am a medical epidemiologist with the New York City Department of Health. That is, if the damn city ever lifts its hiring freeze. Anyway, I have some time before I start and would like to lend my services to the Amerithrax investigation." There was a brief silence.

"Who gave you my name and number?"

The pasta was cold. "Hank Karros, I met him through Dr. Layton." He hoped the mention of Hank's name might thaw her response, and threw in Marci as an extra quilt. However, Agent Chen's reply was no warmer than Alaskan permafrost.

"Dr. Dunn, I appreciate your offer but I am no longer with the Amerithrax investigation. Karros should have known that. I will pass your name and number along to the agent in charge." The line went dead.

Feeling a zap of confidence, Mackey decided to pack it in for the day. Shoving his laptop and notes into his backpack, he set off for the subway. Forty minutes later he was lacing up his running shoes and heading for Central Park. Entering at 110th Street, Mackey followed Central Park Drive west toward Harlem Hill, the steepest in the park. It climbed a mere eighty-four feet but did so in less than a quarter mile and got his heart pumping and lungs burning. Whatever it was that flowed through his arteries during exercise—endorphins, encephalins, or enchiladas—he craved it.

The road crested then dipped sharply to curve past a stand of elm trees that had lost some of their leaves but were not yet wearing their golden autumn attire. The meadow came next; a mosaic of baseball fields now dotted with miniature soccer players in oversized pastel shirts and corrugated plastic shin guards. A majestic red oak announced another bend in the road. A short rise brought him to the reservoir. Mackey turned off the drive, crossed the bridal path, deftly avoiding horse piles, and joined the reservoir trail. He made a mental note of the Yoshino and Kwanzan cherry trees hoping to be long working by the time they again bloomed. Along the reservoir path, two Asian girls asked a passerby to take their photo forcing Mackey to duck to avoid becoming a blurry head in their shot. At 86th Street he followed the path as it turned east, then north.

He was a freshman in high school when he first called a girl for a date. She had smiled at him in the cafeteria line. They shared mutual disgust at the deep fried and greasy offal. He found out her name and one night, after his parents were out of earshot ensconced in their respective reading dens, he stilled the butterfly wings and spun the dial. She didn't know Mackey from Macbeth. He felt her recoil like a slap across a wind chapped cheek. He hung up before declaring his intent. Years later, with Allison, he took a different approach.

He was living in Hershey at the time, playing baseball, and working part-time at the medical school. Armed with her name and the address of where she worked that he charmed out of her landlady, he made the two-hour trip to Scranton between games and the rinsing of test tubes. On his third try, he found her behind the register at the organic market. In his arms were two pounds of peaches and on his face a grin even the Cheshire cat would admire.

"Hi, Allison!"
"Hello. Did you bring your own bag?"
"I don't need a bag, just your phone number."

"Do I know you?"
"Yes, well, sort of... not yet."

Though polite, she didn't recall their first meeting. Mackey half expected that their previous brief encounter had meant more to him than her. He persisted. She gave him her phone number. Several calls and a peach cobbler later, Mackey had persuaded Allison to give him a chance.

He made a mental note to not give up on Agent Chen and exited the reservoir path to rejoin the park drive opposite the Guggenheim Museum. It was getting dark. It usually took somewhere between twenty and thirty minutes into a run before he felt the groove. When he did, his body, like a rubber band once fully stretched then released, returned to minimal tension. The effect lowered his center of gravity. His stride lengthened and breathing slowed, as did his heartbeat. Like a spinning skater speeding up when drawing her arms inward, Mackey reduced drag and conserved energy. As far back as he could remember it always worked this way. Whether being chased on the playground or leaving the house at full tilt to escape the wars his parents fought over money, running was relief. He next hit the downgrade on the opposite side of meadow. The softball fields were now deserted except for a solitary duffer. Each breath seemed to fill his feet with helium. He veered right to pass by the Harlem Meer on the final leg home. An old man sat on a bench staring at the inert water at his feet. His thick fingers scratched at his face's white stubble and poked the air as if to emphasize a point to an imaginary companion.

Mackey dashed along the sidewalk and covered the final blocks back to his apartment with several gazelle-like leaps. He took a quick shower, opened a can of soup, and warmed it like brandy over a blue flame. He ate out of the pot without a spoon. He rebooted his laptop and pulled up an article he had downloaded earlier.

"Anthrax as a biological weapon, a consensus statement by the Working Group on Civilian Biodefense," read the title.

He fell asleep before his computer did.

.| 4 |.

He first met her between games of a doubleheader the summer after college. Mackey was sitting alone beneath a maple tree just beyond the right field bleachers. He was eating a hoagie and singing a bit too loud to Elvis Costello on his Walkman. Not far from where he sat there was a crafts fair in the park. It was the earthy kind, where you could buy hand carved wooden bowls and jewelry made from semi-precious stones and recycled copper. Mackey's singing drew the attention of a woman sculptress named Allison. She tapped him on the shoulder and spoke to him but he could not hear the words. Mackey gazed agog into her gold-flecked green eyes, framed by honey auburn curls. Before he realized that he was still wearing his headphones, Mackey considered that it took another angel to hear her. In a voice like soft-serve ice cream she asked him if he called to her and what he meant by, "My aim is true?"

Whatever the cat's ransom, Mackey would have gleefully paid it for the immediate return of his tongue. In the absence of speech, his brain proposed answers to her question. Costello's true aim was with a gun, but he thought she might interpret this as an endorsement on his part of violence. Untrue and not the first impression he wished to make. What popped forth next was that as the shortstop for the Class Double-A Harrisburg Senators of the Eastern Minor League his throwing aim was true. In her well-worn sandals and sleeveless, yellow dress patterned with snail shells, she didn't appear the type to be impressed by athletic prowess. After what seemed like minutes, but in reality was scant seconds, speech returned. In a burst of inspiration he replied that it was his heart's aim, and yes, it was true.

They spoke but a few minutes yet Mackey was left in a revolving door daze. All of his senses had fired at once, like a switchboard lighting up after a UFO sighting or a bag of Pop Rocks sprinkled over his gray matter. A tickling sensation played in his throat with each note of her effervescent voice. Her dimpled smiles were dollops of banana pudding caressing his tongue. The roundness of her cheeks and sensuous angle of her jaw filled his nostrils with the fragrance of gladiolus. Mackey thought he heard a string quartet play "Swan Lake" to accompany her pirouetting fingers; the sticky heat dissipating from his skin in their delicate wake. When she reached out to brush an ant off his shoulder Rodin sculptures appeared before his eyes.

While he gathered his equipment for game two, it occurred to him that this must be what smitten feels like. After the game he searched for her. The crafts fair had ended and a cheerless park crew was cleaning up. A man wielding a spike-tipped pole gave Mackey the once over before telling him he didn't know who she was, but directed him to a row of tables next to the path. Beneath one he found a handmade, linen business card for Allison Baran. No phone number was listed, but there was an address.

Wednesday was a carbon copy of Tuesday. Mackey connected to the Wi-Fi signal at Bryant Park and found a reply from Marci in response to his inquiry about the anthrax investigation.

-----Original Message-----
From: Marcelle Layton <marci_layton@doh.nyc.us.gov>
To: MADunn24@yahoo.com
Sent: September 15, 2006 9:50:07 PM
Subject: Re: Anthrax investigation

Mackey,
Be glad to provide you with my files. Why don't you come down to my office, I'm sure there's an empty desk here you can use.

No news on freeze. Hang in there.

Marcelle Layton, MD
Assistant Commissioner
Bureau of Communicable Disease
New York City Department of Health
125 Worth St.
NY, NY 10013

-----Original Message-----
From: Mackey [mailto:MADunn24@yahoo.com]
Sent: September 15, 2006 12:25 PM
To: Marcelle Layton <marci_layton@doh.nyc.us.gov>
Subject: Anthrax investigation

Marci,
I am interested in the anthrax investigation. What info might I access at DOH?
Mackey

The UCLA School of Public Health's department of epidemiology maintained a website dedicated to the Amerithrax investigation. Mackey found what he was looking for: a line list of cases. He clicked through and read about each of the remaining cases. He jotted down notes and computed descriptive statistics. There were eleven inhalation and eleven cutaneous cases ranging in age from six months to ninety-four years. He listed the ages of the cases in a line, counting off eleven to get to the median age of forty-six years. He next marked which were cutaneous and which were inhalation cases, observing that below age forty-three all the cases were cutaneous and above age fifty-one all were inhalation. In between, there were four cases, two of each type. Could this be a coincidence of exposure or a measure of immune system integrity? Mackey would turn forty-three in December. He could go either way.

The ratio of men to women was about even. Nine worked for the government as postal workers and one worked within the Department of State's mail service. Seven of these workers developed inhalational anthrax and two died. Of the remaining twelve cases, nine were employed by the media companies and all handled mail more often than the average office worker. Two developed inhalation anthrax and one died. Three women didn't fit in with either risk group. Two of the women could not be connected to an anthrax-laced letter and seemed unlikely targets. One was a sixty-one year-old hospital worker from the Bronx and the other a ninety-four year-old retiree from Connecticut. Both died. Not only had no anthrax-laden letters arrived at their homes, the Postal Service had determined that no letters that had been processed on the same sorting machine as the contaminated letters had arrived either.

The CDC concluded that their exposures occurred from contact with a letter that passed through a sorting machine after a letter that became contaminated when it passed though the sorting machine immediately after an anthrax-tainted letter. Mackey dubbed this the double cross-contaminated magic letter theory. The third woman was a fifty-one-year-old accountant from South Jersey. She, too, had no known contact to an anthrax-containing letter.

The highest fatality rate for inhalation disease, 67 percent, was in this last group of three cases who presumably had exposure to the fewest spores. The data was limited and Mackey was cautious about assumptions based on small sample size. He considered how extensive the outbreak could've been if people of all ages were equally susceptible to a few spores. How many millions of pieces of mail must have passed through postal machines after the anthrax-filled letters? If only 1 percent had picked up spores that meant there might've been tens of thousands of victims.

Needing a break from Web surfing, Mackey ducked beneath the ground and stepped into a silver subway car heading downtown. He might have thought it was headed to Amsterdam. In addition to the usual Spanish and Chinese, he recognized German coming from a boisterous group seated mid-car, a Slavic dialect from a couple traveling with kids, and French from two women who exited at the next stop.

Less than fifteen minutes later, Mackey stood blinking at the Brooklyn Bridge. He walked to the west tower to admire the intricate brickwork and crisscrossing lattice of cables. A perfect setting for Spiderman III.

The street to the Department of Health passed through an urban canyon formed by the forty-story municipal building and the Surrogate Court Building. It then opened onto Foley Square, the sudden widening of the vertical space filling the scene with glorious sunlight. To the east stood two granite courthouses, their Greek columns and façades looking more natural in a scene from a Cecil B. DeMille epic than a modern city landscape.

At the Department of Health's security desk they made him empty all of his pockets and take off his shoes and belt. Now the shoes he could understand. Richard Reid attempted to blow up an American Airlines Boeing 767 en route from Paris to Miami with plastic explosives hidden in his shoes. But the belt? Maybe folks got the urge to strangle an unhelpful clerk.

A young woman directed him to Marci's suite. Finding no receptionist he poked his head into several offices until he found hers.

"Hi, Marci, am I interrupting?"

"Oh, hi, Mackey. I didn't hear you come in." Marci gestured to an open file cabinet with one hand while continuing to type an email with the other, "That drawer over there has all of my anthrax files. Dr. Sanders is away this week. You can use his office. It's out the door to your left."

"Terrific. I'll grab some files and get out of your way." Mackey knelt next to the file drawer. Each hanging file tab bore a hand-scrawled label: "Anthrax journal articles," "CDC information," "Connecticut case," "Department of Defense," "Environmental," "FBI." He froze trying to decide where to start.

"Did you reach out to Agent Chen?" Marci asked between rapid-fire computer strokes that sent an email out to fifty staff.

"Yeah, I called her. She made me feel about as welcome as emergency root canal."

Marci's head tilted and an eyebrow lifted.

"A reception colder than a January night at Everest base camp," Mackey added.

"Have you been to Everest?"

"No. One doesn't need frostbitten toes to know that 17,000 feet up in the Himalayas is cold and I don't need a thermometer to measure a cold shoulder." Marci screwed her face into a question mark, shrugged and returned to her keyboard.

"But you have been above the Arctic Circle, right? When you were in Alaska?" Marci continued, half joking, fingers drumming the keys. "You do know that is the only reason we hired you?" Marci herself held a special fondness for the state's untamed wilderness having spent time in Point Barrow, the northernmost outpost in America.

Mackey turned grinning with an armful of folders, nodded, and headed for the door.

"I'll send Hank an email. Maybe he can provide you with an introduction that might get you a warmer reception. No guarantee though. You've had a thorough background check to work for the CDC, so that should count for something."

"Thanks," he lifted the files, "I've got enough to keep me busy for a while."

Mackey deposited the shifting pile of folders on the desk sending an avalanche of papers skidding behind the computer screen. The folder that fell to the floor contained a report on the NBC investigation. The letter sent to Tom Brokaw at NBC was hand-addressed and bore a Trenton, New Jersey postmark from September 18, 2001. The address was printed in neat block lettering with all the letters capitalized, the first letter made larger. The penmanship slanted downward as the long line of "Rockefeller Plaza" neared the envelope's edge, as if the author ran out of space or wrote with one hand otherwise occupied. It had been determined that the letter was placed in a mailbox on Nassau Street across from Princeton University. A route postal worker emptied the mailbox on the afternoon of the September 18. He dumped the contents into a bin, loaded it aboard his truck, and drove it to the Hamilton Processing and Distribution Center.

The FBI tested every mailbox that fed into this center for anthrax spores but the drop box on Nassau Street alone was positive. The letter was one of about a million pieces of mail that arrive daily at the Hamilton. The bin containing the letter was unloaded from the truck and tossed onto a loading dock, then hauled by conveyer belt to the reader processing machines. There the handwritten zip code was read by the advanced face-canceller machine which cancelled the postage and printed two bar codes; one on the back that recorded the time the letter was processed and the other placed below the address which converted the handwritten zip code to a digital code. A second machine, the digital bar code sorter, routed the letter to the cubby slot for New York City. Later that night the letter was loaded onto a truck and driven sixty miles to the loading dock of the Morgan

Processing and Distribution Center, located on West 30th Street in Manhattan.

There the letter was again run through postal machines to route it into the proper delivery zone. Rockefeller Center, where NBC has its offices, has its own zip code and post office. From the Rockefeller post office the letter traveled to the mailroom at NBC. It was X-rayed and sorted for its third-floor destination.

The letter likely arrived on September 20 and was opened by a page who handed the oddly worded letter and its powdery contents to her supervisor, a thirty-eight-year-old executive assistant for Tom Brokaw. Her name was omitted from the report so Mackey decided to call her Dhalia. NBC received many wacko letters and their security department was tasked with collecting them. Dhalia slid the letter and envelope into an inter-office envelope and placed it next to her computer to give to security, but she forgot about it.

Dhalia noted powder on her desk. She recalled finding it everywhere—on her keyboard, the chair, her pants, and hands. She brushed it away, but more appeared. It was fine and gritty, like sand, but the particles were smaller, lighter. It stuck to her hands and made them itch. She washed it off and wiped down her desk, but soon noticed more. It was on her lap and she couldn't figure how it got there. Her hand reached up involuntarily and rubbed a spot on her shoulder beneath her bra strap. She opened the desk drawer thinking perhaps the powder had fallen into the drawer. She didn't see any. Dhalia shook out the folders on her desk, but nothing fell out. Now her clavicle itched. In the women's bathroom she examined the spot. Aside from the redness from her scratching she saw nothing. As she turned to leave, something on her skin caught the overhead light and shimmered like the sparkles kids put in their hair. She found powder on her neck and down her top. She washed it off, thinking that she didn't have time for this.

The following Tuesday, a pimple appeared below Dhalia's left clavicle. It filled with fluid, became enlarged, and turned red and swollen. By Friday, it had become an ulcer the length of her thumb. Dhalia felt like she was getting the flu. She was achy all over with a headache and malaise. Her symptoms intensified over the weekend and she retreated to bed. Her collarbone became extremely swollen. She found an old prescription of antibiotics and starting taking it. On Monday, she went to work for the sole purpose of seeing the NBC staff physician. He had received messages from the Department of Health after 9/11 to be alert for infections caused by bioterrorism agents and to call if he saw anything suspicious. He grabbed the phone and dialed the Department of Health. Arrangements were made to pick up the letter and to test the powder. He then took a culture of the fluid oozing from Dhalia's wound and placed her on the recommended antibiotic for anthrax.

Mackey read on. The timeline began to crystallize. By October 1, 2001, the photo editor from Florida was entering the second phase of anthrax while driving home from North Carolina. The mail clerk from AMI was being admitted to a Miami hospital for pneumonia. Doctors in Florida had no reason to suspect anything. A co-worker of Dhalia's, the page who opened the mail, made an appointment with her doctor for a rash. She was diagnosed with impetigo and placed on antibiotics. A seven-month-old boy, whose mother worked at ABC, was being admitted for intravenous antibiotics to a New York City hospital. He had a large, swollen, and ulcerous sore on his upper arm. An editorial assistant at the *New York Post* was in an emergency room receiving surgical treatment for an infection on the middle finger of her right hand. Dan Rather's personal assistant noted two reddish spots on her cheek.

Mackey knew that there was no system in place to connect all the disparate dots. The national disease surveillance system depended on positive culture tests to recognize similar events in different parts of the country. Aside from Dhalia, no one yet suspected anthrax or that their condition was linked to mail and her culture test was negative. Dhalia's ulcer was forming a dark, ominous crust. She was feeling better though, no longer suffering from body aches or malaise. The antibiotics seemed to be working. The letter retrieved from Dhalia's office also tested negative for anthrax by multiple methods at the Department of Health's laboratory.

On Saturday, October 7, the lab results from AMI were made public. Dhalia was flooded with second thoughts. When she learned that her page also had a skin problem she told her boss. Arrangements were made to retest her. Since she had been on antibiotics for more than a week a biopsy was necessary. The specimen was flown to the CDC in Atlanta.

The Department of Health's report read like a Hollywood script minus the melodramatic dialogue. CDC laboratory technologists worked into the night, rubbed tired eyes, sipped stale coffee, and spoke in hushed tones. The tests for DNA elements from *B. anthracis* were negative but interpreting these results was complicated by Dhalia's antibiotic course and the fact that it had been two weeks since the infection began. The envelope and letter tested negative for anthrax as they had in New York the week prior. At close to midnight a snip of Dhalia's skin stained with a dye specific for anthrax lay beneath a microscope lens. There was stain uptake by the tissue, but technicians couldn't be sure. The other tests were negative, but this was a trusted test. They called over the head of the lab, a well-respected scientist and expert microscopist. He scanned the slide while they held their breath.

This is anthrax he murmured.

Mackey wondered what it must have been like in New York City early that morning of October 12, 2001, when Marci got the call from Director Jeff Copeland of the CDC. Perhaps akin to when the first officer told Captain Smith that an iceberg had ripped a gash in the hull of the Titanic. He flashed back to the Boston apartment. Allie was upset with him because he'd again left a wet towel on the bed. Suddenly the cold waters of the North Atlantic threatened to pull him under. His breath became short and his skin flushed. He stood, walked out into the open hallway wiping beads of sweat from his brow. In the bathroom, he splashed cold water across his face and neck and swallowed a Xanax with a palmful of water. He stared at his reflection in the mirror. He knew exactly when the dark circles beneath his eyes first appeared and how they marked the years like the rings of a tree trunk.

The mayor and the health commissioner held a press conference at NBC's studio on October 12th to announce that anthrax was in the city. Within hours of the press conference four more cases surfaced. Buildings were closed. A hoax letter held the staff of the *New York Times* for several hours in quarantine. Anxious staff were interviewed, had their noses swabbed, and antibiotics flowed like Pez. Environmental teams mobilized to test target buildings while the public viewed their mail and the sugar dust at the bottom of their Little Debbie Snack cake packages with apoplectic suspicion.

Mackey reached the law enforcement paragraph of the report but found no details on the criminal investigation. He tossed it onto the pile of folders.

"I need to know what the FBI knows."

.| 5 |.

The courtyard of 26 Federal Plaza, home of the FBI's NYC field office, was a winding maze of curved benches and humongous Chia shrubs. Across Lafayette Street sat the squat cube of the Department of Health, his future employer. Separating the road from the sidewalk was a fence of cylindrical vehicle impact barriers. No such terrorism deterrent protected the Department of Health.

Marci had reached out to Hank who got Agent Chen to consent to a meeting. Mackey figured this spot qualified as neutral turf. He took a seat on an empty bench hidden by the bushes at the southeast corner of the courtyard as instructed. The sky was clear and the air tasted of hotdogs. Mackey was scouting for the grill cart when Chen appeared from behind, the clack of a boot heel against the bench announcing her arrival. Special Agent Charo Chen wore sunglasses, a flattering black turtleneck sweater, and crisp gold slacks. She was slender, five-foot-four, and with sweeping, brown tresses that framed a serious, yet winsome face.

"Dr. Dunn," she began, pausing long enough for Mackey to nod an acknowledgement of his identity, "the FBI appreciates your interest in the Amerithrax investigation. I left the team five years ago and am no longer in the noose. As I indicated on the phone, I cannot provide you with any information that is not already in our media releases or posted on our website. I also cannot discuss an ongoing investigation or show you any of our files. In fact, I am violating protocol by even speaking with you. I do not know how I can possibly be of assistance to you."

"Thanks for meeting with me, Agent Chen. I'll not waste your time. My hiring at the Department of Health has been delayed." Her face was as readable as Gabriel Garcia Marquez prose. Mackey continued, "The anthrax letters were both a crime and an outbreak and I believe as an epidemiologist I have something to contribute to solving the case."

Chen turned to leave but Mackey put a hand up to interrupt her departure.

"Please, this will just take a minute."

It took five for Mackey to plead his case. Starting with a reminder that five years had passed without an arrest was perhaps a poor choice. Chen remained stone-faced. When he explained that epidemiologists are trained to investigate disease outbreaks in much the same way agents are trained to investigate crimes he thought she bristled. The series of analogies weren't meant to amuse, but Agent Chen's lips pursed when Mackey suggested that the FBI would consult an expert in Egyptology if somebody stole a sacred Tutankhamen artifact and a gemologist to help hunt blood diamonds smuggled out of Liberia. When he finished he stared at his diffident reflection in her sunglasses uncertain if he'd made an impression, good or bad.

"The thing is, Agent Chen, I need to keep busy, for, uh, personal reasons. I've been so bored I've taken to writing limericks about former managers of the New York Yankees."

Chen laughed, exposing snow-white teeth and crescent dimples. She took a seat next to Mackey, removed her sunglasses, and stared at the courthouse across the park. The solemnity returned to her face.

"Let me hear what you've got."

"I don't have any theories yet but I've—"

"No. Let me hear the limerick."

"Ooo-kay."

> There once was a man from Cleveland,
> To baseball he put a meddling hand
> Lemon, Michael, Berra then Pinella,
> Who'll be the Yankees' next fella?
> Fourth time is charm to all's alarm, Billy Martin is the man.
> He thrice re-hired and then canned!

Chen smirked and shook her head. "Not bad, but I believe if you are starting with Lemon in 1982, he was followed by Michael, Clyde King, Martin, Berra, Martin again, then Pinella. Martin was actually hired and fired five times."

"I won't quit my day job. Can't. Don't have one. Agent Chen, you know your baseball."

"Call me Charo. It's short for Charlotta," she added before Mackey could ask about or utter the famous non-namesake's trademark phrase. "My dad is from China. Baseball was how he assimilated. My mom learned a thing or two about the game growing up in Venezuela with four brothers. I was the son my dad always wanted but had to wait a few years for."

Mackey envisioned an eight-year-old Charo, baseball cap pulled down low over bangs, tossing a ball against a tenement wall until well after midnight.

"Can we talk about anthrax?" he asked.

Charo's eyes darted toward the doors of 26 Federal Plaza and her back straightened. "I don't know. I need to think about this. I've got your number." With that she got up, turned on one heel, and dashed off leaving Mackey with a lingering impression.

Charo scanned the courtyard and street without moving her head as she walked back to the office. A trace of paranoia was healthy, too much, pathological. In fact, since the day she stepped into the FBI Academy classroom at Quantico, people *were* watching her.

Instructors leered, male cadets jeered, and her female colleagues feared she might handle the strain better than they did. Many of the women did learn to trust each other and became friends, once they realized that competing was counterproductive. They were in it together, a small island nation surrounded by hostile waters teeming with sharks.

Charo was a rookie agent in the NYC field office in 2001. After 9/11 she was assigned to the Joint Terrorism Task Force (JTTF), a team made up of FBI agents, New York City cops, and New York State officers. Her tasks were to take notes at meetings, run errands, and ensure chain of custody for evidence. There wasn't much. The closest she got to the anthrax investigation was on October 12th when she assisted in the search for the second threat letter at NBC, the real one that contained spores. Her partner CJ was a no-show. Typical. Another agent, Diego, who was not much more senior than her, went down to the mailroom where the letter was sent to be X-rayed again. Charo waited in the security office. Diego returned with a plastic shopping bag. Inside was an inter-office envelope and inside of that the missing letter and envelope. With a gloved hand one of the JTTF officers she didn't know removed the letter and placed it into a Ziploc bag. He then did the same with the envelope. Both were then placed into a larger Ziploc bag. Holding it at arm's length, he glanced about the room. Charo examined the printed block lettering of the letter through the double layers of plastic. She could read the last line, "Allah is great."

He turned and handed it to Charo and told her to run it over to the city lab. Diego drove, Charo placed the bag at her feet. That's when CJ called ordering her to swing by 26 Federal Plaza to pick him up. Diego had the good sense to split as soon as CJ opened the car door.

"What's in the bag?"

"We found the second letter."
"Did you make me a copy?"
"No."
"Go, I'll wait here."
"My orders are to rush it to the lab."
"Make me a copy first."
"I'm not going to do that."
"Stupid bitch."
"CJ, no!"

He snatched the bag and took off with Charo in hot pursuit yelling for him to stop. She caught up to him in the copy room where a frightened secretary held the letter at arm's length while CJ tried to punch a passcode into the copier. The commotion caught the attention of the Deputy Chief.

The floor was immediately evacuated and shut down. Both CJ and the secretary tested positive for anthrax spores as did the copy machine. They all took sixty days of cipro. That was the last day Charo worked on the Amerithrax investigation.

The office was empty when Charo returned. She swung into her desk chair while eyeing the wall clock. Three o'clock in the afternoon. She was just getting home from school. Charo brought up the website LowLita.com and logged in as Qtpye_grl13. She entered a chat room and perused the list of screen names already there. She was hoping to find TheBigOmar69.

After being *excused* from the anthrax investigation, Charo worked in counterintelligence for thirteen months and then, in 2003, joined the Innocent Images National Initiative. Innocent Images, as it was known in the bureau, was created in 1995 to combat the proliferation of child pornography on the Internet and to protect children. Agents posed as underage girls or boys in chat rooms as bait or as undercover predators trying to infiltrate distribution networks.

Charo met TheBigOmar69 in the LowLita chat room. He wanted to relieve Qtpye_grl13 of her virginity. Like it was a book bag too heavy to carry. The true depth of male depravity was relatively unknown to the general public until "Dateline NBC" began airing their undercover sting operations and showed in prime time predators going to homes where they believed underaged girls were waiting to have sex with them. Working for Innocent Images only served to diminish Charo's already low opinion of men.

Justice for sex offenders was slow and irregularly applied. Charo was in favor of a more immediate penalty. Testicles teed up on a fairway, a golfer with a name like Dent or Crush stepping up with a one-wood separating the offending gonad from its miscreant owner. TheBigOmar69 wasn't in the chat room. Charo remained logged in, but her mind drifted back to her meeting with Dr. Dunn and her first year with the bureau.

New York City was her first choice of assignments out of Quantico. Most agents saw New York as a punitive assignment. It was expensive, crowded, and noisy. One couldn't easily manage with a car. For Charo it was like tossing Brer Rabbit into the briar patch, it was home. It gave her the opportunity to be near her dad, a priority since her mother was spending more time in Venezuela.

The first two years for new agents is spent on probation. An apprenticeship of sorts. Rookies were assigned to a more experienced agent who was to serve as a teacher and mentor. That is how Charo got paired with CJ. He was a first-class fuck-up, an example of how New York City served as the bureau's Devil's Island. He was one base from the four-bagger after having already been transferred, placed on probation, and censured. The last step being suspension. Being assigned a rookie female agent was supposed to be further punishment. Charo wondered though who was being punished. He treated her like his personal assistant, the type that does all the work while the boss goofs off. When he wasn't investigating some bogus lead in a bar, he subjected Charo to a constant diatribe against the FBI administration, immigrants, and women. She bit her lip so often it looked like an old-time catcher's mitt.

The anthrax attack was her first major case and one she had barely begun before she was sacked and reassigned. She chafed at how she got sucked into the maelstrom of procedural mishaps that day. The next year, CJ finally drank his way into that suspension and then, as far as she knew or cared, oblivion. After CJ she wasn't given a new mentor, which suited her fine. Now this friend of Karros had shown up with ideas about the anthrax case.

The bureau took a beating in the New York City press over the failures of the investigation, and more than once Charo had given thought to how she might help restore her own and the bureau's tarnished reputations. There were a lot of good men and women in the bureau. Dedicated, hard workers, toiling to prevent such heinous acts from terrorism to child abduction. CJ was an anomaly and Karros the norm. If you ignored the sexual innuendos, crass remarks, and chauvinism, it wasn't a terrible place to work. Truth was she enjoyed her job, especially the freedom of reporting directly to the regional Cyber Division Chief.

She couldn't officially return to the Amerithrax investigation without requesting a transfer, which would take months and mean being reassigned to headquarters in Washington, DC. Getting involved otherwise was a significant breach of protocol. She'd worked hard to become a respected agent. Special agents didn't take others meddling in their cases lightly and there was considerable risk involved, especially if she allowed Dunn into her confidence.

.| 6 |.

Mackey and Allison dated the rest of that summer. She moved in with him when he started medical school and in October of his fourth year, while he was doing an elective in New Hampshire, they got married. The honeymoon was a three-day weekend in a cabin on a secluded lake in Vermont. They were early risers and took walks along the shore as the sun rose and mist lifted. At night he'd read to her until she feel asleep with her head on his lap. The place was drafty but he never once felt cold.

Every anniversary they rented the same cabin. On their third anniversary, Allison made Mackey a basket from pine twigs she collected so he'd always know where he put his keys. Nowadays that image only reminded him of where he'd left his heart.

Mackey had done his best to try to block out any reminders of their anniversary date to keep from dragging himself under but as September 18th approached he found it more difficult to block the thoughts from invading his mind. He wandered the aisles of the supermarket but couldn't remember what he had come for. It didn't help that it was also an important date in the anthrax investigation; the date the first group of letters were postmarked. Nor did it help that he had both too much time on his hands and didn't know anyone in the city. He tried contacting a medical school classmate, an orthopedic surgeon on Long Island. She told him she'd try to carve out some time for him. Codewords that meant she'd only see him if he had a cartwheel fracture of the femur with a disarticulation of his hip joint, the kind of case worthy of a write-up in the *Journal of Bone and Joint Surgery*.

He tried walking in Central Park but the canopy and fragrances reminded him of Vermont. Riding the subway, something Allison seldom did, worked for a spell. But having no destination other than to kill time was somehow worse than the alternative: thinking about Allie.

At least Mackey was cognitive of why he was feeling blue. There were people who wallowed in their anniversary reactions neither recognizing nor understanding why. It was on September 18, 1996 that Allie disappeared. Mackey came home from a run-of-the-mill overnight shift at Boston City Hospital. He was thinking about writing up the gunshot wound victim he'd treated for heart failure because the bullet had traveled from the right femoral vein to lodge in the left pulmonary artery when he saw that Allie had left him a note. She had biked down to the harbor and taken a ferry to Cape Cod for the day. Allie loved the beach and relished having it all to herself with the high tourism season over. It was a trip she had made several times, taking an early morning ferry across the Atlantic to Provincetown, returning in the late afternoon. The ninety-minute ferry ride often passed pods of humpbacks and less often, right whales. She'd take a sketchpad and some charcoals, walk the beach picking up interesting pieces of driftwood and sit on a dune and draw.

Mackey ate a bowl of cereal and went to bed. He awoke at three in the afternoon to the sound of a jackhammer outside his window. He figured Allie should be just getting on the ferry to come home. He went for a run, showered, and picked up some cod for dinner. In his mind he could still see the cat clock on the kitchen wall that Allie had sculpted and constructed using assorted items from a shoebox she kept in the hall closet. She painted it tabby orange and white. Mackey installed the mechanism for it to tell time. Its oversized eyes were made of dissimilar marbles, producing an effect that was both quirky and eerie. They stared down on him like twin crystal balls portending an ominous future as he diced Allie's favorite, string beans.

Allie never came home for dinner. She didn't own a cell phone so he couldn't call her. Mackey went down to the wharf to meet the last ferry. When the final passenger disembarked, he stood alone on the darkening pier. It as when he turned to ask someone at the ferry office for help that he noticed Allie's bicycle propped against the ferry station wall. A deck hand told him the bike was found on the ferry, though he couldn't say when or how long it had been on board. The Boston Police Department tried to reassure him. An officer advised him to go home to see if she left a message. She probably lost track of time and got stuck on the Cape. She'd be home by morning. But the bike, he insisted, why was it on the ferry without her? They came up with distantly plausible explanations.

The Coast Guard said much the same, except they went as far as to interview the ferry operators and show them the photo Mackey had produced from his wallet. The one in which the camera caught Allie unawares, with paint on her cheek, and strands of auburn hair in her eyes. No one recognized her. Mackey felt paralyzed. Nothing made sense. Sure, Allie could lose track of time, but it wasn't like her not to call. If she made it to the ferry to load her bike, then why wasn't she on it, too? He called their answering machine, no message. He considered renting a boat to search for her. That seemed crazy, he didn't know how to pilot a boat plus it was dark. Did she fall overboard? Surely someone would have heard or seen her fall? Unless they were busy whale watching. He was making himself sick. The thought of her out there in the cold, dark Atlantic waters pierced him with the force of an errantly hurled javelin. He convinced himself that she couldn't have fallen overboard. There were too many safety features to prevent it. Maybe, he hoped, she lost track of time and missed the last ferry and went in search of a yachtsman or local fisherman to get a ride back. But the bike, why was it there?

For no other reason than the ominous feeling he had in his bowels, he stayed at the dock. Every half hour he called the apartment, but there was no message from Allie. When he returned home after dawn the next day she wasn't there. He couldn't sleep. He suffered his first panic attack, initially mistaking the sudden shortness of breath for a spontaneous pneumothorax. The minutes passed like all the sands of Cape Cod sifting through the eye of a needle. He called in sick to work. One of Allie's friends, who he called to inquire if she had heard from her, offered to help in the search. She went to Provincetown with photos to alert the local police and ask around. Mackey badgered the Coast Guard until they agreed to take him out on a patrol boat tracing the ferry route.

Among the thousands of agonizing thoughts that cycled through his mind was the revelation from Allie's brother that their mother had committed suicide, not breast cancer as Allie had told him. Did he miss the signs of depression? The weeks passed. He didn't return to work. Instead he spent the days at the docks, until, weeks later, he overheard a tour guide include him as part of her speech to Japanese tourists. Allie's body was never found.

His soul wandered aimlessly through despair, anger, and guilt. Most of all he felt lost. A rudderless ship set adrift on a vast ocean of loneliness. Mackey couldn't muster the courage to have Allie declared dead. Allie's father, a whimsical toy maker with too large of a heart, was shattered. He died two months later. Her brother went back to Europe and Mackey was left alone with his grief. Grief so large and omnipresent that it rolled over him day after day, relentlessly crushing him into pea-grade gravel.

He packed up his stuff, their stuff, and shipped it to his mom's place. All except her studio, on which he still paid the $2,000-a-month mortgage. He then rode out of town on his medical degree signing up with a locum tenens outfit and lived in two to six week stints, never staying anywhere long enough for his memories to find him. He was a medical pinch hitter, the consummate utility infielder, filling in at practices across the Midwest, South, and Southwest for physicians on vacation—a family practice in Lawrence, a doc-in-a-box in Duluth, and a generalist in Indianapolis. He stayed in boarding houses and with old widows who rented rooms. His services were in high demand. Doctors outside the East Coast were few and far between and they needed long vacations.

Practices asked him to come back, some even offered him full-time positions. He preferred to keep moving; to another town, to places where no one knew his name or asked him why he chose to be a nomad. He did four dark and dreary February weeks on Kodiak Island, Alaska. Fried his own breakfast outside a trailer in Silver City, New Mexico. Delivered babies in Shattuck, near the Oklahoma panhandle, and stitched bar fight wounds in Texas border towns. With stethoscope in hand, he was the Paladin of pediatrics, the Mark Twain of pain, the Gunga Din of emergency medicine, Ernest the internist and the Heinlein of Ob-Gyn—an ex-patriot stranger in his own land.

Work occupied eight to twelve hours of the day. He tried filling the rest by running and reading, but found he couldn't muster sufficient endurance or attention span. He took in local sights but still struggled with the long evening hours. Those were the times he and Allie used to spend together at home, in their parallel, yet synchronized orbits. Mackey took to hanging out in local bars; nursing a beer or two until closing time, and making sure to over tip the bartender so he wouldn't wear out his welcome.

Sometimes another patron would strike up a conversation. It was a relief that the person wanted an ear to bend, asking no more of him than an agreeable nod or an occasional "uh-huh."

Alcohol did nothing to numb Mackey's pain. A Scottish genetic tolerance he supposed, not that he was curious to find out how well it might work in higher doses. Pain was the sole thing he had left and he clung to it like moss to a cliff.

The weather on Sunday turned damp and cool so he set up shop in a Starbucks, ordering an uncomplicated cup of coffee to the puzzlement of the perky counter girl. He was at 118th and Frederick Douglas Boulevard, the farthest north Starbucks had ventured in the city. The place was not crowded and he found an open table near the window with room for his laptop and notes.

The FBI dubbed the anthrax investigation "Amerithrax," a combination of America and anthrax. Whenever an agent referred to the investigation or suspects they used Amerithrax, as if it was a stalwart brand name like Kleenex or Skippy. But whenever Mackey heard Amerithrax he cringed, thinking of a high-fiber breakfast cereal with a fading sports hero emblazoned across the front of the box. Like high-fiber cereals he couldn't stomach it. Any word with "Ameri-" in it should be a good word, a proud word, a word that invokes images of purple mountains, spacious skies, and amber fields of grain. A word that stands for freedom, not fear. Courage not cowardice. Tolerance not terrorism. The investigation, and certainly the crime, didn't deserve to be so christened. Mackey refused to call the investigation or the perpetrators Amerithrax. He preferred Mailthrax.

A young woman in a green smock leaned against the window on the other side of Mackey's roost. She lit a cigarette and turned to adjust her hair in her reflection. She appeared to be in her young twenties, not unattractive, with brown hair and big-boned Midwestern features. She held the cigarette between her middle and index fingers and took a deep draw from the corner of her mouth twisting into a squint-eyed grimace that was half Bogart and half Popeye. The squint was a reasonable attempt to keep the smoke out of her eye while siphoning nicotine into her bloodstream. The delicate optical organs being susceptible to the hot, irritating gasses emitted by the burning tobacco. Mackey yearned to ask why she cared so little about the lining of her lungs? Did she not realize that the single-cell walls of the terminal air sacs of her lungs were not only highly sensitive to the toxins in cigarette smoke, but they had the unremitting, life-sustaining task of transferring oxygen to and waste product carbon dioxide from the blood stream? The woman, as if sensing Mackey's disdain, stubbed out the cigarette, and returned to work pushing a different legal drug.

. . .

When Charo started at the FBI in 2001 she shared a computer with two other rookie agents. It wasn't a PC but an IBM 3270 terminal. She had not seen one like this since high school and even then it seemed obsolete. The computer didn't use Windows, but a DOS-like program designed by a German company. The screen was green and blinked incessantly. She at first thought it was part of the new agent hazing process, but soon realized this was state of the art for the FBI. It had no Internet browser software or connection beyond the mainframe network.

For word processing and Internet access there was an equally antiquated and shared Compaq 386 computer. The IBM terminals were for ACS, the Automated Case Support system. ACS tracked investigation information and indexed the whereabouts of paper files. Navigation was through a combination of keystrokes. There were separate systems for telephone data, informant interviews, and surveillance on organizations. The system was introduced in 1995, which must have seemed like buying a brand new '65 Dodge Dart with a push-button transmission at the time.

The system was the computerized extension of J. Edgar Hoover's 1920s scheme of having agents record information on the people they investigated on index cards. The computerized version offered little more than the original and immediately showed its shortcomings. It failed to locate key documents in the Oklahoma City Bombing case. Many agents found it too cumbersome to use and relegated the tedious chores they had to perform to clerical staff. But there was one special agent who made expert use of the system. Robert Hanssen employed it to locate the files he sold to the Russians.

The anthrax letter mailings in the fall of 2001 launched simultaneous investigations all over the country. Nearly 700 agents conducted over 8,000 interviews and served 1,700 subpoenas. Emails were sent to 40,000 members of the American Society for Microbiology asking them if they had any clues to the identity of the anthrax mailer. Half a million letters blanketed southern New Jersey inquiring if any of the residents recognized the handwriting or style of the anthrax letters. But there was no electronic mechanism to synthesize and analyze all the data that was collected.

Charo was well aware of the Amerithrax investigation's missteps. Potentially the most dreadful was when the Iowa State University Lab called right after the outbreak worried that they could not secure their stocks of anthrax cultures and wanted permission to destroy them. The field office in Des Moines called headquarters and the message got passed around. The University called back, headquarters replied it was okay to destroy their stocks. Into the autoclave they went, along with them an opportunity to trace the heritage of the spores in the anthrax mailings.

The FBI lacked sufficient knowledge of bioterrorism agents and microbial forensics to solve the case alone. The image it conjured in Charo's mind was of a 10,000-piece jigsaw puzzle with only a few thousand of the pieces randomly divided among the Amerithrax agents, each of whom was trying to solve the puzzle in solitary confinement.

Charo ran Dunn's name through the FBI databases and Internet search engines. He was born in Baltimore and was an only child. His father was a classics professor and his mother a school librarian. Not surprising, since he was a federal employee, his fingerprints were on file. He had no criminal record. His government status was terminal leave. She made mental notes. He received his medical degree at the Pennsylvania State College of Medicine in Hershey, graduating in the top 10 percent of his class. His residency and fellowship training were both at Boston City Hospital. He held medical licenses in four states: Alaska, Massachusetts, New York, and Pennsylvania. He had no lawsuit or disciplinary action on his record.

On the Web she found his name associated with several outbreak investigations. Two intrigued her: "An outbreak of methicillin resistant *Staphylococcus aureus* in a traditional Native American sauna," and "Foodborne botulism following a change in traditional fermentation practices in an Eskimo community." Botulism was an agent that could be used as a bioweapon. Charo clicked on the link. It led to a report of a foodborne outbreak investigation. The outbreak occurred in a fishing village on Chichagof Island. The traditional method of fermenting "stink heads" was to bury the fish heads in the ground wrapped in leaves, but a change in preparation had occurred. The people who contracted botulism had modernized and used plastic buckets. In doing so they created an environment devoid of oxygen, the preferred growth condition for botulism. A team of epidemiologists, including Dunn, interviewed the family members of those ill along with a sample of community members that were not ill. By comparing the ill to the well, they were able to determine the cause of the outbreak.

The other investigation Charo read about traced a series of serious skin infections to rotting wood in traditional Eskimos saunas. Charo began to realize there was an element of detective work in what Dr. Dunn did for a living.

She next widened the search to mentions of Dunn in media stories. Several hits were related to the outbreak investigations in Alaska she had already viewed. His named appeared on a list of physicians who worked for Locum Tenes America. She then found a photo of a minor league baseball team with the caption: "The 1986 Harrisburg Senators." She recognized Mackey third from the left in the first row, listed as an infielder. She entered his name with MD in quotes and scanned the results. Her eyes were drawn to the words "wife of Boston physician MacPherson Dunn missing." She brought up the link. It was a brief *Boston Globe* article from September 20, 1996. All it said was that Allison Dunn was missing and was presumed to have drowned in the Atlantic Ocean in a ferry mishap. No other details were provided.

She hadn't initially thought to search ACS for Mackey's name in connection with an FBI investigation, but there it was, a missing person's file marked as a maritime investigation in the name of Allison Barak

Dunn. A single paragraph summed it up. Mrs. Dunn went out on a ferry ride and never returned. There were no witnesses, no body, nor any evidence of foul play. Although no note was found the case was closed as a suicide. The investigating agent made one curious entry writing that Dr. Dunn was at home asleep at the time of his wife's disappearance and that no one could verify his alibi. Charo decided to place a call to the Boston field office.

.| 7 |.

Mackey formulated a plan to make it through the day. To still his inner voices he needed an activity that absorbed his mind and body. So he put the day in the hands and feet of what he knew best: baseball, or the closest thing he could find—softball. When it got dark he'd try his luck offering an ear at a bar. The anthrax investigation would have to wait.

He headed to Hecksher Fields where the Broadway Show League played in the morning before their evening performances. The season was over but there were still pick-up games. He passed on his usual pregame ibuprofen, glad to suffer physical aches in order to avoid the emotional ones.

He got the requisite who's-the-new-guy stares as he laced up his cleats and stepped out onto the field during warm-ups. The actor who played a bowling alley lawyer in a cancelled TV show and was in a play called *Urinetown* picked him. The guy insisted on playing shortstop, Mackey acquiesced and played third. In the sixth inning of the second game, with his team down two runs, Mackey got a text message. He was on deck and about to ignore it when the batter popped up to end the inning.

MEET 2NITE 4-10 SPLIT BAR WMSBRG 1800H CC

The second game ended and the actors dispersed leaving Mackey alone and anxious. He popped a Xanax and headed out of the park to locate an Internet café. The 4-10 Split Bar was located on Hope Street in Williamsburg,

Brooklyn. Mackey had spent a fair amount of time on Hope Street. His view of hope lay somewhere between Emily Dickinson's: "It strange invention/ a patent of the heart/in unremitting action/yet never wearing out," and Friedrich Nietzsche's: "Hope in reality is the worst of all evils because it prolongs the torments of man."

Hope is a minuscule thing, invisible even to the strongest electron microscope, yet possesses strength beyond measure. It has no moving parts and cannot be broken. Hope is pliable and can be compressed to a fraction of its already molecular size, but not so far as to crush or divide it. Each nidus of hope is singular, independent, and unique. Like a virus that's sole mission is to reproduce itself, hope too has a singular goal. To persist. In the face of overwhelming odds and insurmountable obstacles, hope holds steady. A jetty in the storm. It could be two outs in the bottom of the ninth, down by six runs with the ace reliever of the league on the mound, or a lottery ticket for a hundred million dollar jackpot, hope is there. Steadfast, inexhaustible, indefatigable. Hope doesn't do anything. It doesn't unravel mysteries or save you from yourself. It is not a superhero. It cannot perform miracles. Hope just is. A placeholder. The bookmark for that which is missing. Something that perhaps once was, but is no longer. Something that never was but perchance may still yet be. Hope has no use for resources. It neither consumes nor produces them. It renders no opinions, makes no faces, rolls no eyes, clears no throats, and shrugs nary a shoulder. It can't be forsaken and most certainly doesn't float.

The 4-10 Split Bar was a bar-bowling alley populated by the young and painfully pierced. It was the second to last place a cop or fed would go, a gay bar being the last. It sported four reduced sized lanes, a video game arcade, and sofas that looked to Mackey as if the proprietor had raided the trash on the day you are allowed to put out oversized items. He spied Charo sitting in a molded plastic chair facing the lanes. She was reading a book. A beer sat on the table next to her and she neither looked to be alone nor as if she was waiting for someone.

"Nice to see you again, Charo," Mackey said as he slipped into the adjacent chair.

"Hello, Dr. Dunn."

"I prefer Mackey. After several days of reading the public health literature, media accounts, and culling the various sleuth websites I've come to a realization."

"You figured out who did it?" Charo asked.

"No. Epidemiologists, while skilled at investigating outbreaks to discover the agent, vehicle, and mode of transmission of disease, haven't contributed much to finding the anthrax villain."

"Why is that?"

"It's the types of questions we get caught up with. Like how many spores can cause infection or if you open an envelope containing powdered anthrax, where will it disperse? Important to protecting the public's health but irrelevant to catching the culprit."

"I thought you came here to convince me of the value of your insight?"

"I did. Epidemiologic methods can contribute to the investigation. I just have to readjust my focus."

"Explain."

"Suppose you had a hundred sick people who all ate food at a banquet. One approach might be to gather information on all the ingredients used and trace them back along the route they took to the dinner table. Then test the foods to see if contamination occurred at any point along the route from farm to fork."

"Isn't that what is done?"

"No. First we interview the attendees, both the ill and well, asking them which foods they ate. We then narrow suspects using statistics. Focus on the most suspicious foods, conserving precious personnel resources and time."

"Makes sense. The FBI doesn't have unlimited resources either, but I don't yet see how this applies to the investigation."

"Several hundred agents went door to door in the Princeton area showing photographs of the suspect Hatfill to residents. This is tantamount to searching for a needle in a haystack on your hands and knees with tweezers. I've not seen any scientific evidence that pointed to Hatfill as a suspect and presume the effort yielded nothing."

Charo put down the book she was reading on the table and turned toward Mackey.

"Because it wasn't him."

Mackey shook his head. "Irrelevant."

"Sometimes you only have the haystack and a lot of hands to pitchfork through the hay," Charo replied. "How can statistics help identify a potential suspect?"

Mackey's mouth was dry from talking. He motioned at Charo's beer.

"Sure, but it's warm," she warned.

He took a sip and leaned forward in his chair. "The analogous approach would be for the FBI to have created standardized questionnaires and entered the responses into a database. Then to interview ordinary people, those without any specific knowledge relevant to the investigation, to act as controls—a comparison group." He took another gulp of beer, wincing.

"I warned you it was warm."

"Several thousand members of the American Society for Microbiology were canvassed by email. How were the responses processed? Were they to have been given a standardized questionnaire, the results could've been entered into a database and analyzed, to see if anything stood out."

"Standardized questionnaire?"

"Yes. A set of questions broadly used to interview witnesses and designed to identify common elements." Mackey looked about for a waitress.

"Police work isn't that simple. Interviews have to be tailored to the individual and situation," Charo said.

"Of course, but I bet there is a routine set of questions you ask. Like where were you on the night of …"

"You've watched too many cop shows, Mackey."

"Perhaps. But how did the FBI process thousands of interviews to pick out clues?"

"I'm not sure how that was done in the Amerithrax investigation."

"Suppose someone at a defense research lab says in an interview that he knows a co-worker who is disgruntled. Disgruntled is pretty subjective, but it could mean something if several people at that lab or elsewhere in the country share the same observation. But how would you know if the same name came up in different parts of the country?"

"We compare notes," Charo offered unconvincingly.

"That's inefficient and hasn't worked in this case. What if you could learn of more subtle connections and examine the intersection of disgruntled and access to anthrax? Using simple statistical software you could narrow down the suspect list to those with motive and means."

"Okay, I get it. Putting aside that this would require a major change in FBI procedure how does it help solve Amerithrax? It's too late to apply this concept to interviews long since completed. You are not suggesting they be redone. Are you?"

"No. And I prefer to call the investigation Mailthrax. There was nothing at all American about it. My point was to demonstrate the advantages of epidemiologic methods."

"That leaves the question of who mailed the anthrax letters and what you or I can do to solve the crime," Charo said.

Mackey leaned back in his chair and ran a hand through his hair. He watched a bowler toss a ball onto the lanes with a loud thunk. It rolled harmlessly into the gutter past the pins.

"Here's an idea. We look for Mailthrax on the Garden State Parkway."

"What?"

"E-ZPass. If the mailer didn't live near the postal box where the letters were mailed he must have driven there and likely passed through a toll booth."

"Now that sounds like a needle in haystack to me."

"Who better to find a needle in a haystack than a computer?"

"How do you propose to do this?"

"E-ZPass records the user account number of drivers as they pass through toll booths. We obtain the E-ZPass data for 2001 then write a computer algorithm to scan for a car that passed through tollbooths to and from Princeton around the two days the letters were postmarked, September 18th and October 9th."

"Hold on. Supposing the data from five years ago is even available there must have been thousands, maybe millions, of cars that passed through those E-ZPass tollbooths. How do we identify our suspect?"

"The concept comes from a technique I learned in college chemistry called Fourier transformation. We used it to extract a faint signal from background noise with a regular pattern."

"Picking out the trees through the forest?" Charo asked.

"Sort of. More like picking out the two white roses in a sea of red ones."

"Hmm. Has this ever been tried before?"

"We used something similar to narrow down the list of health personnel who we suspected was a carrier during an outbreak of *Serratia marcescens* in a neonatal intensive care unit."

"Was it the maid?"

"No. A nurse. She had a chronic nail infection and shared hand lotion with other nurses."

"Intriguing. But what if the unsub didn't have an E-ZPass?"

"Unsub?"

"Unknown subject. Perp. *Mailthrax*."

"A smidge more difficult. Video surveillance captures license plates of toll jumpers. We'll need access to scanning software. And a statistician."

Charo was quiet.

"Do you want another beer, seeing how I drank yours?"

"Yes, a Brooklyn Lager, please. Thanks." Mackey returned with two beers and a bowl of peanuts.

"What if we get 10,000 hits?" Charo asked.

"Assign probabilities and focus on high scorers."

"What if none fit the pattern. Or the unsub was a daily commuter?"

"We're no worse off than now."

Mackey got up and went to the bathroom. He was heartened by the fact that Charo hadn't walked out and was more at ease than their brief first meeting. Was he over-reading the situation and at the end of the evening she'd smile politely and decline? What began as a necessary distraction was becoming an obsession. Every time he dug into one aspect of the investigation something else unraveled. It was hard not to get lost in eddies. But there was too much he didn't have access to. He needed Charo's help like skydivers need parachutes.

"I hope you don't mind me asking, but what made you become an FBI agent?"

Charo smiled but didn't immediately answer. "I was really close to my dad growing up, still am. Guess being the oldest has something to do with it. He was a civil servant, worked for the Postal Service for twenty years if you can believe it. He retired before 9/11. Some of my earliest childhood memories were sitting with my dad on Sunday nights watching TV. My younger brother had already been put to bed and my mom was off painting so it was the two of us. I must have been five or six. He loved the show *Colombo* and would explain all the clues and the methods the character used to disarm his suspects."

"I loved *Columbo*. Peter Falk was great."

"I attended a seminar on criminology at Queens College given by a female FBI agent. I was impressed by how much she used her mental skills to solve crimes. After graduating I worked for the Museum of Natural History, but had it in my head to get into law enforcement. I enrolled at John Jay College to pursue a master's degree in criminal justice but I pretty much knew by then I was going to try to get into the FBI. After the master's I was accepted into the training program at Quantico. I finished at the end of 2000 and began here in New York as a special agent in 2001."

"Hank mentioned you were part of the 2001 investigation team."

"I was still in my probation period, so I was relegated to being a groundhog. I transported samples, kept notes, and made spread sheets. I transferred to counter intelligence and when a position opened up in the Innocent Images National Initiative Project I took it."

"Innocent what?" Mackey asked.

"Innocent Images National Initiative. We hunt child sexual predators and pornography rings."

"What does that entail?"

"Maybe we should stick with anthrax."
"Right."

Mackey shared his research, but what he didn't know dwarfed what he did. Like what was done to track where the spores came from. The anthrax strain was determined to be Ames, and the focus of the investigation turned towards a short list of American scientists with access to the Ames strain. But did the FBI find evidence that the spores were made, stolen, or bought?

"Are you suggesting the focus on domestic suspects was misplaced?"

"Perhaps prematurely narrowed. Russian bioweapons defectors have intimated that the Soviet Union weaponized many strains of anthrax. But we don't need to take their word for it, there is proof. Are you familiar with the accidental release of anthrax that happened in the Soviet city of Sverdlovsk in 1979?"

"I attended a briefing, but continue."

"Sverdlovsk was where the main Soviet plant was located and it produced anthrax spores by the ton."

"By the ton?" Charo gasped. "The total amount used in 2001 was less than ten grams."

"Exactly. On April 1, 1979, at the end of the second shift, a worker donned a protective suit and entered the air exhaust chamber. He removed an air filter and slid it into the automatic scrubber that cleaned and disinfected the filter with bleach. The cycle took forty minutes. He then left a note for his supervisor and went home. But the supervisor never saw the note and started up the exhaust fans without the filter. Spores spilled out into the night air and somewhere close to a hundred people were infected, maybe more. The exact count isn't known."

"Disturbing, but what does it have to do with the anthrax mailings?" Charo asked.

"After the dissolution of the Soviet Union some US scientists got access to pathology specimens from the victims. They reported finding at least four different strains."

"You think the Russians mailed the anthrax?"

"I don't know. The Russians claim to have destroyed their stockpile of anthrax spores but I haven't been able to find an accounting of all of it."

"Are we back to considering foreign terrorists?" Charo asked.

The list of nations supporting terrorism in 2001 was long and included Iran, Iraq, North Korea, Libya, Syria, and the Palestinian factions of Hamas and Hezbollah. Several had approached the Russians looking to buy biological weapons or to recruit their unemployed scientists. Mackey wasn't the only one to worry about the whereabouts of Soviet bioweapons and technology. President Clinton and the State Department were concerned enough to fund programs to convert the weapons plants for domestic use. The money employed some of the scientists, but it was not nearly enough. There were huge gaps in intelligence and Mackey believed it was of little consolation that a terrorist group hadn't yet used a biological weapon. Or had they? Could 2001 have been a test run?

"Aum Shinrikyo tried liquid anthrax as a weapon," Mackey said.

"I think they were out of the terrorism business by 2001," Charo replied.

"I'm stuck on the motive," Mackey said. "It would narrow the suspects."

"Money, hate and revenge are the top three," Charo said.

Mackey and Charo grew silent. The occasional crack of bowling balls marked time like a drunken pendulum. At first the timing and wording of the anthrax letters had thrust al Qaeda into the spotlight. The administration was on record that Iraq participated in 9/11 so they were on the short list of suspects, too. After critical analysis of the letters and the identification of the Ames strain, the Iraq/al Qaeda suspicion shifted toward pro-Israeli groups seeking to capitalize on the anti-Arab furor caused by 9/11 and to push the US toward war with their enemies. This quickly faded in favor of homegrown terrorists—both right-wing extremists groups and the disgruntled lone scientist.

"Where is the investigation now?" Mackey asked.

"There is a new suspect, but insufficient evidence to indict at this time."

Mackey's shoulders sagged. Maybe there was no need to continue.

"Not everyone in the bureau is convinced. I think the SAC—the special agent in charge— is being ultra cautious because of what happened with the last suspect." Charo stood up and lifted her jacket from the arm of the chair.

"Where does that leave us?" Mackey asked.

"I'll see what I can find out," she replied.

"Does this mean we are teaming up?"

Charo reached into her jacket pocket and pulled out a business card. She scribbled her cell phone number and an email address on the back and dropped it into Mackey's lap. He met her unreadable eyes before she turned for the exit.

"Consider yourself a person of interest," she called over her shoulder.

Charo didn't go straight home. She could have used the free gym in 26 Federal Plaza but that meant heading back into Manhattan and being subjected to stares, come-ons, and sexual innuendos from her male co-workers. She got her fair share of leers at the local gym, but no one approached her or said more than, "How you doin'?" This she could tolerate.

She went right for the speed bag. Boxing was something she took to at Quantico. It was a way for her to work out her aggressions and turned out to be a superb exercise to tone her upper body strength and improve her cardiovascular endurance. Her instructor wanted her to try out for the FBI's version of the Golden Gloves. Charo saw no reason to bruise another person without probable cause and cared to compete only with herself. She adjusted the bag height, tied her hair back, and then taped up. She got into the rhythm, switching hands every three to four hits. After ten minutes her heart was racing and she glistened with sweat.

What were the risks? She didn't know of any agent who had gotten caught performing an unauthorized investigation. In fact she knew of only one agent who was ever disciplined and suspected it took a laundry basket of wrongdoing to get dismissed. It was her observation that if you displeased your superiors you were passed over for promotion or transferred. It would be horrible to be sent to a field office in the Midwest. Worst of all, if she was caught accessing files she had no reason to see, she could be branded a security risk. Her mixed heritage already made some nervous. As if being a Chinese-American, or more specifically, a Chinese-South American, made her an automatic candidate for turning double agent. This was the most distasteful of consequences. She might be forced to leave the bureau in disgrace like Aldrich Ames and Robert Hanssen.

What was there to gain? Mackey was right, the FBI was not proficient at sharing information. He went easy on her. She knew firsthand how the FBI failed to communicate within as well as with other security agencies. Perhaps if she demonstrated how inter-agency cooperation could benefit the bureau, and the nation, Hoover's antiquated culture would begin to change. Then there was the current suspect. If they didn't have the right one, she could save the bureau a world of further embarrassment and ridicule.

She moved on to free weights, doing biceps and triceps curls before the floor-to-ceiling mirror. More than allowing her to monitor her form, the mirrors gave a view of who else was in the gym. Another Quantico lesson she learned well. If you can't have your back to the wall, find a way to have a view of who else is occupying the same space.

Charo wanted to believe that the main reason for taking the risk was to ensure that justice was served. It did bother her that the perpetrator had thus far gotten away with murder. The events of 2001 still made her bristle. Although the transfer did not have any perceptible impact on her career she knew it was there—a black mark in her file that she didn't earn or deserve.

There was something about the gym that made it hard to fool yourself. It could be that your gym clothes hid nothing, or that the mirrors on every wall revealed unflattering angles of your body. Or that it's just plain hard not to be honest with yourself when trembling with fifty pounds suspended above your chest and neck. As she lay on a bench with dumbbells extended she conceded that this was her motivation.

. . .

It was a chilly night for September. The cold air was a prelude to winter and caught Mackey unprepared. From the first melancholic note of the solo piano he recognized the song "Winter[3]." But as the jukebox was in his mind, he knew all the songs. *Little Earthquakes* was by fellow Baltimorean Tori Amos and a CD Allie used to play. He never gave the lyrics much thought but he now wondered why his mind picked those words to play over and over.

Maybe it was because he couldn't remember the whole song. He checked his watch, still a few hours left to September 18th. The chill seeped closer to bone.

He tiptoed into the factory of his guilt. The foundry of molten regret provided no warmth. He had failed to meet her needs. The independence that had served him so well earlier in his life had pushed Allie away. He wanted to need her but he didn't know how. He knew he loved her. He had proof. The time she fell off her bicycle and broke her collarbone—the anguish overtook him like a tsunami. The panic he had never before felt petrified him. Allie, with her arm pressed to her breast to quell the pain, was the one to do the consoling. Mackey had seen far worse at the hospital, but when someone you love is hurt you lose all objectivity.

What he feared to his core was that he was emotionally distant like his father. A man who found himself in a life he never expected. At the age of fifty-five he married a younger woman who invaded his narrow, structured, yet comfortable existence. A child came a year later. The man did his best, but after years of living alone he didn't know how to relate to a small boy. Mackey rationalized that as a professor he dealt with "kids" all day, hence when he came home to his family he preferred to be alone. He knew there was more to it than that. His father was a kind, patient man and a reliable provider. But no amount of reasoning could prevent the hurt he suffered when the man retreated to the quiet solitude of his study rather than spend the time with his family.

The din of the approaching L train was a welcomed distraction. Two young men carrying conga drums entered with Mackey. They unfolded stools and set up an impromptu stage in the center of the subway car. Their fingers and palms raced effortlessly across the drumhead from center to edge and back again. Mackey had no musical aptitude, an irony not lost on him whenever his jukebox fired up. The drummers' syncopated beat was denser than the angst in his head. As the infectious sounds flowed through the car they squeezed out the deprecating thoughts and chased Tori back into the CD rack. Mackey tossed a five into the upturned cap though the service provided was worth more than an autographed, first edition of Sigmund Freud's, *The Interpretation of Dreams*.

At home, in bed, staring at a spot on the ceiling that resembled a nesting bat Mackey was again serenaded by his subconscious. It was a few lines from "Golden Slumbers," an old Beatles tune[4]. He wondered if John Lennon had ever found the way and if Paul McCartney still carried the weight.

The feeling was most akin to bursting to the surface with a desperate hunger for air after holding your breath too long under water. It was lying in bed next to Allie when he had first felt the sensation. Long before the self-diagnosis and self-medication of panic disorder, it took just the soothing distraction of Allie's voice to calm his breathing. All he could do now was pop a Xanax and trade anxiety for insomnia.

.| 8 |.

The difference between their reasons for pursuing the investigation was inconsequential, yet as palpable as a depressed skull fracture. If the solution to some riddle or puzzle was knowable, as Mackey believed the identity of the person or persons responsible for the anthrax mailings was, his compulsion drove him to pursue it to the near exclusion of all other aspects of his life. Like coming across a pistachio nut with no perceptible opening, Mackey had to figure out a way to crack it and the tougher the challenge the more fervent his efforts. The nearer he got to the solution, the closer his patience approached that of an electron.

Charo viewed the crime as just that—a violation of law. Hers was a world of order, honor, duty, and consequences. Her commitment was to principle and the specifics of any crime and often failed to incite any passion beyond what she felt as an agent of federal law enforcement. She possessed the ideal temperament for a job dominated by bureaucracy and male egos.

The FBI's leading suspect, and the entire focus of the FBI investigation in the fall of 2006, was a twenty-seven-year-old US-born man of Palestinian heritage who was an assistant instructor of microbiology at Rutgers University. As an undergraduate student at Lehigh University, Joseph Erekat participated in a soil study on a Pennsylvania farm where, seventy-five years earlier, there had been an outbreak of anthrax amongst its cattle. After graduating Lehigh University in May of 2001, Erekat did a summer internship at the US Army Medical

Research Institute of Infectious Diseases (USAMRIID) at Fort Detrick in Maryland. The FBI learned of him through a tip from someone who met him during the summer of 2001 at Fort Detrick. Erekat had told the scientist that he had been a member of the Palestinian Independence Freedom Foundation, a nonviolent group that was in favor of a peaceful land settlement with the Israelis. The FBI placed Erekat under surveillance, convinced he possessed the requisite skills and equipment to have grown anthrax.

There was a faction within the FBI, including Special Agent-in-Charge Calvin Martinez, who were certain that Erekat was the anthrax mailer. Others did not share this view. They were leery of previous "false starts" as they preferred to call them. Charo told Mackey this as they strolled along the Battery Park walkway in the early morning hours of September 20th. The morning sun glanced off the waters of the Hudson River like the accusations cast against Steven Hatfill; producing heat but not much illumination. To the casual observer Charo and Mackey were a couple out for a morning walk before heading to their respective offices.

"Why hasn't Erekat been arrested?" Mackey asked.

"I don't have an answer. There are two things about an agent that provokes suspicion. Asking a lot of questions about another agent's investigation and being a woman. I had to be careful to learn what I told you, which you cannot repeat."

Mackey agreed.

"I suspect there is additional evidence but not yet enough to meet the director's new standards," Charo continued.

"What additional evidence is there to find by following Erekat around? Do they think he'll lead them to the lab? Or blog on how he did it?"

"Criminals have been known to do stupider things, but no, the bureau does not expect any significant breakthroughs. The sad reality is that he may never be charged."

"You guys need help. If not to prove it was Erekat then to redirect the investigation toward the real culprit," Mackey said.

Charo eyed him like the X-ray machines at the airport scanning for hidden contraband, but she had already made up her mind. Mackey didn't notice; he was gazing across the river at a clock the size of a Ferris wheel. He turned back to catch the last of Charo's gamma rays. Her sunglasses were off, arms folded across her chest, and lips puckered to one side like she was about to spit out something distasteful.

"Meet me this afternoon at 4:55 PM at the African Burial Ground National Monument. Bring your CDC identification card and put on a suit. You do own a suit?"

Mackey nodded.

"If we are going to do this it has to be on my terms. I need to know I can trust you not to jeopardize my position with the bureau. It is easy enough for a woman to get tossed into the FBI dog run, I don't need any help from you. One simple rule, you don't talk to anyone unless you clear it with me. Got it?"

Mackey held up two fingers. "Scout's honor."

"The scout's pledge is three fingers," Charo said.

"I'm saving the other one to seal my mouth."

Mackey approached the construction site of the African Burial Ground National Monument from the east and Charo from the west like a pair of gunslingers. It was 4:55 PM. With his CDC ID card and Charo leading the way they entered the federal building without a glance from the Homeland Security Police. Charo waited until they could board an elevator alone before ushering Mackey into the car.

"I gave some thought to your idea. I still think it's a long shot. I might be able to get the E-ZPass data but that would attract unwanted attention and I wouldn't know what to do with it anyway. I can't give you access either." They exited onto the 26th floor. The stencil on the glass door read: Criminal Justice Math Lab.

"However, if Geetangali Reddy does it..." Charo slid her card through a scanner. The door buzzed and then unlatched. Two men hunched over computer screens jerked their heads as if caught browsing porn. They waved at Charo and went back to their screens.

"God bless civilian data wonks," she said, "the FBI would be lost without them." From the corner of her eye Charo noticed a retort forming on Mackey's lips. She placed the three-fingered scout's pledge to her ruby lips. Then removed two fingers.

Mackey swallowed his words. Around a corner they came to a cubicle where a petite woman with waist-length onyx hair sat staring at a pair of giant computer monitors.

"Hi, Geeta. I'd like you to meet Mackey Dunn, he's a physician with the CDC and we've come to ask for your help. Mackey, Geeta has a master's degree in computer science from MIT and is a trusted friend. She's working on fixing some of our archaic databases."

"Have you heard of VCF? The Virtual Case File?" Geeta asked.

Mackey shook his head no.

She cast a conspiratorial glance over his shoulder and lowered her voice, "It was a $170-million debacle of a database that was supposed to replace the ACS and bring the FBI into the twenty-first century." She waved her hands about the unit. "We are up here trying to help patch something together."

"We've got a different sort of problem; more like finding a needle in a haystack."

Geeta flashed a quick smile and pulled up a couple of chairs.

“I’ve got to… attend to some things,” Charo said. “Mackey, I’ll come back for you.” Mackey watched her leave, a twinge of remorse lingering like lemon zest on his tongue.

“Okay, Dr. Mackey Dunn, what is it I can help you with?” Geeta said.

Mackey explained the E-ZPass idea, going into greater detail than he had done for Charo.

“If it works, we’ll have a short list of drivers who drove to and from Princeton in the days before each mailing,” he concluded.

Geeta nodded. “I might be able to program this in SAS, or better O-Matrix. Where is the data?”

“We were hoping you could assist there as well. Charo thought you might be able to get access to the E-ZPass data?”

Geeta glanced over Mackey’s shoulder at her co-workers. They were consumed at their own workstations, out of earshot. When she turned back Mackey saw a gigahertz size gleam in her eye. She slid her chair closer to Mackey.

“Charo warned me this might be risky. You think that buried within that Mt. Kangchenjunga of data there might be a clue to the anthrax killer?”

“Yes. We know the unsub was at a mailbox in Princeton to mail both groups of letters. Assumption number one is that the perpetrator would not mail the letters from his backyard. Coming by train or bus while carrying anthrax-laden letters would be far too risky. Renting a car would leave a record, so assumption number two is that he used his own car. He likely lives in a neighboring state or in Northern New Jersey, so he might have an E-ZPass account. That’s the third assumption. If he doesn’t have an E-ZPass, tollbooths take photos of the license plates of every car that passes through.”

"We have optical character recognition software of course," Geeta said. "Supposing the data is available I am not yet clear on how you intend to use it to identify the anthrax mailer?"

"That's the analytical challenge. Daily commuters will make up the bulk of travelers. During weekdays the flow is like the tide, one set of commuters heading in one direction in the morning, and the reverse in the afternoon. Within the monotonous repetition of the tide there are eddy currents, aberrations, trips that don't fit the pattern. The question is can we identify travelers whose E-ZPass footprint on the days before each mailing fit with a trip to and from Princeton but differ from that of a regular commuter?"

"Isn't that another assumption?"

"What?"

"That our killer was not a regular commuter and his trip to Princeton was not along his normal route."

"Yes, I suppose you are correct. I expect that we'll either not find anything or have too many matches to check out," Mackey sighed.

Geeta contemplated her computer screens. "Let me work on getting the data then I'll call Charo to get your help defining the model and parameters. In case anyone asks, Charo instructed me to say this is for a child pornography case investigation," Geeta said.

"A cold one," Mackey added.

Charo led him back out onto the street. "It's not a good idea for you to spend too much time in the building."

Mackey shrugged.

"I'll see what else I can find out about the new person of interest."

The phrase brought a smile to Mackey's face, which provoked a smirk from Charo. She gave him a playful slug on the shoulder, propelling him up Broadway.

At Worth Street he turned right. A block later he stared up at the names etched into the frieze of the Department of Health building. How could anyone not be inspired to come to work each day by the sight of such stalwarts of public health. Paul Ehrlich, who dreamed up the magic bullet theory that became the basis of the antibiotic revolution, had his name carved in granite. A tireless researcher with a background in chemistry, he rarely stopped working long enough to eat. Ehrlich spent much of his life testing thousands of compounds for antibacterial activity. Mackey saw a parallel in the task of picking one E-ZPass user from among the millions. Failure did not deter Ehrlich. Sadly, although he won the Nobel Prize in Medicine in 1908 and discovered a now antiquated treatment for syphilis, the magic bullet eluded him.

Next to Ehrlich on the building's façade was Anton Van Leeuwenhoek, the Dutchman who advanced microscopy making Ehrlich's work possible. A tradesman without scientific training, Leeuwenhoek ground lenses that could magnify 300 times.

Moving along the frieze he came to Louis Pasteur. Remembered best for the process used to preserve milk that bears his name, not many knew that he invented the first vaccine to prevent rabies and pioneered the process of virus attenuation still in use today.

A man noticed Mackey frozen to the sidewalk. "You okay, buddy?"

"Yeah. Just climbing onto the shoulders of giants."

9

Her cubicle mates had left for the day. Charo didn't miss them. She could handle their over-the-top machismo, the pet names such as G-spot and Breast Fed, their juvenile sexual innuendos and lame double entendres. If it wasn't football or basketball they discussed at excessive decibels it was the size of the knockers of some new secretary or waitress at the diner. But Charo found it hard to work while they didn't.

It had occurred to Charo on more than one occasion that the office was not unlike her high school in Stonesend, Queens—foreign and isolating. Charo was born and raised in the US, but they were the only things she had in common with her classmates. The boys, under the influence of hormones, alcohol, or drugs had become alien. They called her "Chinezuelan," a nickname she might not have minded if it hadn't been delivered with vehement derision. The girls hated her because she cared about her grades, was talented at sports, and popular with teachers—especially the male ones. The boys disliked her, too. Charo's self-esteem, a product of a dutiful father and artistic mother, inured her to their belittling attempts at subjugation. They got drunk or stoned at any and every opportunity while Charo abstained. They viewed sports as a get-out-of-jail free card played whenever their drunken exploits went too far. To Charo, it was a way to escape the toxicity of her environment and see how other teens lived.

There was the summer after graduation when she worked as a lifeguard and had gotten to know one boy well from the hours they spent together up on the stand.

Away from his friends, Danny wasn't so beastly. They talked about music and plans after high school. His father was a fireman and Danny planned to enroll at the academy. They both liked the A-ha music video for "Take On Me." Vanishing into the pages of a comic book was for some the lone way out of Stonesend. It surprised Charo that Danny wasn't dumb, that he liked poetry, and wanted to be a musician like his idol, Billy Joel. He had a real talent for putting together words, but was forced to abandon music lessons after his father got hurt on the job and went on disability.

It seemed to Charo that the kids she grew up with always ran into one obstacle or another. The six-foot-six kid who received honorable mention All-New York City basketball honors and who was supposed to go to Notre Dame on a full athletic scholarship didn't even graduate from community college after he hurt his knee falling off a motor scooter. The last time Charo saw him he was wearing a stained apron and slicing salami at Louie's Deli.

The girl two years ahead of her who played lead in all the theatrical productions dropped out of high school during her senior year after getting pregnant. She never made it to Broadway except years later as a chaperone for the school's drama club.

It is not like Charo had any advantages. Her father supported their family of four and her mother's struggling painting career on Postal Service wages that kept them just north of the poverty line. But Charo never saw this as an obstacle.

When the summer ended Charo got busy with college, and she and Danny fell out of touch. She wondered every now and then how his life turned out. Did he become a fireman or return to his passion music? Maybe he was married and had kids, falling into the well-trod routine of previous generations. Did he still live in Stonesend? As irksome as her teenage years were, they turned out to prepare her well for a career in law enforcement.

Charo logged into her alter ego's email account. There was an email from TheBigOmar69. He had taken the bait, searched MySpace, and found her email address. He invited her to IM so they could have a private chat session. Charo typed a message:

Qtpye_grl13: hi, im home fr skool
TheBigOmar69: ive been waiting, why so late?
Qtpye_grl13: d
TheBigOmar69: wha?
Qtpye_grl13: detention. I dont do my hwrk
TheBigOmar69: ur a bad grl, eh? lol
Qtpye_grl13: how did you get my email?
TheBigOmar69: I saw your MySpace page
Qtpye_grl13: o. bad pics.
TheBigOmar69: No, I think ur very cute. Do you have other pics? Can't see your face and bod too well.
Qtpye_grl13: nah, 2 fat n ugly
TheBigOmar69: I don't think so, ur bu t ful
Qtpye_grl13: u sound like my da
TheBigOmar69: he must be a gud man
Qtpye_grl13: he lives in Grmany
TheBigOmar69: soldier?
Qtpye_grl13: y
TheBigOmar69: u must miss him. I was in Desert Storm.
Qtpye_grl13: ☹
TheBigOmar69: so u just live with mom?
Qtpye_grl13: + brat bro, 11
Qtpye_grl13: gotta go, shes home. dont wanna another fight
TheBigOmar69: u fight with yur mom?
Qtpye_grl13: duh
TheBigOmar69: she treat u like a kid?
Qtpye_grl13: uh-huh
TheBigOmar69: I wouldn't
Qtpye_grl13: bye
TheBigOmar69: write me later?

Charo logged off. For the first contact the protocol was to keep it brief. The Big Omar was a live one, grooming her with complimentary remarks and angling to take advantage of the absent father. Charo saved a copy of her chat session. Before shutting down she checked her email account. There was a message from Mackey. While Geeta worked on getting the E-ZPass data he wanted to meet to go over the evidence. If she hurried, she could make it to the last evening spinning class.

.| 10 |.

Mackey watched the rain cascade in sheets from the comfort of a Starbucks table. He didn't bother to buy coffee, instead plucking a used cup out of the waste bin as table decoration. Not that the staff ever bothered to roust a rooted person, patron or not. He did it to deflect the impatient glares of customers, who, like him, had sought shelter from the storm. The pages of his *New York Times* were wet. There was an article based on a FBI report that New York was the safest big city in the US. The overall violent crime rate had increased by 2 percent in other parts of the country while in New York it was down 2 percent. The epidemiologist in him was not impressed. Results like that wouldn't get you National Institutes of Health funding.

On another page was the story of a fourteen-year-old girl in South Carolina who outwitted her kidnapper and abuser by swiping his cell phone while he slept and texting her mother. The chirp of his own phone announced a text message from Charo. The weather had cancelled her plans to help paint her dad's hardware store so she had the day off. She invited him to her apartment to go over the mail problem.

When he became tired of reading the scientific literature about spores, Mackey read about the FBI. There weren't many facts about the criminal investigation on the Internet, so he hoped he might find clues in a retired agent's memoir. He found several books written after the outbreak, two by former agents, but none had chapters on the anthrax investigation or even listed anthrax in the index. He remembered what Karros and Charo told him—that they couldn't discuss an open investigation. He perused the books anyway, finding the history of the FBI and J. Edgar Hoover's legacy relevant to how the investigation was handled.

Hoover was a peculiar man at a minimum. He never married, was devoted to his mother, and fastidious in habit and routine. The cross-dressing thing seemed to be a rumor proffered by one of the many enemies he made in his almost fifty years as FBI director. When it came to the bureau, he didn't respond well to direction or interference from anyone, including the long list of attorney generals who served as his boss. He had no qualms about using agents to gather information on congressmen, public officials, and celebrities if he thought it might one day serve his needs or strengthen his hold on the bureau. Hoover enjoyed catching an elected official in a salacious liaison with someone other than his spouse. Although he often spied on elected officials he didn't prosecute them for corruption, choosing instead to keep the leverage for future situations such as a favorable vote on a bill authorizing increased funding for the FBI. He had so many public officials in his pockets that he had to carry his keys and wallet on a chain from his belt.

Hoover had created a self-propagating environment of intimidation and mistrust. The official motto may have been "Fidelity, Bravery and Integrity," but the tenets were fear, bluster and insecurity. Provoked by a deluge of Freedom of Information Act requests, the FBI scanned parts of their secret files and posted them on their website. Mackey found it amusing and frightening whom the FBI maintained files on. Many of the links weren't yet live, but it made him wonder. Muhammad Ali, Count Basie, Louis Armstrong, W.E.B. Dubois, Arthur Ashe, Wilt Chamberlain, Pearl Buck, Cab Calloway, Roberto Clemente—and he was only up to the letter D. Clemente was listed because an irate Met fan sent him a death threat. Dubois and Buck were painted as communists, an attempt to silence their dissonance. Not all of the files were on people of color. A number of entertainers from Lucille Ball to the Doors had files. Even America's first environmentalist, Rachel Carson, had a FBI file though the link wasn't yet live. It sure seemed like investigations were opened in a capricious manner. Hoover had been dead for over twenty-five years when 9/11 happened but the mark he left on the agency was more indelible than Krylon on a brick wall. Mackey was beginning to understand why terrorism leads before the attacks on the World Trade Center were mishandled.

Mackey thumbed through an FBI exposé on the subway ride to Charo's apartment. It was a thick book covering the agency's creation through the present. Turning to the index he again failed to find an entry for anthrax. The table of contents did have a chapter on 9/11.

The two frequently cited gaffs by the FBI before 9/11 had to do with individuals with ties to Islamic extremist groups who where in the United States taking flying lessons. An agent in Phoenix notified FBI headquarters about his discovery in July 2001 and suggested that the bureau check all other flying schools in the US to see if this was a pattern. The other tip came from a flying school in Minnesota where Zacarias Moussaoui, later called the 20th hijacker, showed up demanding to be taught how to fly jumbo jets. Mackey recognized a bizarre yet recurring theme: the arrogance with which the terrorists demanded things. As if they were taught in al Qaeda training camps that in the land of freedom all you had to do was ask firmly and you would receive.

Mohammed Atta, who piloted one of the planes into the towers, walked into the US Department of Agriculture in South Florida office seeking a small business federal grant of $650,000 to buy a plane and retrofit it with "crop dusting" equipment. When the clerk didn't reach into the cash box and start doling out hundred-dollar bills he became incensed. A bitter irony that the very freedom Americans defend with their lives made it possible for hijackers to learn how to fly planes. The thought of a society without such freedom made Mackey queasy.

Thankfully, the school in Minnesota thought Moussaoui's request and behavior were suspicious, so they reported him to the FBI. Moussaoui was in the states without a visa. French intelligence connected him to al Qaeda and he was arrested. The blunder occurred with his laptop. Agents confused about the law covering search warrants based on intelligence versus criminal evidence could not agree that a search warrant could be issued, so one wasn't requested. The information on Moussaoui's laptop did not come to light until after the attacks.

When a trauma patient comes into the emergency department the priorities are breathing and circulation followed by a rapid head-to-toe assessment. Minutes can matter for survival. Rarely the unseen fatal injury doesn't come to light until post mortem. The knowledge that several men of Middle Eastern descent were suddenly requesting and taking flying lessons should have been enough to go head-to-toe on Moussaoui's laptop. The fact that these tips were overlooked disturbed Mackey but gave him hope that something overlooked would allow them to solve the anthrax crime.

With his backpack loaded with his laptop, books, journal articles, and notes, Mackey exited from the L train stairs huffing. Coming toward him down the rain-slick sidewalk were two boys on scooters. The younger one was leading the race pushing hard, one foot on his Razor the other slapping the pavement. His head was turned watching his brother, who, with much less effort, was gaining on him. The lead kid was making a beeline for a lamppost and a collision forceful enough to propel him to the emergency room for stitches and perhaps a tooth reimplantation. His mother was more than half a block away, pushing a stroller and calling after them to no avail. Mackey quickened his step and reached the lamppost before the kid did. He nabbed the boy beneath his arms lifting him from the scooter and swinging him around the pole as the shiny Razor crashed into the rusted metal. The boy's face contorted from nervous excitement to frightened panic to dazed confusion. Mackey lowered him to the ground. His brother skidded to a stop peering at Mackey with head tilted as if trying to place a distant relative. The scooter was damaged but functional. The mom came upon the scene, ushered her boys down the block but didn't say a word. Mackey watched them leave. The older boy turned back and waved.

The sun was sinking below the jagged steel outline of lower Manhattan. Mackey stood before floor-to-ceiling windows overlooking the Williamsburg Bridge. The south faces of the buildings glowed like hot coals, while the north sides were dark and featureless until incandescent lights popped on like stadium flash bulbs during a Barry Bonds at bat. Behind him Charo emerged from the bathroom running a towel through her wet hair. She was wearing an oversized gray sweatshirt and skimpy gym shorts. Mackey was mesmerized by the vision of a cuddlesome co-ed that stood in stark contrast to the hardened G-Woman persona Charo ardently cultivated. The sweatshirt collar was pulled seductively to one side exposing a tan shoulder and playful collarbone that skimmed the surface like a dolphin beneath a cotton wave.

"What are you doing?" Charo's voice interrupted his reverie. Caught in an admiring stare by the spotlight of Charo's glare, he blushed. He ran through possible explanations until he noticed she wasn't intent upon his face but the pad he was holding. He raised it to his face to hide the reddening hue he suspected still lingered there.

"An outline. I want to focus on the criminal part of the investigation."

Charo plopped down on her sofa, crossing her calves on the coffee table. She tossed a bag of corn chips on the table and pulled a laptop onto her lap. She tapped the keys and then looked up.

"Ready."

"Back in a minute." Mackey ducked out her door into the hallway returning with a wardrobe box he had passed on his way in that he disassembled into a makeshift blackboard. He leaned it against the window opposite the sofa.

"Got a marker?"

Charo sprung from the couch and returned with two markers. Mackey tried them but both were dry. She disappeared again, this time Mackey heard her in the bathroom rummaging in the medicine cabinet. She bounced back onto the couch and laid three lipsticks on the coffee table. Mackey picked up a cylinder of lipstick and removed the cap. Bubble-gum pink. Wearing a wry smile, Mackey held it out to Charo. She batted her eyes. Mackey tossed it back. The next was a ghoulish shade of purple. From the pristine angled faces of the sticks he could tell neither had ever brushed the lips of Charo Chen. He tossed that one back too. The third was burnt-torch auburn.

On the first cardboard panel nearest the wall, he printed in small block letters "FBI." Writing with lipstick required that he put the pad down, press lightly and hold the cardboard with his other hand. Beneath it he scrawled his outline:

FBI
Interview recipients of letters
Forensic examination of letters

- *Fingerprints*
- *Fibers*
- *Chemicals*
- *The envelopes*
- *Pharmacy fold*

Handwriting analysis

- *Wording*
- *Style*
- *Compare to other letters on file*
- *Psychological profile*

"Both the FBI and public health investigators interviewed every anthrax case or the family of those who died."

"Were murdered," Charo said.

"Right. Did this uncover any clues to the identity of the anthrax mailer?" Mackey paused. "Most never saw or did not recall seeing a letter. And for those who did, the letter was found and their testimony didn't add anything beyond the physical evidence." Mackey returned to his makeshift chalkboard and drew a zero.

Charo typed "no eyewitness" into her laptop notes.

"What about the forensic analysis of the letters? It has been five years, so if any fingerprints were found they must have had no match in either the FBI or Interpol databases and thus haven't led to the identification of a suspect." Charo punched the zero key. Mackey drew one.

"What about fibers, hair, or unusual chemicals that could be used to track the origin of the letter. I couldn't find anything on this." Charo avoided Mackey's laser-beam eyes. "Agent Chen," he said raising his left eyebrow, "are you holding out on me?"

"I was able to find out some information, but you can't ever repeat it. I am not sure how useful it is anyway. The envelopes were sealed with clear tape. Attached to the tape were fibers."

"Fibers?"

"Eight to be exact. Two were cotton—one black and one red; two were wool—one black and one blue; two were acrylic—one red and one yellow; one was black nylon; and one was brown polyester."

"Eight fibers? Is it common to find that many? And to have them be of different colors and materials?" Mackey asked.

"I'm not a fashionista, but I can't think of too many articles of clothing that would have black, blue, yellow, red, and brown fibers. Maybe a scarf?" Charo replied.

"Multiple handlings of the envelopes wearing different clothes?"

"Or there were accomplices."

"I am also guessing these couldn't be traced to a garment or manufacturer." Mackey said.

"No."

"So, they are only of help if there are other fibers to match to them. Which requires a suspect, a search warrant, and a scintilla of luck. What else you got?"

"The tape was 3M brand. Can be bought in any number of stores in any number of states. No help there."

"None indeed." Mackey added another zero to the board. "Anything else?"

"The ink on the envelopes wasn't from a ball point pen. It was from the type of pen where the ink flows freely."

"A fountain pen?"

"No, more like a felt tip."

"Any link to a specific product?"

"Negative."

"That it?" Mackey inquired as he updated the board.

"For now," she smiled.

"Any chemicals found?"

"No chemicals," Charo replied.

"The envelopes measured 6 3/4 inches by 4 5/8 inches in size, were self-adhesive, and prepaid bearing a US Postal Service Federal Eagle. Was any DNA found on the envelopes?"

"No DNA. But the envelopes had a printing defect." Charo said.

"Oh?"

"The postage was an illustration of a bald eagle in blue perched on a horizontal bar with 'USA' in white block letters and was printed using a flexographic press. She handed him a color enlargement. "Look between the *U* and the *S* and then the *S* and the *A*. See the eagle's talons? They aren't the same. One is broken."

"The one between the S and the A looks like it is missing a pixel," Mackey said.

"The manufacturer confirmed that approximately 45 million envelopes with this defect were produced and sold between January 2001 and June 2002 throughout Maryland, Virginia, West Virginia, Delaware, Eastern Pennsylvania, and the District of Columbia."

"Hmm, the envelopes weren't sold in New Jersey."

"Perhaps your E-ZPass idea isn't so far fetched," Charo grinned.

"All the letters were photocopies," Mackey moved on.

"No ink for analysis," Charo added.

"The mailer used a pharmaceutical fold to contain the powder. The paper used to write the letters was standard, unlined ordinary copy paper, 8 1/2 by 11 inches. And it was trimmed," Mackey said.

"Pharmaceutical fold?" Charo asked.

"Yes, like a pharmacist does to keep pills or powdered medicine from escaping." Mackey pulled a sheet of paper off the pad and laid it on the coffee table. He grabbed an empty bag of chips and shook out the crumbs onto the page, positioning them in the middle. He then folded down the top third followed by folding up the bottom third. He next folded a half-inch from each open horizontal edge to make a semi-sealed packet. Charo examined the packet, then walked into the next room returning with two envelopes, one letter size, the other the size used in the mail attacks. She first placed the folded packet in the letter-sized envelope. It fit easily. There were several inches on either end of the packet. The letter shifted back and forth inside the envelope. The top flap cleared the folded letter upon sealing. When she placed the folded packet into the smaller envelope, the width was a snug fit, but the top flap could not be sealed. Charo handed it to Mackey.

"If it doesn't fit, we must acquit?" she said.

"That's why he trimmed the paper."

Mackey examined the envelope from every angle. The corner seals did not form a tight barrier; the glued flaps leaving spaces large enough to pass the bent prong of a paper clip. Mackey demonstrated this for Charo.

"The pharmaceutical fold suggests Mailthrax knew how potent this stuff was," Charo said.

"Or she," Mackey added.

"This was not the work of a woman," Charo said. "Not with a wardrobe of brown polyester."

"My dear Watson it is a capital mistake to theorize in advance of the facts," Mackey said.

"You can quote all the Sherlock Holmes you like, but you won't convince me that the letters were mailed by a woman," Charo replied. Mackey wrote on the cardboard the words "Knew potency." Mackey stepped back to view what they had thus far. It wasn't much. "What did the FBI make of the handwriting?" he asked.

"That the person attempted a style unlike his own natural handwriting to obscure the evidence. He used block letters because script is more distinctive. All the letters are capitals, perhaps to limit comparison to other samples had we ever gotten to that point."

"Why do you suppose he didn't use a typewriter or printer?" Mackey asked.

"Both are traceable."

"The Senate letters were mailed after the first Florida case but before the New York City cases were known. I remember the media circus when the news broke. It wasn't called an intentional act at that time. The timing of the letters could be an important clue."

"Say more," Charo said.

"I'm thinking the second group of letters was mailed because the first set appeared ineffectual. It wasn't until October 7th that the laboratory tests from the AMI building confirmed bioterrorism."

"You're saying the Florida case didn't achieve the mailer's goal so he sent more letters?"

"Yes, and added the phony return address to keep them from being tossed out unopened."

"Perhaps he upped the potency, too," Charo added.

"That's it, Charo! The fatal mistake and how we'll catch him!"

"Spore purity?"

"No, the two trips to the mailbox in Princeton. A single point can be anywhere, but two points make a line. Straight to Mailthrax's door!"

.| 11 |.

Senator Byron Dorgan called the meeting to order. He sat before a microphone in the middle of a semicircular oak dais flanked by fellow Democratic senators. He was chairing the tenth hearing of the Democratic Policy Committee on contracting waste, fraud and abuse in Iraq. In their previous sessions the committee had heard from dozens of whistleblowers; former employees of defense contractors and government officials who shared stories of greed that made even Charles Ponzi seem honorable for bilking his countrymen. Dorgan had christened the hearings three years earlier with a cautionary tale of a young Republican congressman who warned in 1966 that the lack of oversight of a war contract was an invitation for profiteering and waste. That congressman was current Secretary of Defense Donald Rumsfeld and the company was Brown & Root. Brown & Root became Kellogg, Brown & Root, a subsidiary of the embattled Halliburton, and a major recipient of taxpayer dollars.

While latecomers filed in Senator Dorgan reminded the audience that the Democratic Policy Committee, like its Republican counterpart, was created by legislation in 1947. Dorgan had tried and failed to implement oversight in the Senate committee system and the present "paper tiger" gathering was as close as he could get to an official audit.

Dorgan concluded his opening remarks by recapping the findings of the first nine meetings beginning with the $1.4 billion in charges submitted by Halliburton for which no services or equipment could be verified as delivered. Gasoline which could be imported for less than a dollar a gallon was billed to the US taxpayer at more than twice the cost. There were SUVs being leased at $7,500 a month and a case of Coca-Cola that cost $45. And waste. Lots of waste. Vehicles with repairable malfunctions were junked in "torch pits." New ones were purchased at $80,000 apiece. When twenty-five tons of nails of the incorrect size arrived in Iraq, instead of returning them for the correct size they were buried in the desert and another order was placed.

As if these acts were not dreadful enough, contractors were placing the health of American soldiers in jeopardy. Wastewater was recycled for showers and oral hygiene and when tests showed the presence of dangerous *Escherichia coli* bacterium, the vendors claimed that it was normal practice. And then there was the food. Meals were prepared with frozen ingredients that were months past their expiration dates, held at unhygienic temperatures, and shot through with bullets or embedded with bits of metal from IEDs. These meals were then served to our brave sons and daughters fighting for the American way of life.

The first witness was a divorced mother of two who wanted to serve her country and did so as an employee of Halliburton. She was a coordinator of morale, welfare, and recreation. Her name was Julie McBride.

> "Good afternoon. It is truly a privilege for me to be here today and to speak to this honorable committee. I would like to thank the members for taking the time to investigate how American tax dollars are being spent in Iraq. I was 'over there,' and I will share with you some of my observations and concerns...
>
> I was hired as an 'MWR coordinator.' MWR stands for Morale, Welfare and Recreation. MWR facilities organized recreational activities for off-duty troops. I became the camp mom to many of the troops while I was there, and that

meant a great deal to me.

The two MWR facilities at Camp Fallujah were a fitness center and Internet café. The fitness center had gym equipment, pool and ping-pong tables, video games, and a large room for movies, fitness classes, and dances. The Internet café housed telephones and computers, and a library.

...I became concerned about several Halliburton practices. The first...procedures used to compile the headcount for the MWR department. Funding was evidently based, in part, on the headcount that Halliburton reported.

Each off-duty soldier who entered the fitness center or the Internet cafe signed in. This was referred to as the 'boots in the door' count. Halliburton MWR employees were directed to utilize the following methodology to intentionally inflate this count:

To begin, each hour on the hour, Halliburton staff were instructed to record the number of soldiers in each of the five rooms of the fitness center and in the Internet cafe and library. In addition, each person who used any equipment in the fitness center was required to sign a form. This included balls, ping-pong paddles, pool cues, board games, video games, et cetera...To inflate the figure, the coordinators began by adding together the boots in the door count and the hourly totals for each room in the fitness center throughout the day and in the library.

For example, I was present in Iraq on February 27th, 2005, when the boots in the door count at the MWR facility in Fallujah was about 330. The hourly count that day for each room was over 1,300. These totals were then combined for a fitness center headcount in excess of 1,600, or five times the actual number of troops that had come into the facility that day.

...One day in January 2005, they added 240 bottles of water used by the troops that day...This fraudulent head count can then equate to millions of dollars in unnecessary funding...The additional staffing does not benefit the troops, but it does benefit Halliburton...As the mantra at Halliburton camps goes, 'It's cost-plus, baby.'"

The senators, their faces contorted with a mixture of concentration, anger, and dismay, nodded as Ms. McBride spoke. In the back row a thin man wearing a grimace borrowed from the Grinch crossed his legs, the afforded leg space inadequate for his length. The room was warm and his throat dry. Behind the dais he noticed a pair of light fixtures fashioned to resemble torches. Inquisition torches. Each time he shifted in the leather seat his sweaty thighs peeled away from his slacks' polyester fabric. Ms. McBride concluded by explaining that the forty-five-dollar-per-case-soda wasn't given to the soldiers, except when they paid for it. However, Halliburton employees consumed the soda at no cost. She thanked the committee. There was a brief shuffling of paper and then Senator Dorgan welcomed the next witness, Alan Grayson.

> "Good afternoon. Thank you for the opportunity to be here today and to speak before this honorable committee... My name is Alan Grayson. I'm an attorney, and I represent dozens of whistleblowers in cases brought against contractors who have defrauded the government...With this week marking three and a half years since the occupation of Iraq began, it is possible to conduct an appraisal of the role that contractors have played in Iraq. It is not a pretty picture. While US forces are praised for their professionalism and their discipline, there have been countless reports of government contractors in Iraq undermining the mission, wasting money, and stealing money. Half of the $18 billion in Iraq reconstruction funds are unaccounted for. Senator Dorgan has said that there is an orgy of greed among contractors in Iraq, and there is ample evidence to back that up.
>
> Out of all the cases filed by whistleblowers regarding fraud in Iraq, only two of them have been litigated. The Bush administration refused to participate in either one of those. In the first case, a suit that I helped whistleblowers to bring against Custer Battles, the company's own internal audit report found the company guilty of criminal fraud. The US military suspended the defendants, finding adequate evidence of that fraud. Yet the Bush administration did literally nothing to recover the millions of dollars that the defendants stole. We brought that case to trial without the help of the Bush administration, and won a jury verdict worth more than $10 million for taxpayers. But the judge then ruled that the Bush administration had messed up the

> contract paperwork, and now the issue is on appeal.
>
> The second case is Ms. McBride's complaint against Halliburton. Her case was filed over a year ago. The Bush administration sat on it for that period, investigated only one of the five allegations of fraud in her complaint, and then, without explanation, refused to participate in that case as well. In both the Custer Battles case and the Halliburton case, the defendants' intimate connections with the Bush administration are well known.
>
> …Abraham Lincoln, had this to say about war profiteers when he proposed enactment of the Whistleblowers False Claims Act seven score and three years ago.
>
> 'Worse than traitors in arms are the men who pretend loyalty to the flag, feast and fatten on the misfortunes of a nation while patriotic blood is crimsoning the plains of the South, and their countrymen molder in the dust.'"

Having heard all he could stomach the thin man slipped out unnoticed through the bronze double door at the back of the hearing room. He steadied himself with a hand against the wall, hiding his face with his hat that he slipped over his sparse scalp once he was out of the building. At least Senator Dorgan omitted mention of several projects his contractor clients had messed up. There was no mention of the prison at Khan Bani Saad. The one the Iraqis didn't even want built because it was too close to the Iranian border. The Iraqis got their wish. After $40 million the roof wasn't finished and much of the plumbing and electrical work was absent or shoddily constructed. Speaking of shoddy workmanship, he was fortunate not to have to listen to Dorgan recount the incompetent electrical work that had nearly electrocuted several soldiers.

A sharp pain knotted his gut causing him to double over as he reached his car. Only 20 of the 150 medical clinics contracted were actually built and a good number of them were still unfinished. Thankfully the doctor from Diwaniya wasn't flown in to testify. If he ever showed photos of the pediatric and maternity wards of the hospital built with Iraq reconstruction funds showing sewage backing up through floor drains and the premature infant incubators that were manufactured in the 1970s held together with bailing wire he'd be out of a job.

He grabbed the bottle of Pepto-Bismol he kept in the glove compartment box and gulped what remained. Dorgan hadn't covered the half of it. There were Dell laptops marked up more than 100 percent in price, the $7-million road-to-nowhere, and the over-priced helicopter pad. He could only dance so long to those folksy adages of how the Army always overpaid for things like hammers and toilet seats.

Then there was the dichromate debacle. More than a hundred Iraqis and Americans were exposed to the carcinogen at a water treatment plant. The attempt to downplay the severity of the incident blowing up when dozens of soldiers became ill and reporting to the hospital with breathing problems and nose bleeds. That lawsuit would soon hit the fan.

He shuddered at the recollection of how the money charged for school air conditioner units at several hundred dollars a pop became eleven-dollar fans at installation time. The unspent money pocketed by the contractor, or the recycled forklifts abandoned by Iraqi Airways that were repainted and given to the troops instead of new, reliable John Deeres. He felt like OJ's attorney rather than a lobbyist advocating for the best supplies for American troops. He dialed a number on his cell phone. A secretary answered.

"It's Timothy Ryan, is he in? Good. Tell him I am coming over to see him."

.| 12 |.

Mackey's unfocused stare landed in Charo's lap.

"What are you thinking?" she asked, shaking garlic powder on her pizza.

"About spore powder. Where's that demo envelope? Do you have a pair of scissors?"

Mackey trimmed a sheet of paper to be the same size as the anthrax letters. He then poured a mound of garlic powder into the paper and performed a pharmacy fold. Sealing the envelope he clapped it between his hands."

"What are you doing?"

"Simulating what happened when the anthrax letters passed through the postal sorting machines."

Mackey clapped again, this time harder.

"I can smell the garlic," Charo said.

"And the anthrax spores were less than 1/1000th the size."

"Our lab team believes the spores were made in two batches. With experience the second run produced a higher spore count," Charo said.

"Both before the first mailing?" Mackey asked.

"I think the second batch was believed to have been made between the mailings."

"I would think Mailthrax would've laid low after the first mailing, but then why didn't he go with the first-rate stuff?"

"Limited supply? The first letters were a trial run?" Charo said.

"The senators were the real targets? People with the power to decide whether we go to war or don't, lose liberty or preserve it."

"I think the news anchors were definitely intended targets," Charo replied.

"What did Tom Brokaw, Peter Jennings, and Dan Rather have in common with Senators Daschle and Leahy?"

"My mom loves Peter Jennings. If he said it was raining arepas she'd run outside with a plate," Charo said.

"My point exactly," Mackey chuckled, "the anchors were trusted national figures who played a role in forming public opinion."

In the aftermath of 9/11 many called for blanket retaliation against all our enemies, especially those in the Arab world. Mackey postulated that the timing of the letters was curious and could have been part of a plan to sway public opinion in favor of war by using the anchors as involuntary spokespersons and the senators as legislative pawns. Charo was dubious. She thought relying on the reactions of the targets was too unpredictable. She argued that the perpetrator would have known that by using the Ames strain the focus would be on domestic evildoers.

"Yes, I suppose you're right, unless… unless Mailthrax didn't understand that the strain would indicate a US source."

"Seems unlikely he wouldn't have understood basic microbiology."

"No, I mean where the strain came from."

"You mean he didn't know the provenance?" Charo said.

"Huh?"

"The provenance, like with works of art. You think he didn't know the spores' origin?"

"Yeah, that does seem a bit far fetched."

Mackey returned from a bathroom break and laid on the living room floor with his head propped against the leg of the sofa. He closed his eyes. In the moments before he dozed off he thought: *If I were a terrorist, would I make my own anthrax or pursue it ready-made?* The advantage of ready-made spores was that no source culture had to be stolen or otherwise obtained. Spores made by a bioweapons program would be of known quality and the evidence would point to a state sponsored program. Mailthrax would still have to stuff the envelopes though—meaning that some sort of biosafety equipment was necessary. This task might be more safely accomplished in an existing facility than a makeshift basement lab. But that entailed other risks.

"Mackey? Hey, Mackey. You want something to drink?"

"Yeah," he croaked.

Charo disappeared into the kitchen and returned with two ice-filled glasses, a pair of bullet shaped cans and a two-liter bottle of Dr. Pepper under her arm. She poured the glasses half full with Dr. Pepper. When the foam subsided she topped them off with Red Bull.

"I've never had a Red Bull," Mackey said.

"Honestly? What do you do when you need to stay awake? Double shots at Starbucks?"

"In my line of work it hardly ever comes up." He stood and Charo passed him a glass.

"Really?"

Mackey shifted from one foot to the other. A shy smile creased his face. He was leaning against the wall and staring off, lost in distant memory. His index finger traced the rim of the glass absently like a car on a track. Mackey possessed no late-night stamina. Between midnight and two in the morning he wilted faster than a boutonniere in a sauna. When people observed this they'd invariably ask how he made it through medical school. His stock reply was that he was a talented cheater.

Charo was sitting on the arm of the sofa. She poked Mackey's calf with her toe.

"I used to chew gum."

"Chewing made you more alert?"

"Not exactly. It was nicotine gum. You know, what smokers use to quit. If you've never been a smoker, it can give you a rad brain jolt."

Charo set her glass down on the coffee table and stretched. Mackey averted his eyes to a pile of papers on the floor. In his field of vision Charo's left hand appeared. It was small with long, slender fingers. She rolled her wrist revealing wrinkleless skin, lithe veins, and clear lacquered nails trimmed to bureau specifications. When she arched her head backwards it thrust her chest forward. Mackey's eyes were drawn sideways like iron filings to a magnet. The thickness of her sweatshirt revealed little of what lay beneath. Charo flexed each hip and then threw a leg over the top of the sofa. With a suppleness that made Mackey's hamstrings, and a few other body parts ache, she lowered her head to her kneecap and worked the muscles of her leg. After repeating with the other leg, she dropped behind the sofa. From Mackey's vantage, all he could see was the bobbing of her ankles. When she stood up she wasn't even breathing hard.

Mackey poured himself another glass and took a large gulp.

"Better go easy on that stuff, Mackey, you'll never get to sleep." Charo said. "While you were napping I read up on Daschle and Leahy. They were major prickles in the side of the administration. If this is what made them targets, it points to right-wing extremists."

"Why not the administration?" Mackey said twisting like a tree in a hurricane to un-kink his back.

"Now that's a stretch."

Mackey and Charo soldiered on. They reviewed the FBI's psychological profile. Mackey thought the FBI had recycled the Unabomber file. Charo didn't disagree. She detailed for him the methods used by the FBI to canvass the Princeton area for suspects. He tried hard not to show his appall. The hour neared midnight. In contrast to Mackey's vanquished countenance, Charo's shone like a well-hydrated sunflower.

"I am losing steam. We could tackle the details of the spore evidence or call it a night," Mackey offered.

Charo nodded, her concentration focused on her laptop. "Take a look at what I've summarized thus far," she said.

Mackey walked around behind the sofa. As he leaned forward his cheek brushed against an aromatic tress before coming to rest aside Charo's cherubic cheek. His pupils dilated momentarily and vision blurred as if looking through a pane of frosted glass.

"Mackey?" Charo turned to stare into his eyes. The proximity revealed to Mackey the hidden intricacies of her brown eyes. The shade was somewhere between almond butter and coffee with swirls of cream.

"Do you think I've missed anything?"

He looked at the screen with a contemplative pause.

"Looks good," he wheezed. Retreating to the other side of the sofa, he kneeled and began stuffing papers into his backpack. "Hey Charo, before I forget, there is one thing we really need."

Charo pulled her legs up to the lotus position. Mackey's eyes followed the line of her tan calf all the way until it disappeared into white thong.

"And what might that be?"

"Er, where was I?"

"I believe mid-thigh, on the way back from Crotchville," Charo deadpanned.

Mackey's second blush of the evening was redder than the hindquarters of a baboon in heat.

"Um, um. Oh, yeah, the FBI's list of suspects."

.| 13 |.

The tires thumped at eighty-eight cycles per minute. Tim Ryan had made this ride over the Potomac numerous times before and knew the sound had to do with highway joints and not a flat tire. That knowledge did nothing to stop his stomach from flipping like an unbalanced load in a clothes dryer while the empty bottle of Pepto-Bismol hopped around the back seat like a squirrel in the bear paddock at the National Zoo.

He believed in the war. Had it not been for his pigeon chest deformity and lax joints he might have even been a soldier. He wanted to believe he was helping; an ersatz equipment manager for a championship team. He joined Van Owen Syndicate as a senior consultant in 2002, hired to lobby Congress to allow the administration a free hand in deciding contracts for rebuilding war-torn countries. The war in Iraq hadn't even begun. He didn't represent the government rather a licentious conglomerate of defense contractors and investors who, recognizing the scent of blood-splattered earth, lined up for no-bid contracts. He should have become suspicious when he asked his boss, whose name wasn't Van Owen, where the firm's name came from. The reply was a line from a Warren Zevon song about war mercenaries.

"Mr. Farrington, the gentleman from VOS is here to see you."

"Voz!?"

"Tim Ryan from Van Owen Syndicate."

"Oh, wonderful. Send him in."

Farrington stood behind his desk. He was a large man with broad shoulders and a Catholic-school posture. He met Ryan's slender dactyls with a firm grip that matched the directness of his blue eyes.

"Thanks for seeing me, John. I've come from the DPC hearings, and I must tell you I am worried. The clients I represent are understandably nervous and I don't know what to tell them. They have serious exposure in Iraq and as you know Senator Dorgan is parading an assortment of whistleblowers and lawyers before the committee. I'm concerned he's digging around in freshly disturbed dirt."

"Timmy, there is nothing to worry about. We call the shots in this town. The public doesn't give a damn about cry-baby whistleblowers."

"It's not the public I'm concerned with John, it's those damn senators on a witch hunt."

"That dog won't hunt. The Dems have been trying for years to pin conflict of interest on us. They haven't gotten any traction. They won't get any here either."

"Perhaps, but it won't be long before Dorgan gets his hands on a list of investors—people who we've worked very hard to keep out of the spotlight. People with ties to the administration, who have... special relationships... and would be rather angry if they were dragged into a hearing or courtroom."

"You needn't concern yourself, the ship is leak-proof."

"But what if Dorgan succeeds in attracting media attention? With the upcoming midterm elections, that could upset the Senate's party balance and he might be able to push through a full Senate hearing with more Dems in office."

"It's under control."

"I wish I shared your confidence. I think Dorgan is intent on using this issue to make a name for himself. He may have his sights on higher office."

"See here Tim, this is a nonissue. There are leveraged parties on both sides of the aisle. I, myself, have stock options and deferred compensation from AmCon. I assure you it's in no one's interest for this to ever go beyond the impotent DPC. Now, if you will excuse me, I have to run. My daughter has a soccer game."

.| 14 |.

Mackey had dealt with death more than most people his age. One grandparent died before he was born, two more died before he was twelve, and the last one when he was in medical school. His father died when he was sixteen. Magnus Osgar Dunn III had the good sense to name his son something other than Magnus IV, but not to have a colonoscopy when the blood in his stool first appeared. The adenocarcinoma was in an advanced stage when it was diagnosed. Mackey witnessed the cancer drain the man's vitality. It was like watching time-lapsed photography of wetlands withering into desert. He had a year to get used to being fatherless. Not enough time, but it stood in stark contrast to the time he had to adjust to being a widower.

Mackey worried that Allie was beginning to fade from his memory. Last week he couldn't recall the word she'd use when he was being brusque. Like the time before they were married and discussed her changing her name.

You're going to change your name right?
Why?
For the kids sake.
I haven't given it much thought.
Well, we're not going to hyphenate them.
Baran-Dunn isn't so bad.
They'll get picked on by other kids.
Mackey, stop being surly.

If it weren't for music Mackey feared he might soon not remember anything about her. Songs reignited feelings, both good and bad, as vivid as when first experienced. Mackey's jukebox appeared soon after the day in junior high school when he heard his first mixed tape. The jukebox played songs upon waking that could only have been remnants of forgotten dreams. While out for a jog he'd suddenly find himself singing along to lyrics running around in his head. The jukebox faded the words in as subtly as the sun rising over the horizon. After Allie disappeared the jukebox changed. Though not quite malevolent it played with a new urgency and no longer spun frivolous tunes. It was as if melancholy, emptiness, self-loathing, apprehension, sadness—virtually every bad feeling he had ever felt—were stored in individual jars on a shelf in his Limbic system. Tied to the lid of each jar was a string the other end of which connected to specific bars of a piano solo, guitar lick, or lover's lament. Every lyric was selected to make a point. Not allow him to forget.

The color of the dusk sky that night was a mix of cobalt and coal, like the skin of a miner pulled from a collapsed West Virginia shaft. The words of Jackson Browne often brought a tincture of comfort salted with pain. The song was "Sky Blue and Black," and the line that kept repeating would define his life for years[5]. He kept searching for her.

For months he saw Allie everywhere in the specter of other women. Her hair, her style, and the way she walked. The memories would then melt leaving him to wrestle with the tricks of a grieving mind. Like an amputee who's missing limb still seems to be attached, the warm pain was the lone reminder of what was lost. The years as a medical nomad avoided painful questions about his past, but there was an endless stream of new faces to search.

Mackey was on the subway heading downtown to meet Charo and Geeta. His mind was using the interlude to tear down the steel girders that propped up his stoic façade. The wrecking crew was hard at work. The guilt jackhammers succeeded in giving him a headache and he was perspiring from the should-have-done acetylene torches. After years of demolishing his psyche, some insight had been found. Self-reliance, a skill cultivated in childhood, honed as an adolescent, and once viewed as an indomitable strength, emerged as a fault in his foundation. But he was not yet ready for reconstruction.

Two songwriters who met in a bar, formed a band, and then fell in love cued up in his jukebox. He wondered what experiences prompted them to write the words to "World Spins Madly On."

> Woke up and wished that I was dead
> With an aching in my head
> I lay motionless in bed
> I thought of you and where you'd
> gone and let the world spin madly on
>
> Everything that I said I'd do
> Like make the world brand new
> And take the time for you
> I just got lost and slept right through the dawn
> And the world spins madly on.[6]

He met Charo outside New York's FBI headquarters. They split a cloud of cigarette smoke and entered. Upstairs he followed her through the maze of cubicles to hers, almost stepping on a white rabbit on the way. Two others appeared and they seemed to be following Charo.

"What are they for? A search warren?"

"Ha, ha. They're moles," Charo replied. Mackey looked closer. Fluffy, white fur, floppy ears, large hind feet, and twitchy noses.

"I am pretty sure those are rabbits."

Sensing someone behind him, Mackey turned. It was a man in a dark suit, holding a carrot, and walking like he had another shoved up his butt. "Here kitty, nice kitty." He stopped and gave Mackey a quick once over.

"Brad, they're rabbits, not cats," Charo said.

"Aha! I was right." Mackey said.

"Who are you?" Brad asked.

"Dr. Dunn, Centers for Disease Control and Prevention." Mackey rarely used his medical title, but he sensed this was a situation that demanded such formality. He extended a hand. None was returned.

"Mackey, this is Special Agent Bradford Johnson. Brad, Mackey is helping out with a child pornography case." Brad continued to stare at Mackey with raised brow. Mackey pondered if Brad's scrutiny was about his presence as an interloper or rival.

"Why is the CDC involved in child pornography?"

"The case is connected to an outbreak of measles in illegal immigrants," Charo replied without missing a beat. Brad gave an insincere head nod and redirected his attention to the rabbits beneath Charo's desk.

"Guess they came to be with their own kind," he clucked reaching under the desk to grab one by the nape of its neck. He lingered to sneak a peek at Charo's legs but hastily retreated when she drew her foot back as if to launch his head toward a goal post.

Brad turned to Mackey and confided with a smirk, "Women are like rabbits, only good for one thing."

"Brad you've found your evidence now I suggest you get back to your desk before the rest of the litter scamper down the hall to the SSA's office."

Brad threw a sneer in Charo's direction before disappearing around the corner juggling balls of fur.

"What was that all about?"

"Drug bunnies, one in a long list of methods used to smuggle cocaine. He's waiting for his evidence. The rabbits will defecate several hundred grams of Colombian Snow."

"I mean, does he have a thing for you?"

"Brad?"

"The way he gawked at you."

Charo shrugged. "FBI protocol."

Charo led them back to the Criminal Justice Math Lab where Geetangali was waiting for them. Beaming, she explained that her initial analysis had yielded over 200,000 hits.

Mackey's eyes narrowed.

"It took a little refinement to find fewer needles," she explained.

She double-clicked an icon on her computer screen and a database sprang open. "Here, I've extracted the E-ZPass data for all the toll booths into and throughout New Jersey for the year 2001. We were able to use scanning software to abstract license plates from those that paid in cash. This is the master file of account numbers seen during the year by the system. Linked to this file are separate files for each of the thirty-seven tollbooths in a fifty-mile radius around Princeton. The program I've written requires two user inputs—the threshold value and the scanning window."

Mackey sat down. His face crimped in concentration. Geeta's fingers flew over the keys and a new window appeared:

FBI MATH LAB

ALGORITHM TO LOCATE SEED IN HAYSTACK

INPUT THRESHOLD __

"Let's say you were seeking a vehicle that appeared once in the system, anytime during 2001—a driver who drove through New Jersey back to college." She keystroked the number *1* and then hit *Enter*. A series of dots marched across the screen and in a matter of seconds the answer returned:

ELEMENTS = 2634

"Not too bad," Mackey said.

"We are not done yet," Geeta grinned.

"What if the driver made a return trip? She entered the number *2*. This will return vehicles that passed through the system twice, traveling in opposite directions, anytime during the interval." She hit *Enter* and the screen changed.

ELEMENTS = 121,677

"Whoa, at this rate it will be 2011 by the time we find the needle," Mackey said.

"This is just to demonstrate how the system works, and that there are many more round trips than one ways. We must set the scanning window. It is like booking air flights online—you choose a date range and then it brings up the trips that meet your criteria. Since we have two events, we enter two intervals."

ENTER TRIP PARAMETERS 1: START __/__/__
ENTER TRIP PARAMETERS 2: START __/__/__

"Okay, I need you to narrow the possible date ranges of the two mailings. Mackey, what are the dates for the first set of mailings?" Geeta asked.

"The first letters were postmarked on September 18, 2001, which was a Tuesday. Therefore the letter could have been placed in the box late on the 17th or early on the 18th."

Geeta typed in those dates.

"And then October 7, 2001 through October 9, 2001 for the second mailing," Charo added.

Geeta added the dates and hit enter.

ELEMENTS = 444

"Cool," Mackey said.

"What if the mailer stayed overnight and returned the next day?" Charo asked.

"I've programmed it to scan by date and to use a forty-eight-hour range. So, as long as the return trip was made within two days it will count it as the same trip in the system. If either criteria is met, it flags it."

"What if the trips were made with different cars?" Mackey asked.

"That's actually easier. It turns out that a pair of cars making the identical trip on two different dates is less common than the same car making the trips. I found three dozen that matched that scenario, but I'll have to rerun the analysis with your modified dates."

"What if Mailthrax made a trip before the actual mailing to scope out the drop box or for some other reason?" Mackey asked.

"Mailthrax?"

Charo nodded toward Mackey. "His name for the unsub."

"That complicates it somewhat. I could narrow the entire data file to the period from September 17th to October 9th, but it would become harder to recognize the regular commuters. I am going to play around with this some more, see if I can optimize. I'll give you the results early next week."

Charo looked at Mackey and he shrugged his shoulders. "Four hundred is still a big number."

"Are you afraid of a little leg work? Don't wimp out on me now," she said.

. . .

Sitting on a bench in Foley Square, Mackey pulled out his laptop. The old hard drive whirred like a phlegmatic about to spit. Like his brain it was filled to near capacity with MP3s. He listened to one, a political pundit podcast called *The Firing Squad*. Mackey had no love of politics. He could trace his indifference to family dinners as a child where his father spoke of actors becoming president while Mackey yearned to talk of Orioles becoming All-Stars.

The administration wanted to invade Iraq and overthrow Saddam. The rest they say is history but parts of the story caught Mackey's ear. Saddam the dictator had amassed weapons of mass destruction, used them on his own people, thumbed his nose at UN sanctions, and posed a threat to the flow of Middle East oil. Surely that was enough to want him dead. Mackey had read enough Web chatter dating before 9/11 to accept this was an executive priority. The fraternity of neocon advisors was also on the record as advocates for war and they were challenged after 9/11 to get the justification needed to garner public support for the invasion. Could the anthrax attacks have been perpetrated to drum up support? To highlight the Iraqi threat, real or imagined?

. . .

The sole noise was the click of her own heels on the tile floor as she exited the elevator to the lobby of the 28th floor. She should've worn flats. Charo slid her badge across the sensor and entered the darkened suite of offices. Her eyes adjusted and senses were on hyperalert as she made her way down the unlit corridor. Turning right without breaking stride, Charo flicked on the copy machine and headed to the bullpen area that served as the workspace for visiting agents. She swept her hand over the top of the file cabinet. A red file folder peaked out and she grabbed it. Emblazoned on the front was a child's handprint in blue ink within a circle of orange fading to yellow. Around the circle, in a font designed to imitate the writing of a child were the words, *Crimes Against Children* the logo of the Innocent Images National Initiative.

"Yup, just where I left it." Charo had used the 28th floor conference room earlier in the day to brief the NYC Innocents Task Force. One member, a grizzled NYPD detective, asked why they weren't in their usual space. Charo replied coolly that it was in use. He remarked that he hadn't been to the 28th floor since the anthrax investigation.

Charo worked by the twilight ebbing through the windows. She removed a bobby pin from her hair and walked over to the secretary's cubicle. She lifted the dracaena plant by its stalk revealing a small copper key lying between the pot and a saucer. With the bobby pin she speared the small ring and lifted the key from its ill-conceived hiding place. She replaced the plant and removed one sheet from a Post-it pad. Pinching it into a U-shape she grasped the key between the sticky surfaces. She then headed over to a row of file cabinets in the bullpen. She checked the corridor and then her watch. One by one she opened each cabinet. In the first drawer she located agent notes from old interstate cases but nothing from 2001. In the file cabinet nearest the window she got warmer—brochures on microbiology labs. She next found an email from an agent who was responsible for the victimology assessment of the anthrax targets. He came to the conclusion that what the news anchors and senators had in common was the fact that they were all middle-aged white men in positions of leadership.

Charo found and speed-read a brief report on the examination of photocopy machines. The Senate letters had trash marks, idiosyncratic imperfections that can identify where the copies were made. The agent reported that his team had retrieved and examined examples of copies from 1,014 machines at or near every lab that was known to have a stock of the Ames strain. Nothing matched.

Moving with vulpine efficiency, she scanned file labels when they existed and slid out and shuffled through groups of folders when they didn't. In the second-to-last drawer she found what she was looking for: a two-page summary list of suspects. It was dated from 2004 but would have to do. She marked the file location and strode to the photocopier. She strained to hear above the noise of the machine cleaning its wires, which sounded like a marching band against the soft hum of the air conditioning. She pulled a sheet of white paper from the Innocents' file folder and placed it into the manual feed tray and punched the key for a two-sided copy. She returned the output between two pages in her folder and then retraced her steps to replace the file and key.

One stride before the intersection of corridors that led back to the elevators she heard the door unlatch and whistling. Women didn't whistle. She had checked the duty log and there were no field investigations planned for the day, no reason for an agent to be returning to this suite after hours. She next heard the distinct sound of male footsteps coming her way. There was nothing she could do. Running to hide now would draw attention and mark her presence in the office as illicit. She'd have to stick with her cover story. Compounding matters was that she had forgotten to turn off the copier and had to double back. She held her hand over the switch and hoped that the man's whistling would cover the sound. Charo turned in time to see the man sharply round the corner on his mission. He wore gray overalls and swung a spray bottle in his hand. He jumped at the unexpected sight of Charo.

"*Dios mio*!"

"I'm sorry, I didn't mean to startle you. Retrieving a misplaced file."

Charo felt silly but held up her folder for the maintenance man to see. He leaned against the wall panting and holding one hand to his chest.

She stepped around him. "Are you alright?"

"I will be as soon as my heart stops pounding."

Charo didn't wait for his reply, she was already at the lobby door, "Have a pleasant evening."

In the elevator she breathed an inaudible sigh of relief. Robert Hanssen popped into her head and the thought made her shudder.

Back in her office, Charo placed the Innocents' file back in its drawer. Before closing the cabinet she slid out the copy she had made. At the top left corner she identified her pencil marks. Both sides of the sheet appeared blank. But at the top of the paper she wrote "Bread, butter, eggs, tea, and yogurt." She folded the paper and placed it in her shoulder bag and headed out to meet Mackey.

. . .

Foley Square was dark and his laptop was low on power when Mackey turned his attention to the spore evidence. Powder samples were recovered from four envelopes, two of which had been opened and the powder dispersed. These were retrieved from NBC and Senator Daschle's office and the envelopes had scant powder remaining. The letters delivered to the *New York Post* and Senator Leahy's office were found unopened and containing less than two grams of anthrax spores apiece. All the strains were a match but contradiction existed in the description of the powders giving rise to theories that the first batch of mailed letters utilized a less refined grade of anthrax spores. As Charo told him, the FBI believed that sometime between September 18th and October 9th, Mailthrax made further refinements to the weapon by brewing up a second batch. This troubled Mackey. It meant that the perpetrator or perpetrators had easy access to a sophisticated lab and still managed to leave no trail. The FBI had traced all sales of the necessary lab equipment and found no recent purchases out of the ordinary.

The spores sent to Senators Daschle and Leahy were first described as "professional" and "weapons-grade" by the scientists at Fort Detrick. This rankled the White House so they backpedaled and described the spores as "energetic," as if describing a classroom full of kids with ADHD. They further clarified that the spores had low attractive forces resulting in stuff that had no inclination to remain still. It flew in the air like dandelion fluff. Mackey decided that whoever made this stuff knew what they were doing.

The Ames strain of *Bacillus anthracis* was in its twentieth year of laboratory life when it was thrust into the national spotlight. It was initially institutionalized in 1981 at the Texas Agriculture & Mining University after having caused the premature death of a cow. A subculture was sent to the US Department of Agriculture Laboratory in Ames, Iowa. Later that year, the US Army Medical Research Institute for Infectious Diseases asked the anthrax community to send them strains to test as possible vaccine candidates. The Department of Agriculture sent USAMRIID the Texas killer-cow strain only it wasn't labeled. A scientist at USAMRIID followed the tradition of naming a strain for the location of its discovery and christened it the Ames strain mistakenly thinking it was isolated in Ames, Iowa.

Only 180 or thereabout strains of *Bacillus anthracis* were known, not many by bacterial standards. Although all of the samples of anthrax found in the letters and affected patients were Ames and the same by conventional molecular analysis, there wasn't enough known about anthrax genetics to conclusively match the attack strain to one in a laboratory. It wasn't until 2002, that researchers began the laborious task of identifying genetic sequences that could be used to forensically distinguish one anthrax strain from another.

With no system to fingerprint anthrax strains, the Amerithrax investigation quickly stalled. The fact that there was a new suspect suggested the lab work was complete. But what did they find?

.| 15 |.

"May I have the eggplant and garlic in black bean sauce? And can I get that with broccoli?" Charo unwrapped her chopsticks, broke them apart, and rubbed them together.

"Uh-huh. You want brown or white rice?"

"Brown."

"Kung Pao chicken," Mackey said, "with white rice. And can you bring some hot sauce?"

"Uh-huh."

Mackey poured two cups of tea. "I've read all I care to about spores. And I keep getting just two facts that I don't think are of any consequence to solving this. One, all of the samples from patients, letters and environmental swabs were the same by limited DNA analysis and two, the strain was Ames."

"We checked fifteen US and three foreign labs holding the Ames strain. Other than a few specimens from the early 1990s at USAMRIID, that we couldn't prove were Ames, no one reported anything missing," Charo said.

"Microbiologists swap bacterial samples like kids trade baseball cards. The CDC didn't begin keeping transfer manifests until 1997. It had to come from somewhere."

Mackey was feeling edgy. A sure sign he needed to eat. "What we really need to know is if genetic sequence analysis found a match to any of the eighteen known labs in possession of Ames. There is no mention of it on the Internet."

“Several academic and research labs assisted Quantico. I doubt I’ll be able to access that information though,” Charo said.

The food arrived and Mackey beckoned to Charo to help herself to his plate.

“Alternatively, knowing who was on the suspect list might get us the same information,” Mackey said between mouthfuls.

Charo forked a floret of broccoli with her chopsticks, dipped it in some bean sauce, and took a bite. Mackey explained that pinpointing the origin of the anthrax spores used in the mailings wasn’t as easy as some people first expected. With a gun, every bullet will bear the distinct markings of the inside of the barrel. But bacteria mutate and change their genetic “barrel markings” over time. The field of microbial forensics didn’t exist in 2001.

“Microbial forensics?” Charo asked; glad to be off the topic of suspects.

“Suppose as the prosecuting attorney I go into court and say that we found blood from the victim on the shirt of the alleged murderer. When I say there is a DNA match there is a body of research to assign a statistical probability of the match occurring by chance. Typically the chance of a random match is less than one in several million. Virtually nil. No comparable science existed for anthrax in 2001.”

Mackey poured hot sauce on his chicken and continued shoveling it into his mouth by the forkful.

“It depends on the number of alleles. The more that match, the less likely the defendant is innocent,” Charo said.

“You paid attention in genetics class at Quantico.”

“I paid attention in all my classes. One allele match that occurs in 20 percent of the population is a one in five chance the person is the right suspect.”

“Not much for the district attorney to build a case on.”

"Right, but we never use a single allele. I recall one statutory rape case where we had a match on six alleles. The population frequencies were 20 percent, 10 percent, 2 percent, 5 percent, 1 percent, and 10 percent."

Mackey jotted the numbers down on the napkin then did math out loud, "$^{20}/_{100}$ x $^{10}/_{100}$ x $^{2}/_{100}$ x $^{5}/_{100}$ x $^{1}/_{100}$ x $^{10}/_{100}$ equals... $^{20,000}/_{1,000,000,000,000}$. The chance of an accidental match would be one in fifty million. That perp would be better off buying a lottery ticket than banking on acquittal!"

"He got fifteen years."

What was known back in 2002 was that the mailed anthrax powders had four mutations when compared to the original Ames strain. But it wasn't known how often these mutations occurred in the larger family of Ames strains, the equivalent of the human allele population frequencies. The field of microbial forensics needed to be created. Without a comparative library for the anthrax genome there was no way to present evidence in court. Specific genetic assays had to be created, tested, and validated before this evidence could ever hope to stand the scrutiny of cross-examination. The work done to establish the field of microbial forensics began appearing in the scientific literature in 2005.

Mackey shared his prior minor epiphany. "Since Joseph Erekat has only recently emerged as a suspect and Rutgers University wasn't on the list that had the Ames strain, it must mean that the lab found a matching anthrax sample at USAMRIID. Erekat was an intern there in the summer of 2001," Mackey said. "What doesn't fit is as an intern Erekat shouldn't have had access to the anthrax stocks."

"There are many things that shouldn't have happened, Mackey."

"True enough, but to also have access to the lab and other supplies to grow and refine the weapon seems beyond possibility," Mackey said.

"His job could have been to acquire the specimen," Charo offered. "Then turn it over to someone to grow and purify."

"There is more to the spore story though."

Charo eyed him with a bang hanging across her face. "What does that mean?"

The check arrived. Mackey nabbed it, relieved that it was less than twenty dollars and waited until the Chinese waiter was out of earshot.

"There were other analyses performed. For one, carbon dating."

"Like with fossils?"

"Yes. Living organisms maintain a balance of carbon-14 and carbon-12. The ratio stays constant. While you're alive that is. When an organism dies, or stops replicating in the case of a bacterium, the amount of carbon-14 declines."

"So, that's how scientists came to the conclusion that the anthrax powders were made within the last two years?"

"Yes, except the technique is not that precise. By my calculations, the ratio of carbon-14 in the anthrax powder compared to living organisms was 99.976 percent. A measurement error of as little as 0.1 percent translates to it being off by ten years!"

"A red sardine?"

"You mean red herring. Perhaps. They also did trace element analysis. Waters from different parts of the world have different trace element signatures. The water used to make the spores was said to have originated in the Northeastern United States."

"That includes both the labs where Joseph Erekat had access. It's not looking too good for him."

"Not necessarily. I think the number of known water signatures is limited. The analysis couldn't rule out that the pattern doesn't match water from some other part of the world, say the Amazon jungle or Siberia."

Charo stood. "Feel like going for a walk? There is a homemade ice-cream place nearby. You can tell me the rest over some lychee-nut-fudge-brandy ice cream."

The best-preserved letter for analysis was the unopened Leahy letter. This was where the trillion spores per gram estimate came from. The Armed Forces Institute of Pathology used X-ray spectrometry to detect two elements unseen by other methods. Silicon and oxygen were found in a ratio of 1:2.

"Glass?" Charo held a dripping cone in one hand and a napkin in the other. Her bag slipped dangerously down her shoulder.

"Yes, one assumption was that it came from the test tubes the spores were stored in."

Mackey grabbed Charo's bag before it slid down her tan bicep and collided with the ice-cream cone.

"Is that common? Contamination from glass containers?"

"I doubt it is something that has been routinely considered. I don't think anyone knows."

"You don't sound convinced, Mackey."

"When I try and put it together with the other evidence, I arrive at a different hypothesis. Do you remember when you were a kid at camp and someone put itching powder in some kid's shorts as a prank?"

"Sorry, I never went to prank camp."

"Lucky you. Fire ants in your pants uncomfortable. Ordinary fiberglass, the kind used for insulation, ground up causes intense itching."

"Are you suggesting itching powder was added to the spores?" Charo asked.

"I don't know. Maybe to the first group of envelopes to prevent the inhalation of the spores." he replied.

"To deliberately cause skin infections?"

"Aiming to scare, but not kill. Its just one theory."

"Wouldn't that have been obvious? And what about the Florida cases?"

"Yeah."

They passed a fish shop closing up for the night. Whole catfish and snapper lay in buckets filled with murky water. An old man dangling a cigarette from one corner of his mouth was shuffling the buckets from the sidewalk into the store. He stopped to eye Mackey and Charo and wipe his hands on his stained smock.

"Something is rotten in the state of Denmark," Mackey said.

"Are you still on that government conspiracy notion?"

"It may not be a conspiracy."

Charo tossed the bottom half of her cone in the trash. "Are you seriously suggesting that the mailings were done by a member of the administration?"

"You did the research. Daschle and Leahy had clout and were big pains in the administration's ass. It's conceivable that the senators were targeted to influence theirs and others' votes on the Patriot Act and the war in Iraq."

"Anthrax as a method of lobbying Congress? A bit over the roof don't you think, Mackey?"

"You mean 'over the top,' and I haven't found any supporting evidence, but I haven't ruled it out. We also can't exclude a right-wing extremist group seizing upon the opportunity to strike at perceived enemies."

"The FBI has had some experience with those groups," Charo said.

Mackey frowned. "I don't wish to disparage you or the many fine agents of the FBI, but after 9/11 the FBI wasn't in much shape to investigate a paper cut let alone a case as complex as the anthrax mailings."

Charo stiffened. "No offense taken, but you're going to have to explain."

"There were serious problems with how the FBI handled intelligence. This included reluctance, no, an actual sanctioned impediment to sharing information. And not just with other intelligence agencies, like the CIA and NSA, but within the FBI itself. You may not be aware that there were teams of agents investigating criminal activities of possible terrorists while other teams were collecting intelligence information on the same individuals. The two teams didn't even talk to each other."

Charo stopped as if struck by a beam from Mr. Freeze's ice gun. She stared out into the street, but the villain wasn't there. "Why on earth not? I know agents protect their case files to ensure no one else gets the credit for their work. This practice is as common as jokes about women, but it shouldn't interfere with getting the job done."

"In this instance it did. It had to do with Rule 6(e) of the Federal Rules of Criminal Procedure."

"Rule 6(e)? That exempts disclosure for federal and state officers during grand jury proceedings. I don't see how it applied to the events that preceded 9/11."

"Information uncovered by FBI agents in Phoenix and Minneapolis about Arab men taking flying lessons didn't fall under Rule 6(e) but still wasn't shared throughout the bureau. There are those in the intelligence community who saw the FBI's overuse of Rule 6(e) not as a protection of civil liberties but as an excuse to maintain the culture of secrecy and independence."

Mackey had kept walking but stopped and looked back at Charo who remained frozen to the sidewalk.

"In your world," Charo paused as if waiting for dyspepsia to pass, "this would be equivalent to a patient being transferred from one hospital to another and the doctors at the first hospital refusing to disclose the patient's medical information to the doctors at the second hospital due to a misguided belief in doctor-patient confidentiality."

Mackey chuckled, "Perhaps to cover their substandard care."

He walked back and looped his arm in hers, nudging her gently forward. "There have been some grave complaints of incompetence and lax security leveled at you guys in the past few years."

"You're referring to problems with the Counterintelligence Division. There was a translator connected to Turkey's intelligence agency who left out key information and a supervisor who delayed translations to give the appearance of his unit being overworked. It was a colossal scandal in the bureau," Charo said.

"And those weren't the only incidents. I read of a former attaché of the Pakistani embassy, a place reputed to be a cover for espionage, who was hired despite the red flags in his past. A leak of classified information occurred weeks after his hire."

"Mackey, you shouldn't believe everything you read on the Internet."

"It wasn't a single blog post. Plus, there exists a preponderance of examples. What about Behrooz Sarshar?" Mackey asked.

"You're referring to chatter about an al Qaeda plan to attack five American cities?"

"It was five months before 9/11 and the chatter mentioned the use of airplanes and that the plotters were already placed inside the US," Mackey exclaimed.

Charo removed her arm. "You must realize that this, and many other types of intelligence, flood into the FBI daily. It is literally hundreds of informant leads, anonymous tips, and surveillance reports daily. You know how all of this gets used nowadays? A press release occurs and the national alert indicator goes from yellow to orange. Not terribly helpful, is it?"

"No. Not unless you own the patent rights to ciprofloxacin. But Charo, come on. Are you honestly going to defend the position that independent reports of a plot to use airplanes as weapons, several Middle Eastern men taking flying lessons, and a known member of a terrorist organization making demands to learn how to fly a 747 don't add up to a need to take action? Civil liberties be damned, these weren't even American citizens. The FBI flat out blew it!"

Charo crossed her arms over her chest. "I am keenly aware of our missteps but can't believe you are trivializing how difficult it is to interpret intelligence information and that you are blaming 9/11 on the diligent agents who have dedicated their lives to protecting both our safety and our freedoms. It's getting late and I better be going."

"Charo wait. All I was trying to say is that I don't think every stone was overturned in following leads in the anthrax investigation."

"So, get busy poking your nose under rocks and find the ones we failed to overturn." With that, Charo turned abruptly and with determined strides disappeared down a side street.

.| 16 |.

He'd done it again. Allowed his opinions and emotions to mix in toxic proportions then spill all over Charo like a novice bartender with a leaky shaker. He hoped Charo would forgive him, unlike the hospital administrator in Missouri who was so offended she saw to it that his contract was not renewed. Looking up, he had no idea where he was. He guessed that Charo went west, toward 26 Federal Plaza and the subways to Brooklyn. That meant north was behind him.

A few blocks later he came to Canal Street where the avenue became a wide plaza. There were Greek columns and replica of the Arc de Triomphe. Cars sped between the pillars, exiting from the Manhattan Bridge.

He considered calling her. Experience taught him that this often made matters worse. The affront usually loomed larger in his own mind than in the recipient's and his clumsy attempts at apology were often interpreted as insult upon injury. That is if Charo wasn't too annoyed to even speak with him. Best to let it go for now. Allie always needed time to sort out the cerebral from the emotional. But that was different. His rough edges never seemed to poke through as often with Allie or perhaps it was her softness that cushioned them.

But was Charo committed to this? He needed her help. Up until now it was going well. Geeta was whittling down the E-ZPass toll data to a manageable number and there was still a chance it could lead them to a suspect.

The street was quiet. He had just his thoughts and the streetlamps for company. His mind returned to the problem of spores. What if Mailthrax had filled envelopes with two grades of spore powders that were prepared well before October and held for the right moment? Perhaps sending out the first batch a week after 9/11 to suggest a link to the hijacked airplanes. This first batch contained the less pure spores, perhaps even adulterated to cause only the milder skin infection. The letter to AMI was then an anomaly because it resulted in two cases of inhalation anthrax, none cutaneous, and spores scattered throughout the building. Maybe Mailthrax forgot which powder he filled that letter with? AMI was the parent company of the *National Enquirer*, *Star*, *Globe*, and *Weekly World News*. Supermarket tabloids specializing in shock journalism. The address for the *National Enquirer* had changed in 2001 so it was possible that the letter had not reached its intended target. Since no letter was ever found, there was no way to know how the letter was addressed and the real target. Still, it didn't seem to fit with the pattern of the other recipients.

Mackey checked the wrong way down a one-way street while crossing against the light. He froze as a cab raced by from behind, the displaced air flapping his jacket like the cape of a matador. It was another one of his traits that could either be a positive or a negative. The ability to focus on one task to the exclusion of all else. It worked for baseball and got him through medical school but didn't alloy well with relationships. Or walking in New York City. Allie had a way of calmly reeling him in like a kite in a hurricane.

He saw himself in the lines of the Bruce Cockburn song that whispered in his inner ear[7]. The need to keep moving. Air hunger. A life out of balance.

It struck him like a sudden summer downpour. At least one of the anthrax envelopes had gotten wet. That would explain the clumping and difference in spore particle size. Mackey closed his eyes and tried to visualize the images of the four recovered letters, but the only one that appeared was the Brokaw letter. He squeezed his lids tight. Did it have a water stain? He tossed his backpack onto the sidewalk and tore through it like an unemployed actor searching for a ringing cell phone. He found the folder and shuffled through the papers. It was the Daschle letter that had gotten wet.

Mackey spotted a crowd. People smoking out front of McSorley's bar. He'd been to the historic haunt once, while in med school. It had charm and plenty of characters. Allie would have liked the place despite the fact that it didn't allow women until 1970. She had more friends with 501s than 401ks.

The different spore powders nagged at him. The *New York Post* letter had not been opened and its contents were likened to Purina dog chow: coarse, brown, and clumped. The Leahy letter was also found unopened, but that powder was composed of very fine, whitish, flyaway particles. Mackey didn't want to admit that the FBI was right in their belief that Mailthrax made two batches. The only alternative he could think of was that something undetectable was added to the spore powder placed in the first group of letters. The Florida letter was an anomaly.

Mailthrax must have believed that the letters sent to the news anchors were either discarded or duds and so decided to mail the more potent spores to the senators. A powder with a spore count that exceeded anything the US made in its bioweapons program by fifty-fold. Purportedly ten times higher that the best-known anthrax powder made by the Soviets. A trillion spores per gram. The particle size was a few microns, with infinitesimal mass such that they were influenced more by air currents than gravity. Meaning they could remain airborne, invisible to the eye, yet nonetheless deadly. Particles small enough to bypass the respiratory defenses and reach the smallest airways, where, in sufficient number, the advantage was theirs.

As Mackey sailed up Broadway, the Flatiron Building passed by almost unnoticed. From his vantage point, the prow of the twenty-two story, terra cotta facade appeared to be cruising along side him. It was looking pretty spry for its 104 years.

Advanced techniques are needed to refine spores to micron size without forming large clusters of spores that fall to the ground quickly when airborne. Once you have a pot of replicating bacteria, turning them into spores is like convincing a bear to hibernate. It takes adverse conditions like insufficient nutrients or too much oxygen to make the vegetative cells form spores. This isn't even the hardest part of weaponizing anthrax. After stripping away the unwanted cell material with solvents, and the liquid with centrifugation, the hard part is drying without clumping. Some state-sponsored bioweapons programs use lyophilizers—vacuum systems that operate at cold temperatures—while others favor hot-air jet sprayers. This process requires specialized equipment you couldn't find in a lab supply outlet. Other options to maintain small particle size were grinding, which left telltale marks on the spores, or adding an antistatic additive. Both of these processing methods were detectable during analysis.

The consensus was that the spores were intact and weren't milled. The official FBI stance was that no additives were used. This didn't jive with the earlier report that silicon and oxygen were found, but majority opinion favored that the spores weren't made by a known bioweapons program. And what of the extreme purity? It didn't make sense that such purity could be achieved without significant experience and resources—the kind of resources only available to governments. Mackey struggled with the contradictions.

The Empire State Building was wearing its dress white lights. Mackey passed without taking notice. Former head of the biological weapons team for the United Nations Special Commission on Iraq and retired USAMRIID microbiologist Richard Spertzel was quoted as saying that only he and a few others in the US were capable of making anthrax spores as pure as those sent to Senators Daschle and Leahy. In his opinion it was a task requiring a cadre of experienced lab staff and expensive hi-tech equipment. He discounted the FBI's theory of a disgruntled loner working in a makeshift basement lab. Spertzel hadn't ruled out a state-sponsored terrorist though, specifically in the nation where he had spent many months in the 1990s. Iraq. As far as a domestic source, the list of who had the skills to make the anthrax spores was a short one and it included himself, William C. Patrick III, Ken Alibek, and several unnamed scientists at the US Army Dugway Proving Ground in Utah.

At 42nd Street, Mackey passed a woman wearing heels that would make the Empire State building acrophobic, a skimpy halter-top corralling two weathered balloons, and a leopard skin print dress that couldn't see her knees with a telescope. She didn't bother to proposition.

William Patrick III was the father of the US biologic weapons program. He seemed the logical person to interview although the FBI hadn't thought so. Not at first. They didn't question him until March of 2002. They came back twice more, once even with bloodhounds to sniff around his home for the scent of growing bacteria. Satisfied that Patrick wasn't the anthrax mailer, the FBI then invited him to be a consultant. This was a common problem for the FBI. The experts they needed to help solve the case were also on the list of possible suspects. It must have put them in an awkward if not untenable position.

It was after midnight when Mackey reached the fountain at Columbus Circle. A marble statue of Columbus peered down upon him from a seventy-foot-high granite pedestal. At eye level was a winged youth holding a globe representing the genius of discovery. Mackey circumnavigated the fountain, crossed traffic to Central Park West, and continued his own journey to discovery beneath a canopy of oak and maple trees. To the east lay the vast expanse of Central Park, its interior as dark as the mystery he was trying to solve. Even the dark had somewhere to belong.

Patrick was a mentor and friend to Steven Hatfill. In the late 1990s, while serving as a government contractor, Hatfill awarded Patrick a grant to prepare a classified report on how anthrax might be disseminated through the mail. This is how suspicion was cast upon Hatfill. He was eventually exonerated as the evidence against him proved shakier than an alcoholic in delirium tremens. It did make Mackey wonder who might have had access to Patrick's report and what it contained.

Patrick was the grandfather of US bioweaponry and had the spirit of P.T. Barnum in him. He loved to show off his handiwork and kept a jar of fake anthrax at hand to show guests. In an interview with the *New York Times* and *NOVA*, Patrick showed them the jar containing weapons-grade *Bacillus globigii,* a harmless bacterium that also formed spores and was used to simulate anthrax. He demonstrated how it flowed like a cloud with the slightest provocation. He boasted that the particle size in the jar was near one trillion spores per gram. With a crude spray device he puffed some into the air of his backyard, remarking that it could travel several kilometers before falling to the ground. Mackey imagined the scene. The old man and his perfume atomizer spraying bacteria out over the rolling hills of Western Maryland while two antsy reporters edged toward the driveway.

Patrick created the US process to make weapons-grade anthrax. It didn't use milling to reduce the particle size. Instead, the process involved freeze-drying to get the particles down to the desired individual spore size. In 1998, he was hired to teach scientists at the Dugway Proving Ground how to make weapons-grade anthrax from bacteria and broth. When the FBI asked he was quick to point out that while the pound that was produced from his instructions was potent stuff, it was not the Ames strain.

Both Spertzel and Patrick mentioned Dugway Proving Ground. Scientists there had the know-how to make weapons-grade anthrax spores. Located in the desert outside Salt Lake City, Utah, the Dugway Proving Ground was built by the army during World War II as a research, testing, and training site for chemical and biologic weapons.

Mackey came upon the four-block-long American Museum of Natural History. The main entrance was on Central Park West facing the park. Between two of the four Ionic columns hung a banner announcing an upcoming exhibit on gold titled, *Greed.* The frieze was inscribed with prophetic words: "Truth, Knowledge and Vision." He needed a heaping helping of all three. At the foot of the stairs stood a statue of Teddy Roosevelt riding upon his horse Little Texas. Roosevelt, in addition to serving as president and vice president, was a New York City police commissioner. Teddy once quipped, "This country has nothing to fear from the crooked man who fails. We put him in jail. It is the crooked man who succeeds who is a threat to this country." Mackey couldn't agree more.

Mackey continued north along the exterior of the park. Saddam Hussein was a crooked man and he had a motive—avenge the 1991 US invasion and expulsion of Iraq from Kuwait. The chaos after 9/11 was an opportunity. And there was a precedent—Saddam invaded Iran in 1980 when he perceived a weakness following the Islamic Revolution. His use of chemical weapons against the Kurds, his own people, demonstrated that he was bound by no moral code of conduct. What's more, not all of the Iraqi bioweapons were believed to have been destroyed after the 1991 US invasion. There were some, including those in the administration, who believed he still possessed biological weapons, including anthrax.

The evidence was circumstantial. American weapons inspectors knew Iraq had purchased several spray dryers, one of which was unaccounted for during the bioweapons inspections. Shortly after the 2003 US invasion it was reported that two mobile bioweapons laboratories were found in Iraq. The administration announced this to the world as justification for the war. They kept using the information long after it had been determined that the vehicles were not equipped for making biological weapons, but hydrogen for weather balloons.

The Iraqis also had no natural source of anthrax. In 1986, during the Iran-Iraq War, a US company shipped three strains of anthrax to Iraq. It was later learned that they had been weaponized. Whether Ames was among the strains, Mackey couldn't find out. No anthrax, however, was found after the 2003 invasion.

Iraqi anthrax was identifiable by the anti-clumping additive they used, a type of clay containing aluminum called bentonite. The analysis of the spores used in the mailings found silicon and oxygen, but not aluminum. It would have been clever of the Iraqis to make spores without bentonite to throw investigators off the scent. Iraq had purchased tons of fumed silica in the 1990s.

Fumed silica was a German invention in which silica was heated in the presence of oxygen to form tiny micro particles of glass. The molecular beads fit between the spores and functioned like a lubricant to prevent clumps from forming. The Iraqis had experimented with silicon dioxide in making weaponized anthrax. So had the Soviets.

When a researcher at USAMRIID examined the Daschle letter spores under an electron microscope he described what he saw as goop resembling the white of a fried egg. Fumed silica under an electron microscope resembles cotton balls arranged in a chain. Could what the researcher saw have been the silicon dioxide micro particles? This would mean they weren't just looking for a domestic terrorist. In the course of an investigation, the list of suspects is supposed to narrow, not expand. Mackey gazed up. He was standing before the stoop to his apartment. In the mailbox he found a bank statement and a red-bordered past-due mortgage notice. Mackey sighed. His mounting debt was pursuing his assets with a velocity to match that of the boulder chasing after Indy, Willie, and Short Round in *Indiana Jones and the Temple of Doom*.

.| 17 |.

The next morning Mackey awoke late. He headed out to Columbia University's courtyard and managed to find an unprotected wireless signal. He spent the early afternoon reading transcripts of interviews with former Soviet bioweapons scientist, defector, and author Ken Alibek.

The FBI showed Alibek electron microscopy images of the mailed anthrax spores. According to Alibek they were not milled. The particle size was small, 1–10 microns and there was a mix of single spores, clumps, and large conglomerates. But he didn't agree that the anthrax concentration was 1 trillion per gram. Alibek went on to say that skilled professionals did not produce the powder; it wasn't a Russian or American-made weapon. With respect to the question of additives, Alibek stated that the Soviets didn't concern themselves with additives and that coating spores was not necessary.

Mackey searched online for evidence that the Soviets weaponized the Ames strain. He didn't find it, just a peculiar admission from Alibek that the Soviet's had spies within the US bioweapons community.

At the height of the Cold War there were over 60,000 people employed in Biopreparat, the Soviet bioweapons program. Not all were scientists with technical know-how. After the dissolution of the Soviet Union, most facilities were downsized, closed, or converted to other purposes. More than twenty-five former Biopreparat scientists defected to the West and the whereabouts of other scientists was a concern shared by the US and its allies. Alibek stated that the Soviet stockpile of bioweapons, specifically anthrax spores, was destroyed. Mackey had read this account before. Cargo trains shipped canisters of anthrax from the facility at Stepnogorsk to Vozrozhdeniye Island where they were destroyed with bleach and then buried.

In the transcript of Congressional testimony from December of 2001, Alibek appeared to draw a distinction between the Soviet Union's bioweapons program and any program undertaken by the nation of Russia that emerged after the Soviet Union break up. He had no knowledge about or even if Russia had kept an offensive bioweapons program after he returned to Kazakhstan in 1991 and then immigrated to the US the following year. Something from Alibek's testimony poked Mackey in the ribs. It could have been the Kazakh's incomplete mastery of English or perhaps a subliminal clue. Alibek had stated that the powder wasn't a *Russian* weapon. Since he admittedly knew nothing about Russian bioweapons, was this a backhanded way of suggesting he recognized it as a Soviet one?

The anthrax experts couldn't agree on the powder used in the mailings. Spertzel and scientists at USAMRIID believed the powder was a sophisticated weapon and couldn't have been made by a lone scientist. William Patrick and Alibek both thought it was a good product but not up to standards for a bioweapons program. Sergei Popov, another former Soviet bioweapons researcher who defected to the United States, was on record agreeing with Spertzel that weaponizing anthrax could not be fashioned outside of a state-sponsored program. There was one former Soviet scientist now in the US whose opinion Mackey couldn't find published anywhere on the Web—that of Yuri Chenko. Perhaps he had nothing to add. Mackey decided to find out. But it would have to wait. Charo had texted she wanted to meet. Would she tell him she was backing out of their illicit investigation? What would he do then? He called Marci.

"Hi, Marci, it's Mackey. Just wondering if you have any news on my hiring?"

"Not much, other than learning that the glitch isn't with the city. The problem is in Washington. They aren't releasing the grant money."

"Is this common?"

"It's never happened in my years here."

A pang of paranoia struck. Was this somehow connected to his nosing around in the Amerithrax investigation? Other than Geetangali, no one knew the full extent of what Mackey and Charo were up to. What about the agent he met at Charo's desk chasing drug bunnies? Brad something. He acted suspiciously. Mackey patted his pockets, but found no Xanax was there.

Charo was already waiting for him in Columbus Park on the edge of Chinatown. As he approached she held out a folded piece of paper. He took it while trying to read her expression. She nodded at the paper but did not make eye contact. Mackey unfolded it slowly as if it might be filled with spores. The page was blank.

"What is this? A letter of reference for my next job?"

"That's a list of all the suspects who had access to the Ames strain. It's only current to 2004, the best I could get my hands on."

Mackey turned it over. On the reverse, across the top, there appeared a shopping list. "Yogurt was a suspect? Eggs I can believe, they've used *Salmonella* as a weapon. And butter, they are only in it for the bread." He held it up to the light and at an angle but no watermark or list was visible. He cast a puzzled eye at Charo.

She took the page from him and removed an atomizer from her bag. She sprayed the paper. The air filled with a faint acidic odor. Typing appeared wherever the mist landed on the paper. Charo sprayed both sides, waved it in the air, and handed back to Mackey. While she did this the apologetic lyrics from the Tom Waits song, "Please Call Me, Baby," rushed into his head[8]. He took the opportunity to exorcise a demon.

"Hey, about yesterday. I'm sorry if I came across too strong. I can get carried away sometimes. A temperament I didn't inherit from my parents. Maybe I developed it in medical school," he said unconvinced.

"I appreciate that and respect your passion," Charo said.

"By the way," Mackey said with a renewed smirk, "do you get many second dates with that fragrance?"

He scanned the list of names. It continued on the second side; over sixty he guessed. Some he recognized. Steven Hatfill, the most publicized person of interest, had already been exonerated and all that remained to resolve was the dollar figure on the damages award for the FBI's misguided pursuit. Egyptian-born scientist Assaad Ayaad was on the list. He was the target of a slanderous, anonymous letter that was sent weeks before the anthrax letters were mailed claiming he was a terrorist. His co-worker and alleged tormentor, Phillip Zack, was also on the list. Both had worked at USAMRIID, had alibis, and were long ago forgotten by the FBI. Next to the suspects were the names of the labs at which the person worked. Almost all of the names bore an *X*. The FBI had determined them to be cold leads. There were two names on the list that did not bear an *X*— Arthur C. Lavigne and Oren Waldman. Joseph Erekat was not on the list.

Charo read his mind. "Lavigne is dead and we have been unable to locate Waldman. He dropped out of eyesight in 2001, months before the attacks. But he didn't possess the requisite skills or fit the motive profile."

Mackey sat on a park bench. "I was hoping this would point us to the labs with the matching strain.

Without that, we don't know which of these *X*'s might deserve a second look."

"Sorry."

"Where does this place the official investigation now? Are there any suspects other than Erekat? Is the FBI close to an indictment?"

"That's going to take me more time to learn. I don't have any contacts on the investigation team any longer and it is being run out of the Washington bureau. I've got to tread carefully. While my SSA does not look over my shoulder, if I start asking questions about an investigation that is not mine, I will attract unwanted attention. After Robert Hanssen everyone is a tad jumpy and attentive to unauthorized accessing of the databases."

Twilight rolled down around them like a Broadway curtain. They watched children in the park run giggling in between the monkey bars and a caterpillar slide. Around the periphery sat their parents and grandparents looking like dolls on a store shelf. On the other side of a fence, Mah Jong games were finishing for the evening while the card players shuffled on, the bent and smudged cards resembling roofing tiles. Mackey felt their stares and whispers. The presence of an Anglo man and an Asian woman speaking English in this homogeneous enclave provoked curiosity. None of the children playing had mixed features, which further fueled the intrigue. When he next spoke he lowered his voice.

"Al Qaeda. Another terrorist group, foreign or domestic. A domestic hate group. A disgruntled lab worker. A nut job like Kaczynski. A scientist trying to bring the risk of biological weapons to the forefront of the national consciousness."

Charo added, "A foreign government, like Iran, seeking revenge or attempting to destabilize our government and economy. Israel, instigating war to eliminate a mutual enemy."

"Who besides Israel profits by war in Iraq, Afghanistan, or the Middle East?" Mackey asked.

"Oil companies. War contractors." Charo answered.

"All supporters of the administration."

Charo didn't answer but Mackey read her dubious expression. They spent the next half hour in gray silence watching the last of the children leave the park holding hands with fathers, mothers, grandmothers, and grandfathers.

.| 18 |.

It was chilly in Bryant Park. Although no clouds obstructed the late September rays the sun had already hightailed it too far south to warm the Canadian air mass delivered to the city the night before. Mackey hadn't shaved and with sunglasses and the hood of his gray sweatshirt pulled over his head, he resembled the famous sketch of the Unabomber. Aside from the occasional groundskeeper and sweater-clad Scandinavian tourist, the plaza was empty.

For the moment he ignored the suspect list Charo had given him the night before. It was clipped to a strap of his backpack and flapping in the morning breeze. In his notebook he made a list of the leads the to follow:

1] Why Joseph Erekat?
2] Which labs had matching strains?
3] Fort Detrick-USAMRIID and Dugway Proving Ground
4] Suspect list from Charo
5] Yuri Chenko
6] E-ZPass data

That the FBI was considering Joseph Erekat was the best clue he had. But what to make of it? If Erekat was Mailthrax then all that remained to solving the case was collecting enough evidence to prove it. Perhaps the FBI was waiting for the completion of the anthrax genetic library before presenting to a Grand Jury the evidence against Erekat. If this were true there would be little need for him to continue. Without access to all that the FBI had ascertained he decided to work backwards from what little evidence was available.

If Erekat wasn't Mailthrax then how did the FBI's suspicions otherwise inform the investigation? It had to be through the spore evidence. As far as he could tell Erekat had access to three labs in his life—the rudimentary one at his college that didn't possess anthrax, the one at USAMRIID that did, and the one at Rutgers University that as far as he knew didn't either.

Knowing that Erekat's link was through USAMRIID didn't narrow down the list of other suspects when he considered that the Army shared interesting strains like teens swapped spit. Mackey shut his eyes. On the whiteboard in his mind he saw a hypothetical map of where USAMRIID sent Ames samples. At each site the spores would have been subjected to different conditions, therefore they might have evolved different mutations. He crafted pie charts to represent the genetic changes, using the slice size and color to denote the divergent DNA. Since anthrax was slow to mutate, these differences would be subtle. Thus the need to develop the forensic tools to say with near absolute certainty that two strains shared a common ancestry. Since records of *Bacillus anthracis* transfers began in 1997, the FBI should know where USAMRIID had sent the strain that matched the one used in the tainted letters. But what if the strain was shipped the other way, from a lab that had worked with the Ames strain and sent a sample to USAMRIID? If it happened before 1997 there might not be a record, yet the spores used in the attacks could have originated at a lab other than USAMRIID.

He rifled through a 2002 *Science* article. In the days before microbial forensics a team of researchers compared genetic sequences recovered from the first anthrax victim to several "stock" *B. anthracis* strains. Five of them were Ames but not all the sources were disclosed. The analysis was limited by the amount of the genomes available for comparison, but similar to human DNA forensics, enough was available to conclusively discern when strains didn't match.

Porton Down Lab in the UK received Ames from USAMRIID around 1982 and at the time of the analysis the strain differed at four loci. Not much divergence over 5.2 million nucleotides after almost twenty years but enough to establish its innocence.

Another strain, denoted as A, was missing a chunk of the chromosome responsible for virulence so it was ruled out as the source of the attack strain. That left three strains.

The strain referred to as D differed at a single nucleotide. But the two remaining strains, denoted as B and C, were indistinguishable from the strain found in Florida.

Mackey dug deeper. He deduced that of strains B, C, and D, two likely came from USAMRIID and the other from Dugway Proving Ground. What the authors of the *Science* paper couldn't say, since they examined a mere five strains, was how many other strains in laboratories and the natural environment also matched to the Florida strain and if the matches would hold up as more of the genomes were sequenced and compared. Regardless, Mackey began to see the noose tightening around someone at either Fort Detrick or Dugway Proving Ground. He couldn't very well show up at either lab pointing fingers. They'd surely throw him out on his ear and he couldn't spare the cash to fly to Utah. Besides, the FBI appeared to have ruled out the scientists as suspects. Why?

Out of the jumble of laboratory names that were swirling around the neurons in Mackey's brain there emerged a thread. He pulled on it gently, afraid that it might break before he reached the nugget of insight tethered at its far end. Since the Ames strain got its name at USAMRIID, any lab holding a descendant also named Ames would have gotten it from USAMRIID or from a lab that received it from USAMRIID. There might also be labs with Ames strains, but didn't know it, getting their isolate from a lab in possession of the pre-Ames moniker Texas cow culture. Labs using the strain for research would have surely corrected the name discrepancy but a lab that stockpiled it in their freezers along with the rest of their collection might not know its true identity. This complicated Mackey's narrowing of the laboratory suspect list. Anthrax occurs in nature and at a minimum was on the Texas farm where the cow encountered it in 1981. There still was a slim chance that the source of the attack strain was soil. Regardless, he had to hope Charo could extract from the FBI the information on which labs held matching strains and how suspects were ruled out. He also needed to know the evidence that implicated Joseph Erekat.

A replica Michelin man, his treads made from layers of discarded clothes and inflated by putrefaction, ambled over to where Mackey sat in the park. His weathered and grimy hand jingled a few coins in a crushed paper cup.

"Spare some change?" he mumbled through missing teeth.

Mackey patted his pockets and shook his head guiltily. The man shuffled off but had pried loose a memory. On a ride back to Boston from Baltimore they stopped in New Haven to eat. Allie picked the place, a retro luncheonette complete with linoleum countertops, trimmed in corrugated steel, and vinyl stools that spun to endless delight at the hands of children. While they checked out the menu at the counter an old man entered. His clothes were worn but not unclean. Rope held loose pants about a gaunt frame. Burnished hands the color of shoe leather fumbled nervously. In a low voice he spoke to the waitress behind the counter. With a glance to assure the owner wasn't watching she wrapped the two ends of a loaf of white bread in a paper napkin and slid them across the counter. Mackey looked away so he would not have to witness the man's shame. The old man shuffled toward the exit, mumbling, and genuflecting his gratitude. Allie stepped between the old man and the door. Before long the three of them were sliding into an open booth.

Bartel Williams was sixty-four. He ordered an egg salad sandwich and told Allie and Mackey, while hiding his rotting teeth with his hand, that Cookie's egg salad was the best he'd ever tasted. Bartel had worked in a zipper factory, but it closed down. At fifty-seven he was too young to retire and too old to be re-hired. His wife Dottie got breast cancer and died. Bartel had given a substantial portion of their savings to a friend to invest. Both disappeared and the mortgage was soon past due. He defaulted, lost his home and now lived in one of two men's shelters, alternating when he reached his consecutive day limit. Allie listened, all the while beholding Bartel's face. He had a son who lived in California, but they had a falling out and he didn't have a current address. Bartel wanted to work, was handy with tools, but arthritis had taken most of his dexterity and without new glasses he couldn't spot a quarter at his feet. He ate with the speed of one not wishing to overstay a welcome and refused to take any money. Allie got the addresses of the shelters before he was out the door with a wave of a sun-bleached baseball cap.

After Allie was gone Mackey found a letter from Bartel among her things. It was a Christmas card thanking her for her concern and help getting him much needed glasses and dental services. He was going out to California to see his grandchildren and might stay there. Allie's touch was as light as a hummingbird's feather, and as fleeting. He missed her terribly.

Two names. Oren Waldman and Arthur Lavigne. One missing, the other dead. Mackey looked up Waldman on the Internet and it turned out he wasn't missing but had moved out of the country. Waldman retired from research and joined Doctors Without Borders. His last known destination was Kenya and its AIDS epidemic.

Lavigne had been employed at USAMRIID from 1965 to 1970, long before the Ames strain was even discovered. He taught microbiology at Marshall University in West Virginia and died in November 2001.

Yuri Chenko was not on the suspect list. But his name kept popping up whenever Mackey researched the Soviet Union's bioweapons program. Chenko was the last émigré to the US from Biopreparat and lived outside Baltimore. Having arrived after Alibek and Popov, his value to the American intelligence community was vastly diminished. A defecting Soviet bioweapons expert was as novel as a twist-off beer cap. If the Soviets had acquired the Ames strain either through a laboratory exchange or theft from USAMRIID, Mackey reasoned that as one of the last to leave the program, Chenko might know. Like his predecessors, Chenko worked for a biologic consulting firm. Mackey found the number for Arbus Research, Inc. on the Web and, forgetting it was Saturday, dialed the number. He was expecting a receptionist to answer, followed by a personal assistant who he'd have to talk his way past to speak to the man. But a gruff, accented male voice came on the line after two rings.

"*Da*?"

"Hello, I am calling for Dr. Yuri Chenko."

"I am Yuri Chenko. What do you want?"

"Dr. Chenko, my name is Dr. Dunn, I am with the Centers for Disease Control and Prevention and I would like to speak with you about anthrax." There was a long pause. Heavy breathing on the other end reassured Mackey that he had not been disconnected.

"Come by my office tomorrow. You know how to find me?"

"Yes, sir. What time would be good?"

"No matter." With a click, the line was dead.

Mackey purchased a Metroliner ticket with his scissor-bound Visa card figuring that if Chenko was confused about it being Sunday he'd instead surprise his mother with a visit. He got off at BWI Airport stop. After a short taxi ride he stood before 100 Aberdeen Road. A chain-linked fence surrounded a gray concrete block building. The constant roar of ascending jets and their hot, fuel-soaked exhaust lifted Mackey's breakfast uneasily from the pit of his stomach. The landscape, devoid of vegetation, put him in mind of a Siberian gulag that wasn't far off from Chenko's Uzbekistan homeland.

Mackey pushed opened the gate but it swung crooked on one hinge and dug into the sandy soil. He squeezed through the gap. The entrance was a faded green steel door with a slot for mail. He pressed the buzzer. Hearing no noise, he pressed again, this time with more force. The buzzer dislodged, fell to the ground, and tumbled away in the breeze coming to rest in a pile of shredded newspapers caught in the bottom of the fence. He retrieved and replaced it, knocking with the other hand. From within he heard shuffling, but it was several minutes before the latch turned and the door opened.

Yuri Chenko was a large, bearded man. He thrust a hairy hand out that Mackey attempted to shake, but it gripped his forearm instead and yanked him into the darkness. Mackey was pinned against a veneer-paneled wall by the barrel of Chenko's barrel finger.

"You are you?" he bellowed.

"Dr. Chenko, I'm Dr. Dunn. We spoke yesterday. You invited me to see you today. You said anytime. I hope I am not inconveniencing you."

Mackey glanced past the man's shoulder. There was a metal desk, a chair, a brown Naugahyde sofa, a fire extinguisher, some books, and little else. The sole illumination came from a tiny desk lamp. Chenko released him and motioned him to the sofa.

"Dr. Dunn, please have a seat. Excuse my boorishness. In my line of business you have to be careful, you understand Yuri?" Mackey nodded but fretted over the line of business in which such a greeting was customary. Yuri removed a small glass from the desk drawer and poured Mackey a shot from a nearly empty vodka bottle, spilling the rest into his own glass.

"I am sorry, this is last of vodka."

With considerable effort Mackey jackknifed using his ankles as a fulcrum to emerge from the crevice of the couch. He grasped the glass and kept it between his knees, remaining on the edge of the sofa, rather than have to repeat the gymnastics.

"What is your business with Yuri?"

Mackey explained that it wasn't business so much as information he sought. "We are reopening the Postal Service anthrax investigation of 2001 and I have been sent here to make use of your extensive knowledge and expertise. I have a few questions that won't take up too much of your time."

Yuri stared at his vodka longingly then took a sip. He leaned back, folding his hands behind his head.

Mackey continued, "I've read your book, *Cold Terror…*" Mackey hesitated, remembering that Russians were often offended by the frankness of Americans. "You worked at a bioweapons plant in Berdsk, is that right?"

"*Da.* Siberia, Novosibirsk Oblast. I was a civilian scientist for Biopreparat. Soviet Union top-secret bioweapons program." He paused to draw a breath.

"There were three facilities in Berdsk—an assembly plant where biological agents were loaded into bomblets, a mobilization facility for producing large quantities of bioweapons in the event of war, and a research facility—the Technology Institute of Biologically Active Substances. I worked at Institute."

"Did you work with anthrax?"

"In Soviet Union there were, uh, I believe you call them fiefdoms. I was part of the serfdom. I worked on what I was told to work on."

"Did your research involve anthrax?" Mackey repeated.

"Have you heard of strain 836?"

"No," Mackey lied. Strain 836 was in Alibek's book but he wanted to hear Yuri's unvarnished testimony.

Yuri drained the little that remained of his vodka. He stared at the empty glass like a child about to swipe a finger around the bottom of a pudding cup. He sighed heavily. The simple act of expanding his massive chest appeared to be a source of tremendous fatigue.

"Strain 836 is hypervirulent strain. We recovered it from rats in the sewers of Kirov. We believe that after several growth cycles in the rats it had mutated to a more virulent form. I was one of many scientists trying to discover what made it so deadly."

Mackey considered the implications. If they knew what made it so virulent and had identified the genes coding for virulence they could transfer the element to other anthrax strains with favorable characteristics or perhaps even to other bacteria to make a catalog of super strains. The thought gave him a chill.

"Did you ever determine why strain 836 was so virulent?"

"*Da*. Strain 836 is very hardy. It produces a thick capsule that renders it resistant to many disinfectants and ultraviolet radiation. It also produces more toxin than other strains. We never determined the genetic basis that allows strain 836 to produce more toxin."

Mackey breathed a sigh of relief. "Did you develop any other strains of anthrax as weapons?"

"We had stocks of every known anthrax strain. Our collection was the most complete in the world."

"Did you ever work with the Ames strain?"

"*Nyet.*" Yuri shifted in his chair, turning to face Mackey, and placed his hands on his thighs. "The facility at Sverdlovsk could produce 5,000 tons a year of pure anthrax spores." Yuri paused and raised a bushy eyebrow at Mackey who was struggling with the concept of 5,000 tons. Five thousand tons of anthrax equals ten million pounds, equivalent to 4,545,000 kilograms or 4.5 billion grams at one trillion spores per gram, with the human lethal dose of about 20,000 spores, equals... game over. If only one of every hundred spores reached the lower airways it was still an amount sufficient to kill the entire world population 250,000 times over.

Yuri remained quiet. He rubbed his face with both hands, then smiled broadly. "I am hungry. You will buy Yuri lunch."

From behind the building Yuri wheeled his truck around in a spray of gravel. Mackey hopped into the front seat of the Toyota pickup next to a greasy carburetor wrapped in a torn shirtsleeve. They pulled into an employee parking lot behind the airport terminal. Yuri entered through a service door and navigated narrow corridors until a staircase emerged by a row of garbage cans in the food court.

He headed straight for Sbarro and ordered four slices of pepperoni and a large soda. On Mackey's tray lay a limp brown salad and a beige slice of plain pizza. They sat in the food court next to two rotund women in stretch pants who were sucking down frozen coffee drinks topped with whipped cream and chocolate syrup. Nodding his head at the table, Yuri admonished Mackey.

"Americans are spoiled by excess and too much freedom. It is both your greatness and greatest weakness. Free market is how your economy goes into, how do you say, freefall. In Soviet Union you don't buy your house. If you are fortunate you will get a place to live because of the importance of your job. There is no choosing. Americans buy houses they cannot afford. Then they steal from their employers. Bad for business. Businesses can't compete, so they move jobs overseas. More unemployment. Soon the man loses his home, his wife, his self-respect."

Between words, Yuri took delicate bites of his pizza, as if bypassing a bad tooth. Mackey pushed through his salad searching for a firm morsel. Finding none, he excused himself. At the duty-free shop he grabbed two bottles of one-hundred-proof Stolichnaya vodka. In the men's room he opened one and poured half down the sink. He thought better of it and decanted more and then refilled it with tap water. With his keys he made a small dent in the cap.

Yuri was leaning back in his food court chair, eyes closed, hands folded over his belly. At Mackey's approach he got up and led the way back through the maze of the building's intestines to the parking lot. The ride back to Yuri's office was short, but gut churning, affirming Mackey's light choice for lunch.

"Where were we?" Yuri asked. Mackey removed one of the two bottles of Stolichnaya, careful not to grab the one with the dented cap and slid it across the desk. Yuri flashed a bearish grin and reached out to shake Mackey's hand. Mackey's glass was still full but his host topped it off anyway before filling his own, drinking half in a single gulp. Mackey worked on his more leisurely. When the glass was near empty he reached into his bag to produce the second bottle of Stolichnaya. He saluted Yuri with a tip of the bottle and refilled his own glass. He kept the bottle next to him on the edge of the desk with the label turned toward Yuri.

Mackey had read enough to suspect that the Russians had the Ames strain, the question was did they weaponize it? With strain 836 in their arsenal, why would they bother? The vodka was loosening them both up, so he decided to put the question to Yuri.

"At Sverdlovsk, four strains were found in the victims. Was the Ames strain one of them? Did you ever weaponize it?"

"In Soviet Union we produced many anthrax weapons. A single strain not the best weapon. Many strains with different properties and resistance much better. No one defense can stop weapon."

"Resistance, you mean to antibiotics?"

"*Da*, and vaccine, too." Mackey poured himself another diluted vodka, but did not drink. He wanted to remain in Yuri's confidence, keep him talking yet retain his wits about him. He was already feeling lightheaded, uncertain if it was the vodka or the stark realization that if the US had engaged the Soviets in a biologic war he'd either be dead or performing testicular exams on Kuznetski coal miners right now. He moved on to the main reason for his visit.

"When the FBI questioned you, did they ask you about additives?" Yuri looked puzzled.

Additives might not have existed in Yuri's English lexicon. "What was used to prevent spores from sticking together?"

"I know what is additives, but I have never spoken to the FBI."

"What types of additives were used to improve particle aerodynamics?"

Yuri again grinned and poured more vodka. He studied the glass as he held it up to his lips. Mackey checked what remained of Yuri's vodka hoping his comrade's supply would last the length of the interview. The bottle had a little less than half remaining and Mackey dearly hoped that Yuri himself was more than half in the bag.

"You want Yuri to reveal Soviet secrets, eh?"

Mackey wore his most attentive look but said nothing, a technique borrowed from Charo. Yuri stared at the wall. His eyes were bloodshot but Mackey thought he saw them welling. The big man turned and regarded his drinking buddy. Wearing a wrinkled white button-down shirt, paisley tie, and threadbare sports jacket across his lap, Mackey looked more like a college baseball player on game day than a person who could improve Yuri's financial status.

Yuri rubbed his nose, cleared his throat and let out a roar. Bursting into laughter, he exclaimed, "We put wool over America's eyes."

Mackey feared the vodka was affecting his hearing. "I beg your pardon?"

Yuri was still convulsing. It took some time, but he calmed down and told Mackey that the Soviets had experimented with many ingredients to improve the aerodynamics of the anthrax product by reducing the attractive forces that cause stickiness. One of the additives the Soviets found useful was finely ground lamb's wool. Some Soviet scientists figured if working in a wool processing plant was the greatest risk for contracting occupational inhalation anthrax there might be something about the wool itself that promotes transmission. The best additive though, the one that turned spores into a powder that floated like the clouds, was fumed silica. With the sudden clarity of a college physical chemistry professor, or a man with a spare liver, Yuri detailed the process.

"Spores were first milled then sprayed with super heated air and fumed silica to produce sub microscopic particles with weak attractive forces to each another. The spores weren't coated. The fumed silica makes the powder behave like a gas. It was dramatic, like the difference between hail and snow."

The half-strength vodka had begun to affect Mackey's wherewithal, making it more where-without, but there was still more he wanted to find out. He pushed back the nausea and pressed on.

"Have you reviewed the descriptions of the powder found in the letters sent to the US senators?"

"I have seen the electron micrographs."

"Do you think it was the work of a bioweapons lab?"

"Perhaps."

"Could it have been produced in a makeshift basement lab?"

"Perhaps." Yuri rose and left the room. Mackey heard a toilet flush. When he returned his host's eyelids were at half-mast and he retired to the couch.

"What about all of the stockpiled Soviet bioweapons?"

"Gone."

"All of them?"

"Yesssss." He was now breathing slow and deep.

"How? Where?"

"*Vozrozh…de… ni…ye…*" Yuri faded off into a deep slumber.

It was almost dusk when Mackey slipped out the door, leaving Yuri snoring on the couch. Half a bottle of diluted vodka was the equivalent of six beers and more than his poor liver had seen since college. Walking as if searching for firm ground but finding golf balls instead, Mackey made his way to the road. He could see taxis on the airport drive but there was no way to get there short of climbing a fence and crossing a field so he set off in the direction of the train station. For a moment he considered spending the night at his mom's but then thought better of it. Inebriated as he was, it being a Sunday night, and *she* having a job—it didn't seem like a good idea.

The 6:48 PM Amtrak Northeast Regional left without him so he had an hour to kill until the next train. Locating an Internet kiosk, he swiped his credit card and thought about how much his cash flow resembled a NASA rocket booster. It went very fast in one direction and then burned up. He typed "Biopreparat" into Google's search engine. He was about to click on a Wikipedia link when another link caught his eye:

ANTHRAX ATTACKS AND MICROBIOLOGIST DEATHS
Sibir Air Tu-154 was shot down by a Ukranian missile, on board were fice Russian microbiologists from Novosibirsk...More microbiologists have turned up dead in the wake of the US anthrax attacks...
www.anthraxconspiracy.com/fivedeadmicrobiologists.html

Mackey vaguely recalled the plane crash. He clicked on the link and it brought up a blog entry. An errant missile fired by the Ukrainians during a military exercise over the Black Sea struck a Russian commercial plane killing all on board. He clicked on the source link. The flight originated from Israel and five of the passengers were alleged microbiologists from Novosibirsk, a Biopreparat site. The Ukrainians at first denied any role but when fragments of the Ukrainian-made missile were found in the wreckage they admitted their mistake. The date was October 4, 2001, the same day the first US anthrax case was confirmed and announced to the media.

The post was linked to another about a string about microbiologist deaths that the author believed was part of a conspiracy. In mid-November 2001 a Miami infectious disease researcher got a call on his cell phone after which he departed his lab. He was found dead not long afterward in the lab's parking lot. A mugging was suspected but no trauma was evident. Four days later a well-known Harvard AIDS and Ebola researcher disappeared; his car found abandoned on a bridge spanning the Mississippi River near Memphis, Tennessee. The authorities postulated suicide, though no one who knew him could believe it. The link to anthrax was through his groundbreaking work in X-ray crystallography.

The next day, in a remote area of West Virginia, sixty-six-year-old Marshall University microbiology professor Arthur Lavigne was found shot to death. Next to Lavigne's body was a .38-caliber Smith & Wesson revolver registered in his name. Four days after Lavigne's death, Vladimir Pasechnik, an ex-Biopreparat bioweapons scientist who defected to England in 1989, was found dead in his home. No autopsy was performed. The cause of death for the sixty-four-year-old was said to have been a stroke.

Things were getting weird. The next death was of an American whose expertise was in the DNA sequencing of pathogenic organisms. He was fifty-seven and was brutally stabbed by a group of self-described Goth teens. Four days later, across the world in Australia, a scientist walked into a refrigerator and collapsed. A liquid nitrogen tank used to keep lab samples cold had leaked displacing oxygen from the room. The scientist suffocated. The lab had been manipulating the genes of poxviruses.

The blog entry went on to report several additional deaths that the author believed were related to the US anthrax cases. Two scientists were murdered in Moscow in January 2002 and another in England the following month. The Brit was stripped naked and stuffed beneath a piece of furniture. That same month, in San Francisco, a pizza deliveryman shot an expatriate Russian woman involved in AIDS research. Mackey spotted the word Ames. An astrobiologist from the Ames Research Center in the UK specializing in microbial adaptation was struck and killed by a car while jogging in March of 2002.

Mackey wasn't the first to latch onto conspiracy theories, but he didn't discount them either. Maybe it was the liquor, but he felt a sudden wave of apprehension. He had dove head first into the investigation without much thought as to the possible repercussions. He hadn't before considered that there might be consequences to his actions.

The last person in the macabre series was the most famous. Dr. David Kelly was a biological weapons expert and former UN inspector who made several trips to Iraq. His body was found near his home. The police concluded that he had slashed his own wrists after being despondent over the recent publicity he had received regarding statements he made about the war in Iraq. His resume listed Porton Down, one of the labs that received the Ames strain.

Was the anthrax killer or killers going around murdering microbiologists who might suspect their identity? Or were these attempts to rid the world of contributors to bioweapons research? If true, wouldn't Chenko, Patrick, Popov, and Alibek have been targets, too? The PA system announced the final boarding call for the 7:48 PM train to New York City.

.| 19 |.

Mackey was awakened from deep sleep by an irksome noise. Hung over and disoriented, it took him too long to recognize the ring of his new cell phone. The call was from Charo. After a few missed attempts he found and hit the callback button.

"Hey, where are you?" she asked.

He cupped his eyes and peered out the window into the darkness. "On the train back from Baltimore. Looks like we're stopped in the Meadowland swamps."

"Get down here as fast as you can. Geeta has made some wicked curry you've got to try."

"Huh?" Charo had already disconnected.

Mackey's blood alcohol level was on the down slope and the few dry neurons he had began to make sense of Charo's words. Both Charo and Geetangali were at work late on a Sunday night. The E-ZPass analysis must have found something.

When he emerged from the subway at Chambers Street it was 11:30 PM. A fuzzy full moon hung over the Woolworth Building. Mackey nearly collided with a couple exiting a bar but managed to turn east then north on Broadway. A block from 26 Federal Plaza he pulled out his cell phone and dialed Charo.

"Hey, I'm here for the curry."

"I'm coming down now."

She was waiting for him as he trudged up Broadway. If the moon was aglow, Charo was as radiant as the northern lights in an Alaskan sky. She had come straight from a workout when Geeta called her with news. She was wearing a zippered hoodie low enough to reveal the top of a pink sports bra and a pique of cleavage. If Mackey had ever wondered why they were called tights, Charo answered the question once and forever. Through his vodka-steeped and sleep-deprived stupor he hoped his tongue wasn't hanging out too far.

"You look like crap."

"Wish I felt half that good," he mumbled. The guard barely glanced at Mackey's ID, devoting his attention to Charo's derriere. They rode the elevator in blessed silence. They found Geeta in her cubicle; the dual video display terminals were scrolling continuous code. Charo guided Mackey into a chair.

"Hi, Mackey," Geeta looked with concern to Charo who rolled her eyes.

"He's okay."

"Yeah, I'm all right. You got any coffee to go with the curry?"

Geeta gave Charo a puzzled smile to which Charo just nodded toward the computer screen.

"I think I may have found something. You recall when we last spoke that I ran the E-ZPass data and I had filtered the results down to 444 hits?"

"Uh-huh."

"With refinements I got it down to 431 hits."

"Oh."

"Then I cross referenced the license plates with our databases. We have access to the DMV, terrorism watch list, hate groups, parole board, and some others. I filtered out soccer moms and senior citizens. We can go back and review them later if you'd like. By the way, I found several parole violators who crossed state lines."

"Wait. How did you know the person was a soccer mom?" Mackey asked. Geeta looked to Charo.

"It's okay to tell him," Charo said.

"I used 2000 census data. It is handy for ruling out suspects, but not much use for ruling in."

"Census data? You have access to household-level census data?"

"Uh, yes, the Patriot Act has been interpreted to allow this in matters of national security. I figured this qualified."

Mackey winced at his participation in the shredding of the US Constitution. All he could muster was a weak groan. Charo motioned to Geeta to continue.

"I've assigned probabilities to each E-ZPass account based on their demographic," she lowered her voice. "… and other profile data. Unfortunately, I was only able to eliminate about a hundred."

"That means we are still left with more than 300 E-ZPass accounts?" Mackey emitted an Eeyore-like moan.

"Yes, but there is more," Charo chimed.

Geeta continued, "I also ran the two-car scenario we discussed last time and it found a pair of government plates fitting the dates and pattern. They are registered in Washington, DC."

"Really?" Mackey said with renewed interest.

"One of the cars made a round trip though Princeton, New Jersey area toll booths on September 17th. Wanna guess when the other did?" Charo asked.

"October 8th?"

"Close. Sunday, October 7th. Came into New Jersey early in the morning and exited before ten."

"Hmm. Do we know where the cars originated from?"

"We didn't think to ask for all the East Coast data, but both cars came across the Delaware Memorial Bridge," Geeta replied.

"And which government agency owns these cars?" Mackey watched as Geeta's face changed from that of an explorer who expected to find coyote footprints to one who fell into *T. rex*-sized craters instead.

Charo answered. "For that I'll have to go to Washington. I suggest Mackey that you head home, get some sleep, and take a day off."

"No way. I'm going with you."

"I don't think that would be a good idea. I'm taking enough of a risk with you here. I can't have you hanging around headquarters without receiving some serious scrutiny."

"There are a lot of loose ends that lead to Washington," Mackey knew he was stretching it. Though there were plenty of loose ends, he neither knew where they began, led, or ended. "I'll be incognito, blend in with the tourists."

Charo considered this at length and then carefully replied, "It would be nice to have company on the drive down. You'll have to be here tomorrow morning at seven sharp and promise to stay out of sight."

Mackey responded with an enthusiastic yawn.

Charo and Mackey exited the building together and walked to Chambers Street.

"Were you visiting your mom?"

"Er, no. Yuri Chenko."

"Learn anything?"

"I'm not sure. Maybe at the train station."

"Train station?"

The turnstiles spun like an oil-starved combine. On the uptown express platform Mackey slumped onto a bench. His tie knot was irrevocably askew, his shirt more rumpled than a Shar-Pei's coat, and his weary jacket looked like it had lost a wrestling match to a porcupine. At the sound of an approaching train Charo grabbed Mackey's forearm and hoisted him to his feet.

The only unoccupied seat on the subway car faced backwards which was enough to loosen Mackey's tenuous hold on his nausea. The train driver, in what seemed to Mackey to be a deliberate attempt to cause him to puke, was alternately stomping on the subway train's brake and accelerator. The solitary thought Mackey was able to form was the need to get off the train and drink water, somewhat incongruous with the busting pressure his kidneys were inflicting on his bladder. Charo recognized Mackey's wasted state and left him to his own detritus. Before hopping off the train at 14th Street to switch to the L train, she poked him to see if he'd be able to make it home alright and reminded him *sans voce* when to meet her the next morning.

Mackey closed his eyes. Tom Waits was about to whisper whiskey breath into his inner ear when the pounding in his head jiggled loose the jukebox power cord. He opened his eyes in time to stumble out the doors as they were closing at 116th Street. He didn't think he could feel any worse until he played his lone phone message. It was from his mom. She wanted to know when he'd be by for a visit. He forced down a quart of water and several aspirin before burrowing under the guilt.

.| 20 |.

After the reward for information about who was responsible for the anthrax mailings was doubled to $2.5 million in January 2002, US embassies and consulates around the world were flooded with people trying to cash in. From Abidjan, Cote d'Ivoire to Ulaanbataar, Mongolia, people rushed in with claims that they possessed evidence vital to solving the case. An elephant in Lahore was said to have a bloodhound-like trunk and could sniff out the origin of the putative spores. Dozens of powders allegedly linked to that found in the letters were paraded in rolled leaves, animal hides, clay pots, and urns. A letter written in Arabic, turned up in Riyadh. Its recipient claimed the handwriting matched that of the letters posted on the FBI website. Another man from Dar es Salaam brought in a letter postmarked in Florida. It was from his cousin, but it wasn't expected. In Germany, a man reported to the authorities that his Algerian neighbors were dealers in black market anthrax. He was half right. They were dealing in black market, knock-off Lange & Söhne watches. A number of these reports came from countries that were formerly part of the Soviet Union. Each person's name and address, if they were willing to divulge, was dutifully recorded by US Foreign Service staff, who then passed along the tips to their superiors, who then passed them on to the FBI. On the subway ride to meet Charo he reminded himself to add the task of checking with the State Department to their DC trip list.

Charo pulled out of the underground garage in a crimson Camry at seven o'clock. Mackey slid in and she turned west in the sparse morning traffic. Minutes later the Holland Tunnel spat them out into the cheerful sunshine of the Garden State. After the Statue of Liberty waved them good luck, the infamous New Jersey refineries belched approval, the malodorous support nearly bringing Mackey to tears. As soon as they cleared commuter traffic on the turnpike, Charo reached behind her seat and produced an identical pair of foil-wrapped spheres. She handed one to Mackey.

"Egg and cheese on a toasted English muffin," she said. With a nod to the backseat she added, "There's juice and coffee, too." Mackey placed his sandwich between the seat and car door. His stomach was still too jittery to accept nourishment and he hoped it would roll away when they stopped for gas. Charo attacked hers.

The cover for their impromptu junket to Washington was that Charo needed to brief the Legislative SSA on her child pornography investigations. She laid out their real mission to Mackey: "One, identify which agency the vehicles belong to. Two, find out who drove the cars on the dates in question. Three, turn the evidence over to the SAC of the Amerithrax investigation."

Mackey didn't respond, not even to item three. It wasn't so much the hangover, bad as it was, but something from the collection of microbiologist deaths that was dripping like a leaky faucet in his subconscious. He knew one couldn't believe everything posted on the Web. With access to so much information, Internet conspiracy theorists sprouted like mushrooms in a dank, peat-filled cellar.

A neuron sorting yesterday's vodka-marinated memories into cerebral file folders came across a duplicate. It took several more synapses to fire before Mackey made the connection. The third in the macabre sequence of microbiologist deaths was Professor Lavigne.

"Hey, Charo, Arthur Lavigne from the suspect list, where did he work at the time of his death?"

"He was teaching at a college… in West Virginia I think."

"Marshall University?"

"Yes, that's it. Why do you ask?"

Mackey didn't answer. "Charo, can we make a pit stop?"

At a turnpike rest stop with Wi-Fi, Mackey typed Arthur Lavigne, PhD into Google. The first entry was from an anarchist website. It listed excerpts from Lavigne's self-published manifesto, *Cookbook for Terrorists: Biological Weapons for Dummies*. Although it found its way into the hands of anti-governmental groups it was not a "how-to" manual of biological weapons but a diatribe against a lackadaisical government that failed to regulate and prohibit the purchase of dangerous biological agents. At a minimum, it seemed that the anarchists misunderstood Lavigne.

The next hit was a story about Lavigne's arrest for purchasing bacterial cultures on the select list of bioterrorism agents from a US microbiology supply house. His position as a professor and member of the American Society for Microbiology raised no suspicion at the supply house. Through these purchases he sought to demonstrate how anyone could, with minimal concealment of his true identity, make such a purchase. If he hadn't announced it at a press conference he might well have never been noticed by the authorities. But then that would have not furthered his cause. The publicity generated by his arrest caught the attention of Congress and they passed laws regulating the sale of select agent bacterial cultures.

Mackey found Lavigne's obituary in *The Baltimore Sun*:

> November 19, 2001, Morgantown, W.V.- Dr. Arthur C. Lavigne, Professor of Microbiology at Marshall University, was found dead in his Sweetland cabin reported Thelma Lassiter, spokesperson for the West Virginia State police in a statement released today. The cause of death is believed to be suicide. Lavigne was found by his daughter. The coroner believes he had been dead for several days. A handgun was found next to his body.
>
> Lavigne sparked controversy in 1997 when he successfully purchased bacteria that could be used to produce biological weapons. The stunt was done to draw attention to the lax oversight of sales of these agents and in doing so he had broken no laws. He also was a frequent lecturer on the danger and availability of bioweapons arguing that the US was not prepared and was not doing enough to protect its citizens.
>
> Arthur Clark Lavigne graduated from University of Maryland in 1957 with a degree in biology. He received a PhD in microbiology from Rutgers University in 1962 and worked for the United States Army Medical Research Institute for Infectious Diseases from 1967 to 1970. He left to take a position at Marshall University where he was a professor and former chairman of the biology department. He is survived by a daughter, Lorraine Bilderback, and two grandchildren of Pikesville, Maryland.

Lavigne's death a month after the anthrax attacks could be a coincidence. However, his former employment at USAMRIID, his political activity against bioweapons, and his presence on the FBI suspect list argued otherwise. Lorraine Bilderback lived just outside of Baltimore.

Mackey didn't turn out to be much of a driving companion. If he wasn't sleeping or requesting a pit stop he just stared straight ahead as if any movement would cause him to become violently ill. Charo opted for the companionship of Tom Petty and the Counting Crows on her iPod. As they neared their destination she concentrated on staying off the road that went in circles around Baltimore. When they got within DC city limits she roused Mackey with a poke to the ribs.

"I have to meet with SSA to establish the reason for this trip. I can drop you off wherever you like. Sorry."

"No sweat. Drop me at the Lincoln Memorial."

If brutalist architecture needed a poster child, it couldn't do any better than the J. Edgar Hoover Building, the national headquarters of the FBI. Completed in 1974, it squats halfway between the White House and the Capitol on Pennsylvania Avenue and is a featureless fortress of concrete and glass. True to its genre, it is repetitive, appearing to be constructed from identical concrete cubes. Above the seven main floors on the E Street side hovered four additional floors like a giant stool. Oversized concrete flowerpots guard the ground floor from car bombs.

Charo's meeting was at one o'clock. She had forty-five minutes and the cover of the lunch hour to get the needed information. The last thing Charo wanted as she made her way to the office of the assistant director in charge of the Innocent Images Task Force was to attract attention. She didn't help matters by wearing a dress that revealed her tanned and toned legs and a blouse buttoned to mid-breast. Who was it she dressed for this morning anyhow? She closed a button on her blouse and tugged at her dress hem to no effect.

She was met by a plump, rosy-faced secretary who greeted her with a southern accent. The nameplate said Aubrey Hagar and she appeared to have been at her post for half of her adult life. Seeing that her boss was out, Charo put her plan into action.

"Good day, Aubrey. Is ADIC Wilkerson in?"

"No, ma'am. I'm afraid he's gone to lunch. May I help you?"

Charo scanned her desk for clues, spotted a framed picture of Elvis Presley and a coffee mug emblazoned with "Volunteer State" and the Tennessee flag.

"I'm Agent Chen, from the New York City office. I am working with the Innocent Images Task Force and I need some information."

Aubrey's pleasant features contorted to cautious curiosity.

"I'm down here for some pretty intense meetings and I was wondering two things."

"How may I help you?"

"I expect to be have to work through lunch and then I have to drive back to New York City. I don't know how much you know about New York City, but there isn't a decent barbecue place up there. Not a Memphis-style place, that is."

Before Charo could lay it on any thicker, Aubrey broke into a pulled-pork grin and reached into her desk drawer and grabbed a take-out menu.

"Oh, you'll want to go to Dexter's, best ribs east of Tennessee."

Charo reached for the menu.

"Agent Chen, you can keep that. I have the number and specials memorized," Aubrey giggled self-consciously.

"That is very kind of you." Charo stood before her desk, scanning the menu as if she was at the counter of Dexter's trying to make her selection.

"Hmm, cornbread."

"Their cornbread is to die for. Was there something else, Agent Chen?"

"Oh, I don't want to bother you, you've already been too kind."

"Please, it is no trouble."

"My SAC asked that while I am down here I get some information on two vehicles. They are government vehicles. I think it has to do with some parking tickets or something silly like that, I don't know."

Aubrey leaned across her desk to peer down the hallway. Charo followed her gaze to an empty cubicle.

"Should I return later, when the boys are back?" Charo leaned on *the boys*, playing the solidarity card.

"That won't be necessary," Aubrey quickly responded.

Charo reached into her jacket pocket and withdrew a crumpled piece of paper. She read off the two license plates. Aubrey logged into the system. The minutes dragged by, it was almost one o'clock. Charo tapped her foot, thinking about how she'd explain herself if any of the agents or the assistant director returned. Aubrey's face sagged with disappointment.

"I don't see those plates listed, can you read them to me again?"

Charo fought the urge to jump over the desk, shove Aubrey aside and do the search herself. Instead she repeated the license plates slowly. The corners of Aubrey's mouth still pointed down, then, she broke into a smile.

"Those cars are no longer in service. However, they were in the executive office car pool. Looks like your SAC is doing somebody big a favor."

"Does it list any more information? What part of the executive office?" She was pushing her luck. The longer she hung around the greater the risk she could get caught.

Aubrey's eyed searched, and then she pointed at the screen. "Office of the Vice President."

. . .

Mackey sat on the steps of the Lincoln Memorial looking out at the reflecting pool. He leaned against one of the Doric columns that represented the thirty-six states in the post-Civil War Union at the time of Lincoln's assassination. Groups of tourists with bad haircuts, shiny walking shoes, and digital cameras strolled by, their noses buried in maps and guidebooks. To passersby he was just another tourist taking a break to rub sore feet.

He got up and walked through the portico and stood before Lincoln's likeness in white Georgia marble. It couldn't hurt to get Abe's help. It occurred to Mackey that although Abe was a lawyer by training he knew a thing or two about infectious diseases, having lost three of his four sons to tuberculosis and Typhoid fever as well as the countless other young men to an army of microbes during the Civil War. If anyone would appreciate the gains made over disease in the 20th century it would be Abe. What advice might he give on their investigation of the intentional use of anthrax? Lincoln stared out over the water with his index finger distractedly tapping as if contemplating Mackey's question. Perhaps he might offer Mackey the advice that to chop down a tree one would be wise to spend most of the time sharpening the ax. Mackey returned to his grindstone.

He stared at a blank page in his notebook. A pile of clipped articles sat half out of his backpack and another bundle was flapping atop a marble step in the late afternoon breeze. The sun was going down behind the monument, casting a yellow glow on the water. The reflecting pool turned to orange before Mackey's pen moved again. He'd been trying to come up with the means, motive, and opportunity to narrow down the possibilities but was getting nowhere. He needed a new approach: eliminate the impossible. Lincoln might have added, "No man has a good enough memory to be a successful liar."

He reviewed the facts he knew. At least seven letters were sent; five to media sites and two to the Senate. The senators were both high-ranking Democrats at odds with the direction of the administration. The letters were timed one week and four weeks respectively after 9/11. A defect in the envelopes put their purchase in a Midatlantic State other than New Jersey. The letters were mailed from an ordinary postal box opposite Princeton University. The spores were of two grades of purity and had at some point originated in the US. The spore molecular evidence and the fact that Joseph Erekat was the number one suspect pointed toward USAMRIID as the lab source. A few experts didn't think anthrax of this quality could have been produced by a lone scientist while others thought it could. What should he make of the use of the Ames strain and its susceptibility to penicillin? Did that suggest it wasn't from a bioweapons cache?

In the five years since the crime no fingerprint, chemical, fiber, or microbiological piece of evidence led to an arrest. He leaned back. Unable to eliminate any means, motive, or opportunity he couldn't hope to extract the improbable from the morass.

. . .

A male agent caught the flash of Charo's brown skin as she hurried to her meeting. An hour later he was there as she exited the Innocent Images Task Force briefing. The secretary who had endured his musky presence gave Charo a sympathetic frown when the agent hopped off her desk after Charo wearing a grin borrowed from a hognose snake.

As Charo turned the corner she heard the squeak of shoes and caught a glimpse of a pant leg out of the corner of her eye. The elevator doors were closing. She called out, but the doors shut without reopening. She reached to call another but a hand shot forth from behind and covered the button.

"Hey, what office are you from, sweet cheeks?"

"New York field office," Charo replied stonily.

"Ooo, the Big Apple. Can I have a bite?"

Charo stared at the light above the elevator, willing it to light.

"Tony Carbonaro, Fraud Unit. I like your moves, what's your name?" He stood beside her, leaning with an arm outstretched against the wall. Close enough for Charo to detect onion on his breath.

"Special Agent Chen," she replied.

"Whoa, why so formal? We have a rule down here that visiting agents need to have an escort. How 'bout I show you Washington, you know, show you a good time?"

"Does that apply to male agents, too? I think I saw a lost soul down the hall." Charo didn't make eye contact, though she hoped Tony could see from the side her *get lost* expression.

"A bra full of piss and vinegar means a pussy full of honey. What you say, babe?"

Charo decided to use the time waiting for the elevator to practice her perp recognition skills. It would keep her from saying or doing something that she might later regret. Perhaps she'd have to pick Agent Carbonaro out of a lineup one day or go to the morgue and identify his body. From the corner of her eye, without turning her head, she could see that he was about six feet tall with brown hair that was slicked back and thinning. He was muscular and wore a white button down shirt with the sleeves rolled up. The tie was red and ragged at the bottom. From the crags on his face she surmised that he had either been a boxer with an 0-23 record, had bad acne as a teen and self treated himself with a soldering gun, or had volunteered for a live smallpox vaccine trial that went horribly wrong. She could see him tense and move closer. He lowered his voice and spoke menacingly inches from her ear.

"It isn't polite to ignore a fellow agent when he is speaking to you." Carbonaro reached out and placed a clammy paw on Charo's shoulder. It lay there for a second, then two before Charo spun, grasped his thumb and twisted his arm around until he spiraled to his knees like a flushing toilet.

The elevator light blinked on simultaneously with the electronic ping. The doors slid back to reveal a filled car, the blank faces of the occupants changing to stunned curiosity as they took in the scene. Charo's hold was tenuous, but no one got off or moved to make room. As the doors started to close, Tony reversed Charo's move. It was then that a voice from the back of the elevator called out.

"There's room."

The doors reversed and the crowd split like an oak tree struck by lightning. The owner of the voice was none other than the director of the FBI. So much for a low profile Charo thought as she squeezed in. Exiting at G1 she gave a quick scan of the garage before heading to the car and speeding off Steve McQueen style.

She headed up Pennsylvania Avenue and turned left onto 17th Street NW passing the White House. At Constitution Avenue she turned right and the lights of the Lincoln Memorial swung into view. She was looking forward to seeing Mackey.

Maybe he was being too literal. Mackey decided to try to develop a solution to the problem by crossing out that which his *gut* told him was impossible. The targets and delivery mechanism didn't fit with usual acts of terrorism. That eliminated several suspects. He didn't think the outcome would be satisfying enough to quench a vengeful thirst. Under motives, he crossed out revenge. What did this leave? Still more questions than answers.

The attack was limited. Was that because supplies of spores had run out or because the perpetrator was fearful of getting caught? Or maybe the mission was accomplished? But what was the mission? Expose a weakness in laboratory security, the mail system, or emergency preparedness? Was the motive political? To scare liberals into voting to eliminate constitutional protection of civil liberties or to invade Iraq? What was the origin of the spores? Were they manufactured or stolen? Was there a conspiracy with someone on the inside at Fort Detrick? Could the Soviets somehow be involved, either by providing technical assistance in the production of anthrax, in the theft anthrax from Fort Detrick, or to give the US an apparent self-inflicted black eye? There was one coincidence that kept circling back in his mind. Arthur Lavigne died a month after the mailings. He was an outspoken critic of bioweapons and once worked at USAMRIID. Mackey reread Lavigne's obituary. He looked up Lorraine Bilderback's address. It was not far from his childhood home.

"How did it go?" Mackey asked.

Charo shared the findings of her day, the helpful secretary and her tip on the best Memphis-style barbecue in the area, but spared any mention of her run-in with Agent Carbonaro.

"Veep's car pool? Huh. How do we find out who drove them in 2001?"

"That's going to be more difficult," Charo said.

"Where to now? I'm famished."

Charo handed him Dexter's menu. Thirty-five minutes later they were getting greasy and loving it.

.| 21 |.

Mackey savored the garlic, tomato, and molasses on his tongue while trying to poke an extra hole in his belt with a fork. There wasn't a clean napkin to be found within fifteen yards, but one soaked with barbecue sauce sat beneath the table like a penalty flag thrown for illegal use of the hands. Topside was a brimming bowl of chicken and pig bones, a plate of cornbread crumbs, and the milky remains of a double side of coleslaw. Charo had gone to wash up.

Between the wings and ribs they discussed where the new information fit. Charo argued that the government cars belonging to the VP car pool put them at a dead end. It was most likely a coincidence and the VP's office security was impenetrable. They had no choice but to turn the information over to the Amerithrax team and go back to their seats in the audience. Mackey had designs otherwise.

The FBI recruited informants from inside organizations, couldn't they see if there was a disgruntled driver or garage attendant who they could turn? Charo informed him that this technique took weeks, even months, to execute and required an experienced handler. It was risky and beyond what she was prepared to do. Mackey's next idea veered from crazy to criminal. He proposed they hack into the FBI's computer network. Charo pointed out that the file from 2001 might no longer exist even if he managed to access the network. That discarded Mackey's next idea to join a tour of the VP office and while Charo feigned illness he would search for an unguarded computer. His last idea was to submit a

Freedom of Information Act request. Charo told him that the information was likely covered by executive privilege and not to hold out much hope.

The night air was cool. Hickory smoke mingled with the scent of pine as they strolled the parking lot back to the car. Mackey shared with Charo the curious series of deaths of microbiologists that followed the anthrax letters he read about on a blog. He focused on Arthur Lavigne, highlighting his appearance on the FBI's suspect list, his former employment at USAMRIID, and his activism against the proliferation of biological weapons. Charo admitted that the coincidences were intriguing but offered no next steps.

"Why was Lavigne ruled out as a suspect?" Mackey asked.

"I don't know, maybe because the leads ended when he committed suicide."

"I don't see how death exonerates him if he was guilty," Mackey said.

"Guilty? You think he's Mailthrax?"

By the time they reached the car it was 9:30 PM. Too late, Mackey argued, to make the long drive back to New York. He suggested that they stay the night at his mother's home, about an hour's drive along the route back to NYC. Charo agreed without debate. A tinge of regret flicked at Mackey's subconscious as he envisioned his mother divulging embarrassing details of his childhood. It would be worth it if he could get Charo to make a stop on their way home and keep them on the trail of spores.

Back on the road Mackey dialed his childhood home, the one phone number he always knew by heart. He also knew his mother would be awake: her geriatric insomnia usually kept her awake past midnight.

"Mom, it's me, Mackey."

"Yes, sweetie, I recognize your voice. I'm not senile, at least not yet, and I recognize your new number on the whatchamacallit."

"It's called caller ID, mom."

"Yes, dear."

"Mom, I'm driving back from Washington and thought it would be best to spend the night at home, is that okay?"

"Of course it is. I'll make up your bed."

"And the guest room, too, I have a friend with me. I'll explain when I get home. We should be there in about forty minutes. See you soon."

Rose Dunn was a gracious host. She prepared a pot of herbal tea and apologized for serving store-bought biscuits. She sat with Mackey and Charo in her parlor decorated with old lithographs depicting scenes from the early American life. In the print hanging askew over the sofa a horse was dragging a log up from the river's edge. Tracing the river past a bend there was a dairy farm and farther in the distance low mountains reminiscent of the Cumberland Valley. Mrs. Dunn had been a school librarian until recently and still worked part-time at the local public library. Although osteoporosis and arthritis slowed her step, her mind was sharp and her stamina was surprising.

Mackey and Charo sat on a floral print Victorian sofa, the sole remaining furniture from Mackey's childhood. Mrs. Dunn sat in a mismatched armchair within reach of the coffee table where she monitored their cups and told tales of Mackey's childhood.

"When Mackey was six his father came home to find him sitting on the roof. My husband questioned him on how he had managed to get up to the roof without a ladder. He climbed a tree in the backyard and shimmied out onto one of its branches that extended over the house. Then crab-walked to where his ball was lodged in the gutter but was unable to reach the tree limb to climb back down. I was inside preparing dinner and had no idea he was up on the roof. Had I known half of what he got himself into I doubt very much I would have made it to eighty years old."

"He was a mischievous child?" Charo asked.

"No, I wouldn't say mischievous. A daredevil. When Mackey was nine he was struck by a car while riding his bicycle. It was the longest moment of fear I have ever felt."

"Old Mrs. Perkins ran the four-way. I walked away with several scratches and minor bruises. It was the end of my stingray bike though," Mackey said.

"I was in the front yard tending to the garden when I heard tires screech and looked up to see my son catapulted twenty feet into the air landing in Mrs. Wilson's azaleas."

"It was the end of Mrs. Perkins' Ford Fairlaine, too. I left a gigantic dent in the hood and cracked the windshield," Mackey added.

"Of course we took him to the hospital to have him checked out. Sitting in the exam room with all those machines I think is when he first got the notion to become a doctor." Rose became quiet. "The only other time I ever had a similar feeling was when the first tower fell," she said.

The numbness in his fingers and soreness in his neck made Mackey realize he had been sitting on his hands with shoulders hunched.

"I bet he was a cutie when he was a kid. Did he have many girlfriends?" Charo asked catching a sideways glimpse of Mackey's face knotting like a crimson necktie.

"Some. I remember when he was twelve he had a crush on a neighborhood girl. Susie, I think her name was. He made her a big Valentine's Day card and picked some of my roses to give to her. He was met at the door by her rather strict father who sternly told him his daughter was not old enough to date. Do you remember that, dear?"

His mom used to regale him with endless stories of comings and goings in the neighborhood. She must've unsubscribed from the town weekly.

"Mom, it's getting late. We've got a long drive tomorrow."

"Nonsense. This is your first visit since moving back from Alaska. Don't be antisocial."

Mrs. Dunn turned to Charo. "So, Charo, how long have you two been dating?"

Mackey nearly sprayed the room with tea. It was nothing compared to the look on Charo's face. Her eyebrows hopped up like meerkats sensing a cobra while her jaw headed for cover in the opposite direction. She blushed cranberry then drained faster than grain punch at a frat party. It was the first time Mackey had ever seen her lose composure.

"Mom, we're not dating. We are working together on a case."

Before Mrs. Dunn could ask another question Mackey stood, kissed her on the cheek, said goodnight, and whisked Charo off to the guest room, returning moments later with towels and a fresh toothbrush.

Mackey nosed around his old room. The baseball trophies on the top shelf wore a layer of dust that made the hair appear gray, as if they too had aged. In the desk drawer he found a faded yearbook from high school and the scrapbook his father had kept until Mackey was sixteen when it abruptly ended. He took it out of the drawer and stroked the worn leather cover feeling transported to a familiar yet agonizing time. He put it back in the drawer.

"Glory days."

His mother had moved much of his father's clothing into his closet ostensibly to make room for hers but he suspected the real reason. The suits of brown and gray did not fit Mackey. His father was taller and of a slighter build. Mackey slid his hand inside one of the suit jacket pockets. His father would leave items there for him to find, such as a pack of baseball cards or a flashlight with a magnifying lens in one end. The pocket was empty. He flopped down on the twin bed. The mattress sunk nearly to the floor. No wonder he never brought a girl up here. Before falling asleep his thoughts drifted to Charo's reaction to his mother's question. What had prompted such a dramatic redistribution of cranial blood flow?

Mrs. Dunn awoke early and prepared them scrambled eggs and toast with homemade marmalade. She remarked, for the umpteenth time, how breakfast was the most important meal of the day and that Mr. Dunn never left home without it. Mackey winced whenever his mom spoke of his departed father with such detached candor. It reminded him that he had lived more years without his father than he had with him.

.| 22 |.

Mackey directed Charo to the highway, choosing a route that would pass the exit for Pikesville.

"Arthur Lavigne's daughter coincidentally lives just up the road," he said. "Since we're in the neighborhood, it might be a good idea to pay her a visit."

Charo smiled but kept her eyes on the road. Behind her shades Mackey thought he saw her eyes roll.

"I suppose you already have her address and phone number?"

"Right here."

"Let's see if she's home. When we get there I'll conduct the interview."

Lavigne's daughter lived on a residential street with minivans parked in driveways and toys abandoned on lawns. Mackey's and Charo's presence in the neighborhood was closely watched by two preschoolers in a doublewide stroller. As they came up the walkway Lorraine Bilderback met them at the door. A small, plump woman, she had curly brown hair, freckles, and lines around her mouth when she smiled. A tear-stained toddler was perched on one hip.

"Hello Mrs. Bilderback, I'm Special Agent Chen and this is Dr. Dunn. Thanks for agreeing to see us on such short notice."

"Please excuse the mess; I haven't had time to clean up this morning." Mrs. Bilderback led them to the living room, moving toys, shoes, and mislaid clothes out of the way. The couch crunched when they sat.

"Who is this little guy?" Mackey asked.

“Little Artie.”

“We appreciate you taking the time to speak with us about your father, Mrs. Bilderback. We are sorry for your loss,” began Charo.

“Thank you. I didn’t get to see my father often but I very much miss him. I lost my mother when I was in college.” Mackey felt a sympathetic pang.

“I understand you were the one to find him? That must have been difficult for you. May we ask you some questions about that day?”

“Yes, anything to help. Are you reopening the investigation?”

“I can’t promise anything. Please tell us how you came to find your father on that day back in 2001.” Mrs. Bilderback set the child down and removed the dishcloth from her shoulder, balling it up in her hands. Little Artie waddled over to Mackey to show him his truck.

“My dad didn’t do this. He didn’t send those letters. He may have been a strange, sometimes angry man, but he wouldn’t hurt anyone. If you could have seen him with my kids.” Tears came to her eyes and Mackey searched for a tissue, finding none, he handed her a small T-shirt he found stuffed in the cushions of the couch. She took it, thanked him, and recomposed herself.

“Were you told he was a suspect in the anthrax letters investigation?” Charo asked.

“Yes. And the State Police and FBI came here several times to interview me.”

“I know this is difficult, but what can you tell us about that day you found your father?”

“My dad always came here for Thanksgiving. About a week or two before Thanksgiving in 2001 I called to remind him. Artie would forget his own birthday. Remembered the kids’, but not his own. After several tries I couldn’t even get through to his voice mail.”

"The voice mailbox was full?" interjected Mackey. Charo shot him a sideways glance. Mrs. Bilderback nodded.

"After the kids were off to school, I drove out to his place. I had a bad feeling."

Mackey was giggling. Little Artie was rolling his truck up one thigh and down the other. Charo pressed the nail of her forefinger deep into his thigh.

"Ever since 9/11 my father became more paranoid, secretive."

"When was it you went out to see him?" Charo asked.

"November 19, 2001."

"Please continue," encouraged Charo.

"He lived way out in the West Virginia woods. When I drove down his road I didn't see any smoke from his chimney so I thought he wasn't home. There was a bad smell though when I reached the porch, like spoiled food. I thought perhaps he'd been hunting. The front door was unlocked, which wasn't like my dad. He was pretty paranoid about intruders. I saw him from the foyer, at his desk, slumped in the chair." She began to tear up again. "There was blood everywhere. Then I saw his gun on the floor." She began to weep softly into the towel and T-shirt. Little Artie had crawled into Mackey's lap leaving sticky grape juice prints on Mackey's pants.

Charo reached out her hand and touched Mrs. Bilderback on the wrist reassuringly. "Do you believe your father killed himself?"

"No. There was no note. My dad was a crusader and had unlimited passion for his causes. I didn't always understand or agree with his politics, but I don't believe he would take his own life. And not that way."

"What way?" Mackey asked.

"He was shot in the mouth. Like in the movies, you know, a mafia hit, where the message is to shut someone up. I was hysterical, frightened, and I panicked. I must have been in shock because I did something irrational, without really thinking. I started opening drawers, looking for a towel to clean him up. Then I stopped and called the police. FBI agents came to question me. They asked me about my father's work, if he ever mentioned anthrax, or getting even with anyone. The state police came back in early 2002, then that was it. I never heard anything more from the FBI or police until you called." She faced Charo. "Do you think my father killed himself?"

"No," Mackey answered with conviction.

Charo dug the heel of her shoe into his ankle. "You mentioned your father was passionate about his causes. Do you know what he was involved in at the time of his death?" Charo said.

"I'm not sure. He often spoke out against the development and use of biological weapons. He wouldn't make anthrax."

Mrs. Bilderback turned to Mackey. "Do you think he was the anthrax mailer?"

Charo put her hand up to stop Mackey from responding. "Testing at your father's house found no traces of anthrax and there was insufficient evidence to connect him to the crime."

Mrs. Bilderback sucked in her lower lip and stared off into the dining room.

"Is there something more you wish to tell us?" Charo asked.

Mrs. Bilderback got up and disappeared into the dining room returning with a Ziploc bag. She removed two folded sheets of paper and handed them to Charo.

"Agent Chen, I found these at my father's house. You are the first people I've shown them to."

Charo unfolded the papers and considered them for some time. She showed them to Mackey but motioned for him not to touch. She secured them back in the Ziploc bag.

"Where exactly did you find these?"

"I found my father near his writing desk. When I opened the center drawer these were poking out in such a way that you could see some of the writing. Do you think these are originals?"

"I can't say. I'm going to have to take them for analysis," Charo answered. "I will do what I can to shield you but your removing these from the crime scene is itself a crime. I can't make you any promises. In all likelihood you will be visited by agents from the Washington office.

"They wouldn't put a mother in jail, would they?"

Charo forced a half smile. "Would you happen to have any samples of your father's handwriting?"

"I have the birthday cards he sent the children. I'll go get them."

Mackey, still bug-eyed, turned to Charo. "Do you think these are the original anthrax letters? The ink looks to be from a pen, not photocopied."

Mrs. Bilderback returned with a plastic bag in which she placed the cards from her father. "I'd like to get these back, please."

"You have my word," answered Charo.

"Please clear my father's name. He didn't do this. My father was never understood in life, I'd like that his memory rest in peace."

They got up to leave. At the door, Mackey turned back.

"Mrs. Bilderback, one last thing. Did Artie use email?"

"Yes."

"Would you happen to know his email address?"

"I think he may have had several email addresses." She scribbled on a slip of paper and handed it to Mackey. "This is the one he used to correspond with me."

Mackey navigated Charo to the interstate but she took the ramp south, back toward Washington. The main FBI laboratory is located in Quantico, Virginia, but Charo didn't drive there. She explained to Mackey that she needed to know the validity of the letters and to identify any latent prints before announcing to the bureau that she was interloping in the Amerithrax investigation. There was a small lab at headquarters. The guy who worked there had a crush on Geetangali. He might do this for her. Leo, was his name, like the actor in the movie *Titanic*.

"The agents who investigated Lavigne's death searched his computer. I came across a report that a powerful magnet had wiped out the hard drive. Usually the technical boys can recover some files, but not this time."

"I'm not surprised," Mackey replied. "Artie sounded like he was pretty paranoid. He probably kept a magnet around for such purposes."

"They never found the magnet but it left an imprint where it tore off bits of paint. And the search of his office at the university turned up nothing."

Mackey looked down at the slip of paper Mrs. Bilderback gave him and read:

ALavigne@marshalluniversity.edu

"This was his work address at the university. Mrs. Bilderback mentioned she thought he had a number of email addresses."

Charo was studying the road signs.

"If I was the anthrax killer, I don't think I'd leave incriminating evidence in plain view like that," Mackey offered.

"You might, if you wanted to confess your sins," replied Charo.

"You think Artie got religion and offed himself from the guilt?"

"It's one theory. I expect the forensic evidence at the scene found gunpowder residue on Artie's hand that supports the conclusion of suicide."

"Hmm. Any evidence of other shots? You know, the classic bullet embedded in the door frame found by the curmudgeon detective?"

"Sorry, I don't know. That information would be in the West Virginia State Police records."

Charo pulled into the underground garage at FBI headquarters, parked the car, and proceeded to step out of the vehicle. Mackey remained seated. She turned and poked her head in through her open door.

"What are you doing?"

"I thought I couldn't come in?"

"You can't wait here; you're liable to get shot. After I drop off this evidence the cat will be out of the basket."

"Bag."

"What?"

"The cat will be out of the *bag*."

"Who carries cats in a bag?"

Charo swiped her badge through the reader and led Mackey up the building's stairs to an empty conference room and drew the shades. She left him to drop off the letters and Lavigne's handwriting samples at the lab. Mackey pulled from the bookshelf a manual on ballistics. He cracked open the blinds enough so a passerby would know the room was occupied, but not be able to see by whom.

He flipped to the chapter on gunshot residue. Pulling the trigger of a gun causes the firing pin to strike the shell, which ignites the primer that contains a concussive sensitive compound like nitroglycerin. This in turn ignites the gunpowder explosion and expels the bullet. Along with the bullet, unburned gunpowder, primer, pieces of lead, and even bits of metal from the gun are expelled from the barrel.

The old paraffin test detected nitrite residues from the gunpowder, but was not specific enough as it also picked up nitrites from other sources in a person's environment. Paraffin was replaced by two newer technologies. The one he'd seen on TV uses cotton swabs soaked in diluted nitric acid to wipe a suspect's hands. These swabs are then analyzed by atomic absorption spectroscopy for lead, antimony, and barium. The combination of all three is conclusive for gunshot residue.

The other method involves using adhesive tape to remove particles from the suspect's hands, then using a scanning electron microscope to visualize the residue. The immense heat generated in the gun barrel vaporizes the elements that then fuse upon cooling. The presence of tiny spheres of lead, antimony, and barium is again evidence of being in proximity of a recently fired gun. The tests are most accurate if performed soon after the gun is fired.

The trouble with both analyses is that they can't discriminate if the gun was in the suspect's hands or just nearby. But some information can be gained from the quantity of gunshot residue and the spray pattern found at the scene of a crime.

Charo returned to the conference room with coffee and sandwiches.

"What are you reading?"

"Ballistics manual. So I can make sense out of the West Virginia State Police report on Artie's death."

Charo tossed a manila folder onto the table.

"What's that?"

"The FBI Lavigne file with a copy of the West Virginia State Police report."

Mackey put aside the ballistics lesson and began sifting through the file. There was a twenty-six-page inventory of every item found in Lavigne's house, from paper clips to dust bunnies. There was a copy of a West

Virginia license for the .38-caliber handgun found next to Lavigne's body. It indicated that Lavigne had purchased it in 1997 at a gun shop near his home.

"West Virginia is a good place to buy a handgun," Charo said. "No background checks, no waiting period, and no concealed weapon prohibitions."

Mackey raised an eyebrow. He thumbed through the report until he located the ballistics report. Gunpowder residue was found on Lavigne's right hand and the report indicated that the quantity was consistent with having fired a gun.

To his novice, sleuth eyes the West Virginia State Police part of the investigation had been thorough. They performed an analysis of gunpowder residue on Lavigne's clothing, a tough task with the amount of blood that was present. Mackey couldn't be certain, but it appeared that the forensic specialist determined that the pattern was consistent with the barrel being placed in Lavigne's mouth. The specialist identified GSR on the upper part of the shirt—by the neck and chest. But that wasn't all. While no GSR was found on the abdominal half of the shirt there was some on the thighs of his pants. Mackey could not find an interpretation of this finding anywhere in the report, but he read a curious comment about the spent shell.

"What do you make of a GSR on the upper part of the shirt and pant thighs but not in between?"

"GSR? You sound like a TV cop. Let me see that." Charo studied the report then handed it back to Mackey. "I suppose something could have been lying across his chest that blocked the gunshot residue? Clothing, maybe some papers?"

"There's nothing mentioned in the report. And what is the significance of the spent shell falling out of the cylinder when it was opened?" Charo thought about that for a moment.

"When a gun is fired there is a considerable release of heat. This expands the shell and can cause it to stick in the chamber. But Lavigne was found some time after he died, and it was November, plenty of time for the shell to cool."

"Could the shell have been removed and then put back?"

"I suppose, why?"

"I noted on the inventory report that one of the items found in Lavigne's house was a box of .38-caliber blanks."

"Where are you going with this?"

"The box was described as 'new' and only one blank was missing."

Charo read the file over Mackey's shoulder.

"The West Virginia State Police were rather thorough at documenting if nothing else."

"Why would Lavigne have a box of blanks?" Mackey asked. "And why were they on the bookshelf on the day that he died? The live rounds were found in a drawer."

"All good questions. Stop me if I lose you. We have a GSR spray pattern that appears interrupted by something and two boxes of .38-caliber shells present at the crime scene, bullets and blanks. When a bullet is fired a lot of pressure and heat builds up in the barrel due to the resistance of the bullet in the barrel. When you fire a blank, the heat and pressure are less."

"Stands to reason, without the bullet to cause an obstruction there'd be less pressure and heat. It's Boyle's Law. I'm with you."

"If the gun was fired twice, once with a bullet in the chamber and once with a blank in the chamber, I believe that would result in two different spray patterns," Charo said.

"So, to avoid the police detecting that two shots were fired, the bullet shell would have to have been removed and the blank placed in the same chamber. Then after the second firing of the gun, the spent blank shell was removed and replaced with the spent bullet shell. That would explain both the split GSR pattern and why the shell slid out easily when the officer opened the cylinder."

"So, where then is the blank shell?" Charo asked.

Mackey flipped the pages of the report. "It is not listed on the inventory list. But I know how we can find out if this is what really happened," Mackey said.

Charo regarded him with surprise.

"You said it yourself, less heat with the blank. The particles from the two firing patterns should give different results on scanning electron microscopy. Any chance the clothing evidence is still available?"

They headed to the elevator and descended to the sub-basement level. Charo swiped her badge and they entered the evidence storage area. A gray-haired clerk scrutinized her badge as she filled out a request form, sliding it beneath the thick glass window. They took seats in molded plastic chairs as the clerk shuffled off to retrieve the evidence box.

"If someone were to fire a gun with blanks, would there still be gunpowder residue found on their hands?" Mackey asked.

"Yes. I can't say if it would be more or less than if there was a bullet in the chamber, but yes, the GSR test would be positive."

"But I thought residue didn't last that long. Wouldn't it have dissipated before Lavigne was discovered?"

"You took college chemistry. These are heavy metals. They don't dissipate. GSR can be wiped off or washed out, but it won't sublimate."

"Right, then it is possible this wasn't suicide. *Lavigne was murdered.* Come Charo, the game is afoot!"

"Hold on Sherlock. Let's take this one step at a time. If this was murder, it seems rather careless for the killer to leave the box of blanks lying around," Charo said.

"Maybe something startled him and he left prematurely?"

"Mackey, let me see the file again." Charo thumbed through the pages then stopped. "Body temperature was 53°F, same as ambient, rigor mortis was no longer present and there was evidence of body decay and insect larvae. That puts time of death more than seventy-two hours prior."

"Okay, so it wasn't Mrs. Bilderback who startled the killer. Perhaps it was something else." Mackey said.

An electric buzz sounded indicating that the door to the evidence storage area was about to open. The clerk emerged and handed to Charo a brown cardboard box marked with case number and Lavigne printed on it. Charo took it over to the table against the wall and donned a pair of rubber gloves. Mackey put on gloves too, though from the amused look on Charo's face he realized it was unlikely he'd handle any evidence. It turned out that much of the physical evidence was in the possession of the West Virginia State Police; however, inside the box was the Smith & Wesson revolver along with a quarter-full box of .38 shells. The single used shell casing found in the chamber was in an evidence bag and under that Charo found the once used box of blanks.

"Someone thought this stuff was worth hanging onto," Mackey said.

Charo picked up the box of blanks and turned it in her hand until she found the bar code. It was stamped with "Jack's Gun and Sport Shop, Route 33, Elkins, West Virginia." She slipped the shell box into an evidence bag and put it in her jacket pocket. She signed the evidence manifest and returned it to the clerk. "Feel like going for a ride?"

.| 23 |.

The drive to Elkins was long. The first leg took them along the famed Route 66 and cut through DC suburbs then farmland, the latter reminding Mackey of his Midwestern travels along the same highway. They next snaked their way up the eastern side of the Appalachian Mountains climbing through hairpin turns that offered spectacular views of the valley below. After descending the western slope they entered a deep evergreen forest and passed from Virginia into West Virginia. The road that split the Monongahela National Forest consumed time and fuel but didn't seem to put many miles behind them. The unincorporated towns too homogenous to gauge much progress. They emerged from the forest four hours after leaving FBI headquarters on the outskirts of Elkins. Their first stop was the West Virginia State Police station; they arrived stiff-legged and weary at a quarter to five.

The sheriff, coroner of Lincoln County, and representative of the West Virginia State Police Department were the same person, one J. Parker Lemontyne. A sinewy man in his late fifties, Lemontyne was bald with wild tufts of hair protruding from the sides of his sheriff's cap. His most striking feature was a pair of closely set, cold grey eyes that viewed Mackey and Charo with the intensity of a mountain lion. He greeted them warily as Charo flipped open her badge and asked to see the Lavigne file.

"New evidence has come to light," she explained.

"What new evidence might that be?" Lemontyne replied reaching for his coat from a rack behind his door.

"I am not at liberty to say."

Lemontyne frowned. He had done the investigation himself and assured Charo it was conducted by the book. Charo assured him in return and emphasized that some details that were previously overlooked by the FBI might be crucial to solving another crime. Lemontyne's demeanor changed from obfuscation to curiosity.

"You Fed boys didn't seem all that concerned at the time."

"All the more reason you should get that file for us."

Lemontyne did as he was asked, though not with anything approaching enthusiasm. When he returned, Charo managed to commandeer the man's office with a puma-like glare to equal his. Lemontyne remarked about some business at the mortuary and instructed his secretary to see to their needs in his absence. Mackey assumed these were codewords for keep an eye on those two.

The file was indeed by the book. Several black and white photos of the crime scene were clipped to the inside flap. It was a bloody mess. Arthur Lavigne was found by Mrs. Bilderback as she had stated. The exit wound was large and blew away most of the back of Lavigne's skull. Charo handed Mackey the coroner's report.

"Exit wound was through the right occipital area," she said.

Mackey held his right index finger to his mouth. "That's a bit awkward."

"Exactly my thought."

The bullet was found and dug out of the wooden wall behind the desk. The gun, a nickel-plated, .38-caliber Smith & Wesson Classic, was found on the floor next to his right hand. It was registered in Lavigne's name and purchased at a gun shop in a neighboring town. Gun shot residue was found on his right hand and the only prints on the gun were Lavigne's. A single shell was found in the gun's chambers and rounds matching the one fired were found in a box in Lavigne's desk. Ballistics on the bullet matched to the gun. There was no suicide note. No evidence of forced entry or a struggle. Nothing appeared to be taken. Mackey sifted through the file photos. Lavigne's house was filled with newspaper clippings, magazines, scientific journals, and books. Every bookshelf was over packed. There were books stacked in corners, on tables, on countertops, even in the bathroom. In the bedroom two large mounds fused to form a replica of the pyramid at Giza. Mackey considered that Lavigne suffered from compulsive hoarder disorder. Absent from the photos were the requisite fifty cats. Mackey did spy in one of the photos of the kitchen an empty dog-food bowl.

Charo asked Lemontyne's secretary to make a copy of the coroner's report and the gun registration paperwork and to retrieve the physical evidence taken from the crime scene. In the boxes, dusty from their basement crypt, they found a bag containing Lavigne's clothing. Charo completed a form to have the clothes analyzed at the West Virginia State Lab by electron microscopy to compare the GSR on the shirt to that found on the pants. The results would be delivered to Sheriff Lemontyne. She handed it to the secretary, who doubled as property and evidence clerk.

They left for Lavigne's cabin without waiting for Sheriff Lemontyne to return. The place was set well off the main road, accessible by a gravel drive that wound through a transition forest of conifer and deciduous trees.

A shred of yellow crime scene tape was still stuck in the doorjamb as they pushed through several years of decay. Lavigne's daughter had the place cleaned up. The blood on the floor was gone, as was Lavigne's haphazard library. Mackey roamed from room to room until he found himself in Lavigne's study standing before his desk. He sat in the chair, trying to position it as he saw it in the photo. It was a wooden banker's chair. The seat swiveled, tilted, and the chair rolled on casters. He searched the desk for something weighty, finding an old-style, hand-crank pencil sharpener. It wasn't the size or weight of the .38 Smith & Wesson but it would have to do. He held it in his right hand and brought it up to his open mouth, trying to mimic how his body would react to the shock of the bullet entering his brain. Charo watched from the doorway.

The pencil sharpener fell to the floor and bounced forward landing at Charo's feet. Charo immediately dropped to her knees, her head coming to a point between Mackey's thighs, her eyes locked on the wood floor.

She raised her hand up toward Mackey's chest. "Look in the drawers for a magnifying glass and pen knife."

Mackey didn't have to look in the drawers because there was a magnifying glass on the desk. He wiped the dust off on his pant leg and handed it to Charo and then opened the penknife attached to his key chain and handed that to her as well.

"What is it?" he asked.

"Might be a burn."

"A burn? Like where the hot end of a gun barrel might have struck the floor?"

"No. It is not a single mark, more like a spray."

"Spray?"

"Yeah, like you might see in close range GSR."

She dug and scraped with the penknife at the black grains, then slid them into a small evidence bag.

"Might have been overlooked with all the blood," Mackey said.

"Yes, that's what I was thinking."

They didn't arrive at Jack's Gun and Tackle Shop until nightfall. Jack was sitting on a stool behind the far end of the counter with his reading glasses perched on the tip of his nose and a newspaper spread out before him.

"Always a pleasure to serve law enforcement," he said as Mackey and Charo approached.

"Special Agent Chen," Charo said, "This is Dr. Dunn. Are you the owner?"

"I am. Are you here to make a purchase, or is this official business?" Jack asked.

Charo produced the box of blanks from her pocket. She placed them on the counter and pushed them over to Jack. He regarded them like a rattlesnake found coiled in the tool shed.

"Can you tell me if this came from your store?" Jack picked up the bag containing the box, and then placed in on the counter. He took off his glasses, letting them fall to his chest suspended by a chain.

"I never heard of a murder committed with blanks and you didn't drive all this way to ask me questions you already know the answers to Agent Chen."

"Murder? How do you know we are here about a murder," Mackey asked.

"Small town."

"What can you tell us about this box of .38-caliber blanks?"

"We don't sell many. Mostly for starter pistols and stage props, usually .22 caliber."

"Might you remember selling this box back in November 2001?" Mackey interjected.

Jack shook his head. "Sorry, Doc."

"Did you know Arthur Lavigne?" Charo asked.

Jack smiled ruefully. "Yeah, I knew Artie. We used to target shoot together sometimes. He was wrapped a pinch too tight, but I liked the guy."

Charo unfolded the gun license she copied from the state police's investigation file.

"Did you sell Artie a .38-caliber Smith & Wesson Classic?"

Jack glanced at the page, then went to a file cabinet and returned with a matching page in canary yellow. He passed it across the counter to Charo.

"Sure did, you're two for two."

"Do you believe he committed suicide?" Mackey said. Charo's cool glare grazed his temple.

"That's what the papers said."

"You knew him. Was he the type to put a barrel in his mouth and blow his brains out?" Mackey asked.

Jack shrugged. "Dunno. Rumor was he was having financial troubles."

"How long have you had those up?" Charo pointed to the security camera mounted on the wall behind the counter.

"My nephew Pete put them in right after 9/11. He's sort of a technical wizard."

"Digital?" Mackey asked.

"Yeah."

"You have the files from November 2001?" Charo asked.

"Might, I don't think Pete erased anything. He's a little like Artie, paranoid."

"We are interested in the files from mid-November 2001," Charo said.

"I don't suppose you have a warrant?"

"We aren't here to make trouble for you," Charo advised. "Artie was your friend, we are trying to establish how he died and we would appreciate your cooperation."

In the back office Charo sat next to Pete as he searched through the archived security files. Mackey paced behind them.

"I designed this software myself," Pete said. "What were those November 2001 dates again?"

"November 12–19."

"Okay. Now the camera has a time-lapse feature, taking a five-second sequence every fifteen seconds, and the images are stored in a compressed format. Still we are talking about hours of footage. Can we narrow the period any more?"

"Are your sales computerized?" Mackey asked.

"Yes, we began shortly before the dates you mentioned."

"Charo take out that box of blanks. Can you scan the bar code and tell when it was sold?"

"That'll work. It records the day, not the time, so you may still be facing hours of footage to review."

"Can you check if they were bought with a credit card?" Charo added.

Pete scanned the box, taking several scans to read the faded bar code. He hit the keys of his computer to search the inventory log. The screen flashed back in return, "Searching." An invoice then appeared with the date of November 12, 2001.

"Sorry, cash."

"On the morning of November 12th," Charo announced, "American Airlines Flight 587 crashed in Queens shortly after takeoff."

"How did you remember that?" Mackey asked.

"The crash site was not far from where I used to live."

"A clever distraction. A murder in the backwoods of West Virginia would be sure to go unnoticed," Mackey added.

"It was also Veteran's Day. We were open ten to five," Pete said.

Pete brought up the digital file. The video was low quality and included an audio track. The images alternated views from three cameras—one behind the counter, one aimed at the front door, and the third a view of the register from the opposite corner.

"It's still a long shot that we'll find who bought the blanks, Mackey," Charo said.

Charo was right. The five-second images weren't long enough for them to see entire transactions. They could tell if someone bought a gun or nothing, but they realized that a box of blanks on the low-resolution images wouldn't look any different than a box of live rounds. Charo removed the box of blanks from her pocket and regarded it closely. The choppy motion on the monitor was making Mackey feel nauseous and he turned away. Each file captured an hour of real time and took a little more than fifteen minutes to view. Mackey stared at the grain pattern of the wood floor while Charo remained intent on the computer screen. It had been nearly two hours and they were coming to the end of the 3:00–4:00 PM file when Mackey's ears perked up.

"Did you hear that? I thought I heard someone say, '.38 caliber blanks.'"

Pete stopped the file and played it back.

"Turn up the volume, please," said Charo.

The first image was an empty shot of the register from the corner camera with a great deal of static that sounded like squirrels wrestling in the attic. They could barely make out Jack's voice talking to a customer about .38-caliber blanks, but the image shifted to the front-door camera, which showed a young woman exiting and then to the view from behind the register with Jack standing alone.

"Looks like you are out of luck," Pete said.

"Wait," interjected Charo. "Run it back five minutes before the audio about the blanks, and play it forward at half speed."

Pete obliged. Charo perched motionless on the edge of the chair like a hawk scanning a field for the movement of a rabbit. Mackey tried to watch but the slower speed only worsened his motion sickness. It was quiet for too long, he thought. The person who purchased the blanks must've eluded the cameras. Mackey turned to say something to Charo and he saw it. On a sequence from the front door camera a tall man entered. He wore a fedora that obscured half of his face. A red feather was stuck in the hat's band. The next shot, from behind the register, showed the young woman at the register. Behind her, was a profile view of the man in the fedora standing next to a display case. He walked out of the shot and didn't appear again. Then came the empty shot of the register with Jack's voice off camera saying, "38 caliber blanks." This was followed by the image of the young woman exiting the shop.

"That must be him!" Mackey exclaimed.

They replayed the sequence several more times, but didn't see anyone else.

Mackey handed Pete a flash drive. "Copy that sequence for us."

. . .

Leo stayed late. It was safer to do this work after hours. He had met and fallen for Geetangali in an FBI civilian training course they took. Even though she didn't return his amorous attention and lived in another city he was still of the mind to do whatever he could to curry her favor. The request from Agent Chen, though risky, fit with the plan formulated by his love-stricken brain. The letters, he reasoned, must be fakes. As part of the deal he made with Agent Chen, that included a lunch double date in NYC, she'd have to inform SAC Martinez of their existence. If discovered, he would simply say he did the preliminary analysis without alerting the SAC because he figured Martinez was too busy to deal with such an inconsequential finding.

Leo first examined the letter sent to NBC under a microscope. It was handwritten in black ink, cropped, and folded in the same locations as the original. The paper was ordinary copy paper. Quantico would do chemical tests to see if they could identify particular markers of its manufacturer. As in the photocopies sent to NBC and the *New York Post*, the *T* in lines one and two and the *A* in line five were double traced. Nice touch he thought. He scanned and loaded the image into the digital recognition software. Leo pushed a button and the computer began the laborious task of comparing every dot on the letter Charo gave him to the image of the NBC letter stored in the computer system's memory. The greater the differences the longer it took. He figured an hour or more. He left the computer humming like a tenor and went out for a smoke and a candy bar. Upon return he found the computer quiet. He must have forgotten to set a parameter or punch start and cursed himself for wasting an hour. He would miss *CSI-Miami* now.

Leo stared at the screen. The program had completed the analysis and returned an identical match. Disbelief squeaked across his face like a worn windshield-wiper blade. He ran it again and again, but each time the program failed to detect any differences. A perfect match? He repeated the process with the second letter Charo gave him, the one addressed to the senators. Same results: exact match. Even the steadiest trace was inexact. Leo reached for the phone to page Martinez then thought better of it. It was late. He couldn't be sure he hadn't overlooked something. Missed a calibration. Better to sleep on it and try again with fresh eyes in the morning.

He took a deep breath and closed his eyes conjuring his favorite fantasy. Lying in bed next to Geetangali after lovemaking. His hand lying across her abdomen and face nuzzled against her cheek. Then Geetangali grew a moustache and morphed into Martinez. She did not look happy.

.| 24 |.

They spent another night in Mackey's childhood home. Mrs. Dunn made them tomato soup and tuna fish sandwiches due to the extreme lateness of their arrival. They awoke early, said their good-byes again, and headed north. The déjà vu continued when they stopped to see Mrs. Bilderback. Charo had received a call from her before they left Elkins asking that they pay her another visit.

Mrs. Bilderback met them on her driveway, child in tow, heading toward her car. She handed Mackey a book explaining that her father had sent it to her before he died. After Mackey's and Charo's visit she remembered its unusual inscription inside the front cover.

"I recall thinking at the time it was odd but that was my father."

"Do you recognize this email address?" Mackey asked pointing to the inscription.

"No, at least not in my father's correspondences to me." She pointed at the book, "but Charleston was his middle name."

Mrs. Bilderback started the engine and was about to put it in reverse when Mackey stopped her.

"Mrs. Bilderback, wait. Did your father have a dog?"

"Yes, Goldie. Why do you ask?"

"What happened to Goldie?"

"She disappeared after my father died. She wasn't at the cabin when I got there. I figured she got badly spooked and ran away."

Little Artie was fussing in his car seat.

"Sorry, I have to run. I'm late for a doctor's appointment." She backed out of her driveway to the chorus of a cracked muffler and a howling child.

"I've heard of dogs that stay beside their master after death," Mackey said to Charo. "Odd that Goldie ran away, don't you think?" Charo shrugged and headed for the car.

As Mrs. Bilderback was pulling away, Mackey bolted after her. She braked to a halt at the neighbor's silver mailbox, its red flag up.

"One more thing. How tall was your father?"

"Five-foot-eleven, I think."

"Oh, and did he wear hats?"

"Hats? You mean like a baseball cap?"

"No. A fedora. You know, 1920s-gangster style."

"No."

The book cover was paper-bag brown with the title printed in an unadorned type, *What Einstein Told His Cook: Kitchen Science Explained*, by Robert L. Wolke. It was a pre-publication proof copy. Inside the front cover Lavigne had printed a note to his daughter. Below the words, "Looking forward to seeing you all on Thanksgiving," were two rows of odd numbers sandwiched around an email address:

$59\ 8\ J\ 5\bar{4}\ \widetilde{43}\ \ 5\ 57\ 6\ 19\ \bar{6}6\ 3\bar{4}\ \bar{7}9\ 90$

ACharlestonL2001@yahoo.com

$59\ 53\ 42\ \bar{5}7\ 2\bar{6}\ 23\ 53$

Mackey interrupted the drone of car wheels on paved highway. "A few things stand out. All of the characters except for one are numbers. There is a *J* in the middle of the first word. Several of the numbers have symbols written over them—either a dash or a tilde."

"Huh?" Charo snapped back to the moment.

"The inscription has a tilde."

"An accent mark?"

"Yes. It looks to be code."

"Maybe it says Happy Thanksgiving," offered Charo.

"Okay, there's already a comedienne named Charo. Besides there are too many words and why include the mysterious email address?"

Mackey proceeded to examine each page of the book for clues. He had to do so in short bursts, stopping whenever carsickness appeared on the horizon. He turned to a dog-eared page. The lone postproduction mark in the text of the book was a handwritten dash, similar to those in Lavigne's coded message. The dash was over the letter *A* in the word "Aluminum" in the summary of Chapter 4. Other than this and the inscription, the book was clean cover-to-cover. He had been so engrossed that he failed to notice that Charo was again driving back toward Washington. Minutes later they were turning onto Pennsylvania Avenue.

"I think it would best if I tell SAC Martinez in person about what we've found—the letters Mrs. Bilderback gave us and the new evidence in the Lavigne case. I'm going to stop by the lab first though, to see what information Leo has learned before he sends the letters and material off to Quantico."

"I thought you seemed preoccupied," Mackey said.

"I am not sure how our snooping is going to be received. I knew this was a risk, but I didn't think we'd ever get this far." Charo stopped the car at the Eastern Market Metro station.

"You should make yourself scram for the rest of today. I'll call you later."

Mackey let the mixed idiom pass. "What about the book?"

"Hang on to it. For now."

Leo had his back to the door as Charo entered the lab. He didn't turn around until the click-clack of her footsteps came to a stop. He was both anxious and relieved to see her and ushered her into an empty office. He closed the door and latched it.

"I think your memorabilia are authentic," he began. Charo stared at him in disbelief. "I am logging them in this morning and sending them off to Quantico. If asked, I will say you brought them in late yesterday afternoon and I didn't have time to process them until this morning. Have you spoken with Martinez yet?"

"I am on my way to his office now."

"My assessment of their authenticity is off the record. Officially, I never examined them. I've deleted the files. You understand?"

"Yes. It will be up to Quantico to make that determination. Leo, do me one more favor. Don't send it off to Quantico just yet in case SAC Martinez should decide he wants to examine the letters himself."

"You have until noon."

Charo knew little about Calvin Martinez, the special agent in charge of the anthrax investigation. He was a rising star who began his career in the San Francisco field office. Her heart dropped a beat when a perky secretary told her he was in and to have a seat. She bolstered her resolve by telling herself it was best to get it over with as quickly as possible, like pushing an arrow through flesh until it comes out clean on the other side.

"Agent Chen, what is the nature of your business with SAC Martinez today?"

"I have come across evidence in the Amerithrax case."

"May I ask the nature of that evidence?"

"Letters. They could be the originals of the anthrax letters."

"And is that evidence in your possession now?"

"No. I dropped it off at the lab."

"Just a moment." The secretary poked her head into Martinez's office but Charo could not hear the content of her conversation.

"SAC Martinez would like you to retrieve the evidence from the lab and bring it to his office."

When Charo returned Martinez was standing in his doorway. He was a muscular man, several inches taller than she was, with a Marine crew cut and a narrow moustache. Old school. He beckoned her to enter. She sat down opposite his desk with hands folded across her knees, holding the manila envelope with the letters like a bad report card. On the wall behind his desk was a photo of Martinez with the FBI Director, next to it one of the Princeton University crew team. She recognized Martinez third from the left.

He was pleasant but all business. He listened quietly as Charo told him how she had come to visit Arthur Lavigne's daughter. She explained that her interest in the case persisted since her involvement back in 2001. Lavigne's suicide had stuck in her mind. She figured that as long as she was in DC to report on her child pornography work she might as well pay Lavigne's daughter a visit. She didn't expect the woman to have anything useful to tell her, let alone hand over evidence.

Martinez studied the letters. He took several minutes, meticulously inspecting them with a magnifying glass not unlike the one Charo used while trespassing Lavigne's house less than twenty-four hours ago. Charo studied his face looking for signs of annoyance, agitation or excitement. She found none. Martinez slid the letters back into the envelope and handed it across the desk back to Charo.

While awaiting the inevitable reprimand and litany of disciplinary actions, Charo reconsidered Leo's certainty—the unofficial analysis she couldn't reveal. Martinez was staring at her.

"If there is nothing else, Agent Chen, I thank you and ask that you return these to the lab. Good day."

On her way out Charo failed to notice Tony Carbonaro eying her menacingly through a conference room window. She wanted to feel relieved but that wasn't how she felt. Martinez's cursory dismissal of the evidence puzzled her until the sinister implications wrapped around her like a *Boa constrictor*. For the first time in her life she *needed* a drink.

In the courtyard of an apartment complex on Jefferson Street, Mackey located an unprotected wireless signal on his laptop. He checked his email but found no news from Marci regarding his paperwork. Setting his computer aside he opened what *Einstein Told His Cook* to the inscription hoping that Albert, like Abe, might have some inspiration for him.

The cryptogram used a number substitution code but what of the superscripts? The first line perhaps was a message and the last line he hoped the password to the yahoo account. He grabbed his laptop and typed an email to the address. For the subject line he wrote, "Artie, can you help us solve the anthrax mystery?" He hit *Send* and set the computer aside.

From his backpack he pulled out a pad of paper and copied the cryptogram. From the spacing he deduced that letters were represented by numbers 5–90. Too many numbers to represent a simple one-to-one, number-to-letter substitution. Then there was the letter *J* suggesting no corresponding number for it in the code. That didn't make sense. Cryptograms were self-created codes. Why wouldn't Lavigne assign a number for the letter *J*?

He approached the code systematically by listing the frequency of every number. Three numbers appeared twice—*59*, *57*, and *53*. But one of the 57s had a dash over it, whatever that meant. All the other numbers appeared once. The three most common letters in the English language are *E*, *T*, and *A*, but which was which? There were no single number-words or repeat number-pairs to provide clues. Not enough characters to make an educated guess. He put the pad down and checked his email. No bounce back message from the Yahoo *MAILER-DAEMON.* The email address was legit. Maybe Lavigne knew something and was worried he'd be killed for it so he left a clue. Or maybe it was a crazy old man's way of screwing with folks after he'd passed on. But the timing. It could contain a suicide note, confession, or will. But then why the subterfuge?

His cell phone went off. It was Charo. She wasn't calling from behind bars but from the bottom of a tumbler in a Georgetown bar.

When Mackey arrived Charo was sitting in a booth facing the door. Her hands embraced two fingers of liquid the color of jet fuel.

"How bad is it?" he asked. "Did you have to hand over your badge and gun?"

Charo tilted her head, the afternoon sun pouring through the bar's open door made her squint, concealing the disillusionment in her eyes.

"Leo is convinced the letters are the originals."

"Seriously? What happened when you told this to the SAC?"

"Total indifference," she replied. "Leo's analysis was off the record so I couldn't tell Martinez. He examined the letters and said nothing. Didn't seem to care that I visited Lavigne's daughter and asked her about his suicide. He didn't even care that I meddled in his investigation." She took another gulp of high-test.

"Isn't this good news? It means you aren't in trouble and we can keep investigating."

"No, no. It means I just opened a can of gummy worms. Martinez's response didn't make sense at first, until…"

"Until what?"

"Until I considered the possibility he is involved somehow in this mess. Maybe you are right, this is one big government cover-up."

"Aw, what do I know? I'm just a paranoid, unemployed epidemiologist. Where are the letters now?" Mackey asked.

Charo checked her watch. "Quantico."

"I haven't gotten too far on the puzzle," Mackey said changing the subject. "Other than to send Lavigne an email. It didn't bounce back."

Charo wrinkled her nose. Mackey pulled the book from his pack, laid it open on the table to the inscription, and spun it around so it faced Charo. With her chin resting on her hands she contemplated it through the crystal facets of the tumbler, but offered no interpretation. Her lids sagged under the weight of the liquor. Mackey swung the book back to face him and pulled out his notes and read them aloud for Charo's benefit.

- Four words: three before, one after an email address
- Five, four, four, and seven-letter words
- Letters represented by numbers from 5–90, except for the letter J
- Suggests no number corresponding to the letter J?
- 59, 57, 53 appear twice
- No doublets
- Seven superscripts in three of the words: six dashes, one tilde
- Purpose of superscript characters?

Charo's next stop on the whiskey train was Sleepy Hollow, the alcohol having been invited in to mingle with her brain cells. Mackey stared at the inscription. Rather than try to guess what Lavigne was trying to communicate he thought about the man. Who was Arthur Lavigne? He was a college professor of microbiology. An activist who spoke out against the dangers of biological weapons. Eccentric, reclusive, and perhaps misunderstood. But was he a zealot or a terrorist? Did these numbers have some significance in microbiology? He booted up his laptop managed to locate a weak wireless signal from the café next door to the bar. He plugged the first numerical sequence into Google. The page loaded excruciatingly slow, returning pages for a Long Island Railroad schedule, a mathematical table of hyperbolic functions, and a box score from a 2003 Houston Astros versus the St. Louis Cardinals game. He browsed a couple of the 15 million hits. Nothing suggested a key to the code. He tried the sequence in quotes. No hits. He couldn't enter the superscripts. That might explain why he wasn't picking up anything from his search.

The second word in the first line had no superscripts so he tried that one. This time it pulled up over 100 million hits, the top ones for replica handbags, a blog, and a voting district map for Puerto Rico. He clicked on the blog. On the archive page link he saw that the blog began in 2004. Lavigne died in 2001. He went to Amazon.com and keyed in *What Einstein told his Cook.* He studied the cover of the published edition. An egg was suspended in quotes over a frying pan that sat above a Bunsen burner. The blue flame brought back memories of high-school chemistry class.

He next typed the book's title into Google, followed by the word cryptogram. He tried it with each of the numerical sequences. He repeated using the author's name. He got plenty of hits, but nothing relevant. He returned to the webpage showing the book's cover. The author had written another book called, *Chemistry Explained.* Chemistry. Lavigne was a microbiologist, yet the image was of chemistry. Mackey lunged for the book, madly turning to the page that bore the only other post-publisher marking aside from the cryptogram. Someone, perhaps Lavigne, had over-lined the letters *Al.*

"Aluminum?" Mackey said out loud.

"A-roomi-then? It bedder have two beds," Charo mumbled surfacing from her stupor.

"No, *aluminum*. The element."

"Ar-uminum, symbol Al, atomic number 13, valence +3. Sh-ilicon, symbol Si, atomic number 14, valences -4, +2, +4. Phos-fo-us, symbol, P, atomic number 15, valences –3, +1, +3, +5…"

"Charo, what are you doing?"

She didn't answer but kept spilling elements from her booze-fogged, library carrel. "Su-fur, symbol S, atomic number 16, valences –2, +2, +4, +6." Mackey stared again at the cryptogram.

"Wait, Charo, that must be it! The code is from the Periodic Table. The atomic numbers correspond to the letters in the element symbols!"

"Ch-orine, symbol Cl, atomic number 17, valence –1, +1, +3, +5, +7…"

Mackey pulled up a periodic table off the Web.

"Argon, symbol Ar, atomic number 18, valence zero…"

"Hush, Charo. Atomic number 59 is praseodynium, symbol Pr." He wrote down *Pr*. The next number in the first sequence was *8* for oxygen, he added an *O*. Then came the *J*. He stopped, scanned each row of the periodic table twice for the letter *J*, there was none. In fact, he found that every letter in the alphabet was present in the elemental symbols except for the letters *J* and *Q*. His heartbeat did a jig. He must be on the right track. Charo began to snore softly. The next number in the coded sequence was *54*—xenon, symbol Xe. The final number was *43*— technetium, Tc. He stopped and viewed the translation of the first word.

Pr O J Xe Tc

"Projectasy?" he asked aloud. "Was Lavigne into designer drugs?"

Charo's cheek was pressed against the wooden table; a dribble of drool connected her to the crater of a cigarette burn as if her spit could dissolve wood. Mackey inspected Lavigne's inscription again. There was a dash over the *4* of *54* and a tilde over the *43*. In computer language a tilde was sometimes used to denote an inversion of bits. What if Lavigne meant to switch the order of the letters? And the dash was over the second digit, so he dropped the first letter, the result was "Project." Following the same rules he decoded the rest of the first line in a flash:

Project Black Death

"Hey, Charo, you ever hear of Project Black Death?" Charo's response came as a rumble of her soft palate as air rushed back and forth. The second line translated to *Primolevi*.

"Very clever," Mackey, proclaimed.

Primo Levi was an Italian of Jewish heritage who was a learned chemist and an Auschwitz concentration camp survivor. Levi wrote several books, among them, *The Periodic Table*.

Mackey brought up the Yahoo mail login page, keyed in Lavigne's account name and was about to type in Primolevi as the password when the screen went dark. In his excitement he had ignored the reserve battery power warning and now the computer had shut down. The mystery of the Black Death Project would have to wait. He helped Charo into the back seat of the car and found a decent enough Holiday Inn near the beltway, opting not to show up at his mother's with a drunk FBI agent in tow.

Charo awoke hours later looking like she had just tumbled off the Coney Island Cyclone. "What time is it?" She asked.

"Six."

"AM or PM?"

"Six in the morning."

She stumbled past Mackey who was seated at the foot of the bed. A moment later he heard water filling the bath. He knocked to make sure she was okay, interpreting the tone of her indecipherable grunt as affirmation that she was.

"Hey, Charo!" Mackey shouted over the roar of the water. "I've been thinking. If Martinez was involved and suspected the letters were authentic, wouldn't he have acted differently? I mean he wouldn't have allowed them to go to Quantico."

Charo's reply sounded like, "I suppose."

Primolevi was the password to Lavigne's secret email account. Lavigne was paranoid, but that didn't mean he wasn't under surveillance by the FBI, CIA, or the NSA. Mackey surmised that Project Black Death was the most surreptitious of secret projects, veiled in enough camouflage and misdirection to make Blaine and Copperfield look like cocktail-party card tricksters. Lavigne recorded his digging into germ warfare projects conducted by the United States government in a diary of emails he sent to himself from the anonymous account.

Lavigne's first entry was from August 2000 and the subject line read, "Loophole." In the fall of 1969 President Nixon ended the US bioweapons offensive program. One year later Lavigne was out of a job. The email contained Article I of the 1972 Biological Weapons Convention treaty:

> Each State Party to this Convention undertakes never in any circumstance to develop, produce, stockpile or otherwise acquire or retain:
>
> (1) Microbial or other biological agents, or toxins whatever their origin or method of production, of types and in quantities that have no justification for prophylactic, protective or other peaceful purposes;

The Biological Weapons Convention only allowed research with agents of biological warfare to be done if it was for peaceful defensive purposes or vaccine development. The United States, Great Britain, and the Soviet Union all signed in 1972.

The next email detailed research that became public after the dissolution of the Soviet Union in 1991. Russian scientists had spliced genes from *B. cereus* into *B. anthracis*. The new anthrax strain was resistant to vaccine. A news link said the CIA had a cow over this.

The next email wasn't from Lavigne to himself. The author, Armadillo90120@hotmail.com, titled the email, "Treaty Violations," and simply wrote, "Project Black Death 3x worse," and included a link to a *New York Times* article from September 4, 2001. Mackey clicked on the link.

The "3x" in Armadillo's email referred to three secret US bioweapons projects from the 1990s. The first was Project Clear Vision. Initiated in 1997 by the CIA, the goal was to learn the Soviet technology used to disseminate anthrax through missile warheads. An anthrax simulant with an exceptionally high spore count was also made as part of the project.

Project Bacchus came next. With a budget of $1.6 million, a small group of researchers in the Nevada desert set out to see if they could outfit a basement bioweapons factory. From a French company they bought a fifty-gallon fermentation tank to grow the bacteria rapidly. The centrifuge came from Pakistan and was critical for separating the bacteria from its nutrient broth. A Yugoslavian company shipped them an industrial spray drier to prepare aerodynamic spores. All the pipes, tubing, and support structures were bought at a local hardware store in Nevada. The only thing that wasn't purchased was the starter culture of anthrax spores. In less than nine months the Bacchus team succeeded in producing two pounds of spores. No one in the US Intelligence Service detected the operation. It was a successful proof of concept. The concept being the intelligence community's deficiencies.

The third secret project was called Project Jefferson. It came about as a direct result of the Soviet gene splicing research. The Pentagon and CIA set out to create a US superbug. USAMRIID provided a strain of anthrax recovered from the soil of Vozrozhdeniye Island that had survived the dumping of bleach and extreme temperatures. The results were classified.

Mackey heard the tub drain and the fan come on in the bathroom. He was sitting on the floor with his back to the wall outside the bathroom. The steam no longer wafted out. The final two emails in the inbox were an exchange between Lavigne and Armadillo90120@hotmail.com. Lavigne wrote:

> What became of Project Black Death?

To which Armadillo90120@hotmail.com replied:

> Advise not digging in the Nevada desert without a mask.

Charo emerged transformed. Wrapped in a towel hair her brown calves passed at Mackey's eye level as she grabbed clothes and returned to the bathroom. Mackey summarized the emails for Charo through the door while she dressed. He had slept poorly on the grimy carpet and had eaten only vending machine peanut butter on cheese crackers that tasted like they were made in the 70s. He had a headache, was in need of a full body massage, and clean clothes.

Charo re-emerged from the bathroom, her metamorphosis complete. "Let's get some breakfast."

Charo received a text message at the same time the pancakes arrived. "It's from Leo. Quantico confirmed the letters were the originals."

Mackey attempted to read Charo's face. It was an expression he had not ever seen her wear. Her eyes were wide and unfocused. Tiny wrinkles appeared in her forehead as well as pinch lines on either side of the bridge of her nose. Her mouth was drawn into small, tight line. They finished the rest of breakfast in silence.

They were back on the road to New York and Mackey was battling the urge to doze. The carbohydrate load about to be dumped into his blood stream would stimulate an insulin release and bottom out his blood sugar while the car wheels serenaded him with "Route 95 lullaby."

"Yee-aah! Excuse me," Mackey exclaimed. He shook another yawn loose and sat up in the seat. "Suppose Lavigne was murdered because of what he knew about Project Black Death. Then the image from the gun shop video could be the link to solving both his murder and the anthrax mailings. The clue from the E-ZPass data connects to the VP's office. We need to connect that to Lavigne. What's our next move?"

"Exit," Charo said.

Mackey looked around. They weren't even in Delaware yet. "What? You mean quit?"

"Mackey, at a minimum, our involvement in the Amerithrax investigation could cost me my FBI career. At a maximum, we've uncovered a cover-up that stretches from the FBI to the executive office. This isn't Shaggy and Scooby-Doo anymore."

"But—"

"I've gone to the lead investigator and he didn't seem to care. Either he's involved, has convincing evidence on Erekat, or wants no part of this. I expected anger, not indifference. And frankly, my resolve has been shaken. I don't know what to expect when I return to the office tomorrow."

"Charo—"

"If we continue this it isn't going to end well; we could end up dead. Or if we are lucky, merely discredited, blacklisted, and unable to find work picking through trash for aluminum cans."

Mackey became quiet. Charo wasn't one for emotional outbursts. He'd seen her rattled but now she seemed spooked. He had his share of career missteps and felt he was on the verge of something sanguine with Marci's team. He already reminded himself several times not to blow it, that is, if their meddling hadn't already triggered the federal funding stall. But they made more progress in a week than the official investigation had made in five years. He turned to face her.

"We're so close. We can't stop now."

Charo's reply came as the jut of a determined chin overshadowing the doubt of a slender neck.

.| 25 |.

Mackey stared at a blinking cursor. He was sitting on a bench in a small park wedged between Broadway and the terminus of West End Avenue. Next to him was a bagel with cream cheese and a carton of orange juice. He was attempting to compose an email, but hadn't got any farther than the subject line: Project Black Death.

He watched a male pigeon puffing out its chest, turning in circles, and cooing as it pursued a female. At each advance the female changed direction to avoid her suitor but then stopped and pecked at nothing in particular on the ground. He thought back to Lavigne's emails. Project Black Death was the culmination of three secret bioweapons projects, but what did that mean? Projects Jefferson, Bacchus, and Clear Vision were uncovered and stories were published about them in print and on the Internet. But there was no mention anywhere of Project Black Death.

Charo was of no help. She wasn't returning his calls or emails. Mackey figured that the secret anthrax projects stretched the permissible limits of the bioweapons treaty, and that the Lavigne's death was connected to his discovery of Project Black Death. The connection was Armadillo90210. But Mr. Armadillo could be Mailthrax, a spy, Lavigne's killer, or all three.

Mackey wasn't able to find Armadillo90210's name through the hotmail account; finding a phony alias and a nonexistent address in Los Angeles. Returning to Lavigne's secret email account he opened the last email from Armadillo90210. He found a pull down menu with the option "view full header." Clicking on it opened a new window with the routing information. There were several Internet protocol addresses. Going back to Google he located a website that connected IP addresses to their owners. He typed in the first IP address: 65.55.74.35. The website returned Microsoft Corporation, Redwood California; the host for hotmail. He tried the second: 208.42.163.9. This returned Vector Internet Services of Eden Prairie, MN; an intermediary provider. The last IP address bore the earliest time stamp. Mackey keyed it in: 140.147.87.144. The IP address belonged to the Library of Congress Information Technology Services.

Mackey pondered what to write. If his plan to flush Armadillo90210 out from the halls of the Library of Congress were to work he'd need a reply to his email. He reread the emails Armadillo90210 sent to Lavigne. Between the lines he read friendship, and the tone was a warning not threat. He'd have to risk that Armadillo90210 was an ally. If he was wrong the email could likely be traced back to him despite his using Lavigne's account and someone else's Wi-Fi. Changing the subject line he composed a two-line email: Artie's murderer should be brought to justice, but we need your help. Is Project Black Death linked to the anthrax mailings? Mackey hit send before thinking better of it.

. . .

Charo thrust herself back into getting pedophiles and peddlers of child pornography off the Web and into jail cells. Her pervs were excited to see the return of her teenage alter ego avatar when she logged in to chat. They asked where she had been. She considered replying that she'd been on field trip to Washington, but opted instead for parental grounding. She stayed out of sight of her FBI superiors; maintaining a profile that dust mites would admire. Mackey had called three times leaving chipper greetings and invitations to continue their discussion. She felt bad about ditching him but she had her career to consider.

Charo had braced herself for the avalanche of questions and censure but none came. No call from Martinez, none from Assistant Director in Charge Warshaw, nor from her supervisor. Lorraine Bilderback didn't call either; perhaps no agents came to interview, search, or take her into custody. That came as some relief. What wasn't a relief was the bureau's response to the new evidence. There was some chatter in the office about the Amerithrax investigation, but nothing specific or connected to the investigation she and Mackey had conducted. What was Martinez up to?

It was later in the afternoon, the last Friday of September, as she ducked low in her cubicle that her phone rang. The single long ring announced it was an outside call. It was Sheriff Lemontyne and he was ticked. Finally, Charo thought, someone had taken notice. Lemontyne had a report from the West Virginia State Forensic Laboratory that was ordered by Charo. He wanted to know who was going to pay for the testing. After some cajoling she got him to read her the results. The particles found on the upper part of Lavigne's shirt differed from those found on the pants. They were smaller in diameter and less numerous. The shirt GSR contained lead whereas the pants did not. Lemontyne was still talking about protocol and his tight budget but Charo had stopped listening. The results confirmed their suspicions that there were two discharges of the weapon, or possibly two weapons. Unfortunately, the results couldn't specify the timing, which shot was fired first, or even if they were fired on the same day or week. But since there was no bullet hole in the floor where she found additional GSR it fit with a second discharge coming from a blank.

Charo persuaded Lemontyne to mail her a copy of the results and to have the clothing shipped to the FBI lab for confirmation. The FBI, she assured him, would cover the expense. That seemed to placate him. He didn't seem to grasp the implication of the test results and Charo didn't bother to enlighten him.

. . .

It was a dreary October 2nd, a month since Mackey's move to New York. It seemed much longer. A cold front had waddled down from Canada and squatted over the city like a bulldog peeing on the sidewalk. A week had passed since Charo dropped him off at his apartment in the early morning hours after their trip to Washington. She hadn't returned any of his communications. Armadillo90210 hadn't replied either. The sinking feeling in his gut was that the investigation was over. The weather or his melancholy spit out a tune from his mental jukebox about disappointment and gray days on the English seacoast[9].

The previous week had been exhilarating, better than any outbreak investigation he'd ever done. They had pulled on a thread and unraveled part of the cloak that shrouded the investigation for five years. They had two avenues to follow that perhaps would intersect. Lavigne's murder and Project Black Death. With an image of the suspect and his putative placement at the highest level of government, it was clear that action was needed. At least to Mackey.

One encouraging development was an email from Marci that she was pushing to have his paperwork moved to the front of the queue as soon as the delay in Washington cleared. But Marci didn't know when that would occur. Mackey's leave time was nearly exhausted and the digits of his bank balance would soon cross those of the ambient air temperature only heading in the wrong direction. He was bored and listing toward edgy. Restlessness would next take root; the oscillations of his mood damping until he became as immobile as a lighthouse perched on a narrow spit of land. His beam of consciousness sweeping monotonously over an empty seascape while the brine dissolved away his foundation.

It was October, the year might have been 1995. Mackey was alone watching the Patriots on Monday Night Football. Allie came home upset. He didn't want to be interrupted. She wanted to talk. There was a student in her class. A troubled kid. Mackey was impatient. She tried to tell him, but he wanted to solve her problem and get back to the game. New England didn't even have a good team that season. Allie gave up.

What would cheer him up would be to continue the investigation. He missed Charo and the adrenaline rush that came with fitting together the pieces of a mystery. Charo's concerns were on the surface reasonable but they didn't make it any easier to let go. Mackey knew the feeling of having your *raison d'être* and livelihood in jeopardy. Endowed with an unhealthy disrespect of authority; defiance had on more than one occasion threatened his own career. But this was different. Charo was an FBI agent sworn to protect the Constitution against all enemies, foreign and domestic. Knowing as much as they now did and doing nothing was tantamount to letting a murderer go free on a technicality.

Wandering from room to room in a three-room apartment is unsatisfying. Whereas the hours spent Web sleuthing had a sense of purpose before, now they were tedious and overwhelming. His mind was unfocused. Disappointment pressed down on his shoulders until his knuckles swung glum alongside his kneecaps. If he weren't trying to understand the meaning of Lavigne's death it would soon again be Allie's occupying his thoughts.

Mackey forgot and took an extra shift at the hospital returning home at eight in the morning. Allie was loading up a rented van with her sculptures. She had a crafts fair in Great Barrington, three hours away and was already late. He had promised to help her but was in no shape to drive after the overnight in the ED. Allie sent him to bed and went alone.

He put on a beaten pair of running shoes and a thin shell and went for a walk. It was the first time in weeks that he left the laptop and backpack behind, though he felt its weight anyway. In a way that only psychologists and depressives understood, Mackey found inclement weather comforting. The walk wasn't to clear his head, far from it. He needed the space for the combatants to work out their conflict. He needed to feel the cold. Water seeped through the cracks in his sneakers and soaked his socks. Numbness advanced like the Russian winter upon Napoleon's army. After cresting a hill he headed into the North Woods of Central Park. Leaves clung to the soles of his shoes and the chill rattled the bones in his ankles.

Anger entered the ring first. Too many things had been taken from Mackey in his lifetime: his father, Allie, the job with the city health department and now the investigation. Guilt countered by telling him these were all his fault. Anger knew this wasn't true, but enough doubt landed to drop him to his knees.

It was the Counting Crows, "Raining in Baltimore," that his jukebox selected[10]. Mackey didn't own a raincoat, and the phone call he knew he needed would never come.

Guilt was in a reverse headlock being pounded with whys. Though less muscular, guilt had guile, and slipped out of the hold with a scathing combination of recriminations.

Mackey pushed past the urge to urinate. He was racing against his mind to the east side of the Meer. Without the cover of trees there was nothing to slow the wind and water. His teeth began to chatter and the dark thoughts crystallized like hail.

Anger was against the ropes. Guilt was raining down should've dones, but it took a lot to knock out anger. Pain was his ally, righteousness his fortitude.

Mackey had sponsored this battle enough times to know it always ended in a draw with both combatants bloodied, unable to see and swinging wildly. He needed guilt and anger to exhaust their energies leaving nothing for anxiety to worry about. Though he never played chicken on a railroad trestle Mackey understood the ache and allure and held a healthy respect for the brink. He knew it was not a place to dawdle and turned back to find indoor plumbing and a hot drink.

In the Starbucks bathroom he slumped against the wall beneath the hot air of a hand dryer until the muscles in his foot cramped. A left-handed barista girl, who looked like Audrey Tautou, wrote his name on an empty cup of a hot cocoa. Moments later he grasped the steaming beverage like a beggar and eased into a seat by the window expecting a view of the Eiffel Tower. Instead, a mirrored reflection caught his eye.

Lead in Anthrax Investigation

He turned around. The headline was the front page of the *New York Times* Metro section. Before the man turned the page he read: Lead in Anthrax Investigation.

After a half dozen interrupted glances that produced nothing more than queasiness the man offered Mackey the section. An anonymous Department of Justice source confirmed rumors that the FBI had a new suspect in the anthrax mailings and was close to making an arrest.

With minimal effort the reporter was able to deduce from the leak that the suspect's name was Joseph Erekat. Perhaps this explained the disinterested shoulder Charo received from Martinez. The reporter went on to remind readers about prior FBI missteps and didn't provide details on the evidence implicating Erekat as Mailthrax. Interviews with former FBI agents, who now made their living as talking heads, suggested the FBI was being more cautious while the bureau's critics were quick to dismiss the story as anniversary propaganda. Mackey put the paper down and pressed his thumb and forefinger into the spaces above his eyeballs. Caffeine withdrawal, the low-pressure front or the cerebral ultimate fight match was making his head feel like the lump of coal Superman crushed into a diamond.

. . .

Charo read the *Times* article online and pouted. In her mailbox she noticed a thick inter-office envelope left by the mail clerk. It was from the headquarters. The envelope contained transcripts of the vice president's speeches and photo essays of his various trips and appearances. She forgot about the request she made while in DC. There were also policy statements, publicity reprints, and newspaper clippings. Not surprisingly there was nothing specific about his staff.

The last item was an 8-by-10 publicity photograph of the vice president. He wore his trademark smirk, a dark blue suit, and a blood red tie. Stuck to the back of the photo was another photograph. Careful not to damage the emulsion, Charo peeled away the second photo. It was a picture taken on the White House lawn. The vice president stood in the middle of the photo with his staff flanking him. Beneath the picture was a caption listing names.

Charo's eyes were drawn to a figure standing in the last row on the left—J. Farrington. He was tall and wore a fedora. She compared it to the digital clip from the gun shop. The video still was blurry, but there was a resemblance.

She scanned the VP staff photo and saved the image to a portable thumb drive built into the base of a breath-mint container. A breach of FBI protocol, but like Hoover's ban on drinking coffee while on the job, one routinely ignored. She picked up the device at a techie-show kiosk at the Javits Center. It served her purposes. The 100 megabyte memory board was replaceable and it came with a supply of mints that rattled when carried in a pants pocket. She returned the contents of the folder to the envelope and placed it in the outgoing mail back to the DC office.

Stepping out into the sunless day she put on sunglasses and strode down Broadway to the Internet Café. She paid cash for a five-minute-card and flipped on a computer in the far corner of the balcony section. She turned the chair and screen so that prying eyes could not see from behind. She composed an email and uploaded the file. In the text she simply wrote, "Driver?" She removed the USB memory board and broke it like a walnut against the table. With a lighter she melted the circuit board until it resembled a lollipop forgotten in a child's pocket after an hour in an industrial strength dryer. She tossed it into the pit of a garbage truck emptying sidewalk receptacles along Broadway and returned to 26 Federal Plaza.

After her floor mates left for the day, Charo dug up what she could on John Jacob Ellsworth Farrington. He was the youngest son of Edward Farrington Jr. and Bootsy Ellsworth Farrington. He grew up in Old

Melville, Connecticut where instead of riding around his gated community on a bicycle he cruised the Long Island Sound on his sailboat; rather than play little league baseball he received private tennis lessons in his backyard from Patrick McEnroe; and in lieu of piggy banks he and his friends had trust funds. His great-grandfather, John H. Trumbull, was governor of Connecticut and a close friend of his namesake, John Jacob Astor IV.

Farrington attended Princeton; graduating with dual degrees in political science and international studies. He moved to Washington, DC and was given an entry-level position in the Department of Defense. He campaigned for George Herbert Walker Bush's unsuccessful bid for a second term. Before the Clintons took office he departed the DOD and founded AmCon, a defense consulting company that did work for the Pentagon and CIA. With his insider connections AmCon did well landing numerous defense contracts.

Farrington sold AmCon in 1999. Three years later the company ran afoul of US legislation banning the sales of materials that could be used in the weapon production of nations that support terrorism. The more serious charge was that AmCon sold missile guidance systems through a chain of subsidiaries beginning with Cheyenne Global security and ending in Bahrain with Three Yemeni Brothers. The charge was later dismissed and AmCon got off with a slap on the wrist and a two million dollar fine for export violations. Farrington returned to politics in 2000, serving first as an advisor to the vice president on weapons of mass destruction and then as his deputy chief of staff.

. . .

Mackey viewed the attachment in Charo's email. He hoped this meant she hadn't really stopped her investigation after all. Returning to cyber sleuthing he found cursory mention of Farrington moving up to become VP deputy chief of staff that included a synopsis of his Defense Department career. There was a post of his 1992 wedding announcement that included a photo, but little information other than the name of the country club where it was held and his bride's family tree.

He put both the wedding announcement photo and the VP staff photo up on his screen and compared them to a paper copy of the video still showing the man in the fedora at the gun shop. He enlarged the VP staff photo while balancing an improved view of Farrington with the decline in quality. He then meticulously compared the screen images of Farrington to the paper image. He searched for common features but the poor resolution, the fedora obscuring the man's eyes, and differing angles limited what was available for comparison. The fedora appeared to be the same one in both images but he didn't see a red feather in the VP staff photo. The prognathous, chin of Jay Leno proportions was the same in the wedding and gun-shop photos. He couldn't be sure though and he cautioned himself not to see what he wanted to see. That had happened too often in the Amerithrax investigation.

It as reported that after following Steven Hatfill to a pancake restaurant, the FBI released bloodhounds that had been given one of the anthrax envelopes to sniff. Was it possible that any scent remained after autoclaving? The dogs reportedly ran right up to Hatfill and jumped all over him. Evidence of guilt said the FBI. Evidence that he had eaten bacon for breakfast, Mackey thought.

Mackey folded the gun-store photo and put it in his backpack. This was a break. They had a name to go with the face, but more importantly, Charo was back on the trail of Mailthrax. He wrote her back proposing they meet in Brooklyn. He was about to sign off email when he noted three messages in the spam folder. He slid the cursor over the delete button but then hesitated. He double-clicked instead.

The first email bore the subject: "URGENT RESPONSE NEEDED." It was the Nigerian scam, a promise to a share of millions if he put up cash to grease the corrupt government wheels. The plea came from a person claiming to be an embassy official from Sierra Leone who was dying of "pancakes" cancer and asked for help to move a plundered fortune out of the country before the rebels could seize it. The spelling was awful and grammar worse.

The second spam email offered a way to enlarge one of his body parts. He deleted both.

The third was from Armadillo90210. He froze. All it said was, "Who are you?" Mackey clicked to show the header details. Removing a note card from his backpack he compared the series of IP addresses to the previous email Lavigne had received from Armadillo90210 back in 2001. They were the same.

The word embassy now began to loiter in the lobby of his consciousness. Mackey's hands went back to his note cards and he began flipping through them. His notes on embassies were made more out of curiosity than a notion that the information would ever prove relevant. The FBI and Postal Service announced in January 2002 that the reward for information leading to an arrest and conviction in the Amerithrax case had increased to $2.5 million. Yuri had mentioned this, too. One of the more outrageous stories that struck Mackey and caused him to record it was from April 2002. A man showed up at the embassy in Astana, Kazakhstan with the wild claim that he knew where the anthrax used in the 2001 attacks came from. He told the Foreign Service officer that the spores had been dug up from the US desert. Mackey hurriedly logged into Lavigne's email account, mistyping

"PrimoLevi" twice. There, in Armadillo90210's last email to Lavigne, was the advice not to go digging in the Nevada desert.

.| 26 |.

Farrington hung up the phone. The evidence against Erekat wasn't much. He had been a member of a Palestinian independence organization, a possible motive. In 2001, the chap was treated in the emergency department of Hillsboro Hospital for an infected leg. According to Erekat's medical record, the injury was from a fall while wind surfing at Sandy Hook. He was given antibiotics and the infection resolved. But when the FBI interviewed Dr. Nyuk, the doctor who treated him, he recalled that the wound had a dark scab. When prompted by investigators, the doctor could not rule out cutaneous anthrax.

The FBI seized Erekat's computer and Fort Detrick searched their files for security-camera footage from the summer of 2001, when Erekat was an intern with them. Erekat submitted blood samples so the CDC could test for anthrax antibodies and environmental samples were taken from his home and car to look for spores. The results of the tests were beyond the reach of Farrington's contact. He leaned back in his chair, a smile of smug contentment creasing his sun-ripened features.

"Perhaps this tragic case will finally be solved."

. . .

They met up at the Capone Club in the Fort Greene section of Brooklyn. Though there was still light outside he had to search for her in the dim recesses beyond the bar. She was sitting on a plush maroon sofa in the corner reading.

"Are we back on the case?" Mackey asked.

Charo stood. In the dim light Mackey had missed the signs of agitation on Charo's normally placid face.

"I don't talk about it much. How working with testosterone-heads is no picnic. Women have to work twice as hard to be treated half as equal. I've been propositioned, pinched, pawed, gawked at, minimized, ostracized, marginalized and on a good day merely branded a lesbian. We get the end of the barrel assignments, passed over for promotions, reproached for our ideas, and endure relentless condescension for our opinions. A female agent once suffered second-degree burns when a meth lab she was investigating exploded. Instead of going to the hospital, a sign of weakness, she returned to the office with her blouse in shreds. She crossed a room full of male agents who lasciviously stared at her. The next day, her supervisor called her in to reprimand her for parading around the office disrobed. Her co-workers were so distracted by bare female skin that they couldn't function for the rest of the day."

Mackey realized he had been holding his breath and exhaled.

"I still take pride in working for the bureau. Fidelity, Bravery and Integrity aren't just clever uses of the acronym. I take them to heart. As an American and as a woman."

She tossed him what she was reading and marched off. It was a sequel to the *New York Times* article about Joseph Erekat that he'd seen the day before. He skimmed through it. New was that Erekat had an illness compatible with cutaneous anthrax in the summer of 2001 and had willingly submitted a blood sample. His computer was seized and his apartment swabbed for spores.

When Charo returned Mackey tried another subject. "Any luck lately seducing pervs?"

Charo frowned. "Erekat doesn't fit the psychological profile, have sufficient knowledge of anthrax or a believable motive. I spoke with one of the female agents who interviewed him. She described a frightened yet cooperative young man. He knew nothing of anthrax or bioweapons and the Palestinian angle is a stretch. I fear we are heading down the wrong path again."

"Damn. So let's solve this," Mackey said pulling out his laptop and opening the photo of Farrington's wedding announcement. "This photo of John Farrington is from the late '90s. See any resemblance to the image of the man from the gun shop?"

Charo slid over and studied the photo for a moment. "Do you have a wireless signal in here?"

"No. Maybe by the windows?" Mackey began walking toward the daylight and then out the door, his laptop a divining rod for the flow of the information highway. Charo followed. Mackey found a signal halfway down the block outside a café. He sat on the sidewalk with his back to the front window. Charo took a seat next to him and reached for the laptop and logged into the FBI's facial recognition program.

"What program is that?"

"ILEFIS. The Integrated Law Enforcement Facial Identification System. It's a software program designed to analyze surveillance video. For each of sixty-four different facial features it assigns a variant, like alleles in DNA analysis. There are as many as 256 variants for some features. For example, with a nose, there are varying shapes and lengths. The program then compares the image to those in the national database or in our case the wedding announcement photo since it is of better quality than the VP staff photo. Because it uses 3D technology and coverts physical features to numerical data it is extremely fast and can handle angles of view up to 35 degrees."

"Astounding. But it looks like it didn't work?"

"ILEFIS couldn't identify enough facial features from the video to do a match. It must be the hat and the angle. I can override the default setting and see what it returns, but the margin of error will be high," said Charo as she continued typing. "Yup. There is a 47-percent likelihood that the two images are the same person with a ± 33-percent margin of error."

"Not much use," Mackey said. They got up and walked back to the bar.

"No, it isn't. I'm convinced there is sufficient evidence to prove Lavigne was murdered, but these photos aren't enough to implicate Farrington. Besides, what reason would Farrington have to kill Lavigne and send the anthrax letters?" Charo replied.

"The anthrax letters coincided with the debate over the Patriot Act. Attorney General Ashcroft gave Congress a week to pass the legislation, adding that any subsequent act of terrorism would be on their heads if they did not act in all due haste. Senators Daschle and Leahy stood in the way of the expansion of government powers."

"Even if the anthrax letters were an act of foreign terrorism the Patriot Act would not have prevented them."

"True, but that may not have been the conclusion drawn by the American public. I don't think it was a coincidence that the Patriot Act was passed days after postal workers died from inhalation anthrax. The letters achieved one of Mailthrax's goals."

"One of his goals?" Charo inquired.

"The desire to invade Iraq and rid the world of Saddam Hussain predates 9/11."

"Patriot Act, going to war in Iraq, anything else you figure was on Mailthtrax's wish list, Mackey?"

"War profiteering."

A waitress dressed in a Cloche hat, shapeless dress, and baggy silk stockings came by to take their order.

"Do you have Sam Adams on tap?"

"Yes."

"I'll have one. Charo?"

"I'm good."

"Halliburton reportedly received $6 billion in contracts and that was just in the first two years of the Iraq War," Mackey continued.

Charo nodded slowly. "What physical evidence do we have to link Farrington to the mailings?"

"Someone from the VP's office made trips to South Jersey consistent with when the letters were mailed."

"That's not much."

"I still think we should try to get at those motor-pool records."

"Doubt there's sufficient probable cause to get a subpoena. Then there's executive privilege."

"Yes, the cloak of national security. Farrington is a Pentagon and CIA insider. He may have been aware of or involved with the secret bioweapons projects including Project Black Death."

"But how did he get his hands on the anthrax spores?" Charo asked.

"You'd think someone would notice they were missing."

"Lavigne noticed. There's your motive for murder and a frame job."

"That reminds me, I received a reply from Armadillo90210." Mackey showed Charo the one-line message.

"Did you reply?"

"No. I am not totally convinced that Armadillo90210 isn't responsible for what happened to Lavigne. He was killed days after the cryptic email warning him not to go out into the desert without a hat."

"I believe the message was not to go *digging* in the Nevada desert without a *mask*," corrected Charo. "What do you suppose that means?"

"That something bad is buried there. I was able to trace the origin of Armadillo90210's emails to the National Library of Congress."

"Impressive," Charo said.

"I have an idea for how we might discover Armadillo90210's identity and force a meeting," he offered.

"Why am I not surprised?"

Mackey took a few swigs of beer and regarded the bar patrons. He and Charo drew less attention from them than the vending machines.

"First, we go to the Library of Congress. We ask to see surveillance tapes of the computer station used at the time of the reply to my email. Maybe someone will recognize the person. If we don't immediately get identification from the video we send Armadillo90210 a reply that I, I mean you, are an FBI agent investigating Lavigne's death in connection with Project Black Death. We set up surveillance with the Library of Congress security and monitor their computer system for a reply from that email account. When Armadillo90210 shows up to reply we nab him!"

Charo considered Mackey's plan at length. She had to admit it was clever and she couldn't foresee any problems. But it meant another trip to Washington.

"I can't go until Saturday. And we'll have to get a rental, I can't use a bureau car again."

"Oh, and there's one more stop in Washington we need to make. The State Department," Mackey said.

"The State Department?"

"Embassies are under the State Department."

"And embassies connect to this investigation how?"

"I admit it's a long shot but early in 2002 a tip was submitted to a US embassy that the anthrax used in the mailings came from the US desert."

Mackey vaulted the stoop stairs three at a time. He cheered his empty mailbox. When he slid the key in the deadbolt it wouldn't turn, but the doorknob spun freely and the door swung open. He remained standing in the hall peering in. The super had a copy of his key but he couldn't think of a reason why he would have entered his apartment and then leave it unlocked. He reassured himself that an intruder laying in wait would lock the door, too. He flicked on the light. Nothing appeared disturbed. He grabbed a baseball bat from behind the door and cleared each room. It was when he returned to the foyer and bent over to untie his shoes that he saw a red strand lying across the threshold. Under a magnifying glass it had a uniform diameter. Not a human hair. The only red article of clothing he owned was a tie but when he compared it to the fiber it didn't match. It probably blew in from the hall he thought. Mackey slept with one eye open anyway.

.| 27 |.

Mackey spent time in the Rose Room of the New York Public Library's Humanities and Social Sciences Library until Charo could leave town. He had a copy of a journal article open detailing the FBI laboratory methods used to find the Leahy letter. Knowing what they now know, the science failed to hold his interest. Surrounded as he was by young studious women his mind drifted.

Mackey's career path nearly took him into surgery. While in medical school, a fifth-year surgical resident, Dr. Armand Lefaunt, took a liking to him. Mackey believed it was because he mastered the one-handed suture tie before Lefaunt had readied the scissor to cut. Lefaunt did his best to convince Mackey to join the ranks but in the end Mackey's career path was decided by his impatience. The shortest route through the torment of overnight hospital call and the thirty-six-hour shifts of residency training was three years in internal medicine.

Perhaps the real reason he got along well with Dr. Lefaunt was a shared passion for girl watching. Meals during residency were taken whenever and wherever the work allowed. But Lefaunt insisted that his team eat lunch together every day, provided, of course, he didn't find an extra case to scrub in on. They regularly commandeered a table near the back of the cafeteria where they could see women entering from the right or left as well as those exiting the lunch line with their trays. It was always Lefaunt who offered up a sculpture for review. He'd jab a fork filled with potato or chicken in the general direction of the woman and utter, "*Ah, mon ami, regardez cette femme.*" Words Mackey understood despite three years of German.

Mackey would attempt a subtle gaze, with no disrespect to Allie, and share a succinct assessment like "nice buns," or "spectacular cheekbones" to which Lefaunt would boisterously concur. The rest of the team remained silent. The sub-intern was a pasty lad one year ahead of Mackey who was too stressed over getting a surgical residency spot that he never removed his nose from the *Sabiston Textbook of Surgery*. The first-year intern was a comely woman named Slocum who had yet to shed her freshman fifteen and cultivated the appearance of an art history professor. She wore her hair wound in a taunt bun at the top of her head and eschewed contact lenses for spectacles of Teddy Roosevelt vintage. Rounding out the team was a radiology resident who hardly ate and was in constant fear that someone would ask him a question or slap a retractor in his hand.

On one particular slow morning, when patient discharges moved slower than the line at the DMV, they were gathered in the cafeteria before lunch discussing how to decompress their census full of diverticulitis, wound dehiscence, and diabetic ulcers when a bewitching hospital administrator strode in. Having no fork with which to signal, Lefaunt elbowed Mackey and nodded to the left. In doing so he noted that Slocum, in response to his ogling, was concentrating on a collection of crumbs left over from breakfast. Being the Renaissance man that he was, Lefaunt recognized her discomfort and at their next meal apologized for his chauvinistic behavior and vowed that the team would amend their salacious ways.

Slocum found it all amusing. Nevertheless, Lefaunt was not to be denied his chivalry. When the next curvaceous nurse bounced by their table Lefaunt commanded all to, "Look at your plate!" The raucous laughter that ensued had the opposite effect than intended; drawing stares from nearby tables at their odd behavior of examining their meals as if an image of George Carlin had appeared in the mashed potatoes. It likewise did little to comfort the passing women who suddenly realized they were the objects of the affliction. However, for the team's remaining time together, it became their mantra. Thereafter, whenever a woman—any woman—passed by and a head dared to turn, all those present were implored to give the plates their utmost attention.

Mackey's cell phone vibrated. It was Charo.

"What are you doing?" she asked playfully.

"Looking at my plate," he replied. The line went quiet.

"I am reading about—"

"I just got off the phone with Wexler Barnes," she interrupted. "Do you have a passport?"

"Wexler who?"

"Barnes, at the State Department. Passport?"

"Yes, I have a passport. You're talking about a destination other than Washington?"

"Kazakhstan."

"Kazakhstan?"

"Meet me at my place at eight tonight and I'll explain."

Mackey pocketed his phone before the security guard spotted him and typed Kazakhstan into Google uncertain which "Stan" it was while wondering if Charo was pulling his leg. Kazakhstan was the largest landlocked country in the world and anchored the lands between Russia and China. Mackey was hardly comforted to learn the government was stable.

. . .

Queasiness dueled déjà vu for control of Mackey's midbrain as Charo swung the rented Dodge Neon onto the ramp leading to the Holland tunnel. He focused on the car ahead hoping Charo would maintain a safe but constant distance so his motion sickness would abate. The Neon's interior felt like the inside of an egg and his brain the yolk sac swinging back and forth. It didn't help that the curvature of the tunnel created an optical distortion that made it difficult to see straight. They exited the tunnel in time to keep his breakfast from doing the same.

Two nights earlier, over cold sesame noodles and warm Kirin beer, Charo had explained that she contacted the State Department about the embassy desert tip and was put in touch with Wexler Barnes. He agreed to assist in finding the Kazakh man who filed the odd claim for the reward money and advised that a visit would be necessary. He provided Charo the name of Anatoly Zlotnikov to serve as Mackey's interpreter and guide.

Barnes was with the US consulate in 1995 as part of the Department of Defense's Biologic Threat Reduction Program. Charo relayed to Mackey that Kazakhstan's president was eager to deal the kilos of weapons-grade uranium, fighter planes, and bioweapons machinery in exchange for grants to convert its factories of mass destruction to producers of drugs and vaccines.

While in Kazakhstan, Barnes was invited to tour Stepnogorsk, the former jewel of the Biopreparat Program and the world's most prolific manufacturer of death in a vial. This is how he came to meet and become friends with an unlikely ally, Major General Anatoly Zlotnikov, Deputy Commander of the Stepnogorsk facility.

Mackey had packed his duffle bag full with misgivings.

Charo parked a block from FBI headquarters. "I need to retrieve a package. Barnes was going to forward me instructions, your ticket, cash, and how to contact Zlotnikov. I'll be a minute, okay if you wait here?"

Mackey was still uneasy. He very much wanted to discuss the plan face-to-face with Barnes. But it was looking like he was going to have to take his chances with the Kazakhs.

"Sure."

At the entrance to the J. Edgar Hoover building Charo stopped in her tracks. A row of television vans clustered like penguins against a harsh wind. The path seemed clear but she proceeded with caution. The guard gave her a wink and filled her in on the situation. It was a press conference to present breaking news on the new Amerithrax suspect. Although he was under twenty-four-hour surveillance, Joseph Erekat had disappeared and was believed to have fled the country. Charo tiptoed into the back of the conference room unnoticed as Deputy Director Adrian Pastore introduced SAC Martinez to the press corps. Martinez stepped confidently to the lectern. He wore a crisp, tan suit with a starched white shirt and blue necktie with red stars. His close-cropped hair was finely moussed, and mustache trimmed. He adjusted the microphone to his height. The sole hint of nervousness was the way he jiggled his left wrist to free his watch.

"Good afternoon, ladies and gentlemen, and thank you for coming today. My name is Calvin Martinez and I am the special agent in charge of the Amerithrax investigation. We've invited the media here today to brief you on some breaking news in the investigation and to answer some of your questions."

Charo smiled. Martinez had offered to answer *some* of the media's questions.

"As announced last week, the FBI has been investigating a suspect in the anthrax letter mailings and we are close to an arrest. The suspect, Mr. Joseph Erekat, is an instructor of microbiology at Rutgers University. In the summer of 2001, Mr. Erekat was an intern at USAMRIID in Fort Detrick. While he was not working with anthrax, he was in the same facility where the anthrax stocks were stored. Through the new technology of forensic microbiology we have been able to trace the anthrax used in the 2001 bioterrorism attacks to two labs in the United States: the US Army Proving Ground at Dugway in Utah and USAMRIID in Fort Detrick, Maryland. We have thoroughly investigated everyone who had access to these locations and have been able to rule out every person except Mr. Erekat. For the past nine months we have focused the investigation on Mr. Erekat and I will now present to you the evidence which we believe points to Mr. Erekat, and only Mr. Erekat, as the anthrax mailer."

"One. Mr. Erekat is an American citizen of Palestinian descent. His father is a professor of Middle Eastern studies at Princeton University and has been a frequent and outspoken speaker on Palestinian issues. As a young child, Joseph met a number of Palestinian statesmen, including Yasser Arafat. We believe that these early experiences and the frequent topic of Palestinian independence in his home helped form his beliefs."

"Two. While in college, Mr. Erekat joined the Palestinian Independence Freedom Foundation or PIFF. PIFF is an organization whose mission is to create an independent Palestinian state. Mr. Erekat participated in several protests organized by PIFF in Washington and New York. During one protest in New York several PIFF members were arrested. Mr. Erekat was not one of them."

"Three. In the fall of 2000, Mr. Erekat traveled to Lebanon, a country known to harbor terrorist organizations."

"Four. Mr. Erekat is well acquainted with Princeton through his father's job and was a legal resident of

Plainsboro, a suburb of Princeton at the time of the anthrax mailings."

"Five. In July 2001, Mr. Erekat was seen in the emergency department of a New Jersey hospital for an infection of his right lower extremity. He was treated with antibiotics and recovered. He stated he injured his leg while wind surfing in Sandy Hook Bay. During an interview we conducted in 2005 with the physician who treated Mr. Erekat, the wound was described as swollen and inflamed with a black scab. After being shown pictures of cutaneous anthrax the physician could not rule out anthrax as the diagnosis. No culture or other specimens were taken at the time."

"Six. A search of Mr. Erekat's family home found pre-stamped envelopes of the same size used in the anthrax mailings."

"Seven. The FBI has learned that Mr. Erekat attended Greentown Elementary School when his family lived on Cloverdale Road in Biloxi, Mississippi. You may recall the return address on the anthrax letters mailed to Senators Daschle and Leahy bore the fictitious address of Greendale Elementary School, a combination of Mr. Erekat's former school and home address."

"This concludes the presentation of evidence against Joseph Erekat. Mr. Erekat has been under twenty-four-hour surveillance for the past month. On Wednesday, an agent followed him from his home to his office at Rutgers University. At oh-nine-forty-five hours he left that office with a box of his belongings. He returned to the building after which the agent did not see him leave and was subsequently unable to pick up his trail. Searches for Mr. Erekat have not located his whereabouts. We now believe he has left the United States. We are confident he was not able to leave by plane and believe he may have fled to Canada. We are working with Canadian authorities to locate Mr. Erekat and return him to the United States. We will now be happy to take questions."

What followed Martinez's last syllable was akin to a school of piranhas hearing the splash of a boar in the Amazon River. The intense heat from the dozen camera lights added to the rain forest feel.

"Agent Martinez! Agent Martinez!" an excited pony-tailed reporter yelled as she waved her note pad. "Back during the outbreak, the CDC tested the blood of sick patients to detect anthrax antibodies. In your evidence you suggest that Mr. Erekat may have had cutaneous anthrax. Did Mr. Erekat submit to blood tests and can you share with us the results of those tests?"

Martinez had stepped back from the microphone to allow Deputy Director Pastore to take charge. He now edged forward to speak into Pastore's ear. Pastore whispered considerably longer into Martinez's ear before he stepped into the background.

"Mr. Erekat did submit blood for testing. Our colleagues at the CDC have informed us that these tests are not infallible and it is not clear how long antibodies remain after a skin infection. It was over four years after his leg infection that Mr. Erekat was tested and he did not have any measurable antibodies. The CDC is planning to repeat and confirm these test results."

"Can you confirm that Mr. Erekat submitted to and passed a polygraph test?"

Martinez cleared his throat and adjusted his tie. "Mr. Erekat is an accomplished, long-distance runner. His resting heart rate is fifty-four beats per minute and he has a subnormal blood pressure. He did pass the polygraph test, however we are determining whether his athletic conditioning may have allowed him to beat the system."

"Wow, this is not going well," Charo uttered louder than she had intended, attracting the attention of a cameraman near the back of the room. She slipped off her ID and hid it in her palm.

"Agent Martinez, I have two questions."

Charo recognized the woman as a *Washington Post* investigative reporter. Martinez was beginning to sweat. Charo saw he was fighting the urge to reach for his handkerchief, but was forced to relent as a bead of sweat was poised to careen down his nose. The reporter paused, drawing attention to the wipe.

"Agent Martinez, you indicated that Mr. Erekat has fled the US. As I understand, he was not under arrest so wasn't he free to go as he pleased?"

"The FBI suggested that he not leave the state."

"But that suggestion does not have the binding effect of law, does it?"

"No, it does not."

"My second question is about Mr. Erekat's trip to Lebanon. Do you have any information about what he did while there or if he met with anyone known to be a member of a terrorist cell?"

Charo knew by the way she asked the question that she already knew the answer even if Martinez did not. For effect she was making him tell the world.

"We were told the purpose of the trip was to attend a relative's wedding. We have no evidence that at either of the places Mr. Erekat attended he was in or out of the company of an operative of a terrorism cell."

"Thank you, Agent Martinez."

More shouting ensued.

"Can you place Mr. Erekat in Princeton on the days the letters were believed to have been mailed?"

"We are still checking his alibi."

The reporter followed-up. "What about his activity in the weeks before and after the attacks? Any suspicious activity? Late nights in the lab? Nervousness? Retreat from social interactions as suggested by the psychological profile posted on the FBI's website?"

"Not that we have been able to determine thus far. The investigation is ongoing," Martinez replied.

"Have you searched for evidence of anthrax spores at Mr. Erekat's office, lab, home, or car?" asked a portly *New York Times* reporter.

"Please remember it has been many years since the attacks. We did perform testing and did not expect to find any spores. We did not find any."

More beads of sweat were forming, now beneath his nose and across his forehead. The next wipe would be the dreaded mop across the forehead associated with politicians admitting to infidelity, hedge fund mangers of embezzlement, and chief operating officers of safety report cover-ups. To his credit, Martinez didn't do the usual obfuscation dance so often performed by government spokespersons. He answered all the questions directly, offered no vague responses, and didn't hide behind the cloak of classified material.

"Do the records indicate that Erekat, while an intern at USAMRIID, had…"

Charo had heard enough. Her plan was to check her email, pick up the package from Barnes, and exit unnoticed. She got up to leave and caught Martinez's attention. He suddenly looked pale, his eyes dull and lifeless like those of an antelope in the jaws of a lion. When their eyes met his flashed briefly, as if he was going to call out to her. Charo broke away and ducked between two cameras and into the hallway

Mackey awoke at the sound of the car door opening. Charo handed him the package. "Good news, you are flying first-class to London."

Mackey examined the package's contents. Charo failed to mention that the flight from London to Kazakhstan was on a US Army cargo plane. He found contact information for Zlotnikov and an envelope stuffed with 100-dollar bills.

"That's for Zlotnikov," Charo said.

Charo flashed her badge at the Library of Congress security officer. "Where is your chief's office?"

They followed his crooked thumb down a corridor. The head of security was a fiftyish woman named Margaret Westheimer. On her wall was a highly decorated photograph of her in an Army major dress uniform. She welcomed them into her compact and tidy office. Westheimer studied their identification badges before asking what she could do to assist them. Her keen blue eyes focused on Charo as she explained why they had reason to believe a witness had sent an email from one of the Library of Congress computers. Mackey handed her a printout of Armadillo90210's last email with the computer's IP address highlighted in yellow. Westheimer struck some keys then spun the monitor so Mackey and Charo could see. The screen was split into six panels, each showing a view from a different camera. At the bottom of each panel was the location, frame number, time, and date.

Westheimer pointed to panel four. "This one has that IP address." The workstation was empty. She hit a key and camera four filled the screen.

"What was the date and time of that email?"

Mackey consulted his notes. "This past Monday, at 11:54:23."

Westheimer tapped the keys. The images flickered like Keystone Kops fixing a flat tire. At 11:47:50 a middle-aged, red-haired woman sat down at the computer in panel four.

"Armadillo is a woman?" Mackey replied with surprise.

"Do you recognize her?" Charo asked.

"No, ma'am," replied Westheimer.

The red-haired woman remained at the computer station past noon. They continued to watch. At 12:10:19 she left but did not appear in any of the other panels. By 12:30:00 they still did not see her again.

"Can we print that frame from panel four?" asked Charo.

Westheimer printed out the image then escorted them to the reading room where the computer terminals resided. She approached the reference desk and approached the young man who sat there.

"Good afternoon, Tom. How is your day going?" Before he could answer she handed him the image. "Do you recognize this woman?"

"That looks like Mrs. Monroe, the Pentagon librarian. Why?"

"What is her first name?" Charo asked.

"Vivien."

"What's our next move," Mackey asked as they headed back to the car. "Call her at the Pentagon and tell her we are on to her and force her to meet us in a Georgetown bar? Or, we could stake out the Pentagon parking lot and ambush her."

"Mackey, it's Saturday. We need to make what in your business would be referred to as a house call."

A phone call later Charo had an address for Vivien Monroe. Sleepy Hollow Manor did its somnambulistic best to live up to the moniker. Cookie-cutter, single-family homes on well-manicured, quarter-acre lots. The few trees and shrubs dotting the thin landscape did as much as they could, the bad comb-over to a barren pate. It was a vision of suburbia that evoked in Mackey both fond and anxious memories of his Baltimore childhood. It was almost four o'clock when they pulled up to 301 Patrick Henry Drive. A rusted Toyota was parked in the drive.

Charo rang the bell. When she pressed it a second time, Mackey leaned an ear close.

"I don't think it works."

Charo knocked hard. The window drape drew aside, revealing the face of the woman from the Library of

Congress security video. The door unlatched. Vivien Monroe's hair was tied back by a scarf and her eyes sparkled at the prospect of company.

"We are here to speak with Mrs. Vivien Monroe," Charo said.

"I'm Mrs. Monroe."

When Charo flashed her badge Mrs. Monroe's demeanor changed. Her eyebrows pinched and her pale complexion whitened even more.

"We'd like to speak with you about Dr. Arthur Lavigne," Charo explained. At the sound of Arthur Lavigne's name all the wrinkles in Mrs. Monroe's face deepened and she blushed crimson.

"Please come in," she replied in a slight southern drawl, her composure and complexion recovered. They followed her as she led them to a sitting room.

She motioned to the sofa. "Please make yourself comfortable. I'll just be a moment with some refreshments." She disappeared through the doorway.

Mackey tapped Charo's thigh and nodded after Mrs. Monroe. "Think she's heading for the back door?"

"Give her a minute."

Mrs. Monroe returned with a tray, three glasses, a pitcher of iced tea, and a plateful of cookies. She sat down, poured them each a glass with a sprig of mint leaf, then one for herself. She took a dainty sip and placed the glass on a coaster on a lamp table. She sat straight-backed in the chair facing them, her hands folded over her lap.

Charo took this as her cue to begin. "Mrs. Monroe, we are investigating the death of Dr. Arthur Lavigne. Were you acquainted with the deceased either professionally or personally?"

"Oh, my, no. Not personally. Professionally only."

"How did you come to be acquainted with Dr. Lavigne?"

"I am an assistant librarian at the Pentagon," she said pausing to smile. "Dr. Lavigne used to write letters and send emails to the Pentagon. Colonel Seaford Johnston would ask me to research some of the things in Dr. Lavigne's letters."

"What did Lavigne write about?" interjected Mackey.

"He was trying to convince the Pentagon that they should take germ weapons more seriously. He sent citations from microbiology journals, mostly foreign publications. I would have to locate them and arrange for translation."

She stopped and took another sip of tea. Mackey had already drained his and was munching on his second cookie. Charo's glass was untouched.

"Please continue," urged Charo.

"After a while, Colonel Johnston asked me to respond directly to Dr. Lavigne's emails. I guess you could say we struck up a correspondence. He suspected the government was hiding bioweapons research. Research he felt was dangerous."

"Did Dr. Lavigne ever ask you about a CIA/Department of Defense project called Black Death?"

Mrs. Monroe regarded her folded hands. She rotated the bracelet on her wrist until the setting faced up. "No."

The pause that ensued hung like a cumulonimbus of guilt. As the silence stretched Mrs. Monroe appeared to be lost in painful recollection. She smoothed the hair behind her ear with a veined hand. The corners of her mouth pressed downward. She stared into Charo's eyes, her own were moist.

"It was me. I told Dr. Lavigne about Project Black Death."

Mrs. Monroe told them that the Pentagon Library was damaged on 9/11 and moved to a temporary space. After the move, she found at the bottom of a stack of periodicals a report that was not catalogued. It was not uncommon for some of the 70,000 holdings to go missing or show up in unusual locations, but something about this report troubled her. It bore no author or agency identification and although it was marked as top secret and classified, it was printed on plain paper without a binder or cover. She catalogued and filed it, but with Dr. Lavigne's warnings she could not get it out of her mind. She found herself unconsciously wandering in the stacks, coming to a stop where she had shelved it.

"The frightening thing was that it was precisely what Dr. Lavigne had warned about, but I am quite sure he knew nothing about it before I informed him of its existence. My nephew helped me set up the anonymous email account. It's the one I used to communicate with Dr. Lavigne, and what I presume has led you to me."

Mrs. Monroe went on to further explain that Project Black Death made use of technology developed by other secret defensive projects. Project Black Death succeeded in creating an ultra-potent and completely unauthorized biological weapon. The last thing she revealed to Dr. Lavigne was that after reaching a successful conclusion, Project Black Death reportedly buried its terrible product in the Nevada desert.

Mrs. Monroe was sobbing softly. She dabbed at her tears with a lace handkerchief.

"Mrs. Monroe, one more question. Where is the report on Project Black Death now?" Charo asked.

"Gone, I'm afraid. Last time I was in that part of the collection I noticed it was missing. It hasn't shown up since."

"Do you know when it disappeared?"

"No, not exactly. Perhaps in November or December of 2001? It is all my fault. I wanted Dr. Lavigne to know he was right. That the United States government was breaking the law and the treaty. I should have never told him about the report. I should've never involved him. It's because of me that he is dead."

"You don't know that," Mackey said.

Mrs. Monroe excused herself. Mackey waited until she was out of earshot.

"If Lavigne was killed because he knew about Project Black Death, how did his murderer find this out?"

"Recall that Lavigne was a suspect in the Amerithrax investigation. We were monitoring his emails."

"Are you suggesting someone at the FBI leaked the information?"

Mrs. Monroe returned. They thanked her and she led them out. Mackey could tell Charo was working something out in her mind. Perhaps the implication of a FBI leak or that the nearer they got to nabbing Mailthrax the greater the jeopardy they might be placing Mrs. Monroe's life in. Their own too.

.| 28 |.

Mackey was staring at a bowl of pickled vegetables. He was thinking about Alaska. The place where the visions of Allison in the shape of other women finally ceased.

"You've been staring at that pickle for a long while. Do you want one?" Charo asked.

"No thanks. If I understand this, Wexler Barnes, after hearing our evidence decides to assist, makes flight accommodations, and gives us $10,000 in cash to purchase the services of an ex-Soviet Ministry of Defense major?"

"Right. And you leave tonight."

"Charo, doesn't any of this seem at all peculiar to you? We aren't even part of the official investigation."

"Wexler explained it this way—there is a military transport plane leaving England tomorrow making stops in Germany and Pakistan, the stop in Kazakhstan is along the route. Zlotnikov is on a State Department contract to facilitate the dismantling and conversion of old bioweapons plants for civilian use. I got the impression they use Zlotnikov for 'other projects' but Barnes didn't elaborate. The money is payment due to Zlotnikov, or an advance, or something like that. Barnes wasn't too clear on it."

"But who are you to Barnes? I mean, how does he know you are who you say you are?"

"He's ex-CIA and the right-hand man of the Undersecretary of State for Arms Control and International Security. I'm sure he verified my identity before I finished saying my name."

"And the money?"

"Discretionary funds, small tomatoes. Oh, and he asked that we brief him on what you find out as soon as you get back."

"You've heard of Iran-Contra haven't you?"

"Try not to be so paranoid, Mackey."

"And what is it I am going there to find? We already know about Project Black Death."

"We have no proof, Mackey. The report in all likelihood has been destroyed. All we have is Lavigne's anonymous email account and the word of a librarian. We need to connect Project Black Death to a name," Charo explained.

"Farrington?"

"Whoever is responsible for Lavigne's murder and perhaps the anthrax letters."

"And you think an old man in Kazakhstan can do that?" Mackey asked.

"We've run out of trails to follow. Besides, Barnes must think we're on to something."

"I don't know, Charo. There is something I didn't tell you," Mackey hesitated. "After that night at Capone's, when I got home, I found my door unlocked."

"You had an intruder? Charo asked.

"I don't know. My apartment was empty but I found a red fiber. It didn't match to any of my clothes."

"Was anything missing?"

"No, I don't think so. And remember how as soon as we started making progress with the investigation I learned that the funding for my new job was held up in Washington."

"You think there is a connection?"

"I'm *worried* there is a connection," Mackey said regretting how paranoid he sounded.

"Well, not to alarm you but I've got another coincidence for you. Farrington and Martinez were classmates at Princeton."

“There are too many coincidences for them to be coincidences,” Mackey fretted.

“Finish eating. We’ve got to get you a toothbrush before your flight.”

.| 29 |.

The British Airways 747 jumbo jet pushed away from the gate shortly before midnight. As soon as it cleared the runway Mackey saw ocean then blue-blackness. He vaguely remembered the sun coming up between naps and the first class hostess covering him with a blanket. On the next leg of his journey he was strapped to a sidewall seat of the C-17 military cargo plane flying over the English Channel. The rumbling in his stomach reminded him that he'd missed breakfast and lunch. He also forgot to bring Xanax. After a brief stopover in Wiesbaden, Germany, he was again clutching the straps and hyperventilating as they thundered on to Kazakhstan.

He arrived in Almaty two calendar days after leaving New York. The letter from the State Department and $10,000 in cash stroked chins at customs but afforded him the courtesy of a US diplomat. As luck would have it, the Alm-Ata Hotel had the Internet registration Charo made and allowed him to check in early. Dmitry, the desk clerk, concierge, and porter guided Mackey to his room. After depositing Mackey's lone bag on the bed Dmitry gave him a double thumbs up sign. Mackey fumbled to figure a tip in tenge. The jetlag, lack of sleep, and a threatening tsunami of a headache befuddled his math. Dmitri ended Mackey's misery by plucking a five-dollar American note from his billfold.

Barnes gave instructions for Mackey to meet Zlotnikov at the Medeo skating rink the next day, October 10th, at noon. He stepped out into the bright afternoon sunshine of what would pass for Indian summer in the Northeast. The snow-capped Tien Shan Mountains to the south reminded him of the Chugach range in Alaska. But it wasn't the scenery that transported him back in time. It had taken two years in Alaska's vastness to crystallize his loneliness into a cold, blue lump that he carried around in his chest, but it took barely fifty-five minutes in Kazakhstan to provoke that same feeling.

An ethnic Kazakh woman had spread her wares for sale on a ragged blanket placed on the sidewalk in front of his hotel. It was a pedestrian assortment: a hairbrush, cracked mirror, worn-leather jacket, a woman's summer dress, and bottles of vodka; not the pirated videos familiar to Mackey from the streets of New York. She displayed each item with a bow and a wave of an arthritic hand.

Mackey's feet took him to Panfilov Park. At the end of a flower-lined path he came to a monument. The central statue was nearly as wide as the square and carved to resemble the Soviet Union. Emerging from the granite were the coarsely chiseled faces of soldiers, more skeleton than human. From the region of the Kazakhstan steppes burst forth a Herculean fighter with his chest thrust forward, shielding the republic from harm.

Hearing music, Mackey turned to see two young men perched on the base of another statue playing string instruments. He then became aware of a presence, someone standing close behind. Watching him. He wheeled around.

"Hello. I am Turgalev Pyak. You are American?"

"Yes. You speak English?"

"Of course. I learned English to attend university in the United States."

Turgalev explained that the men were playing traditional dombras. The dombra was the color and shape of a halved gourd, and emitted a curious, yet infectious sound. Two strings passed over the small hole of the resonant chamber and then ran up a long, narrow neck to the head. The melody was a blend of flamenco and sitar, and the range made the six-string guitar seem opulent.

"Are you in Almaty on business?"

Mackey didn't know how to answer the question. Was this business? "No, I am visiting a friend," he replied.

The young man seemed disappointed. "I went to university in the United States to learn business and I am wanting investors. I plan to manufacture computers and Internet phones right here in Kazakhstan, like Apple, Dell, and Gateway did in the United States. We have cheap labor, plenty of raw materials, and an emerging market. I see the company as a supplier of inexpensive portable computers to the all of the Commonwealth States, Europe, and some day maybe the world."

Mackey had to hand it to the young man, he had vision and a persuasive sales pitch. He considered investing if the company ever went public.

"Do you have a name for your start-up?"

"Koryosaram Computers."

"Koryosaram?"

"The Koryo Saram are Korean refugees. We fled the Japanese into Far East Russia. Stalin did not trust our loyalty and we were forced to move to Kazakhstan. During the war we were put into labor camps, like your Nisei. For fifty years we have been working to regain our status. I am fortunate and received a Muskie Foundation Fellowship to learn business at Vanderbilt University. I have been back home now for one year driving a cab until I can find enough investors."

"Why did you come back?"

"Kazakhstan is my home. There is much opportunity here. My family is here."

"You are not bitter over being exiled twice?"

"Kazakhstan is a country of exiles. Stalin was a despot and xenophile. He exiled many people to

Kazakhstan—the Poles, Latvians, Lithuanians, Estonians, and Volga Germans from the border regions; the Chechens, Ingush, Kalmyk, Karachi, the Balkars from the Caucasus; the Tartars from the Crimea; and the Turks from Georgia. Dostoevsky, Godinov, Trotsky, and Solzhenitsyn were all exiled—to Kazakhstan! I am in excellent company."

Mackey was thinking about exiles when a wiffleball rolled to a stop at his feet. He picked it up and examined it; the ball was just like he remembered from his youth. Half solid plastic, half oval holes. He adjusted his grip and tossed it to the boy running toward him. The boy froze as the ball curved and sailed past him. The kid ran after it, picked it up, and turned the ball over several times in his hands. He ran over and spoke a few words that Mackey didn't understand. He then placed the ball in Mackey's hand and imitated the flight of the ball. Mackey demonstrated the grip and pitching motion, then backed up so the kid could take a try. The kid tossed the ball, which whistled and darted away from Mackey and landed in the grass. Before Mackey could fetch it the kid sprinted past him, scooped up the ball, and returned to a clearing in the trees where his large comrade stood laughing with a plastic bat over his shoulder. Mackey hung around long enough to watch the boy pitch three perfect curveballs that dove under the oversized swings of the boy's Ruthian playmate.

On the way back to the hotel Mackey passed a couple in the glassy-eyed throes of new love. Something he had felt with Allie every day he had her in his life. If Allie hadn't had a miscarriage his child would be about the same age as the boys in the park. Behind that sealed porthole was another lake of guilt, which roiled whenever he thought it was for the best. He was in no condition to be a father, but did wonder if the loss had precipitated Allie's disappearance. He felt the tightness in his chest before Darden Smith's words about love's wounds reminded him of the depth of his loss[11]."

Mackey had dinner at the hotel restaurant and tried to retire early. While he could easily attribute the insomnia to the change in time zones and interruption of his circadian rhythm, he knew it had more to do with the room. The ultra-soft bed had put an apple-sized knot in his back. The room was stuffy and reeked of stale tobacco and cabbage. The one small window provided no ventilation but admitted a squadron of mosquitoes who buzzed his ears in repeated attempts to land.

As he lay unable to sleep, staring at the ceiling fan and wishing that it worked, a coin dropped into his jukebox. Several bars from "Sleeping with the Lights On," reminded him that, dead or alive, he preferred to be with Allie[12].

He awoke with cinched halyards instead of back muscles and itchy ears. Mackey lumbered downstairs to the concierge desk. After several minutes of fruitless pantomime with the woman behind the desk, Mackey grabbed a pen and a napkin and did his best to draw a picture of a skating rink. The woman pulled from beneath the counter a bus schedule and circled the line Mackey needed to take him to the Medeo skating rink. Not knowing how long it would take, or how to ask this, Mackey decided to head off. The less time he spent walking around with 10,000 dead presidents in his pocket the better.

The route to the Medeo headed toward the mountains. Once outside the city limits the road split sparse grasslands interspersed with patches of desert. The bus driver and Mackey, his lone passenger, rode in silence. It was Ben Lee's song, "The Debt Collectors," that faded into his consciousness[13]. Mackey no longer begged for forgiveness, but did he keep a list of things he'd do just to feel like a whole person again.

As the bus climbed the steppe fell away in favor of more fertile-appearing land. They passed a horse then a sheep ranch. The bus stopped at random intervals, first to pick up an old woman and then an old man. The road narrowed. Farmland gave way to foothills dotted with tall, straight pine trees. The bus traversed wrought-iron bridges that spanned jagged streams trickling with mountain runoff. The pine trees grew more numerous. The hillsides were steep and the rock faces craggy. At each turn or bend another set of cliff formations emerged like cartoon rock creatures, shaking off the topsoil to become the walls of a narrow canyons.

The bus then slid around a curve to hug a precipice that opened onto a valley below. Mackey saw the skating rink ahead set in a basin crowned by brown mountain ridges. The driver turned off the highway and coasted down a gravel road to an empty parking lot. With a hiss of air brakes the bus came to a halt and let him off.

The gate to the rink was locked and the place deserted. Adding ten to the digits on his watch, Mackey determined he was about an hour early for his meeting. After scampering up a hillside he was treated to a panoramic view of the valley. He leaned against a boulder beneath a tree and inhaled deeply the pine-scented air. The wind rustling through the trees morphed into the voice of Paul Simon comparing Mackey to his igneous companion[14].

Car wheels on gravel awoke him. A young man got out, unlocked the skating rink's gate, went inside, and locked the gate behind him. Soon more employees arrived and then a van full of children. Mackey skidded down the hill and waited by the gate. Rock music blasted from tinny speakers as skaters took to the rink.

About the time the sun rolled up and over the zenith a dented Lada pulled into the parking lot. A man emerged that Mackey recognized as Anatoly Zlotnikov from the photograph sent by Wexler Barnes. He was short, stocky, with thinning brown hair, and oversized tortoise shell glasses. He approached like a terrapin taking a hairpin turn, his demeanor more at home at a Miami early-bird special than the rugged Kazakhstan countryside.

Mackey could see that Zlotnikov was sizing him up. Had he spoke Russian he would have known that the first thing Zlotnikov asked him was if he knew how to skate and not if he spoke Russian. Zlotnikov shrugged at Mackey's dumbfounded headshake no, then grabbed his hand in a firm, two-handed shake.

"Then you will learn," he said in Russian inflected English. "I am Major General Anatoly Zlotnikov, former deputy commander of Stepnogorsk, the fifteenth directorate of Biopreparat."

"Dr. MacPherson Dunn," Mackey replied.

"So, young man, you are a friend of Mr. Barnes?"

Mackey nodded. With a fatherly arm around his shoulder, Zlotnikov guided him into the skating rink.

.| 30 |.

Charo was fuming. Normally she was able to channel her anger into productive activities like boxing, but this was different. She couldn't figure out what to do. Lavigne's emails had been monitored and she was convinced someone inside the bureau had leaked them. The result was the professor's murder. It brought back memories of her first year with the FBI when the most atrocious espionage case in bureau history broke. Robert Hanssen, a twenty-five-year veteran, was arrested for selling classified US information to the Soviet Union.

What infuriated Charo the most about Hanssen was that he was neither a clever nor careful agent. He wasn't a super spy as the media portrayed him. No, the reason Hanssen wasn't caught sooner was due to FBI complacency. Hanssen had access to so much classified information in part because the FBI saw counterintelligence as the domain of weak men and women. If you weren't unholstering your weapon daily you might as well be wearing an apron, an apish male agent had enlightened Charo.

A month after graduating from Quantico and just beginning her career in counterintelligence, Charo attended a farewell party for the highest-ranking female agent in the NYC field office. The sparse turnout, mostly secretaries, puzzled her as she heard of the legendary send-off parties the field office was said to have thrown its retiring agents. Leonora Stump wasn't your ordinary put-in-your-twenty and then go fishing agent. Tough, smart, honest, and by the book even where a book didn't exist, she had made her share of arrests and moreover enemies within the bureau. Few were sad to see her go after a nine-year stint. At the party Leonora had come over and introduced herself to Charo. In their brief five-minute conversation she gave Charo the lowdown on the NYC office and her fellow agents. If every word she said didn't prove true it was only because Charo had yet to encounter that particular agent or situation. The most comforting advice Leonora Stump gave Charo was an open invitation to contact her if Charo ever got so mad she wanted to quit the bureau.

Leonora was not at home when Charo rang the Puget Sound cottage she shared with her two Labrador retrievers. But soon after Charo left a message she got a call back from Leonora's publicist saying she was on a New England lecture tour and would be glad to make a stop in New York to see her.

They met at the Oyster Bar at Grand Central Station. Charo began at the beginning.

"I got an email from Hank Karros asking if I'd meet with a CDC doctor named Dunn who was nosing around in the anthrax investigation."

Leonora slurped down a clam. Charo's chowder bisque cooled.

"So, I met with the guy and told him that I was no longer with the investigation. I figured that would be the end of it. But he didn't let it go and well, he had a compelling idea so I decided to run with it. His idea was to analyze E-ZPass records from 2001 and look for a pattern that fit with two trips to Princeton in the days before the mailings."

Leonora listened while devouring a slab of salmon.

"While researching the case Dunn turns up the name of Arthur Lavigne, a microbiology professor who was on the FBI's suspect list until he was found dead not long after the anthrax mailings. At first glance the evidence pointed to suicide."

"At first glance?" Leonora repeated.

"Yes. A single shot to the head with his own gun and no evidence of an intruder. We talked to Lavigne's daughter. She doubts the official report of suicide. That's when things started to get weird. The daughter lays a bombshell on us. She was the one who found her father. But that was not all she found. Sticking out of her father's desk drawer were some letters. Letters identical to those included with the anthrax mailings. The FBI lab confirmed them to be the originals. We next reviewed the state police investigation of his death and found that they missed some clues—clues that suggest—"

Leonora dropped her fork into her ice water. "Wait. Back up. You mean this micro professor was the mailer? You solved the case?"

"We don't think so," replied Charo. "After we saw the state police investigation report we went to Lavigne's house. Wasn't much there except some old stains on the wood floor that I suspected were gunpowder burns. We also found in the FBI's evidence locker a box of .38-caliber blanks and traced them to a gun store near Lavigne's cabin. Video footage suggests someone other than Lavigne purchased them."

Leonora stopped eating, giving Charo her un-devouring attention.

"The gun shop owner had installed a digital video system after 9/11. By using the bar code on the box we were able to pull up footage from the day the blanks were purchased. The man who purchased those blanks bears a resemblance to a highly placed person in the executive office. The same office signed out cars that drove through New Jersey Turnpike toll booths near Princeton before the anthrax-laced letters were postmarked."

"You lost me there chief. How'd you connect the man in the gun store to the executive office?"

"Sorry. We serendipitously obtained a VP staff photo and identified what we believe is the same man from the gun store video."

Leonora stared at Charo, her right index finger tapping against her upper lip, a fleck of salmon along for the ride. "What did the autopsy report list as Lavigne's cause of death?"

"Suicide."

"Hmm," Leonora pushed her plate to the side and leaned in closer to Charo, her elbows propped on the table. "Ballistics matched I presume? Gunpowder residue?"

"Lavigne's right hand, the hand next to the gun, was positive for GSR."

"I suspect there's more?"

"The trajectory didn't fit with a right handed person and one blank was missing from the box. There was also GSR on both Lavigne's shirt and pants."

Leonora pondered this for a while. "Your theory is that your murderer knew Lavigne or otherwise got the drop on him. He finds Lavigne's gun and shoots him once, removes the shell, and reloads with the blank. He then fires the gun again, this time in Lavigne's hand, to leave gunpowder residue. He removes the blank shell from the gun's chamber and replaces it with the spent casing. To implicate Lavigne he leaves the original anthrax letters in a drawer for the police to find. I don't suppose they compared the chemical composition of the gunpowder on Lavigne's hand with that from the blanks?"

"No."

"Did forensics check to see if the gun had been fired more than once?"

"No. We arranged for the clothes and residue from the floor to be tested."

"Let me guess. Two different residue compositions and what you pulled from the wood floor matched the blanks," Leonora said.

"Close, the residues on the clothes came from different shells and the stain on the floor was GSR but there wasn't enough to match."

"No matter. Tell me more about the letters."

"Lavigne's daughter found him. She took the letters and their existence has been unknown since."

"Fascinating."

"Wait, there's more. The part that I want to ask for your opinion."

Leonora grabbed a passing waiter by the arm, almost yanking his face into the plate of clamshells and twisted lemon wedges. "I'd like a piece of Oreo cheesecake and some black coffee. Chen, anything else for you?"

"No thanks." Charo waited until the waiter left their table to resume their conversation.

"Lavigne's daughter got a book from her father before he died, an Einstein cookbook."

Leonora's left eyebrow shot up.

"There's a coded inscription inside the front cover; a cryptogram of sorts. We figure Lavigne wrote it. Dunn decoded it, the key had something to do with the book *The Periodic Table*."

"By Primo Levi?"

"Yes, that's it. The message was the login and password to a secret email account. There were also the words, 'Project Black Death.' Mean anything to you?"

"I am not familiar with it, go on."

Charo paused to drink some water. The busboy had removed the untouched soup without her noticing. She glanced about her at the nearby tables. The Oyster Bar was packed with the workweek lunch crowd, cheek to jowl. Anyone hearing this tale would probably figure she was an aspiring screenwriter pitching a script to an agent.

"Lavigne's email account was an electronic diary. There were correspondences from a person with ties to the US intelligence community using the handle Armadillo90210."

"East Texas and Arkansas."

"Pardon?"

"Range of the nine-banded armadillo. I'd bet your deep throat is from that part of the country."

"She's a Pentagon librarian who happened across a classified report that wasn't supposed to be there. It has since disappeared."

"Project Black Death?"

"Exactly. Armadillo90201 read parts of the classified report before it disappeared."

"Of course she did. And may I ask, is Armadillo still alive?"

The question made Charo shudder. "Yes. In a nutshell, Project Black Death used the technology of three other top secret DOD and CIA projects and made—"

"Anthrax spores? I see where this is going."

"Yes, however, the trail has taken off in yet another direction. To Kazakhstan."

Both Leonora's eyebrows leapt like puppets on strings.

"Kazakhstan?"

"Dr. Dunn is there now. The products of Project Black Death allegedly were buried in the Nevada desert. But what's more, some Kazakh told the US embassy back in 2002 that the mailed anthrax spores came from a 'desert in the US' and claimed the $2.5 million tip reward."

"Are you saying someone in Kazakhstan sent the anthrax letters? I thought they were our allies? Didn't the strain point to a domestic source? And what about the cars from the executive office?"

"We don't think it was the Kazakhs or Russians."

"One heck of a coincidence," Lenora said.

"Chance is chaos revealed."

"Beg your pardon?"

"Something a physics professor of mine used to say. That, if several events appear to have occurred by chance, there is often an underlying causal chain that won't appear logically related."

"Uh-huh. I take it then you want to ask me about Robert Hanssen?"

"Yes. Two things trouble me. One might lead to Hanssen, but the other I am afraid suggests a different leak in the bureau. Could the Russian intelligence community have found out about Project Black Death from Hanssen?"

"When did you say Project Black Death was active?"

"Late 1990s perhaps into 2000."

"It's possible. Hanssen passed secrets until his arrest in February 2001, and in November 2000 he is believed to have passed about 1,000 pages of classified documents to the Glavnoye Razvedyvatel'noye Upravlenie or GRU, that's the Russian Military Intelligence agency and rival of the old KGB. Of note, the GRU tended to recruit more non-Russian agents than the KGB, including many from the Central Asian Commonwealth states. Might be a link to your Kazakhstan tip. Okay, what else troubles you?"

"When Lavigne was a suspect the bureau was monitoring email traffic from his computer. I think someone at the FBI leaked this information and it got him killed."

"How did Armadillo come to know Lavigne?"

"She developed a friendship through professional correspondence; she was assigned to answer the warning letters he wrote to the Pentagon on the dangers of bioweapons research. She then used an anonymous account and a public computer at the Library of Congress to conduct clandestine communications with Lavigne. Once we gained access to Lavigne's secret account we were able to identify and interview Armadillo90210. I'm hoping that whoever is behind Lavigne's murder has no reason to harm her. With the Project Black Death report gone there's nothing to support her claim. If we didn't go looking for her, this story would still be unknown."

"Makes sense. But who at the FBI leaked and to whom? And why?"

"That's what I was hoping you could help me with."

.| 31 |.

Mackey knew how to skate. Not like Eric Heiden, more like Bobby Orr. But Zlotnikov appeared impressed nonetheless. Despite his awkwardness on land Zlotnikov was nimble on skates, like a penguin taking to water. Mackey kept his right hand in his pocket the entire time. Zlotnikov had refused to take the envelope stuffed with cash in a public venue.

Light headed from the altitude Mackey took a rest along the rink's railing, opting to gaze at the valley below instead of the spinning skaters. Skating, the vista, and being in a foreign country triggered memories of things he did with Allie. But it was thoughts of Charo that tugged at the drapes of denial like Toto unveiling the wizard from behind his curtain. The denial that he held the key to his emotional prison. Mackey hastened to join Zlotnikov who had procured a table with a view of the mountains and a bottle of vodka.

Zlotnikov was a storyteller. His father was a Kazakh and an officer in the Red Army. After WWII he was stationed at Semipalatinsk, the primary site where the Soviets tested their nuclear weapons. He met and fell in love with a young Russian scientist. They married in 1946 and the stork that brought Anatoly two years later had to battle the fierce winds of the barren steppes to deliver him. His childhood was filled with men in uniforms and skies filled with tremendous clouds of dust.

After receiving a degree in chemistry he was sent to the Technical University at Dresden where he learned synthetic organic chemistry. He returned home to Kazakhstan in 1974, assigned to the state-run Progress

Scientific and Production Association located in Stepnogorsk. He was given a lab and instructed to make herbicides. In 1982 change came to Stepnogorsk.

"There was much new construction and many more soldiers. Walls and an electrified fence were built in addition to many new buildings. Not long after I was brought into the office of the new deputy director. I was transferred from my lab and put in charge of building 231."

"Building 231?"

"The drying and milling facility. After the accident at Sverdlovsk, the Politburo decided to move anthrax bioweapons production to Stepnogorsk. No one knew about the presence of the Scientific Experimental and Production Base (SNOPB), not even the citizens of Stepnogorsk, though they must have suspected what was going on. I was deputy director of production when Yeltsin revealed to the world our existence and the fate of SNOPB was sealed."

"Is that when you met Wexler Barnes?"

"Yes. I was ordered to oversee the dismantling of the plant. It was difficult and slow going. Temperatures in Stepnogorsk can reach 120°F in the summer and minus 40°F in the winter. The winds are severe, like a dragon's breath. Now that the work is mostly complete I help locate missing items."

"Missing items? Like fermentation tanks or anthrax spores?" Mackey asked.

"*Nyet*. Former Soviet scientists. There were twenty scientists with doctorates and a hundred other researchers working at SNOPB when it closed. Many returned to the Soviet Union. Some stayed to dismantle the factory but even they began to leave in 1997 when no money came for the conversion. I also assist Mr. Barnes with finding the occasional American who has lost his way," Zlotnikov flashed a gray, toothy grin.

The sun departed the sky like a wino looking for his next drink. It its place an icy wind rolled down from the mountains. Zlotnikov paused to empty the last of the vodka bottle into his glass. He regarded the mountains lost in a melancholic stupor. After a moment, he returned to the present.

"The man you wish to speak with lives in Aralsk."

"Aralsk?" Mackey's limited knowledge of Kazakhstan geography was sufficient to know this was at the opposite end of the country.

"He is an old man and no longer travels. You will have to go there if you wish to speak with him. Meet me tomorrow at the train station. The train leaves at 7:00 AM. Bring the money. I will meet you in Aralsk in two days."

"Where in Aralsk?"

"The hotel."

"Which hotel?"

Zlotnikov got up, downed the remaining vodka, and threw some tenge on the table.

"There is only one."

.| 32 |.

The story of Robert Hanssen was that of a boil, delayed in recognition, and allowed to fester. The lesson of Robert Hanssen was the unsanitary conditions that permitted him to germinate in the first place. Everyone drawn to law enforcement is to some degree attracted to power and authority. The power to restrict freedoms. The authority to peer into the private lives of others. These were perhaps motivating forces for Robert Hanssen to leave his plebian career as a certified public accountant for law enforcement; first with the Chicago Police Department and then with the FBI.

Charo knew that many of her male colleagues had not matured beyond fraternity life, having only traded in pledge paddles for pistols; and that Special Agent Robert Hanssen was unlike the other male agents. He didn't fit in. He lacked sufficient confidence around physically superior men to be accepted as one of the boys. The peculiarities of his mood, macabre sense of humor, and 50s Goth attire made him the object of ridicule by his fellow agents. Believing himself to be their intellectual superior, this rejection built inside him a monument of animosity toward the FBI. His disturbed psyche sought a way to resolve the conflict, and decided that the best way to even the score with the FBI was to betray his country.

"For the last six years of his career, Hanssen was assigned as the senior representative to the Office of Foreign Missions for the State Department," Leonora said. They had exited through Grand Central Station and were sitting on a bench beneath a tree in Bryant Park.

"He had access to their computer system with no supervision whatsoever. Even after he was caught hacking into an administrator's account he faced no disciplinary action. It was chalked up to paranoia. His own brother-in-law reported that he was spending money beyond his means; buying a Mercedes for his stripper mistress and doling out large sums of cash to pay bills."

"State Department?" Charo interrupted. "Does that mean he was privy to secret documents from agencies other than the FBI?"

"Of course—CIA, Pentagon, National Security Administration—any agency that needed to share information with the State Department."

"He could have then gained access to documents about Project Black Death."

"I suppose, but I don't yet see a motive for killing Lavigne, and there isn't any evidence to suggest Hanssen spied for anyone other than the Russians."

"No, I don't think Hanssen or the Russians killed Lavigne. But it might explain why some Kazakh knew that anthrax spores were buried in the Nevada desert."

"Have you considered that it might not have been a leak that got Lavigne killed?"

"What do you mean?"

"The 'need to know' principle holds up pretty well when it comes to the public, but we both know that FBI agents have loose lips among themselves and around people with power. Maybe this information was shared with someone who inquired about the status of the investigation?"

Charo stared at a sparrow taking a dirt bath in the soft soil at the base of a nearby bush. It wiggled out a palm-sized crater, spraying grains of soil beneath its wings.

"Like our man in the executive office," she said under her breath.

.| 33 |.

Mackey peered through sleepy slits at the train schedule board. He blinked his eyes several times to improve focus. It was 6:55 AM and Zlotnikov was nowhere in sight. If he missed this train the next one wasn't until 4:00 PM the following day. It was over 800 miles to Aralsk, a more than twenty-four-hour trek by rail, and his turned out pockets ruled out flying.

People were boarding and a conductor loped along side the train. Mackey felt a twinge of homesickness; despite her sometimes cool indifference, he missed Charo. While trying to recall the contour of her calves a firm slap on the back almost knocked him over a luggage cart. Grinning, Zlotnikov greeted Mackey with a firm grasp of his shoulders and a shake that loosened a molar or two.

"Compliments of the Kazakhstan government," he said handing Mackey a ticket while blasting him with herring-soaked breath.

Mackey pulled from his pocket the envelope and handed it to Zlotnikov who slid it into his coat without inspecting its contents. Mackey shuffled onto the train. Zlotnikov called after him.

"Two days. *Dosvedanya!*"

Mackey suspected he'd entered through the wrong car. The aisle was less than two feet wide and there were bunk beds on either side. He passed through two more identical cars; the bunks were already occupied. On the right side of the car the bunks ran perpendicular to the aisle. The lower bunks were leather-clad bench seats, whereas on the left side there were two parallel bunk beds. Upon exiting the third identical car he was confronted by a uniformed conductor. The man said something, then gestured for his ticket. Mackey began to ask where he should sit but the conductor punched the ticket and brushed by him, waving an annoyed hand toward the other end of the train. When the same scene was repeated with another ticket taker five cars later, Mackey realized he was on the Kazakh Amtrak hostel.

He found an open bench and took a seat near the window sharing the compartment with a Kazakh family. The mother sat with a sleeping toddler in her lap and the father and daughter were above in the top bunk reading. Mackey returned the young girl's brown-eyed stare with a smile. He judged her to be about eight years old. Across the aisle two young women reclined sharing earphones attached to an MP3 player. They got up and dug into their purses. Mackey soon smelled why. A food vendor was making his way down the aisle selling grilled meats and vegetables.

Out the window the scenery was a postcard from monoton-i-stan. The landscape was composed of alternating patches of grass and shrubs like the coat of a mangy dog. There were no trees or water and only an occasional camel or horseman in the distance disrupted the boredom. Steppe, Mackey decided, was the predecessor of desert as ape was the forefather of humans.

No one had ever mistook MacPherson Dunn for a Russian, but the patriarch of the Kazakh family spoke to him in his adopted tongue.

"I don't speak Russian."

The girl popped her head up. "My father asks where you are going?"

"To Aralsk," Mackey said.

The father spoke again, this time in his native Kazakh.

"My father asks why you are going to Aralsk, there is nothing there."

"To meet someone. Where are you going?"

"To Aqtobe. My father goes to train for the Olympics," she told Mackey with pride.

Mackey returned to staring out the window until he fell asleep. He was awakened by the slowing of the train and a tap on his arm. It was the young girl.

"We stop here for little while," she said.

"What's your name?"

"Zharina."

"That's pretty. My name is Mackey."

She smiled and ran off to join her family. Five hours had passed and he was in the town of Shû. The place could have passed for the American Midwest much like the Italian countryside doubled for the Old West in the "spaghetti western" movies.

From a cart outside the train station he bought a lamb kebab and positioned himself on a bench so he could keep an eye out for the conductor's signal to board. None of the women wore traditional Muslim headscarves and their clothing would have fit in at any suburban mall in America. There was a woman haggling with a man selling melons. Before he reboarded Mackey made a purchase: ending up with a bag of melons when he had only wanted one.

The train chugged on and Zharina seemed as bored as Mackey. With her head propped on her hands she peered down at him from the top bunk while the rest of her family napped. Mackey found a pencil in the cushion of his seat and sketched a tic-tac-toe board in the margin of a magazine. He held it up to Zharina and she hopped down into the seat next to him. They played tic-tac-toe and dots. Zharina taught him the Kazahk-version of hangman where one had to guess the identity of a drawing in five guesses or less. Mackey had one guess left on a drawing that looked like an underfed pig when the train pulled into the Taraz, the old city of Zhambyl near the Kyrgyzstan border.

Mackey disembarked and stretched his legs. The air was cool, dropping a degree or two with each breeze. Other than the Steppe Shrikes perched on the power lines he was alone. He couldn't help but chuckle at the twists in his life that landed him in a land as desolate as the one he fled. The feeling of not being connected to anything, which brought an end to his time in Alaska, again enveloped him. Alaska was a place he loved but never made home. In his five years there he didn't form anything more than a rhetorical friendship. It was more than just trading tundra for steppes that reminded him of Alaska. The native Kazahks resembled Alaska's indigenous Inuits. As if enduring centuries of the harsh land and abrasive wind had slanted eyes and flattened faces.

Mackey never made the effort in any of the places he landed after Allie's disappearance for people to view him as anything other than a stranger. A futile attempt to keep pain and guilt from recognizing him. The jukebox whirred and found an all too familiar song, "For a Dancer " by Jackson Browne[15]. Allie's disappearance. Even after all these years he couldn't fully admit she was dead. The bars of the song formed his prison cell.

Darkness invaded his repose by the railroad tracks. The bearded face of Tom Hanks from the movie *Cast Away* appeared in the eroded surface of a rock. It isn't until Hanks is rescued and returns home that he realizes it is the broken relationships of his prior life that truly make him a castaway.

Allie's studio! The mortgage was two months past due. He had meant to ask his mother for a loan but in all the excitement of chasing Mailthrax he had forgotten. Mackey's heart rate quickened and his breath drew short.

A warm flush enveloped him and settled like a hot coal in the pit of his stomach. He couldn't lose the studio.

A faraway voice was calling to him. It was the train conductor's final boarding call.

.| 34 |.

Leonora's words weighed on Charo. Could Lavigne's death have resulted from loose lips and not a leak? Agents were notorious braggarts, especially when male agents congregated to toss back a few. It did seem too much of a coincidence for the leak to have occurred within earshot of the person who had a reason to silence the professor. She couldn't come up with a way to find out.

Worse was the possibility that an authorized communication got Lavigne killed. That someone the FBI trusted had betrayed them. Charo tried to think of agencies with which the FBI shared information. The list was short and the occasions rare.

To find out which agents were involved in the email surveillance and who was assigned to communicate information to other agencies she'd have to look it up in the ACS system. Leonora hadn't said for sure that Hanssen had leaked Project Black Death to the Russians but the general feeling among the agents who interrogated Hanssen was that he didn't account for all the documents he stole and was lackadaisical at keeping track of his misdeeds toward the end of his treasonous career. Charo now risked her own career as she considered undoing some of Hanssen's harm to catch the anthrax mailer.

She needed to speak with the agent who investigated Lavigne's death to inquire if he or she suspected foul play and the reason for keeping the box of blanks in the FBI's evidence cache. She decided to breach the ACS file under the pretext of Lavigne's murder investigation, a more plausible justification than searching for an FBI leak to the VP's office.

Charo removed her watch and propped it next to her keyboard so she could view the second-hand sweep. She had mere minutes to enter and exit the ACS file on Lavigne and stay beneath the radar. She knew the agents who monitored other agents' activities focused on unusual patterns and duration of activity. She fixed in her mind three questions: the name of the agent assigned to the Lavigne case, which agents performed the email surveillance, and if anyone communicated evidence outside the bureau.

Charo took a languid walk to the water cooler, scoping out the agents nearby while considering the search terms that might yield the highest probability of results. Hardly any agents were in the office. Satisfied she wouldn't be interrupted, Charo returned to her desk and brought up the jury-rigged DOS program that linked her PC to the ACS system.

Within thirty seconds she located the name of the agent who had investigated Lavigne's death—James Washburn. Finding the agent or agents who had performed the email surveillance was proving more difficult. As the second hand swept around the dial for the second time, Charo's pulse quickened. Searching on the keyword "surveillance" brought up several entries but none identified the agents involved. She was desperate to log off but knew this would be her lone chance. Her father's theory on avoiding speeding tickets flashed through her mind. If you stay less than five miles over the speed limit, the cops won't bother you. Scanning the document list her eyes were drawn to a word that seemed out of place— *pacemaker*. Lavigne didn't have a pacemaker, at least she didn't think so. She searched the file and found half dozen identical entries for TC pacemaker SO, with different dates. Her watch was coming upon the three-minute mark. She hadn't yet made sense of the notations or found who performed the email surveillance, but hastily logged out.

"What were you doing—"

"Brad! I've asked you not to sneak around like that." Charo slid a palm over her notes.

"—with that CDC doctor?"

"I told you. We're working on a mumps outbreak that might be connected to child pornography," Charo replied avoiding eye contact.

"I thought you said it was measles?"

"Yes, measles."

"I'm keeping an eye on you, Chen," Brad said poking his index finger in the air at Charo.

"How about keeping an eye on your own cases?"

Charo studied the words she had scribbled down: TC pacemaker SO. *TC* was shorthand for a telephone communication, *SO* were the initials of the agent who made the entry, but what did pacemaker mean? It was not unusual for agents to cover their ass by placing such entries in case files. Charo found four agents with the initials of SO who were active in 2001. Two of the agents were nowhere near Washington, DC. The other two were Stephen Oliver and Sandu Omani.

Special Agent James Washburn transferred from the DC field office in 2003. Charo found him in the Minneapolis Field office.

"Special Agent Washburn, this is Special Agent Chen, NYC field office, how are you today?"

"Fair to middling. What can I do for you?"

Good, thought Charo, all business.

"There have been recent developments in a case you investigated in 2001, and I need to ask you some questions."

There was an ominous pause.

"Why is the NYC office calling about a Washington case? Which one?"

Charo detected no tone of defensiveness. Perhaps cautious curiosity.

"The death of Arthur Lavigne."

"Somebody found the blank?"

"The blank? You mean the box of .38-caliber blanks in the evidence locker?"

"No, I mean yes, sort of. Is this on the QT?"

"On the QT, I don't understand?" Charo asked.

"Agent Chen, I've been with the bureau nearly twenty years and in that time no one has ever asked me about a five-year-old case unless they were writing a book or working on something off the record. What is this about?"

Charo had no choice. She took the chance that she could trust him and gave Washburn a much-abridged version of the unauthorized reopening of the investigation of Lavigne's death, ending with the finding of the box of blanks with one missing. She left out any mention of anthrax or Mackey's role.

"That puzzled me, too. The evidence at the scene suggested suicide, but there was no note, and the box of blanks was newly purchased. I asked myself why would a person who is contemplating suicide buy a box of blank shells? And why was there just one missing? I tried to get authorization for a search of the property for the missing blank shell, but was denied by HQ. I thought you were calling to tell me you found the used shell and lifted latent prints," Washburn said.

"No, we found the box of unused shells in the FBI evidence locker and thought it was strange to have kept them. Now I understand why. Was there anything else about the crime scene that seemed out of the ordinary to you?"

The line grew silent while Agent Washburn considered the question.

"It was five years ago, I'd have to give that some thought. About all I recall was an uneasy feeling that we were closing the case too fast. But orders are orders and we had those two other pressing investigations."

"One last question. What made you move to the Minnesota field office?" Charo was hoping to hear that the transfer was somehow politically orchestrated, a way to get rid of someone with second thoughts who could make trouble.

"I am an angler. Best places to fish in the US are here."

Washburn had been helpful but his suspicions were only able to confirm what they already suspected—that Lavigne's death was not a suicide. What was it he said? He moved to Minnesota because he was an angler? Angler. The Secret Service codename for the vice president. And didn't he have a pacemaker? The thought struck Charo like the post-game, celebratory ice bucket of Gatorade. She looked up Secret Service codenames and found that pacemaker was the codename for the vice president's staff but was Farrington on the receiving end of the agent's phone calls? And which Agent SO?

Charo located Sandu Omani. She was in the Washington field office in 2001 and was translating intercepted electronic communications from Middle Eastern countries. She had no connection to the Amerithrax investigation. Stephen Oliver, it turned out, was a cadet at Quantico at the time.

Had SO left the bureau? She searched the list of retirees since 2001 but none bore the initials SO. Was this a dead end? Another cold bucket of Gatorade. In the history of the bureau, fifty-two agents were killed in the line of duty. The last she knew to die in the line of duty was Leonard Hatton, a colleague from the NYC field office who had entered the burning World Trade Center Towers on September 11, 2001.

Charo pulled up the list of FBI agents killed in the line of duty. Two more deaths had occurred since 9/11.

One died from injuries sustained from a fall during a Quantico training exercise in 2005. The other occurred in March 2002; Special Agent Samuel Onyungaya was killed during a drug raid of a warehouse in downtown Washington. The FBI website listed scant details of the account. Charo checked for media stories online. The news reported that a tip had led local police and the FBI to a warehouse that reportedly was a major supply point for an East Coast heroin distribution ring. Onyungaya had found the warehouse empty, but upon exiting back to the street a single shot was fired from a rooftop striking him in the head. He was killed instantly and the sniper was never apprehended. The investigation suggested murder for hire. The ex-wife was suspected, but there wasn't enough evidence to bring charges. Agent Onyungaya was with the counterterrorism unit of the Washington field office in 2001. He certainly would have been involved in the anthrax investigation.

.| 35 |.

The train lurched north while continuing its trek across the steppes. Mackey watched the sun set. It resembled a bright orange ball rolling down a gently graded slope. Zharina's family began pulling food from their bags. The girls crossed the aisle with several parcels wrapped in white paper. They unwrapped cheese and flat bread, placing them on a table folded out from beneath the window. All Mackey had to share was half a roll of lint-flavored lifesavers and the bag of melons he bought in Shû. Having only his miniature pocketknife he held up his melons impotently. Zharina's father smiled and handed him a real knife.

"Ak-nan," Zharina said, pointing to the pile of round flat bread aromatic with onion and herbs. Her palm hovered over the cheese, "Irimshik," and then over a mixture of rice, nuts, and dried fruit, "Plov." Zharina must have watched many American TV game shows because her sweeping hand gestures mimicked the presentation of what lay behind door number two. "Manty" resembled Chinese dumplings. "Shuzhuk" was snake-like, smoked horsemeat sausage, and "Shashlyk" was a version of the grilled lamb Mackey had for lunch. Zharina advanced two slender fingers toward the back of the table whispering, "Baursaki," but as she was about to pluck one her mother intercepted her hand and shook her head. She instead handed her an ak-nan filled with shashlyk and plov. The baursaki looked like munchkins and Mackey figured to try one before Zharina nabbed them all. There were also apples, or "alma," and beer purchased from an onboard peddler. The Kazakh family brought their own tea bags and mugs and shared with Mackey; hot water being one of the few commodities the train offered in abundance. They used their hands as utensils and the bottoms of their shirts as plates.

The hour approached nine at night when the last baursaki was melting in Mackey's mouth and sleep descended on him and his companions. He gently nudged the girl propped in the corner of his bunk. She got up and stumbled back to her own. Mackey went to find the porter. Pointing to the linens on another bunk he was handed a package containing a cotton sheet and towel. The open window admitted the cool night air making sleep on the grimy, leather bench somewhat bearable. Mackey rolled up in the sheet and used the folded towel as a pillow. It wasn't indigestion but mental dyspepsia that kept him awake. Alone again with his thoughts, they careened off undigested memories like bowling balls tossed into the Grand Canyon. It was the plaintive voice of Ben Harper he heard from "More than Sorry[16]."

There was so much that he was sorry for: his periods of self-absorption, not appreciating the moment and being too scared to talk about his feelings. His vocal cords had been paralyzed by the fear. Fear that the words would come out horribly wrong because he couldn't disentangle Mackey from Magnus, nature from nurture, desire from delusion. Time could do little to deflate Mackey's remorse. He gripped it with the tenacity of a barnacle, knowing that with each passing year Allie drifted further away.

The quest to find an elderly, scrap-metal scavenger who may have overheard a Soviet spy reveal how he purloined an illegal American bioweapon from its crypt in the desert seemed ludicrous when Charo proposed it and not any saner now after eighteen hours on the cross-Kazakhstan local. Aralsk seemed like a place whose vitality had been sucked out and spat in the dirt like snake venom. Not your typical tourist destination.

New York City wasn't yet home. The thought of Charo brought a smile. The way she'd shoot him a stony sideways glance and the cadence of her determined stride. Her bronze calves. Her fingers tucking a tress behind her ear when it fell across her face. He wondered if she had uncovered any clues in his absence or had her supervisor discovered their extracurricular activities and this trip is for naught? As he was drifting back to sleep Zharina's father pointed for him to look out the window.

"Baikonur," he said.

Mackey saw in the distance fences and steel structures resembling high-tension wires, he looked quizzically to Zharina.

"Sputnik!" she cheered.

It was just after noon when the train next stopped. Mackey had been dreaming of cosmonauts and mushroom clouds. He checked the calendar on his watch. Thursday, October 12th, the day he was to meet Zlotnikov and five years to the day when New York City learned of its first anthrax case. He wondered how Marci was commemorating the day. Zharina was trying to get his attention. She was excitedly waving and pointing to the aisle.

"Aralsk! Aralsk! Aralsk!" she yelled.

Mackey grabbed his backpack, spun out of the compartment, bouncing off a porter, and upending her towels before tumbling off the train. He waved goodbye to Zharina as the train yawed and shuddered on its way.

As soon as the train curled out of sight the mass of his solitude returned. It leaned on him like a backpack filled with sand. The station sat on the other side of the town; accessible by an elevated footbridge. Behind him lay old railcars, abandoned warehouses, and a gated factory building that looked like it hadn't heard the footfall of a proletariat since Stalin last banished an ethnic minority to the region.

The first view of Aralsk came as he ascended the footbridge. A neat grid of dirt tracks with low cinderblock and wooden houses arranged like toys in a dusty bin. There was no sea just a few thirsty puddles. Little moved in the town. No cars, buses, or people. The path around the station deposited him in Red Square, a copse within a circular drive of brown dirt. In the overgrown shrubs stood the Red Monument.

Mackey reached into his pocket and removed a slip of paper. He had written down the hotel address: 24 Kirov Street. Twenty-four had been his baseball uniform number throughout high school and college. He followed the directions, turning right as he exited the short street from the square, and then taking the second left onto Kirov Street.

A barefoot child stared at him from an open doorway until an old woman with a straw broom swept her inside. Two blocks later he heard voices emanating from a building he took to be a bar. He peered inside but did not see Zlotnikov. A half a block later he came upon the hotel. It was a two-storied structure of whitewashed brick. Large patches of paint were missing, exposing the brown brickwork. The windows were small and shutterless, with the trim painted in a hopeful robin's egg blue. A young woman sat behind the counter reading a book. She gazed up and smiled at Mackey. He mimed to her for a town map. She produced a crudely drawn, out-of-proportion map that could have been for Bar Harbor had it included overpriced souvenir shops. The map was on onionskin paper with fewer than a half dozen landmarks. After she gave it to him she withdrew a blank piece of paper from a drawer and began tracing another copy. Mackey considered returning the map but decided he needed it more than she needed a coffee break.

Aralsk Port was further down Kirov Street. He headed that way under the watchful eyes of shoal of kids. At Godinov Street he turned right, and spied the mast of a ship above a building. When he turned the corner he came upon a narrow finger of water that was barely enough to float a rubber duck. Two rusty ships were moored, rather embedded, in the mud; looking like naked brothers waiting for their mother to lift them out of the drained bathtub. He lingered at the port long enough for his pint-sized entourage to lose interest and meander away. Sitting on a mooring post facing where the water used to be, Mackey considered it could be low tide. But the Aral Sea had no tides, at least not of the magnitude that would explain that before his eyes. Mackey had been to a few docks in his life, but only one was sadder than this.

He returned to the hotel, passed through the lobby where the young woman was intent on her reproduction, and out into the courtyard. He grabbed a lawn chair and headed back through the lobby. On his way out he stopped to select a book from the coffee nook. Nearly all were in Russian but there was one English translation of short stories by Nikolai Gogol. With it in hand he took a seat to wait for Zlotnikov. The book's page-edges were browned as if it had been roasted in an oven. The translation copyright was from the year he was born, another promising sign.

Mackey sat waiting. Words from Coldplay's "Till Kingdom Come" played in his head[17]. He'd been waiting. Not time spent in anticipation of a future event, such as the arrival of his guide Zlotnikov, but for someone to push the play button and start his life again.

He opened the book to Gogol's famous short story, "The Overcoat." A satirical poke at the life of a civil servant, a group to which Mackey aspired to belong, that is if he ever made his way back to the New York City Department of Health. He was just past the part where

Akaky has finally saved enough money to buy a desperately needed new overcoat. Mackey was reading how Akaky is mugged and the coat is stolen when a commotion drew his attention. A crowd of dust was coming toward him down the block. At the lead was Anatoly Zlotnikov. Behind him, at the end of a length of hemp, was a large beast. The ox was a gift for the old man.

"In America, we bring wine," Mackey said as Zlotnikov came to a stop.

A reward far less than the $2.5 million the US had promised, but this was Kazakhstan, and an ox, after all, was still an ox. Townsfolk who had regarded Mackey's presence as a curiosity hardly worth shuffling down the street for now danced and jostled each other at someone's blessed fortune.

Zlotnikov greeted Mackey warmly with a bear hug. "Hello my friend. How was your trip?"

"Riveting."

"Shall we see if Berkut Ahkubekov is at home?"

They continued on Kirov Street in the direction Mackey had walked earlier, past the dry dock. Minutes later they came to a large empty lot. A road ran perpendicular to the path they were on, beyond which was a brown, dirt crater that extended to the horizon. Anatoly pointed.

"This used to be Aral Sea."

Mackey could see where the water had receded there had once been a beach. It was now covered with a crust of salt and crushed seashells. Further beyond were two of the ponds he had seen from the railroad overpass.

They turned right, toward a decaying building guarded by low, scrubby trees. Passing it, Anatoly explained, "Oceanographic Institute."

They came upon another group of houses set in three rows, like those previously seen. They all were single level, with corrugated tile roofs and whitewashed brick, and were nestled like baklava on a tray. They turned down the first street and stopped before a cottage halfway down the block. Anatoly stepped to the threshold and knocked on the splintered door. A round-faced man sporting a toothless grin and sparse whiskers emerged. His skin was the cracked-orange of a leather glove repeatedly left out in the rain and sun. An old woman emerged, and upon seeing the ox, clapped her hands with delight and hopped off to take the beast into the yard.

Berkut Ahkubekov welcomed Mackey and Zlotnikov into his home. They sat on handmade stools of wood that were upholstered with remnants from an abandoned Soviet government office. Mrs. Ahkubekov served them tea and home-baked wheat biscuits. Anatoly leaned forward, his elbows perched on his knees with his hands steepled under his nose. He spoke to the old man in Kazakh, pausing every three or four sentences to interpret for Mackey.

"Berkut was in a bar in Aralsk. It was the year President Bush was first elected. There was a boisterous Russian buying drinks for the locals. He was telling a story about a foolish American who had come to fish in the Aral Sea."

Mackey mulled this over as Zlotnikov again spoke to Berkut. Anatoly's face grew serious as he listened to the old man. He had stopped interpreting for Mackey. Soon Anatoly and Berkut were howling with laughter. The old man took something off the shelf and showed it to Zlotnikov.

The two continued to speak and laugh and then the old man pulled out a bottle of vodka. Mackey declined, content with the tea. After an hour Zlotnikov got up, embraced the old man, thanked his wife, and guided Mackey toward the door. Mackey shook the old man's hand and they stepped into intense sunshine.

"What did he say?"

"He thinks he found a piece of the missile that shot down Sibir Airlines flight 1812."

"What?"

"The plane that crashed in October 2001."

"I read about that, wasn't it hit by an errant Ukrainian war games missile?"

"*Da.*"

"And weren't there microbiologists from Novosibirsk returning from a trip to Israel?"

"Rumors. The plane crashed into the Black Sea, over 1,500 km from here. It may be a piece of a S-200 missile. There were many military exercises in this region, but I doubt it was from that missile."

"Okay, okay, but what did he say about anthrax?"

Zlotnikov was heading back into town at a brisk pace.

"The man in the bar was someone Akhubekov had seen in Aralsk before. He called himself Sergei. The American wanted a jewel of the Biopreparat. Sergei took him to Vozrozhdeniye Island where they dug up a canister of anthrax. The joke was that it was really filled with sand—sand from the American desert."

"Sand?"

"Yes, this is what Sergei told Akhubekov. But he believes it was anthrax spores."

"How do we find Sergei?"

"The old man told me he has a birthmark. A large red stain like wine over his right eye and forehead."

"A nevus flammeus. There must be thousands of men with this birth mark in Kazakhstan if he's even still in the country," Mackey sighed.

"I know how to find this man," Zlotnikov replied.

They weaved through empty streets back to the rail station. Mackey bemoaned the thought of a train ride back to Almaty.

"Where are we going?"

Anatoly was too far ahead of him to hear. Instead he led them past the abandoned cannery and then down more residential streets. Where the houses ended was a barren plain of dirt extending as far as Mackey could see. Barren except for a man in a leather flight jacket smoking and leaning against the cockpit of a Mi-2 military helicopter. The old bird was retrofitted with extra gas tanks, something its Polish manufacturer did not recommend. Mackey stumbled over an empty bottle of vodka as he climbed into the back seat.

They were airborne for over an hour and yet the aerial view of the steppes was no more varied than from the train window. The pilot passed back a grease-stained bag of sandwiches on white bread, and cans of coke. Mackey ate one sandwich and handed the bag back to the pilot, praying he'd eat and dissuade some of the vodka from entering his blood. Anatoly made calls on his cell phone until the battery died. Mackey wondered how he was able to hear anything above the din of the engine but hoped Anatoly's calls met with success. He was eager to get home. Would there be a foreclosure notice waiting for him or perhaps something worse?

He was treated to a spectacular Kazakh sunset. With the land so flat and a smattering of cirrus clouds the sun sank like a new penny into a piggy bank. The horizon radiated gold, the rising air undulating like wheat in a summer breeze. The beauty, tinged with melancholy, overwhelmed him. Patty Griffin sang to him from the jukebox, but the words to her song "Long Ride Home," could have easily been Mackey's mantra[18]."

The eastern sky turned dark blue. Overhead the blueness lightened like a brush stroke of paint spread across a canvas, turning paler as the paint thinned. It was a mundane trick of nature, but it never failed to bring a smile to Mackey's face. The land morphed from desert to semi-arid and Mackey could make out mosaic farmland. Squares of mismatching shades of green and brown like marble tiles laid by an inebriated mason. Cottages and roads appeared, then small towns. As dusk passed into night all he could see were the lights and outlines of houses until the moon rose and reflected off the still surfaces of ponds. They were approaching Kazakhstan's new capital Astana.

The chopper arrived a little after ten o'clock and landed on top of a downtown building. A crew of anxious doctors and nurses flanking a gurney rushed to meet them. Anatoly brushed past the lead doctor planting the greasy bag on the clean sheet as the man shouted in protest.

"Is Sergei in the hospital?" Mackey inquired as the elevator doors closed.

"*Nyet.* Not many places to land a helicopter in downtown Astana at night."

When they exited to the street, Anatoly and the pilot piled into a waiting Lincoln Continental. Anatoly rolled down the window.

"Meet me in Gorky Park at midnight. By the statues." He sped off.

At the bar of the Astana Hilton, Mackey ordered a bowl of borscht and a brisket sandwich. The televisions mounted over the bar didn't run ESPN. Instead they showed videos in German, Chinese, French, English, Russian, and Kazakhstani about the creation of modern day Astana. Mackey moved his seat beneath the English version. President Nursultan Nazarbayev was telling of the decision to move the capital from Almaty in the far southeast to the more central location of Astana. Photos of crumpled mosques and buried schools told the tale of earthquakes and mudslides implying that Almaty wasn't the ideal location for the seat of an emerging nation of wealth and importance. Mackey read between the steppes. Almaty was too close to a billion Chinese who, if history repeated, might one day overrun the border and invoke a centuries-old territorial claim.

Astana needed a lot of work and the people a lot of convincing, especially the government ministers and civil servants. They were not happy with the idea of leaving their comfortable homes in Almaty for the desolate Soviet era town of Tselinograd, which was known to be unfinished, *yet in an advanced state of decay*.

It was a frontier town like Skagway during the Klondike gold rush; with plenty of vodka to smooth out the rough edges. The skyline erupted like it was constructed from an inexhaustible supply of Lego blocks. The video showed master architect Kurakowa proudly navigating President Nazarbayev through a scale model of the city; the camera focusing on its many architectural marvels.

A man at the bar elbowed Mackey and pointed derisively at a cylindrical building on the screen with slanted roof. "That building there we call, 'The Lighter,' because of how it looks. And it caught fire in May," he cackled.

The most spectacular building was the Palace of Peace and Harmony. A pyramid of glass and steel; it was home to a global center for religious understanding, opera house, research center, and library. Inside there were hanging gardens and its glass atrium floor overlooked the opera pit. At the cost of a mere $200 million, Astana got more for its money than US cities that shelled out more in taxpayer money to build unifunctional, unaesthetic sports stadiums. The video ended and Mackey noted the time. He paid the bartender, threw back the complimentary shot of vodka with a wince, and headed out the lobby. The doorman whistled for a cab and he jumped in.

"Gorky Park."

The driver eyed him querulously through the rearview mirror. The doorman rapped impatiently on the car's hood and the cabby sped off.

Every Soviet City had a Gorky Park and Astana's was in the old, gray, and yet unrefurbished section. The cab slowed to a stop on a dark boulevard across from a bland, square apartment building. Mackey didn't see Zlotnikov. He remained in the cab, to the renewed irritation of the driver. Mackey threw his last ten dollars over the seat and the man became content to wait and chain-smoke Marlboros.

In the time it took for the curls of smoke to make Mackey's eyes tear and nostrils burn the black Lincoln Continental pulled up behind the cab. Zlotnikov and the driver emerged and stepped onto a path entering the park. Mackey followed. The path led to a statue, formerly of Lenin, but now of the three great Khans.

Mackey spied an angular man sitting at the foot of Khan Kenen with a pile of cigarette ash and butts between his feet. He rose to a height of over six-foot-four. Anatoly motioned toward a bench. Mackey sat while the driver waited on the path. Their quarry remained standing in the shadow of the monument.

There were no introductions. The man wore a black, leather jacket and blue jeans with his hair slicked back. He paced like a bull awaiting release into Pamplona. Stubbing out his cigarette on a silver Zippo his hands were the only body parts not hidden in the shadows. He spoke to Zlotnikov in Russian, who nodded toward Mackey. The man then continued in English.

"The man you wish to speak with is not in Kazakhstan. I am his cousin, Ivan. I am former member of KGB. As the major general knows I have come here at much personal risk to answer your questions."

"We are interested in a trip an American made to Vozrozhdeniye Island in 2001," Zlotnikov directed.

"Sergei has never been to Vozrozhdeniye," Ivan replied.

Mackey's hopes plummeted, but Anatoly seemed unfazed. Lying in Russia was as common as exaggerating the size of the fish that got away was in America.

"When did you leave the KGB?"

"We left the FSB in 1995."

Mackey recalled that the Federal Security Service succeeded the KGB after the dissolution of the Soviet Union in 1991.

"And what have you and Sergei been doing since?"

Ivan reached into his jacket pocket. The driver who had been monitoring the scene stiffened. Ivan showed his palms—a pack of cigarettes in one, the lighter in the other. He offered one to Mackey and Anatoly, they both declined. He lit the cigarette, took a puff, and exhaled the smoke in rings toward the stars.

"This and that," he finally replied.

Anatoly remained quiet. Mackey wondered if the discourse wouldn't be better served under the influence of vodka in the plush comfort of an Astana nightclub. Anatoly spoke a few words in Russian that made the gangly man stop pacing.

Anatoly returned to English. "What was your job in the FSB?"

"I had many jobs. I trained other agents, read intelligence reports, prepared briefings for generals… I was also… a handler."

"Was Robert Hanssen someone you handled?" Mackey asked.

"*Nyet*. We all of course knew of him."

"Did you ever see or receive any intelligence passed from Robert Hanssen?" Anatoly asked.

"I don't know. It is possible. We were not always told the source of the information we were given."

"Did Sergei, or perhaps yourself, ever come across information on an American project named Black Death?"

The manner in which Anatoly spoke of Project Black Death suggested that he knew more than the scant details Mackey shared at the skating rink. Ivan stepped forward out of the shadows placing a foot up on the bench between Anatoly and Mackey. The details of the man's features became visible, including a large hooked nose, widely spaced eyes, and a nevus flammeus over the right side of his face. Mackey's suspicion was correct, Ivan was Sergei. It was at this point that Mackey wondered if Zlotnikov, alone or in concert, was attempting to hang noodles on his ears. With no other course to pursue he continued to listen to Anatoly's interrogation.

"We were aware of many foolish American attempts at subverting the International Bioweapons Treaty. Perhaps Project Black Death was one of them."

Sergei was trying too hard to appear nonchalant. Mackey's hands tightened around the edge of the bench. The subterfuge was a ruse and the man knew more than he was saying. Zlotnikov bobbed his head as if listening to Rachmaninoff. After several minutes of silence Sergei stood and cracked his back.

Anatoly again spoke in Russian. The tone was that of a general issuing orders. Sergei stroked his chin then squatted on his haunches before them, passing a hand through thinning brown hair. He studied the pebbles imbedded in the concrete walkway as if looking for a pearl.

"There is not much work for ex-FSB. The Kazakhs do not trust us. We have wives and children to support, just like they do. Maybe in Uzbekistan and Tajikistan, but it is not safe for Russians to stay there long. There were freelance jobs. Russian jobs. Treacherous jobs."

"Did any of these jobs take you to America?" Mackey asked.

Sergei stared off into the darkness, a wry smile creeping across his face. He stood up again and lit another cigarette. He took a puff then held it out for inspection. Viewing the cigarette as if it was both a lover and a betrayer.

"Perhaps. My geography is not too good. I recall we made a trip to desert once, to recover some, how do you say, stolen artifacts."

Mackey was about to ask what he meant but Anatoly put a hand out to silence him. Sergei continued.

"We were given a portable GPS with coordinates and told to dig. We turned them over to the FSB."

"All of the artifacts?" asked Anatoly.

"I don't know. I waited in jeep. Maybe Sergei keep one as souvenir."

More silence surrounded the men. The only sound was the wind through the trees.

"A few years later we got contacted by an Uzbek who knew an American operative. I do not know his real name. He was asking about what might be found on Vozrozhdeniye. Sergei arranged for him a tour of the Aral Sea. Let him dig in the sand on Voz. Maybe he found something. I don't know."

"For a price," Zlotnikov added.

"A finder's fee," Sergei shrugged.

"When was this?" asked Mackey.

"Aah. It might have been in 2001."

"Do you recall the man's name?" Mackey followed.

"Your government likes to put its nose where it doesn't belong. Now you look for Sergei to clean up mess."

"Name?"

Sergei frowned. "I believe he called himself Thompson."

Zlotnikov got up, an announcement that the interrogation was over. Sergei turned on his heels to leave.

"One last thing," Mackey said. "Thompson, what does he look like?"

Sergei turned slowly to face Mackey.

"Taller than you; broad shoulders, like a swimmer…" he paused, "light complexion, red hair and freckles, many freckles." He again turned to go.

"Any distinguishing marks? Scars, tattoos, piercings?" Mackey asked.

Sergei took two measured strides so that he stood a hair's breadth from Mackey. He towered nearly a foot taller and peered down at Mackey. His eyes narrowed and the muscles of his jaw tightened. Mackey stood his ground.

Sergei broke into a tobacco-stained grin, nodding and rubbing his chin. "Yes, as a matter of fact he had a tattoo, on the back of his neck. A bald eagle with an American flag painted on one wing. Beneath the eagle's talons was a bear. A red star inscribed with a sickle and hammer."

.| 36 |.

Farrington stared out his office window, across the Potomac River. He didn't like being so far from the White House and Capitol but had to admit the offices in Crystal City afforded a level of privacy that made their work more efficient. The 19th floor also provided a view of Washington that other executive staffers housed in the Eisenhower Building couldn't hope to see unless they were onboard a Goodyear blimp during a Redskins game.

On the morning ride to work it dawned on him that today was an anniversary of sorts. The best laid plans of mice and men oft go awry, a line paraphrased from a Robert Burns poem, was something his college roommate derided whenever one of his plans didn't work out. So where was he now? Probably teaching gym to some overweight Floridians.

Five years ago he turned the page of *The Washington Post* to an article on the anthrax investigation. While choking on a doughnut he read that the strain was Ames. The FBI made this discovery on October 5th, but failed to inform him. Convinced at the time that the FBI had bungled he reassured himself it was a laboratory mistake. He milled around the office and struck up a casual conversation about it with the boss. The clear implication of the strain identification was a shift in the investigation toward a domestic terrorist.

He tried unsuccessfully for several days to reach his FBI contact. When he finally did it was public knowledge that all of the cases were Ames. Believing that the FBI had neither the skill nor the wit to pull off such chicanery he inquired with practiced nonchalance about the lab results. Confirmed three times by two separate labs, it was Ames all right.

Farrington couldn't understand how Thompson had managed to come back from his visit to Kazakhstan without Soviet anthrax. Had the Russians weaponized Ames?

As the days dragged on the FBI's focus locked in on a homegrown fanatic. He objected to the act being called terrorism. Lives would be saved by ridding the world of despots and their weapons of mass destruction. The tools to fight the real terrorists had to be strengthened. Rules were made for the weak—to keep them out of the way of the powerful. The Washington bureaucrats were clueless.

Professor Lavigne was on the FBI's suspect list. It wasn't difficult to get access to his intercepted emails. The FBI thought nothing of his activities but he turned whiter than his sister's debutante gloves upon reading the words Project Black Death. A claim of bad sushi placated his secretary's concern. If Lavigne knew of Project Black Death who else did? An uneasy picture formed in Farrington's mind. Was it conceivable that Thompson went halfway around the world to dig up what had been buried in their backyard? What's more, how did the Soviets obtain the product from the US?

Lavigne made a credible fall guy but he knew too much to let be captured alive. Once Farrington made the decision the rest fell into place. Lavigne's schedule was posted on the University's website. The cabin was a little harder to find, but not for a man with resources. Farrington waited for Lavigne to leave for campus one morning and then snaked his way down the lengthy drive. Farrington passed Lavigne's cabin and parked his car in a secluded area that led to the fire road. He then doubled back, and as he expected, Lavigne's security was based mostly on his home being hard to find. The dog had put a scare in him but she went down easy.

Snooping through Lavigne's cabin he didn't yet have a plan for eliminating the professor. When he found Lavigne's revolver the idea came to him in a flash. He needed a blank round though. Wasn't there a gun store back in town?

The old man was easy to surprise and didn't put up a fight when faced with his own Smith & Wesson. The rest went according to plan, well almost. He slipped the originals into Lavigne's desk drawer and left it opened a crack so it wouldn't be too obvious. Burying the damn beast in the woods took too much time. He needed to leave before it turned dark and his headlights would attract notice. In his haste he left the box of blanks behind but managed to slip out of West Virginia and return back to Washington unnoticed. Stealth. The master would be proud.

When Lavigne was found several days later there was no FBI press conference. No announcement that the anthrax mailer had been found. Nothing about the letters appeared in the media, or in his weekly update from the FBI. Those bunglers must have thought them fakes and didn't even bother to test them. Idiots.

One week ago the FBI announced they had a new suspect. The fools had stumbled upon a perfect replacement patsy—Erekat. It was more than he could have hoped for, a man of Middle Eastern descent. Though the objective was long ago accomplished this would be vindication for the administration and more importantly the FBI would finally stop looking. The fact that Erekat had slipped through the FBI's fingers was even better. Fleeing colored him guilty. Now, if Thompson could manage to find and neutralize Erekat before the FBI did. That was of course if he could find Thompson.

. . .

He removed the turban to wipe the sweat from his brow. His terrified companions took a break from peeing in their pants to stare. They had never seen red hair before. He'd been running arms for years, gotten into bad jams, but none like this. To the south was a Taliban patrol that had chased them up into the ravine. On the down slope was a unit of the Afghan militia who fired on them as they attempted to descend. He couldn't name the tribe he was squatting with but suspected they had fought against both. With their location known to two enemies and the ammunition running low the situation was dire. It was either the terrain or the fix he was in that brought to mind the last line from the movie *Butch Cassidy and the Sundance Kid.*

"Hey, you didn't see Farrington out there, did you?"

His companions looked to each other and then to him with perplexed and worried faces. None spoke English and even if they had the reference would have surely escaped them.

"Good. For a minute I thought we were in real trouble."

.| 37 |.

Mackey was surprised to find Charo waiting for him when he got off the plane. Before leaving the hotel in Astana he emailed her from a computer kiosk in the lobby; but he hadn't expected a welcome home hug. Jet lagged and unprepared, his central nervous system failed to respond in time to reciprocate. Charo was a stealth hugger. In the instant before she asked him how the trip went he wondered if she made love the same way.

As he stepped into the city's night air, the jockeying cab drivers and aromas of jet fuel and auto exhaust briefly made him long for the arid steppes. On the cab ride home he regaled Charo with tales of Kazakhstan like a father telling bedtime stories. He spared her the monotony of the landscape and concluded with the Gorky Park meeting. By the time the cabbie had navigated the Van Wyck Expressway, Triboro Bridge, 125th Street, and the one-way streets of Morningside Heights, it was nearly eleven and he was finishing the part about how Sergei had sold Thompson a canister of Project Black Death anthrax.

"I suppose no one reported it missing," Charo said.

"If anyone even noticed they very well couldn't report it to international authorities, it being the product of an illegal bioweapons operation and all."

Charo had not yet shared with him her discoveries. She got out of the cab with Mackey in front of his building and told the cabbie to wait.

"I'm glad you're home."

"Me, too."

"You better get some rest. I have to be at work tomorrow for a couple of hours. We can meet up afterward and I'll brief you on what I've learned."

She gave him another quick hug and this time he hugged back surprised by how small she felt in his arms.

Stopping in the vestibule he opened his mailbox and removed a cell-phone bill. He shuffled up the stairs and put an ear to the door for several minutes before entering. Coffee table dust greeted him and then dispersed like an invisible cat when he tossed the bill down. He fixed a bowl of spaghetti and ate it al dente with the last of a jar of tomato sauce, making sure to superheat to neutralize any incubating bacteria. Before crawling into bed he put a fresh battery in his cell phone. The messages were all from Kevin Acker, Marci's administrator. He played the most recent:

Dr. Dunn, this is Kevin Acker again. I keep missing you and it is important that we speak. Your paperwork was approved. The start date must be within two weeks of the approval date, or, I don't know what'll happen, but I am sure it isn't good. We didn't get notified right away and I haven't been able to get in touch with you this week. You have to start this Monday. I bet you are pretty anxious to start anyway, please give me a call as soon as you get this.

Jet lag and exhaustion teamed to tug him toward sleep. At the other end of the rope was the narrowness of his life and feeling homeless in his home. Before the trip to Kazakhstan, in the days when Charo was not returning his calls and the investigation was mired in a box canyon, Mackey had ventured downtown to hear live music just to get out of his apartment. The place was called the Living Room and was around the corner from Katz's Deli, where Sally faked Harry. The stage was a postage stamp. On it were squeezed a piano, amplifiers and a drum set. The singer had to lean into the audience to avoid being kicked by the drum pedal. Mackey arrived as the second act was moving their instruments onto the stage. People were vacating tables and he found a comfortable spot against the wall where the low lighting was the lowest. Kim Richey took the stage and it was her soft vocals and acoustic guitar that he was again hearing now, barring him from sleep. The song was, "The Absence of Your Company."

> I'm just trying to find my way
> And a face to wear and a place to be
> In the absence of your company
>
> If you are better off without me
> If you truly do believe
> That you are better off without me
> That's how you should be
>
> 'Cause I don't have a point to prove
> Or a stand to make
> I'm just trying to find my way
> And a face to wear and a place to be
> In the absence of your company[19].

Try as he might he couldn't keep songs from spinning in his head. Sometimes the meaning was obvious, other times he struggled to make sense of what his subconscious was trying to tell him. The words fomenting thoughts and rubbing the gray matter between his clamshells until a pearl of self-recrimination formed. Shame, guilt, and regret—the holier than thou trio—took turns slapping his psyche until he solved the equation for the unknown.

Ten years and he still couldn't let go. He needed a goodbye. Like a child letting go of a balloon and watching it get smaller and smaller as it sailed off into the heavens until it became a speck, then nothing at all. He was still a kid when his father died and he didn't get resolution or a goodbye. Not with Allie either.

. . .

The Grotto lived up to its name; it was a hole-in-the-wall dive located in Alphabet City. The place met Charo's criteria for a suitable place to have a private conversation. It was dark, empty, and the patrons looked as though they had more to fear from inquisitive eyes and ears than Mackey and Charo. Charo dispensed with the easy stuff first.

"Erekat, the FBI's number-one suspect," she began, "is still missing and presumed to have left the country. No new evidence has surfaced that either implicates or exonerates him."

Mackey studied the menu. It met none of his gastronomic criteria. Over half of the items were fried, including the vegetables. They didn't serve turkey burgers and the lone vegetarian dish was chili.

"What looks palatable?" he asked Charo.

Charo picked up the menu and perused it. "They have Cobb salad," she offered.

Mackey groaned. Salads at bars meant brown iceberg lettuce, unripe tomatoes, indigestible radishes, and at most a shred of carrot.

"I've been trying to figure out how and who leaked the information about Project Black Death. I haven't gotten too far," Charo said.

Hearing the dejection in her voice, Mackey put down the menu as the waitress arrived. He hastily ordered the potato leek soup and a Reuben sandwich.

Charo ordered the Cobb salad. She stared across the table at Mackey. "A Reuben?"

Mackey shrugged. "Tell me, maybe you've gotten further than you think."

"While it is possible that Robert Hanssen leaked information about Project Black Death to the Soviets, I've been unable to confirm it."

“Did you turn up anything to suggest a link between Farrington and the Russians, or the Russians and Lavigne’s killer? Mackey asked.

“No. Nothing. I did find the agent who investigated Lavigne’s death and he was as troubled as we were by the box of blanks. He wasn’t able to pursue it any further, but kept the blanks for us to stumble upon.”

“How did you find the agent?”

“Through ACS.”

“You breached? Wow. While you were in the file did you see anything else of consequence, like the name of person who eavesdropped on Lavigne’s email?”

“No. I poked around as long as I could. There isn’t much more I can do. It’s not likely the agents who did the surveillance are going to walk up to me and start a conversation with, ‘Guess who I spied on?’ ”

“I don’t know, men have been known to confess worse things in the presence of a beautiful woman.”

She cast him a sideways glance. “I didn’t find out which agents performed the email surveillance but did come across several phone calls from agent ‘SO’ to codename ‘pacemaker.’”

“Ooh, that sounds promising.”

“Pacemaker is the codename for the VP’s staff. Unfortunately, SO was killed in action in 2003.”

“Really? Is that common? FBI agents getting killed on the job?”

“No, not often. It was a drug raid. The case was never solved.”

“Sounds fishy to me. What if all these events are related?”

“Has your time away fertilized the conspiracy theories?”

“Hear me out. Suppose the Russians learned of Project Black Death either from Hanssen or a source outside the FBI. They decide to get a look at the stuff. Their spies locate the burial site in Nevada and steal it.

Maybe they aren't impressed or one canister is unaccounted for and ends up with Sergei. Sergei is contacted by Thompson who wants to buy Soviet-made anthrax. Having none Sergei sells him Project Black Death spores."

"Okay, now connect the spots to the Farrington and the Lavigne murder." Charo said.

"You mean dots, anyway, the discovery of Project Black Death likely wouldn't result in any grave consequences to the scientists involved. Look at what happened after Projects Bacchus, Clear Vision, and Jefferson came to light. Nothing. Maybe there would be international scorn and some mild embarrassment. But I doubt the perpetrators would be prosecuted for violating a forty-year-old international treaty."

"So, Artie wasn't killed to keep Project Black Death a secret?"

"No, I believe he was."

"Mackey, you're going in circles."

"If the Project Black Death spores were, by intent or accident, the source for the anthrax letters then the discovery of Project Black Death would place the anthrax mailer in jeopardy of discovery if he was originally involved in its creation. I am betting that Farrington was. It puts the smoking envelopes in his hands."

"Enough jeopardy to commit murder?" Charo asked.

"Hell, yeah," Mackey said.

"But wouldn't anyone with knowledge of Project Black Death be a threat to the Farrington?"

"Only if a sample of Project Black Death was available and matched to the spores from the letters. We can infer that a sample found at USAMRIID implicates Erekat. It could either be the source spores for Project Black Death or a sample not labeled as coming from the illegal project. The scientist involved Project Black Death has no reason to suspect that the spores he made were the ones used in the mailings, so he's kept silent or else admit to violating the international bioweapons treaty. Only the mailer knows the connection. And now us."

"So," Charo sighed. "Professor Lavigne was killed because he was about to expose Project Black Death's illegal activity and this inadvertently would expose the anthrax mailer."

"Yes. And that makes the scientist who made the Project Black Death spores an unwitting accomplice to five murders," Mackey added.

"We might not have seen the end to that string of microbiologist deaths you uncovered."

The food came. Charo's Cobb salad was crisp with fresh turkey and ham, springy greens, and rosy tomatoes. Mackey's meal didn't fare as well. If the colors of the soup and corned beef were reversed the meal might have at least appeared palatable. They ate in silence. Charo put her fork down.

"So, Thompson went to buy Soviet-made anthrax?"

"Yes, Sergei hung noodles on his ears."

Charo wrinkled her nose.

"Pulled the wool over his eyes. Bait and switch? A fool and his money are soon parted?"

Her eyes narrowed.

"Pulled a fast one?"

"Okay, okay, I get it. But why Soviet-made spores?"

"To cast blame on foreign terrorists, specifically the 'Axis of Evil.' To justify our invading Iraq, ridding the world of Saddam Hussein, finishing the job left over from the first Gulf War. Not to mention war profiteering, US cowboys riding to the rescue, oil security, and passing the Patriot Act."

Mackey stared disconsolate at the grease slick where the Reuben sandwich once sat.

"You okay? I can't believe you ate the whole thing," Charo said.

"It's a bad habit. I always clear my plate. My mother taught me not to waste food."

"That was my dad's job," she replied.

The busboy cleared away their dishes and they declined dessert.

"Where does this leave us?" Mackey asked.

"We need to prove that pacemaker is Farrington and connect him to the spores."

"I presume you've already tried to identify if pacemaker is Farrington?"

"Yes, and no luck."

"We could try to find Thompson."

"Men like that make their living on not being found. That reminds me, I know why Wexler Barnes was willing to help us. He's chasing Thompson, too. If the State Department hasn't been able to find him, I am not sure we'll have any better luck," Charo said. "That reminds me, I'd better fill him in on what you learned."

"Okay, forget about trying to find Thompson. Since we now know where the spores came from and have a suspect we could try to tie Farrington, or his co-conspirators, to the laboratory equipment used to fill the envelopes."

"How?" Charo asked.

"The mailer of the anthrax-laced letters needed a safe and secure place to fill them. You can't get Biosafety Level-3 equipment at the Rent-All Center. We look for a biosafety cabinet either homemade or purchased."

"The investigation team has been all over that. They looked for any equipment bought or stolen and found nothing."

"Suppose nobody knew it was missing?" Mackey posed.

"What do you mean?"

"I remember back in Alaska when we got new computers the IT folks scrubbed the old hard drives and then the machines were left unattended in the office for months before they were salvaged. I don't think anyone would have noticed if one had gone missing."

"Hmm, I'm pretty sure that angle was covered," Charo offered.

"There's the possibility that one fell off the truck."

"Wouldn't it break?"

"A euphemism for highway robbery. Or maybe Farrington had an inside man," Mackey said.

"The conspiracy is growing."

"It is logical to assume that Mailthrax didn't prepare the envelopes in his home."

"What about an accomplice from a lab?" asked Charo.

"Too easy to get caught accessing a BSL-3 laboratory."

"I know where I'd go if I needed space where no one would bother me or care what I'm up to," Charo said. "A rental storage unit."

"In the DC area."

"There must be over a hundred," Charo said.

"Yes, but I would be willing to bet he chose a neglected and deserted part of town where the rules are less than rigorous and the prying eyes few."

"We'll need a list of all the storage centers that were in business in 2001; data on the number of units, their locations, and neighborhood information. I can ask my artist friend to draw a sketch of that tattoo you told me about last night to see if anyone recognizes Thompson. And we can use Farrington's wedding photo."

"I'll work on pinpointing hot spots. Oh, I almost forgot." Mackey grabbed a toothpick as they made their way out of the bar. "I'm supposed to start work at the Department of Health on Monday."

.| 38 |.

Charo grabbed a sandwich from the bag. They were sitting on a secluded bench north of South Street Seaport with only seagulls and the Brooklyn Bridge for company. She handed Mackey a story from *The Washington Post* on the VP's elusive staff. Mackey glanced at it and stuffed it into his pocket. They didn't have much time. Charo had compiled a list of storage centers and got the sketch artist to draw Thompson's tattoo while Mackey had used poverty and health statistics from the DC health department's website to narrow down the search.

Charo read the addresses to Mackey who mapped each one on his laptop, then compared the location to his hot-spot ward map. Charo scribbled a check mark in the margin of her list when Mackey called out, "Hit."

It took them three hours but when they were done there were seventeen storage centers in the hot zones. They rented a car and arrived in DC after dusk to begin the search. At each site they executed the same routine. Charo would flash her FBI badge at the person on duty and ask how long the person had been working there. With the exception of one man, none of the workers had been at their jobs in 2001. Mackey showed them Farrington's photo and the drawing of Thompson's tattoo. No one recognized either.

It was Sunday near dawn when they finished checking all the storage centers on the hotlist. They were sitting under a street lamp on a vacant frontage road with a view of the Potomac River. They had run out of gas.

"Where to now?" Charo asked. "Go back to the places that were closed or move on to the rest of the list?"

Mackey was certain that Mailthrax wouldn't have set up his lab in those parts of town.

"The second place we stopped at, the one off Capitol Street, what was the name again?"

"No Bother Storage, 1776 Fairlawn Street, Southeast."

"Was that the place where the man on duty said the dayshift worker had been with the company back in 2001?"

Charo checked her list. "Yes. That's right."

"What was his name?" Charo shuffled through her notes.

"Clayton. Clayton Jefferson."

"Did you happen to ask when his next shift is?"

"Tomorrow, I mean today."

It was 7:10 AM when they pulled up to No Bother Storage. Clayton, they presumed, was sitting in the office with his feet up and the paper in his lap. A thermos of coffee sat on the desk, along with a black satchel. He peeked out over his reading glasses as they drove up. Before Mackey could get out of the car, Clayton yelled out at them.

"The boss ain't here, you'll have to come back tomorrow."

Clayton leaned against the doorjamb as Charo and Mackey approached.

"How do you know we aren't customers?" Mackey asked. Before Clayton could answer, Charo had her badge out for his inspection.

Clayton looked down and ran a hand over his close-cropped, white hair. "For one, your car—New York plate, no permit sticker. And two, you two look like trouble."

Mackey handed him the photo and the tattoo drawing. "We are looking for someone who rented a unit here back in 2001. The person might not have been back since. Recognize either of these two guys?"

Clayton glanced at the wedding photo and handed it back to Mackey. "Nope." He took longer with the tattoo drawing; tapped it against his forehead. "This one I remember, only the bear looked different."

"What can you tell us about the man with the tattoo?" Charo asked.

"Not much. Man rented a unit a few years back. I saw him maybe twice, both times bringing stuff over. The usual stuff—boxes, tools. Then that was it."

"Tools? What kind of tools?" Charo asked.

"You know, hammer, saw. Tools."

"Do you remember which unit?" Mackey asked.

"Nah, but I can check."

He returned with a stained and yellowed index card.

"Here it is, John Washington, unit 31. That's around back, facing the river."

"Is it occupied?" Charo asked.

"Let's see. Mr. Washington prepaid in cash for two years. The unit has been rented since, right now by a Mr. Hopkins."

Charo stepped forward taking the card from his hand. "Can we have a look?"

Clayton contemplated Mackey's cheerful smile and Charo's determined scowl.

"This a federal case?" he asked.

"Yes, sir," Mackey replied.

"I don't want any trouble with the government. I'm a law-abiding citizen. I pay my taxes."

"I am sure you do. May we see the storage room now?" Charo said.

Clayton disappeared into a back room and returned with a large ring full of keys. He shuffled out the door and crept down the drive. Mackey and Charo had to pause so as not to overtake him. He passed two rows of storage units set back to back. At the river the drive

Clayton turned right. Mackey counted down the numbers until they reached number 31, about halfway down. The old man stopped, turned back to gaze back to where they came from. He squinted at the key ring.

"Forgot my glasses, can't see much close up without them."

"Allow me." Taking the key ring from his hand, Charo located number 31 and handed it back to him.

He turned the key and the automatic door opener purred to life. Mackey remained standing in the drive. There wasn't a reason to go further. Unit 31 contained squat. A few boxes, children's toys, an old lawn mower, and plenty of open space. His shoulders sank as Charo strode in for a closer inspection. Mackey went to flip the light switch on but the bulb had burnt out.

"Do you have a flashlight?"

The old man unclipped one from his belt and handed it to Charo. Mackey walked across the drive to the river and sat on the guardrail watching a tug push a barge slowly down river. Charo said something he couldn't hear. When she repeated it, he heard the word powder. He got up and jogged into the unit. On the floor near the rear wall Charo was shining the flashlight on specks of coarse white powder mixed with bits of paper. She knelt down.

"It's drywall."

"How did you recognize it?"

"From my dad's hardware store." She poked around but didn't see any tools or leftover pieces of drywall.

"Hey, let me have the flashlight." Mackey retreated and stood in the drive and shone the light at the unit's rear wall, examining it from top to bottom.

"Charo, come here." The flashlight shed a narrow beam, but he thought that the color of the paint seemed off near the right corner. Charo agreed.

"How large are these units?" he asked.

"These here are the biggest, 20 feet by 20 feet."

“Could we bother you to see another unit? The one next door? Unit 32?” Charo asked.

Clayton hesitated. Charo took the key ring from him, found the key to unit 32 and pressed it into his wrinkled palm.

“Clayton, did you fight for your country?” Mackey asked.

“Korea.”

“Your country needs you again.”

Unit 32 was filled with boxes, a steel bed frame, credenza, lamps, and a bicycle. The usual.

Mackey whispered, “What are we looking for?”

“Can you move those boxes along the adjoining wall to unit 31 and clear an alley to the back wall?”

Mackey obliged. Clayton helped. Charo backed up and stood with one eye looking into unit 31 and the other into unit 32. Mackey caught on and walked to the back of unit 32.

“Charo, go stand facing the back wall next door and put your ear to the common wall.” When Mackey rapped on the wall, Charo heard the sound in front of her.

“There’s a false wall!” she exclaimed.

Mackey hustled to join her and they inspected the rear wall of unit 31. Mackey saw beneath the paint the outline of sheetrock tape.

“This wall has been patched here.”

Grabbing the lawnmower Mackey crashed it into the wall. A few inches behind the first wall was second wall. When Mackey peeled back a chunk of drywall they found a wood door with a padlock. Charo unholstered her gun. Holding it by the barrel she raised it to strike the lock.

“Wait, I have a better idea.” He splintered the lower half of the wood door with the heel of his shoe. Using his hands he widened the dent into a hole large enough for Charo to shine the flashlight inside.

“I see lab equipment,” she gasped.

Mackey took a look.

"We better not go any farther," Charo advised.

They edged back as if they had come upon a sow with cubs. Charo asked Clayton to call his boss and tell him they needed to close for the day, though she knew it would be longer. She dialed 9-1-1 and asked to be connected to the Washington Metro police. She informed them she was Special Agent Chen and requested the hazmat team.

"Why didn't you call in the FBI?" Mackey asked.

"Oh, I'll call them. Right after I dial *The Washington Post*."

Mackey paced along the guardrail that separated the parking area from the river beyond. Word about finding the putative anthrax lab had spread faster than cholera in a refugee camp. In the time it took to remove a pack of cigarettes from a coat pocket, withdraw one, tap it against the box to bunch the loose tobacco, light it, and take a drag, there were three news helicopters buzzing overhead. Mackey wasn't a smoker but at the moment he wished he had an addiction or a Xanax to help relieve the tension.

The helicopters dropped down low enough for the cameramen to peer into storage unit 32 and to cause Mackey's hair to blow about his face like a kid on a roller coaster. Mackey thought about pointing to the right storage unit but decided it best to remain a spectator. The whirring of the chopper blades drowned out the sound of sirens, but soon several metro police vehicles screeched to a halt by the open door. Emergency response vehicles were right behind, followed by more cop cars, then the FBI in unmarked vehicles.

Martinez was in the first FBI car to arrive on the scene and before he even had a chance to look for Charo he was embroiled in a shouting match with a Metro Police captain over whose crime scene it was. It was becoming a spectacle. Every news network had a van parked along Water Street. The clustered antennae looking like a coniferous forest after a fire. Reporters stood with backs to the barricade, giving the same update every five minutes. On nearby rooftops other reporters were posted to get the bird's-eye view. Their zoom lenses fed the world images of cops in riot gear and hazmat workers in moon suits milling around the parking lot.

Charo had joined Mackey by the guardrail. They watched as two FBI agents donned Tyvek suits and affixed respirators. Another agent stood by holding sampling equipment and a camera in a bubble bag. It was now easy for the helicopter to figure out which unit was the one to film. The hazmat team was putting the finishing touches on their staging area. Several men hoisted a heavy, airtight curtain and affixed it to the roof of the storage facility. It was fitted with high-power HEPA filters to create negative pressure inside the storage unit. Martinez stood within earshot of Charo and Mackey, engaged in a briefing with the leader of the hazmat squad.

"SAC Martinez, we're sending in two agents now to perform reconnaissance and take some samples. We'll run them out to the mobile lab to see if the unit's hot. We will also shoot video which you'll be able to watch on closed circuit from the truck," he motioned with two fingers to a nearby van with a saucer-shaped disc perched on its roof. "If it's hot, we'll have to go back and map it out before we can allow the forensic boys to collect evidence."

Martinez was nodding, but his concentration appeared to be elsewhere. He slapped the hazmat guy on the shoulder, shoving him toward the curtain, and turned to face Charo and Mackey.

"Agent Chen, aren't you going to introduce me to your friend?"

Mackey stuck out his hand. "Mackey Dunn, medical epidemiologist, ex-CDC now with the New York City

Department of Health." He opted not to mention that he was AWOL on his first day. Martinez gave him a quick handshake then put an arm around Charo's shoulder and guided her toward the least-occupied corner of the parking lot. Mackey remained by the guardrail watching the curtain sway as equipment was brought into the staging area. An agent burst out carrying double-bagged samples and disappeared into the mini-lab.

"He wants to see us in his office at five o'clock," Charo said as she rejoined Mackey.

"Do you think he's involved?"

"I'm not sure, but no."

"Are you in trouble?" Mackey asked.

"I don't think so. I started to tell him how we came to search this location, but I think it was too much for him to process. He'll read my report when he's ready. I think he's elated about getting a break in the investigation but troubled by what this means about his team."

"The misguided pursuit of Joseph Erekat?"

"Something like that."

An agent darted from the mini lab. Finding the hazmat supervisor they both climbed into the video truck. Martinez then emerged and walked to where Charo and Mackey stood.

"The place is pretty clean, but we did get a positive rapid-test hit for anthrax from the filter on the biosafety cabinet. It needs to be confirmed but I think it is going to hold up. From the visual it sure looks like a BT lab."

Martinez shifted his gaze from Mackey to Charo. "By the way you two look like crap. Why don't you get out of here, get something to eat, and get some shut-eye? It is going to be a long week."

.| 39 |.

Neither of them went to sleep. Charo dropped Mackey off at a downtown hotel, returned the rental car, and then went to headquarters. Mackey didn't make it any farther than the lobby. A waiter brought him a complimentary lemonade while he siphoned off the wireless signal. There were two things about the investigation that still bothered him and he thought they might be important to the difficult part that remained: proving it was Farrington.

The first issue was the powerful magnet that had wiped out Lavigne's hard drive. Everyone knows that a magnet is bad for magnetic media but while it can damage a hard drive enough to render it inoperable it doesn't completely erase the data. But the magnet used had done just that to Lavigne's computer, it erased all the data and the geeks at the FBI couldn't find even a tid byte. No magnet was found in Lavigne's home. So where did it go?

He opened his browser and started reading. A magnet capable of destroying a hard drive had had to have military applications. In April 2001, a US EP-3 Aries II spy plane was struck by Chinese fighter and forced to make an emergency landing on Hainan Island. The crew was held captive for ten days and the plane for another three months. Onboard the plane was sensitive surveillance equipment and data that the crew had no quick way to destroy.

A research team at Georgia Tech was working on this problem and developed a portable magnet that didn't require electricity yet could wipe out computer memory.

It was made of the rare-earth metal neodymium, along with boron and iron. At 90,000 gauss, the magnet developed at Georgia Tech weighed over 100 pounds. It seemed impractical for Farrington to have lugged around a magnet of that size, but Mackey had a tougher obstacle than putting the magnet in Farrington's hand. The Georgia Tech project wasn't completed until 2005.

The online story mentioned that a defense contractor had contributed to the project. Mackey looked up the company Uber-Dyne, Inc. They manufactured magnetic devices for use in the guidance systems of smart bombs. Nothing was mentioned on their website about computer-memory-erasure technology. Mackey clicked through all of the tabs of their home page, not sure where to find the information. Under, "About Us," he learned the company was spun off in 1998, but the parent company was not listed. It took him awhile but he was able to find a website that listed financial details about spinoffs. The parent company for Uber-Dyne was AmCon!

The second thing that bothered Mackey was the biosafety cabinet. He had overheard one of the agents say it was an Esco Airstream Class III model from Zeta Technical Laboratory Supply, Inc. Mackey memorized the serial number. He knew the FBI had searched for purchases of such an instrument back in 2001 and found nothing out of the ordinary, so how did Mailthrax obtain a unit? He looked up Zeta Technical Laboratory Supply, Inc. They were located in Norfolk, Virginia. He keyed the number into his cell phone.

"Z-Tech customer service, this is Aileen, how can I help you?"

"Good morning, I mean afternoon. My name is Dr. Dunn and I am calling from the CDC. I was hoping you might provide me with some information about a biosafety cabinet sold sometime in 2000 or 2001?"

"Please hold."

"Hi, this is Thomas Marinotti of Client Services, I will be out of the office until October 23rd, if you need technical information on the complete line of biosafety cabinets we stock, please…" Mackey hung up and redialed. When Aileen got back on the phone he asked to speak with a shipping supervisor. A man's voice came on the line.

"Yeah, we have that item in stock but not the quantity you need, do you want us to ship what we have and back order the rest?"

"This is Dr. Dunn from the CDC…"

"Oh, sorry, wrong line. Be with you in a minute."

Mackey's cell-phone battery entered the red zone. He thought he packed a spare and was fumbling for it in his backpack when the line clicked dead. He dialed again. Spoke with Aileen once more and was connected back to the shipping department.

"Fred Santiago, can I help you?"

"Yes, I hope so. My name is Dr. Dunn and I am with the CDC. I am inquiring about a biosafety cabinet that was purchased in 2000 or 2001." Mackey read off the serial number and heard the clicking of computer keys in the background.

"You're from the government?"

"Yes."

"This is about that cabinet sent to USAMRIID?"

"Huh?"

"An Esco Airstream III?"

"Yes, are you familiar with it?" Mackey asked.

"Hold, I am going to transfer you to billing."

"Billing? No! Wait!"

The line went to radio fill. Millie in billing was pleasant. She was delighted to hear from Mackey and asked him how he intended to arrange payment. Mackey didn't understand. She proceeded to ask if he was arranging payment for the disputed biosafety cabinet that was shipped in July 2001. Zeta filled an order for four

Esco Airstream III biosafety cabinets and was paid for three. When Mackey inquired further, Millie was able to pull up notes in the billing system that indicated USAMRIID claimed to have ordered and received only three.

"Where did the other cabinet go?" Mackey asked.

"Our records show we shipped four, and none came back. Are you arranging to make payment?"

Mackey felt sorry for her. She sounded like her *raison d'être* was to resolve the matter after all these years. He thanked her for her assistance and promised to have someone from the right government office get back to her. One really did fall off the truck after all. He was staring off into space trying to figure out how Farrington or Thompson had pulled this off when he was tapped on the shoulder. A man in a crisp, blue suit, white shirt, and red tie was standing there. A pair of sunglasses twirling in his hand.

"Excuse me sir, are you Dr. Dunn?"

Mackey nodded once.

"Special Agent Raske, I'm here to take you to meet with Special Agent in Charge Martinez, if you would be so good as to come with me."

. . .

Charo entered FBI headquarters with trepidation. She had run her own secret investigation, involved a civilian, and breached more FBI rules than J. Edgar Hoover had vagaries. True, she attempted to involve the official investigators and was rebuffed, but this was after considerable snooping around with neither jurisdiction nor authorization.

The office was mostly deserted. The agents were either deployed to the storage center site or were watching events unfold on CNN in the lounge. She deposited herself at a workstation reserved for out-of-town agents to begin her report but her mind kept drifting to how she was going to explain everything to Martinez. Where should she begin? Should she tell him how retired agent Karros had given Mackey her name and number? She thought better of that, no need to involve Hank. How about including her first meeting with Mackey, when she told him she couldn't help but then reconsidered and agreed to hear him out and check into a few things. Best to keep it brief and leave out the first meeting. When was it that she made the decision to use FBI personnel and the databases to chase Mackey's ideas? This would be tough to explain. Maybe Martinez was an ends-justify-the-means guy. Charo didn't think so.

Another dilemma was that she shared with Mackey all she dug up from the FBI files. A violation of the FBI's need-to-know rule. Despite his tenuous federal status as a CDC employee on furlough, Mackey clearly didn't qualify. Maybe she didn't have to go back that far? She could start with their first trip to Washington? But the reason for the trip rested on the strength of the E-ZPass clue, and that tied back to the use of FBI personnel and databases. Taken another way, all she did was extend another federal employee the courtesy of an audience. The idea of using the E-ZPass data was reasonable. Her sworn duty as an FBI agent was to defend the Constitution by investigating crime. She followed the natural steps of a lead. Okay, she should have turned the clue over to Martinez, but it seemed such a long shot. Why bother the Amerithrax team with a blind lead?

She'd next explain how Mackey had stumbled upon the online story about microbiologists dying in the period after the anthrax letters. Lavigne's death stood out because he was on the FBI suspect list that Charo had lifted from a secured cabinet and provided to Mackey. She'd have to approach that delicately. Maybe say that Mackey ran the microbiologist names by her and she recognized Lavigne? But that wasn't the way it happened. She couldn't flat out lie.

Her discomfort settled in the space behind her eyeballs and began throbbing. Charo was obsessed with finding the truth and it was anathema for her to speak otherwise. She weighed this against the alternative: reprimand, censure, or even dismissal.

What happened next? Lavigne's daughter surprised them with the letters that turned out to be authentic. Then the visit to the FBI evidence locker, where they found the once used box of blanks from the crime scene. That box of blanks was a huge clue. They traced them back to the gun shop in Elkins and a man in a fedora.

But what should she say about the classified file she requested from the DC office on the VP's staff? The photo gave them a name to the face under the fedora. John Farrington, deputy chief of staff for the VP. She'd better not forget to include how she ordered the West Virginia State Police to conduct an extra forensic analysis on Lavigne's clothes, which ultimately indicated that two different cartridges were fired. Better mention that before the bill landed on Martinez's desk.

And of course the book with the inscribed puzzle gram. Should she allow Mackey to explain how they solved the puzzle gram that led to the discovery of Project Black Death? He might describe how she gave him the answer while in a drunk stupor. Better that she do all the talking. But it was Mackey who traced the email about Project Black Death to a Library of Congress computer terminal, which led them to the Pentagon librarian.

The illegal bioweapons project report that Mrs. Monroe had found was now long gone but Martinez might assign some agents to look for it anyway. The trail then led to Kazakhstan and how Wexler Barnes from the State Department facilitated Mackey's trip. On second thought, that might not sit well with the FBI or the State

Department. Dr. Dunn, an official envoy for the United States. It was Mackey's theory that a lapse in national security had allowed Project Black Death's terrible product to wind up in the hands of spies, only to return to the US in the rucksack of a rogue operative. That was how they came to pull a trick out of Sherlock Holmes's cap and locate the concealed lab.

Voices interrupted her thought gathering. Charo turned to see Mackey's grinning, sleep-deprived face. The agent escorted Mackey into Martinez's office. She got up and followed.

.| 40 |.

Charo was behind the wheel driving across the George Mason Memorial Bridge. Mackey had said little since she picked him up at the train station.

"How's your mom?" she asked.

"Same ol'. She's got an appointment next week to have her knee examined. Bad arthritis. Might need a total knee replacement."

"Oh."

The conversation lapsed. Charo figured he was either weary or dazed from the last twenty-four hours. Perhaps he was taking her strict "no speaking" instructions to heart. She was too lost in her own thoughts to give much consideration as to which. They were on their way to Crystal City, to the office of John Farrington.

It was Martinez, to Charo's amazement, who suggested that they pay a visit to Farrington. The official reason was to formally update him on the new turn in the Amerithrax investigation, a task formerly belonging to Agents "Drab" and "Gall," both of whom had been transferred to the bank fraud division. The real reason for the visit, as Martinez explained, was to nose around. *See if you can trip him up. Get him to tip his hand. Find something to justify a probable cause warrant.* Charo wasn't convinced of the merit of this idea and harbored a renewed doubt as to which side Martinez was on.

Martinez had begun the meeting sternly, stating that he could not condone her actions on a case outside of her assignments. Charo's vision of handing in her gun and badge, like Dirty Harry, never materialized. She was stunned when Martinez added "officially" to his admonishment and then switched to suggesting that they, Mackey being the other part of they, continue working the investigation. No written reprimand, demotion, or transfer to some bleak, backwater office as punishment for her impudent behavior.

What Charo didn't compute until later was that through her and Mackey's efforts they had saved the bureau from another embarrassing and public debacle that promised to exceed the turpitude of the Steven Hatfill affair. Erekat had been profiled and pursued because of his ethnicity. There was precious little connecting him to the crime and that which they called evidence was nothing more than innuendo and coincidence. Then, they allowed their chief suspect to elude surveillance and leave the country. By uncovering the laboratory where the anthrax letters were packaged, media attention was directed away from Erekat.

Martinez wanted to know the details of how the two of them had managed to find the lab the FBI was unable, with a hundred agents and five years of work, to sniff out. She recited the steps of their investigation, opting for the unvarnished truth. Mackey added his own perspective and filled in the gaps in Charo's memory. By the time they were done it was after 8:00 PM. Martinez arranged for an agent to drive Mackey to Baltimore and Charo opted to stay with a Quantico classmate in Georgetown.

Charo didn't think Martinez's plan made a lot of sense. What was there to gain by confronting Farrington this way? They weren't going to accuse him of any wrongdoing or share the evidence suggesting his involvement. Nor would they be asking about his knowledge of Lavigne's death, Project Black Death, or his relationship with Thompson. How did Martinez expect Farrington to slip up? Open his day planner and have anthrax spores float out into her lap? Worse still, Mackey wholeheartedly endorsed the idea. Granted he had little knowledge or experience in criminal interviews he also appeared to have lost all common sense. As they approached the exit to Crystal City she replayed their conversation after meeting with Martinez.

"I don't think it's such a bad idea. Maybe we'll rattle his cage. Shake a clue loose. A microbiology textbook on his shelf with a dog-eared page on anthrax."

"You're hilarious," Charo said.

"He might get spooked and lead the tail team to evidence, like the magnet or better yet, contact Thompson."

"Not likely."

"Maybe I'm just not ready to go back to New York yet. I was granted a one-week postponement of my start date and I'd like to see this through."

"Except that forensics will take several weeks and that might not lead anywhere. This is a long way from being over."

"I think it will be fun," Mackey said.

"Fun? We're interrogating an alleged mass murderer. Don't go having any fun. I'll conduct the interview. You are to keep your mouth shut. Cross me on this and I'll arrest you for impersonating a federal officer."

Before heading to Farrington's office, Charo and Mackey made a stop at *The Washington Post*. Not knowing how their discovery would play out, either with the FBI or the VP's office, Charo took Leonora's advice and purchased an insurance policy: the media. As part of the deal Charo promised to give an exclusive, albeit a limited interview with the investigative reporter; their names were to be left out of the article.

In a lavishly paneled, overly air-conditioned conference room, Mackey stood before the window warming himself while Charo sat at the table with the investigative reporter and her assistant editor. Charo politely declined to answer some questions and gave the innocuous details of their sleuthing that would not hamper the remaining investigation or embarrass the FBI.

Digging his hands in his pockets Mackey found the article Charo had clipped for him. It was the first in a series of stories on the VP. It mentioned Farrington.

"Pardon me, where might I find Eric Abernathy?"

"Second floor, bullpen area."

Abernathy had the face of a kid right out of college. He was long and lanky with slender hands like the kids Mackey knew on the basketball team. He greeted Mackey warmly. Everyone seemed to know about the exclusive going on upstairs.

"Agent Chen and I have been asked to brief the VP's office on the new findings in the anthrax investigation. I was wondering what you can tell me about John Farrington?"

If the kid suspected any ulterior motives behind Mackey's inquiry he didn't show it. Instead he gave Mackey the *Reader's Digest* biography of his quarry.

"The VP is rather protective of his staff. They aren't listed in the federal employee directory and they don't grant interviews." Mackey nodded, having learned as much himself. "But we have resources and sources." The kid grinned and extended his hands to encompass the bullpen area where dozens of reporters sat glued to computer screens.

"The first thing you should know about the VP's staffers are that they are the epitome of loyal. The second thing is the depth of their strategic alignment. There is no dissent, no difference of opinion. They were all handpicked by the VP or his closest advisors. Their allegiance can be disarming and they have a reputation on Capitol Hill for brashness and arrogance. But it really isn't so much arrogance as it is empowerment. They know they carry the weight of the president, through the influence of the vice president."

"What about Farrington?" Mackey asked.

"John Ellsworth Farrington comes from a wealthy and influential Connecticut family. After a stellar four years at Suffield Academy, where he started the sailing club, he broke the family Yale tradition and attended Princeton University. He graduated in 1990 with degrees in political science and international studies. After college he joined the Department of Defense as a junior analyst specialized in interpreting intelligence information and became a self-taught expert in weapons of mass destruction. It is easy to see his mentor's influence on his views on national security. Farrington believes that the greatest threat to America is state-sponsored terrorism." Abernathy grabbed a soda can off of his desk and took several gulps. He leaned back and interlocked his hands behind his head.

"Farrington resurfaces in the public sector in 1999 when he heads up the party's campaign in the Northeast. After the election he took a position as an advisor on WMDs in the vice president's office reporting to the deputy chief of staff. Two years later, after the fallout from the Plame scandal, Farrington got promoted to deputy chief of staff. During my interviews with congressmen and aides who have had dealings with him they were all frank about his views on war and the fierceness in his eyes when he spoke about Iraq. His singular goal was to rid the world of Saddam Hussein. He was one of the more vocal, behind-the-scenes voices that advocated for the invasion."

"Do you think he was involved in manufacturing the evidence used for going to war with Iraq?"

"VP staffers leave no trace. I doubt you'll find any proof."

.| 41 |.

"Mackey, don't allow the man's arrogance to provoke you into doing something stupid." They were pulling into the underground garage in Crystal City.

"I know enough not to get between a narcissist and his reflection."

"Do you?"

"You forget I am a doctor. There is no shortage of arrogance in my profession. There was this doc from the hospital up in Boston where I worked who used to wear scrubs to the gym."

"And this offended you as a physician?" Charo asked.

"No, it offended me as an athlete. He looked like a rube. His scrubs soaked through with sweat and sticking to him like wet leaves to a tree trunk. Okay, it did offend me some as a doctor—the neediness for people to know he went to medical school."

The receptionist led them into Farrington's office. Charo took a seat in front of the vacant desk. Mackey paced the room examining the various knickknacks, certificates, photographs, and plaques on the bookshelf and walls.

Farrington rushed into his office, formal but congenial. He was tall and stocky, more like a former football player gone to seed than a yachtsman.

"My secretary informs me you are with the FBI. May I see some credentials?" Charo flashed her badge.

"And him?" Farrington nodded to Mackey who was engrossed with something on the wall.

"Dr. Dunn is with the CDC," Charo replied. Mackey held his ID up over his shoulder.

"FBI and CDC? You aren't here about that wretched border dispute with Canada over mad cow disease? My secretary—"

"No, we are not," replied Charo. Mackey followed the wall until he was now standing to the left and behind Farrington's chair, admiring a letter of commendation from the VP. Farrington shot a skittish glance at him over his shoulder.

"So then, why are you here?"

The first drops of perspiration appear on the upper lip, beneath the nose, on either side of the filtrum. Tiny pearls too small to see unless you are looking for them. Next comes the chin, under the lower lip, forming a line of anxious infantrymen of the thermoregulatory system. Charo scanned Farrington's face for tells.

"Calvin Martinez, special agent in charge of the Amerithrax investigation, asked us to stop by to brief you on the new developments. I assume you've seen the news?"

"Oh, yes, of course. What happened to those other two agents who briefed me in the past? I forget their names?"

"Agents Crosby and Doyle have been reassigned."

Charo was distracted by Mackey's wanderings. Though he hadn't yet said a thing his behavior was unnerving and violated if not the letter, the spirit of her directive. Mackey's 'nosing' around seemed to also disturb Farrington, too, as he hadn't sat down and kept glancing over his shoulder to see what he was up to.

Charo continued, "On Sunday, we discovered what we believe to be the laboratory used to package the anthrax letters. It was in a downtown storage center. The person who rented the space paid cash and used a false identity." Farrington sat down behind his desk.

"Yes, so I've read," he replied, pointing at the newspaper on his blotter.

"A biosafety cabinet was recovered at the scene and we're examining it for clues," Charo said.

Mackey had to admit Charo was on her game. She was poker-faced and steady. She didn't reveal even the slightest glimmer of emotion, let alone her suspicions of or disgust for the man. One glacial G-woman. When she came to the part about finding fingerprints there was a noticeable change in Farrington's attention and composure. From his vantage point Mackey thought he detected the tiny hairs on the back of Farrington's neck snap to attention. Charo must have noticed the change, too, by the smug expression that curled briefly across her face and then vanished like smoke up a chimney.

"Where were the prints found?" Farrington asked; the crack in his voice ever so perceptible.

"We are not at liberty to say at this point."

Charo appeared to be enjoying herself and Mackey was enjoying her enjoyment. He debated whether to stay behind the desk where he could see Charo's face or move so that he could see Farrington's. It was at that point he noted a photograph on Farrington's bookshelf. It was familiar but he couldn't recall exactly where he'd seen it. Maybe a slide during Marci's lecture? It was a photograph taken after 9/11 outside Bellevue Hospital. An impromptu shrine of letters, cards, and posters had been erected. It was a mix of remembrances and frantic pleas for information about missing loved ones. One of the cards was from a young girl searching for her father. Raindrops obscured the words but the rawness of the loss was palpable. The child's handwriting was the early penmanship of someone learning English at the same time as the alphabet. It featured block lettering with many of the letters capitalized regardless of their position in the sentence. The lines slanted downward. It was signed Nailah.

"Poignant photo. Did you take it?" Mackey asked.

Farrington turned. "No, a friend of my wife, a photographer who lives in New York took it and sent it to us." Returning to Charo, Farrington asked, "How many sets of fingerprints have been found?"

An unusual question. Farrington was too curious about certain details of the investigation.

"I am not at liberty to say," Charo answered.

Farrington huffed. "With all due respect Agent Chen, this isn't much of a briefing. You are not being as forthcoming as Agents Crosby and Doyle have been and I would think the FBI would have learned its lesson by now to be more open. I am sure the vice president would concur with me."

At that moment Mackey came around from behind Farrington's desk, pausing to admire a family photograph perched next to the computer.

"Cute kids." He pointed to the photo but misjudged the distance and knocked the frame to the carpet. The glass pane did not break. That is until Mackey, in his attempt to catch the frame, maintain his balance, and negotiate the cramped corner between Farrington's desk and the sideboard, planted his size 9½ shoe on top of the frame's glass pane. It cracked neatly into three pieces. Apologizing profusely, Mackey sat down with the wreckage in his lap. Farrington feigned indifference and reached for the picture.

"Don't bother, it is an old frame."

"I am really sorry. Careful of the jagged edges, you could cut yourself. Let me secure it, do you have any tape?"

"No, that's quite unnecessary," Farrington replied.

Mackey pretended not to hear and reached across the desk grabbing a tape dispenser.

“Please give that to me,” Farrington begged. Mackey now was pulling strips of tape from the dispenser but it kept sliding off his lap and onto his seat cushion, wedging between his thigh and the armrest. The tape twisted like long-sleeved shirts in a tumble dryer. Mackey was having trouble balancing the broken frame on his knees and aligning the pieces of glass with one hand. The other was wrapped with tape. Charo looked on with a mixture of fright and curiosity.

“I think I’ve got it,” Mackey said.

Farrington did not agree. His patience was evaporating. He got up and walked around the desk. The tape dispenser slid toward the floor. Mackey tried to halt it but instead unreeled a long strip of tape that snapped off like 10-pound test trying to land a marlin. Farrington dodged the dispenser as it bounced toward his Bruno Magli loafers. The tape balled up. Most of it was stuck to Mackey’s hands with some adhering to the glass. None, in any way, mending the situation.

Farrington hesitated, uncertain how to extricate the picture without incurring bodily harm.

“Dr. Dunn, please hold still,” he ordered. Farrington began to separate the tape from the photo. Mackey disobeyed and entangled Farrington’s fingers in the tape. Farrington managed to take possession of the broken picture frame and tossed it onto the sideboard; pieces of glass clattered against the wall and onto the floor. Mackey was left with a fullerene-shaped ball of tape stuck to his right hand. He attempted to shake the tape in the trash but it wouldn’t budge. Sheepishly he placed the hand behind his back.

“Will that be all, Agent Chen?” Farrington growled.

The interview was over. Charo thanked Farrington for his time and assured him that if there were any new developments she would be in touch. Farrington dismissed them with a flick of his hand.

As the elevator door closed, Charo's shoulders slumped. The visit was unproductive and she feared only served to undermine an already shaky image of the FBI. She had maintained her composure and for a while succeeded in deflating Farrington's dirigible-like ego but she couldn't say they learned anything useful.

"Did you notice that photograph in his office?

"The one you broke? How could I not?"

"No, not that one. The one on his bookshelf."

"No, I didn't. What about it?"

"I recognized it." Mackey waited until they were in the parking lot before continuing. "Marci used that photo in a talk about 9/11. I didn't notice it then, but now, seeing it up close, it bears a certain similarity to the handwriting in the anthrax letters. I think Farrington could have used it as a model for the threat letters."

"Nice work, Sherlock. That and an admission of guilt should be enough to convict. And that calamity with the photo of his kids. What was that all about?"

"All that ties Farrington to the anthrax mailings thus far is circumstantial. But he had motive to further his political agenda to invade Iraq and perhaps to push through the Patriot Act. Maybe even for profit as his holdings in AmCon were sure to skyrocket with the lucrative war contracts. He had opportunity. We can place him or someone from his office in the area at the time of the mailings. And he had the means, or at least we think he did, through Thompson's retrieval of stolen anthrax spores."

Charo paid the parking attendant and wheeled onto the highway. "What's your point? We can't charge him with a crime."

"What we need is a sample of Farrington's fingerprints to compare to those found at the crime scene. I was wracking my brains on what we might use and how we could obtain them surreptitiously. The inner doorknob to his office, his desk phone, coffee mug, and then it hit me." Grinning like a kid after hitting his first Little League homerun, Mackey held up his right hand with the still adherent mass.

"Tape!" he exclaimed.

"What is that, a ball of Scotch tape?"

Mackey stepped closer so the lab technician could get a better look at the evidence bag.

"Precisely," replied Charo. "We want you to lift any prints off the tape and compare them to the ones we found at the storage-center lab scene. There should be two sets—his," she jerked her thumb at Mackey who was mugging like Macaulay Caulkin in *Home Alone* after dumping Joe Pesci on his ass, "and the unsub." The technician turned the evidence bag in his hand, viewing the tangled mess apprehensively through his safety glasses.

"Mackey, your prints are on file with the CDC right?" Charo asked.

The technician shook his head. "I want a set."

Mackey inked up while Charo completed the chain-of-evidence form. "Call me when you have the results," she ordered and spun on a heel for the door. Mackey followed, wiping the ink off his fingers with a paper towel. The grin, however, was indelible.

.| 42 |.

Charo spent the rest of the week on temporary assignment at the DC office. While she labored to prepare a flawless report Mackey played tourist. He visited just about all of the nation's monuments and museums, including his favorite—the Truxtun-Decatur Naval Museum.

They reunited on Friday at a briefing in the conference room of the deputy director. When Mackey arrived Charo was already there, weary but in fair spirits. She managed to lift a smile that had two twenty-five-pound weights on each end. A pile of papers and a Blackberry occupied her lap. He hadn't seen her since Tuesday when she dropped him off at the Watergate Hotel. Every time he called to see how she was doing his calls had gone straight to voicemail. The one text message he received said that Martinez was keeping her busy. Before he could make his way over to Charo the deputy director stepped up to a mobile lectern at the front of the room; Martinez stood by his side. Without ceremony or introduction he read from prepared notes. Mackey took a seat in the back of the room.

"*Bacillus anthracis* was recovered from the biosafety cabinet found at the No Bother self-storage center. Molecular typing has shown the samples to be a match to the spores used in the anthrax attacks. What hasn't been released until now and couldn't be determined with certainty until recent developments in the field of microbial forensics is that this specific Ames strain has been traced to two US labs, USAMRIID and Dugway Proving Ground."

Aside from Charo, Martinez, and the deputy director, Mackey thought he recognized one of the dozen other people in the room; a tall, gaunt man in a plaid shirt and khaki pants sitting near him in the back row. Although the man appeared to be listening intently, he kept his head downturned looking at where the carpet met the molding.

"The exact origin of the anthrax is still somewhat unclear, whether the strain originated at USAMRIID or at Dugway. We do know that the strain was used in defense projects testing the efficacy of anthrax vaccines that were conducted at the end of the last decade."

A euphemism no doubt for Projects Bacchus, Jefferson, and Clear Vision. No hint of Project Black Death though.

"At this time there is no evidence to suggest that the spores used in the attack came directly from Fort Detrick or Dugway, and no one at either location is under suspicion. We are actively pursuing leads into the possible theft of the spores and are receiving the full cooperation of authorities in Kazakhstan."

This brought a smile to Mackey's face and looks of utter confusion to others in the room.

"We traced the biosafety cabinet to a scientific equipment supplier in Virginia. The item was allegedly shipped to USAMRIID in the summer of 2001, however invoices at USAMRIID do not indicate it was ever received. An employee who worked briefly at the supplier is being sought for questioning at this time."

Thompson. Good luck in finding him.

"Fingerprints at the scene have not matched to any in the Integrated Automated Fingerprint Identification System or IAFIS. We are pursuing access to other databases. At this time we do not have sufficient evidence to make an arrest. That's all ladies and gentleman, as always, the information you have just been provided is classified and may be shared on a need-to-know basis only."

Other fingerprint databases? Didn't the FBI have access to the universe of fingerprints? And what became of the tape?

As soon as the meeting broke Mackey worked his way to the front where Charo stood next to Martinez who was engaged in conversation with the deputy director. When Martinez saw Mackey approach he broke away and extended a hand.

"Dr. Dunn, glad you could make it. We genuinely appreciate all you've done."

Before Mackey could feign false modesty, Martinez had excused himself, taking off after the deputy director who was leaving.

Mackey gave Charo a playful tap on the shoulder. "Hey, how are you doing?"

"I'm holding up okay. Sorry I have been out of touch, it has been a hectic week."

Mackey broke into an impish smile. "I've been pretty busy, too."

"Yeah, what have you been up to?" she chuckled.

"Oh, just being patriotic. Hey, who was the guy sitting in the back row in the corner? Tall, mustache, plaid shirt? I've seen him before, maybe at a CDC conference."

"He's a consultant. An anthrax vaccine specialist from USAMRIID. I forget his name," Charo answered.

"You know I could use a ride home, any chance you are going my way?"

"Yes, I think I owe you that much. I just need a moment to collect my things and sign out a vehicle."

"Make sure it has an E-ZPass."

Charo adjusted the seat and mirrors, buckled up, and turned the ignition.

"Can we make one stop before we hit the interstate?"

"Mackey, why didn't you go before we left the house?"

"Fun-ny. Up ahead, hang a U-turn. Then make a left at 6th Street Northwest."

"Where are we headed?"

"I want to pay my respects. At Rhode Island Avenue Northwest, where Route 1 splits off, turn right."

They passed St. Mary's Cemetery but did not stop. Charo remembered that Mackey's father was buried in Maryland. Perhaps he wanted to visit his grave, though it must be closer to Baltimore. They crossed over the Metro tracks and passed a station. Mackey craned his neck to the right.

"Turn here! Turn here!"

"Okay, I see it."

The road curved back in the direction they came, toward the Metro station. Then Charo saw their destination: the former Brentwod Processing and Distribution Center. It was a nondescript government building. As she pulled into the parking lot the dome of the Capitol was visible in the distance. They got out.

Mackey walked to the entrance and stopped before a plaque affixed to the brick wall.

In the lobby he purchased a postcard stamp then withdrew from his pocket a postcard and affixed the stamp. Charo came closer, placing her hand on his wrist. It was an aerial photograph taken at sunset. The camera angle placed the Lincoln Memorial in the foreground with a view across the reflecting pool at the Washington Monument that glowed golden in the waning rays of sunlight. She turned the card over. It was addressed to MacPherson Dunn. He had written two words: Mailaise Cured. Mackey walked over to a slot in the wall and deposited the card.

It wasn't until they were past Baltimore that Charo broke the silence.

"I still don't understand why he did it. I mean, what did Farrington hope to achieve?"

"If you are trying to get inside his head I think you first have to understand arrogance, power, and greed. I'm no expert, but I've worked for my share of megalomaniacs."

"I'm listening."

"We know he felt strongly that Iraq was a threat and that there was unfinished business with Saddam Hussein. He felt so strongly that it didn't matter that there wasn't the evidence to support his position. That's arrogance. I doubt he ever gave any thought there would be consequences to his actions, or that he'd face charges if caught. That's power. He also stood to make a lot of money. Correct that, did make a lot of money, as AmCon was awarded millions in defense contracts. That's greed, completing the scoundrel trifecta."

"I can grasp why he thought he could get away with it, but the scheme was so far fetched. How could he think it would work?"

"The way I put it together, Farrington figured a bioterrorism attack using anthrax made in the Soviet

Union would implicate a State-sponsored terrorist organization, like al Qaeda or Iraq. He didn't count on the spores being American made. Hey, I almost forgot to ask, whatever became of the fingerprint sample we dropped off at the lab?"

"Technician is under strict orders not to share the results."

"What does that mean?"

Charo shook her head. "Martinez is playing it safe I guess." They returned to their thoughts for several minutes, then Charo again spoke. "I consider myself patriotic. But I cannot conceive ever doing something like this, even if I believed it was necessary for the protection of my country. It is hard for me to accept that Farrington did this out of a sense of duty."

"Okay, stick with greed. Works for me," Mackey said.

They drove in silence. Mackey watched the trees and houses fly by like images from a kinetoscope until he fell asleep. When they reached the turnpike exit for Princeton, Charo poked his arm to wake him.

"Mackey, there's an envelope for you in my bag." He emerged from slumber disoriented and fumbled behind the seat to find Charo's bag. Mackey came forward with a white envelope bearing the FBI logo.

"What is it? A check for services rendered?" Charo kept her eyes fixed on the road and her lips pursed. Mackey turned the envelope over in his hands and the contents slid from one end to the other. "A souvenir? An honorary FBI badge?"

"Mackey, you should open the envelope." Her voice was cold and sharp like chilled lemon juice. Mackey studied her face in the highway lights as he slipped one finger beneath the flap but the reason for Charo's mood change did not reside there. There was no letter inside, just a two-by-three-inch laminated card. He recognized the backside of the card as a Massachusetts driver's license. He cast a puzzled glance at Charo as he spun the license around. It wasn't a photo of Medusa that turned him to stone, it was Allie's.

"Wha—wha—where did you get this?"

"Boston PD sent it by Federal Express yesterday."

Mackey squeezed back the tears, but his eyes welled up like boiled tomatoes. Words raced though his mind but none exited his lips.

"When you first approached me I did a background check on you. I called the Boston field office and had a brief chat with the agent who handled your wife's disappearance. I guess he remembered my name and called the NYC field office for me this week."

It took minutes for Mackey to regain his voice and composure. When he again spoke his words sounded like a truck rolling over seashells.

"But how? Where?"

Charo took a deep breath. "A couple of months back a skel named Darrell Lee Johnson was found dead in an apartment in the South End. He was an alcoholic and a well-known, small-time thief. When his landlady cleared out his stuff she found your wife's license among several stolen credit cards. She turned it over to Boston PD. From there it was given to the cold case squad who notified the Boston FBI office. The agent reached out and cleared the way for it to be returned to you."

For once his jukebox didn't have a song to play. He remained mum until they reached the oil refinery in Elizabeth pouring dense black smoke into the illuminated night sky.

"Allie didn't kill herself."

.| Epilogue |.

It took Mackey an hour and half on the subway and then twenty-five minutes by bus to get to Far Rockaway, Queens. The day was overcast and cold. It smelled of snow but none fell. The bus deposited him in the empty parking lot of Jacob Riis Park. He walked to the beach and sat in the sand staring out at the waves of Jamaica Bay. At some depth, a place beyond the horizon, the bay became the North Atlantic Ocean. His mind drifted with the currents.

Aside from the passing company of a man and his Portuguese Water Dog, Mackey had the beach to himself. He was not dressed for the weather. His teeth chattered and his nose dripped. He held his arms tight against his body and shimmied his butt into the sand for warmth. Hours passed, the tide turned, and the sun began to set. When the edge of the sun dipped into the waves his jukebox cued up lines from the Tim Easton song, "Get Some Lonesome[20]." Like Dorothy's wish to go home to Kansas, the power to step from the shadows had been with him all along.

From an inner-coat pocket Mackey removed a plastic bag. He withdrew its contents and held it in his hands. The plastic was cracked in several places and the hinges no longer worked. He dug in the sand until it became too hard and too cold for him to move. From his other pocket he withdrew Allie's driver's license. He slid it between the pages of the booklet. He took one final look at a grimacing Declan McManus with a guitar in his hands, spread-legged and knock-kneed.

People who spoke so freely about closure he suspected had never suffered profound loss. If they had, it would've been their mouths that had closure. Maudlin sentimentality and empty sympathies irritated him. He could close doors, windows, and cases. But not his heart.

He heard five sorrowful guitar notes followed by the haunting vocals of Kat Maslich singing "Ghost." The Jell-O song, so named because it never failed to turn him into a quivering mass of water and protein.

> The ghost of you
> has almost faded now
> you're drifting in and out
> of my life
> when leaves fall you'll come right back
> ' cause I was yours for a little while
>
> you will always be
> a ghost who lives and breathes
> and you lay me down in reverie
> every tear that falls
> remember me[21]

Mackey placed the CD in the hole and covered it with sand.

"Goodbye, Allie."

. . .

A month into his new job, while a consultant babbled on and on about database requirements, Mackey's cell phone rang. It was Charo. He stepped out of the meeting and into the hallway.

"Hey, beautiful."

"Mackey, you'll never guess who is in town."

"The Pope?"

"No. Robert Mueller, you know, the director of the FBI."

"Checking on NYPD's security measures is he?"

"Listen, he wants to see us in an hour. Can you come over?"

Charo was waiting in front of the Ted Weiss Federal Building, with the smokers no less, when Mackey walked up. She was fidgety. She smiled and kissed him on the cheek. Mueller and Martinez were waiting in the office of the Joint Terrorism Task Force. After the perfunctory handshakes Mueller invited them to sit. He sat on the edge of the table with Martinez beside him holding a manila folder. Mackey knew it wasn't good to meet with someone holding a manila folder. Invariably there was crappy news in the folder. You got a *D* in mathematics and were being placed with the "slow" kids next year. An enzyme test came back too high, followed by the words, "Your father has had a heart attack." Or when he had to tell a patient, "I'm sorry, the tumor is inoperable." Martinez spoke first.

"We have a problem. Remember that sample you dropped off at the forensics lab last month?"

Mackey and Charo glanced at each other. Martinez opened the folder. He adjusted his reading glasses on the tip of his nose and peered at the paper, moving his head up and down until he found the tidbit of information he was seeking. He closed the folder, removed his glasses, and folded his arms across his chest. The tip of the manila folder stuck out of one side of his body while the reading glasses appeared behind the other elbow. Mackey thought to himself, definitely not good news.

"The ball of Scotch tape, remember that sample?" They nodded. "It was logged as coming from the office of John Farrington, his right and left index fingers and thumbs. How exactly was this sample obtained?"

"I stuck the tape to his fingers," Mackey said.

"You stuck tape to his fingers? Did he agree to being fingerprinted?"

"He was much more agreeable after I took the tape off," Mackey said.

Charo gazed out the window to hide the fact that she was biting her lower lip to suppress a laugh. Now, removed from the scene, she could appreciate the humor. She was thinking what would it be like if she worked in the building across the way. Maybe for a company that designed Thanksgiving displays for stores.

"Then there was no consent?"

They didn't answer. Mueller stood up, took the folder from Martinez, and without looking at it placed it on the desk.

"Aside from Dr. Dunn's, the Scotch prints matched one of the sets we found at the storage facility laboratory. It does seem like Mr. Farrington was involved, however, the prints are not admissible in court."

"What about getting his security file from the White House?" Mackey asked.

"We are pursuing all avenues, but aren't optimistic," Mueller said.

Mackey dared not speak what came into his head: the FBI finally had the anthrax killer yet couldn't make the case, and he was responsible for both.

"Farrington would probably receive a presidential pardon anyway," Mackey said.

Charo and Martinez snorted in unison. Mueller smiled wanly, walked over to the folder, and removed two photographs, handing them to Mackey and Charo.

"We found other prints, more numerous, on the Sheetrock. They belong to this gentleman." One photo was of a young man with sandy-brown hair and freckles. The other was of a tattoo; a bald eagle, its wings painted red, white, and blue, standing over a dead bear with a Russian insignia.

"Hunter S. Scott, ex-CIA. Whereabouts unknown, but we are looking for him."

"Thompson," uttered Mackey.

"Is he connected to Farrington?" Charo asked.

"Hunter worked for Cheyenne Global Security, the defense contractor that bought Mr. Farrington's company AmCon. We are checking to see if the two had a relationship. We got the photos and prints, with some effort, from the CIA. Your man Wexler Barnes was of considerable assistance. It also appears that a man resembling Mr. Scott briefly worked for Zeta Technical Laboratory Equipment, Inc., the supplier of the biosafety cabinet."

Mueller pulled out another image from the folder. It was a security identification card photo from ZTL that bore a doppelganger resemblance to Thompson/Scott.

There was some good news. First, that the FBI had exonerated Joseph Erekat. His fingerprints were not found anywhere in the makeshift, storage-center lab. Mueller showed them the official letter sent to Erekat's family stating he was no longer a suspect in the Amerithrax investigation. The second piece of news had to do with Lavigne.

"We've also cleared Dr. Lavigne from any involvement in the anthrax mailings," Martinez said. "Those letters you found were clean, no prints. And the handwriting didn't match to Dr. Lavigne's."

"And Mrs. Bilderback?" Charo asked.

"She's been through enough. We are not going to pursue obstruction of justice charges," Martinez said as he handed the birthday cards to Charo to send back to Mrs. Bilderback.

"Calvin, there's been something I've been meaning to ask you," Charo said, "that day in your office, when I showed you the letters we Lavigne's daughter gave us, your reaction…" Charo gazed to the floor, searching for the right word.

"My reaction?" Martinez asked defensively.

"You were indifferent."

"I know those letters pretty well. Even see them in my sleep. We knew already knew the handwriting didn't match to Erekat and that if he was our man that he had to have help. But we couldn't connect him to anyone with a motive to mail the letters. Lavigne had been a suspect, so I was actually pretty stoked to see those letters. I thought there was a good chance they'd turn out to be the originals. With all the stops and starts in the investigation I was playing my cards close to the vest."

"We thought that because you and Farrington both went to Princeton that you were involved or were protecting him," Mackey said. The hum of the ventilation system and sound of distant jackhammers stopped and the room became eerily quiet. Charo thought she heard a hand grenade pin drop. Then Mueller and Martinez broke out in hearty laughter.

"That's a good one Dr. Dunn," Martinez said.

"What about Goldie?" Mackey asked.

"Who?" Muellller asked.

"His dog."

"Buried in the woods, skull was bashed in," Martinez said.

"Pistol whipped?" Charo asked.

"Nah, a heavier object; flat and round."

"Which brings us to the final bit of news," Mueller continued.

The Maryland State Police had reopened the Lavigne investigation. The medical examiner upon reviewing the autopsy and other evidence concluded that Lavigne's death was not a suicide. Mueller had spoken with Maryland's attorney general and he believed that they had sufficient evidence to charge Farrington with Lavigne's murder. It would be a tough case to prove, the video quality being as poor as it was.

Mackey thought to himself, Farrington was responsible for six murders. Possibly seven if he had anything to do with the death of Special Agent Onyungaya. He might be held accountable for one out of six, not a respectable average. When Mackey was six years old he first fell in love with and then had his heart broken by baseball. His beloved Baltimore Orioles lost the 1969 World Series to the underdog New York Mets. Al Weis, a lifetime .219 hitter who managed seven measly home runs in ten major league seasons, killed the Birds in the series. Weis hit .455 and blasted a crucial homerun that led the Mets to win the Fall Classic over the much-favored Orioles in five games. The percentages were poor, but Mackey hoped it would only take one swing to put Farrington away for life.

A slow smile crept across Charo's face. Out of the corner of his eye Mackey watched the corner of her lip creep up until it unearthed a darling dimple. He turned to her, confused.

"Mackey, don't you see? We've got him!"

"Maybe, for one murder. But he'll walk on the others and the anthrax mailings will forever remain an unsolved case."

"That's where you're wrong. When the Maryland State Police arrest him they will as a matter of routine take his fingerprints. By protocol the prints will be entered into the Integrated Automated Fingerprint Identification System, where we will have access to them."

"We've already searched Farrington's home," Martinez added. "Found envelopes with the eagle-talon printing defect and fibers indistinguishable with those found on the anthrax letters."

"And the murder weapon," Mueller added.

"But wasn't Lavigne killed by his own gun?" Mackey said.

"Not Lavigne's murder, his dog's," Martinez said. "We found a forty-five-pound neodymium-boron magnet; the blood and hair on it were a match to Goldie. There were also paint chips that matched to Lavigne's computer."

Mackey joined Charo, Mueller, and Martinez who were already wearing identical gotcha grins.

·||·

Mackey's Soundtrack (Song Notes)

1. Dan Fogelberg, "Once upon a time," on *Nether Lands,* 1977.
2. Jackson Browne, "Your Bright Baby Blues," on *The Pretender,* 1976.
3. Tori Amos, "Winter," on *Little Earthquakes,* 1991.
4. The Beatles, "Golden Slumbers," on *Abbey Road,* 1969.
5. Jackson Browne, "Sky Blue and Black," on *I'm Alive,* 1993.
6. The Weepies, "The World Spins Madly On," on *Say I Am You, 2005.*
7. Bruce Cockburn, "Open," on You've Never Seen Everything, 2003.
8. Tom Waits, "Please Call Me, Baby," on The Heart of Saturday Night, 1974.
9. Al Stewart, "Not the One," on *Modern Times,* 1975.
10. Counting Crows, "Raining in Baltimore," on *August and Everything After,* 1993.
11. Darden Smith, "All the King's Horses," on *Trouble no more,* 1990.
12. Teitur, "Sleeping with the lights on," on *Poetry & Aeroplanes*, 2003.
13. Ben Lee, "The debt collectors," on *Awake is the New Sleep*, 2005.
14. Simon and Garfunkel, "I am a rock," on *Greatest Hits*, 1972.
15. Jackson Browne, "For a Dancer," on *Late for the Sky,* 1974
16. Ben Harper, "More than sorry," on *Both Sides of the Gun,* 2006.
17. Cold Play, "Till Kingdom Come," on *X&Y,* 2005.
18. Patty Griffin, "Long Ride Home," on *1000 Kisses*, 2002.
19. Kim Richey, "Absence of Your Company," on *Chinese Boxes*, 2007.

20. Tim Easton, "Get Some Lonesome," on *The Truth About Us*, 2001.
21. Eastmountainsouth, "Ghost," on *Eastmountainsouth*, 2003.

Bibliography

BOOKS

Alibek, Kent. *Biohazard.* New York: Random House, 1999.

Bissell, Tom. *Chasing the Sea: Lost Among the Ghosts of Empire in Central Asia.* New York: Vintage Books, 2003.

Bulloch, William. *History of Bacteriology.* New York: Dover Publications, 1938.

Cole, Richard A. *The Anthrax Letters: A Medical Detective Story.* Washington, D.C: Joseph Henry Press, 2003.

DeLong, Candice. *Special Agent: My Life on the Front Lines as a Woman in the FBI.* New York: Hyperion, 2001.

Dew, Rosemary. *No Backup: My Life as a Female FBI Special Agent.* New York: Carol & Graf, 2004.

Dworkin, Mark S. *Outbreak Investigations Around the World.* Boston: Jones and Bartlett Publishers, 2010.

Ember, Melvin, Carol R. Ember and Ian Skoggard. *Encyclopedia of Diasporas: immigrant and refugee cultures around the world.* New York: Springer, 2005.

Ferguson, Rob. *The Devil and the Disappearing Sea.* Vancouver: Raincoast Books, 2003.

Graysmith, Robert. *Amerithrax: the Hunt for the Anthrax Killer.* New York: Joe Books, 2003.

Guillemin, Jeanne. *Anthrax: The Investigation of a Deadly Outbreak.* Berkeley, CA: University of California Press, 1999.

Kessler, Ronald. *The Bureau: The Secret History of the FBI.* New York: St. Martin's Press, 2003.

Lake, Edward. *Analyzing the anthrax attacks: the first 3 years.* Racine, WI: Edward Lake, 2005.

Mandel, Gerald L, John E. Bennett and Ralph Dolin. *Principles and Practice of Infectious Diseases, 5th edition.* Philadelphia: Churchill Livingstone, 2000.

Miller, Judith, Stephen Engelberg and William Broad. *Germs: Biological Weapons and America's Secret War*. New York: Simon and Schuster, 2001.

Powers, Richard Gid. *Broken: The Troubled past and Uncertain Future of the FBI.* New York: Free Press, 2004.

Preston, Richard. *The Demon in the Freezer*. New York: Ballantine Books, 2002.

Robbins, Christopher. *Apples are from Kazakhstan, the land that disappeared.* New York: Atlas & Co., 2008.

Rosten, Keith. *Once in Kazakhstan: The Snow Leopard Emerges*. Lincoln, Nebraska: iUniverse, 2005.

Smith, I.C. *Inside*. Nashville, TN: Nelson Current, 2004.

Thompson, Marilyn W. *The Killer Strain: Anthrax and a Government Exposed.* New York: Harper Collins, 2003.

Wise, David. *Spy*. New York: Random House, 2002.

Wolke, Robert L. *What Einstein Told His Cook.* New York: W.W. Norton & Company, 2002.

Woodward, Bob. *Plan of Attack.* New York: Simon and Schuster, 2004.

Zajtchuk, Russ, editor in chief, *Textbook of Military Medicine: Medical Aspects of Chemical and Biological Warfare.* Washington, DC: Office of the Surgeon General, 1997.

PRINT ARTICLES

Beecher, D. "Forensic Application of Microbiological Culture Analysis To Identify Mail Intentionally Contaminated with *Bacillus anthracis* Spores," *Applied and Environmental Microbiology* 72, no. 8 (2006): 5304-10.

Budlowle, B., S.E. Schutzer, M.S. Ascher, et al. "Toward a System of Microbial Forensics: from Sample

Collection to Interpretation of Evidence," *Applied and Environmental Microbiology* 71, no. 5 (2005): 2209-13.

Dewan P.K., A.M. Fry, K. Lasserson, et al. "Inhalational Anthrax Outbreak among Postal Workers, Washington, D.C.," *EID* 8, no. (2002): 1066-72.

Dixon, T.C., M. Meselson, J. Guillemin and P.C. Hanna. "Anthrax," *New England Journal of Medicine* 4341, no. 11 (1999): 815-26.

Domaradskij, I.V., W. Orent. "Achievments of the Soviet biological weapons programme and implications for the future," *Rev Sci Tech Off Int Epiz* 25, no. 1 (2006): 153-161.

Dull, P.M., K.M. Wilson, B. Kournikakis, et al. "*Bacillus anthracis* Aersolization Associated with a Contaminated Mail Sorting Machine," *EID* 8, vol. 10 (2002): 1044-47.

Glassman, H. "Industrial inhalation anthrax," *Bacteriol Rev* 30 (1966): 657-659.

Greene, C.M., J. Reefhuis, C. Tan, et al. "Epidemiologic Investigations of Bioterrorism-related Anthrax," *EID* 8, no. 10 (2002): 1048-55.

Griffith, K.S., P. Mead, G.L. Armstrong, et al. "Bioterrorism-related Inhalational Anthrax in an Elderly Woman, Connecticut, 2001," *EID* 9, no. 6 (2003): 681-8.

Hoffmaster, A.R., C.C. Fitzgerald, E. Ribot, L.W. Mayer, T. Popovic. "Molecular subtyping of Bacillus anthracis and the 2001 bioterrorism-associated anthrax outbreak, United States," *EID* 8, no. 10 (2002): 1111-6.

Hsu, V.P., S.L. Lukacs, T. Handzel, et al. "Opening a Bacillus anthracis–Containing Envelope, Capitol Hill, Washington, D.C.: The Public Health Response," *EID* 8, no. 10 (2002): 1039-43.

Inglesby, T.V., T. O'Toole, D.A. Henderson, et al. "Anthrax as a Biological Weapon," *JAMA* 287, no. 17 (2002): 2236-2252.

Jackson, P.J., M.E. Hugh-Jones, D.W. Adair, et al. "PCR analysis of tissue samples from the 1979 Sverdlovsk anthrax victims: The presence of multiple *Bacillus anthracis* strains in different victims," *Proc Nat Acad Sci* 95, no. 3 (1998): 1224-1229.

Jernigan, J.A., D.S. Stephens, D.A. Ashford, et al. "Bioterrorism-Related Inhalation Anthrax: The First 10 Cases Reported in the United States," *EID* 7, no. 6 (2001): 933-44.

Meselson, M., J. Guillemin, M.E. Hugh-Jones, et al. "The Sverdlovsk Anthrax Outbreak of 1979," *Science* 266 (1994): 1202-08.

Olson, K.B. "Aum Shinrikyo: once and future threat?" *EID* 5, no. 4 (1999): 513-6.

Read, T.R., S.L. Salzberg, M. Pop, et al. "Comparative Genome Sequencing for Discovery of Novel Polymorphisms in *Bacillus anthracis*," *Science* 296 (2002): 2028-2033.

Swedish Defence Research Agency. *Conversion of Former Biologic Weapons Facilities in Kazakhstan.* Report FOI-R—0082—SE, May 2001.

Teshale, E.H., J. Painter, G.A. Burr, et al. "Environmental Sampling for Spores of *Bacillus anthracis,"* *EID* 8, no. 10 (2002): 1083-87.

Traeger, M.S., S.T. Wiersma, N.E. Rosenstein, et al. "First Case of Bioterrorism-Related Inhalational Anthrax in the United States, Palm Beach County, Florida, 2001," *EID* 8, no. 10 (2002): 1029-34.

INTERNET SOURCES

AbsoluteWrite, "FBI Slang," URL: http://absolutewrite.com/forums/showthread.php?t=62950 accessed on 10/12/2008.

Advantour, "Taraz, Kazakhstan," URL: http://www.advantour.com/kazakhstan/taraz.htm accessed on 9/15/2008.

Alexandrov, Mikhail, "Russian Migration to Kazakhstan," URL: http://cerc.unimelb.edu.au/bulletin/buljun.htm accessed on 9/18/2008.

Alibek, Kent, Congressional testimony, 1999, "Weapons of Mass Destruction," URL: http://www.globalsecurity.org/wmd/library/congress/1999_h/99-10-20alibek.htm accessed on 11/30/2008.

American Chemical Society, "Tracing Killer Spores," Online News, September 18, 2008 URL: http://pubs3.acs.%20org/journals/ancham/news/2008/09/18/cp_anthrax.html accessed on 9/25/2008.

American Type Culture Collection, URL: http://www.atcc.org/ accessed on 12-2-2008.

Andersen, Martin Edwin, "What's at the heart of the FBI failures," *Insight Magazine* July 1, 2002 from URL: http://findarticles.com/p/articles/mi_m1571/is_24_18/ai_89079382/pg_3/ accessed on 1/24/2008.

Anonymous, "Bad Cop, Bad Cop," letter to the editor, Boston Globe, November 7, 2008, URL: http://www.highbeam.com/doc/1P2-19381197.html accessed on 11/24/2008.

Arul John, "Finding IP Address in Yahoo Mail," URL: http://aruljohn.com/info/howtofindipaddress/#yahoo accessed on 1/3/2009.

Bahal, Aniruddha, "Death of Microbiologists: Conspiracy or coincidence?" URL: http://www.cobrapost.com/documents/Death%20of%20Microbiologists.htm accessed 3/28/2008.

Beecker, Jo and Barton Gellman, "Leaving No Tracks," URL: http://blog.washingtonpost.com/cheney/chapters/leaving_no_tracks/comments.htmlpters/a_strong_push_from_back_stage/ accessed 2/7/2009.

Beecker, Jo and Barton Gellman, "Strong Push from Backstage," URL: http://blog.washingtonpost.com/cheney/chapters/a_strong_push_from_back_stage/ accessed 2/7/2009.

Bioweapons Prevention Project, "BioWeapons Report," URL: http://www.bwpp.org/documents/2004BWRFinal_000.pdf accessed on 3/19/2008.

Blackledge, Brett J, August 5, 2008, Associated Press, "CIA officials deny fake Iraq-al-Qaida link letter," URL: http://www.usatoday.com/news/washington/2008-08-05-4136273082_x.htm accessed on 8/5/2008.

Bohn, Kevin, "Patriot Act report documents civil rights complaints," URL: http://www.cnn.com/2003/LAW/07/21/justice.civil.liberties/index.html?iref=allsearch accessed 10/6/2008.

Boston Harbor Cruises, URL: http://www.bostonharborcruises.com/provincetown-ferry/schedule-rates.aspx accesses on 10-4-2008.

Boyer, Peter J. "The Ames Strain," *The New Yorker*, November 12, 2001. URL: http://www.ph.ucla.edu/epi/bioter/theamesstrain.html accessed on 12/30/2008.

Bozheyev, Gulbarshyn, Yerlan Kunakbayev and Dastan Yeleukenov, Center for Nonproliferation Studies, Monterey Institute of International Studies, Occasional Paper No. 1, "Former Soviet Biological Weapons Facilities in Kazakhstan: Past, Present and Future," URL: http://cns.miis.edu/opapers/op1/op1.pdf accessed on 9/11/2008.

Brain, Marshall, "How Carbon-14 Dating Works," URL: http://science.howstuffworks.com/environmental/earth/geology/carbon-14.htm accessed on 11/23/2008.

Brand, Madeline and Laura Sullivan, NPR transcript, August 6, 2008, "Documents: Bruce Ivins Sent False

Samples," URL: http://www.npr.org/templates/story/story.php?storyId=93341386 accessed on 12/1/2008.

British Broadcasting Corporation, *Newsnight,* "Anthrax Attacks 3/14/2002," URL: http://news.bbc.co.uk/2/hi/programmes/newsnight/archive/1873368.stmaccessed on 11/28/2008.

Broad, William J, David Johnston, Judith Miller and Paul Zielbauer, *New York Times* November 9, 2001, "Anthrax probe hampered by FBI blunders / Agents unprepared for complexities of case," URL: http://articles.sfgate.com/2001-11-09/news/17627256_1_anthrax-investigation-anthrax-attacks-anthrax-samples accessed on 2/5/2008.

Broad, William J, David Johnston, Judith Miller and Paul Zielbauer, *New York Times* November 9, 2001, "Experts See FBI Missteps Hampering Anthrax Inquiry," URL: http://www.nytimes.com/2001/11/09/us/nation-challenged-inquiry-experts-see-fbi-missteps-hampering-anthrax-inquiry.html accessed on 2/5/2008.

Cable News Network, October 4, 2001, "Ukranian missile downed Russian jet," URL: http://archives.cnn.com/2001/WORLD/europe/10/04/russia.plane.crash/index.html accessed on 10/15/2008.

Cable News Network, October 5, 2001, "Russia probes jet crash terror link," URL: http://archives.cnn.com/2001/WORLD/europe/10/05/plane.crash/index.html accessed on 10/15/2008.

Cable News Network, October 12, 2001, *Larry King Live,* "America Strikes Back: Anthrax Alert," URL: http://transcripts.cnn.com/TRANSCRIPTS/0110/12/lkl.00.html accessed on 11/16/2007.

Cable News Network, October 13, 2001, "Ukraine apologizes for jet crash," URL:

http://archives.cnn.com/2001/WORLD/europe/10/13/ukraine.plane/index.html accessed on 10/15/2008.

Cable News Network, October 17, 2001, "Ken Alibek: Preparing for the range of bioterrorism possibilities," URL: http://archives.cnn.com/2001/COMMUNITY/10/16/alibek accessed on 11/29/2008.

Cable News Network, May 10, 2002, "What made the American turncoat tick?" URL: http://archives.cnn.com/2002/LAW/05/10/spy.hanssen/index.html accessed on 10/15/2008.

Calder, Joshua and Jim Lee, ICE Case Studies Number 69, "Aral Sea and Defense Issues," URL: http://www1.american.edu/ted/ice/aralsea.htm accessed on 9/20/2008.

Center for American Progress, "9/11 Commission Primer," URL: http://www.indybay.org/newsitems/2008/09/30/18542046.php accessed on 11/15/2008.

Centers for Disease Control and Prevention-Arctic Investigations Program, URL: http://www.cdc.gov/ncezid/dpei/aip/ accessed on 9/20/2008.

Central Intelligence Agency, World Factbook, "Kazakhstan," URL: https://www.cia.gov/library/publications/the-world-factbook/geos/kz.html accessed on 9/18/2008.

Charette, Robert, "FBI Sentinel Update," URL: http://spectrum.ieee.org/riskfactor/computing/it/fbi_sentinel_update accessed on 10/26/2008.

Chamberlain, Casey, September 19, 2006, NBC News, "My anthrax survivor's story: NBC News employee speaks out for the first time on her ordeal," URL: http://www.msnbc.msn.com/id/14785359/ accessed on 3/8/2009.

Chowdawg, "The boats," URL: http://realtravel.com/e-214075-aralsk_entry-the_boats accessed on 9/19/2008.

Columbia Broadcast System News, February 19, 2004, "Years of FBI Agent Crimes Detailed," URL: http://www.cbsnews.com/stories/2004/02/19/national/main601135.shtml accessed on December 1, 2007.

Cornell University Law School, "Federal Rules of Crinimal Procedure, Rule 6. The Grand Jury," URL: http://www.law.cornell.edu/rules/frcrmp/Rule6.htm accessed 11/26/2008.

Deedrick, Douglas W., July 2000, *Forensic Science Communications,* vol 2(3), Hairs, Fibers, Crime and Evidence," URL: http://www.fbi.gov/hq/lab/fsc/backissu/july2000/deedric3.htm accessed on 1/24/2010.

Democratic Policy Committee, "An Oversight Hearing on Accountability for Contracting Abuses in Iraq," URL: http://dpc.senate.gov/dpchearing.cfm?h=hearing37 accessed on 2/13/2010.

Democratic Policy Committee, "DPC Hearings on Waste, Frad and Abuse in Iraq," URL: http://dpc.senate.gov/dpcoversight-hearings-iraq.cfm accessed on 2/13/2010.

Department of Defense, "Richard B. Cheney," URL: http://www.defense.gov/specials/secdef_histories/bios/cheney.htm accessed on 8/5/2008.

"DG Jargon," URL: http://asmrb.pbworks.com/w/page/9958786/DG%20Jargon accessed on 10/12/2008.

"Dick Cheney Exposed," URL: http://www.stateofday.blogspot.com/2005/11/dick_cheney_exposed.html accessed 2/24/2010.

District of Columbia Department of Health, URL: http://dchealth.dc.gov/doh/site/default.asp accessed on 9/17/2008.

Doherty, Patrick, "Why Bush Went to War," URL: http://www.alternet.org/world/19472 accessed on 2/28/2010.

Dolan, Jack and David Altimari, *The Hartford Courant*, May 16, 2004, "FBI Retracing Steps in Anthrax Investigation," URL: http://www.ph.ucla.edu/epi/bioter/fbiretracing.html accessed on 9/20/2008.

Doyle, Charles, "The US Patriot Act: A Sketch," URL: http://www.fas.org/irp/crs/RS21203.pdf accessed 10/6/2008.

Dreyfuss, Robert, "Vice Squad," URL: http://prospect.org/cs/articles?articleId=11401 accessed on 2/16/2009.

Dunn, Katia, NPR, September 18, 2008, "Emotional Wounds Linger for Anthrax Survivor," URL: http://www.npr.org/templates/story/story.php?storyId=94681346 accessed on 9/18/2008.

Elias, Paul, October 16, 2010, Associated Press, "Oil change reignites debate over GPS trackers," URL: http://www.msnbc.msn.com/id/39699243/ns/us_news-security/t/students-oil-change-reignites-debate-over-gps-trackers/ accessed on 10/16/2010.

Epstein, Edward Jay, Januray 24, 2010, *The Wall Street Journal,* "The Antrhax Attacks Remain Unsolved," URL: http://online.wsj.com/article/SB10001424052748704541004575011421223515284.html accessed 2/3/2010.

Evident Crime Scene Products, "Forensic Chemicals," URL: http://www.evidentcrimescene.com/cata/chem/chem.html accessed on 2/6/2008.

Federal Bureau of Investigation, "Amerithrax Final Report," URL: http://www.justice.gov/amerithrax/ accessed on 2/19/2010.

Federal Bureau of Investigation, "FBI Records: the Vault," URL: http://vault.fbi.gov/reading-room-index accessed on 11/25/2008.

Federal Bureau of Investigation, "Forensic Science Communications," URL: http://www.fbi.gov/about-us/lab/forensic-science-communications/fsc/july2000/index.htm accessed 12/21/2008.

Federal Bureau of Investigation, "Innocent Images National Initiative," URL: http://www.fbi.gov/about-us/investigate/cyber/innocent/innocent accessed on 1/12/2010.

Federal Bureau of Investigation, "Our Oath of Office," URL: http://www2.fbi.gov/publications/leb/2009/september2009/oath.htm accessed on 1/4/2009.

Federal Bureau of Investigation, "The Amerithrax Investigation," URL: http://www.fbi.gov/about-us/history/famous-cases/anthrax-amerithrax accessed 1/21/2008.

Federal Bureau of Investigation, "The FBI Academy," URL: http://www.fbi.gov/about-us/training accessed on 10/12/2008.

Federal Bureau of Investigation, Killed in the line of duty, "Hall of Honor," URL: http://www.fbi.gov/about-us/history/hallhonor accessed on 2/5/2009.

Fenner, Austin and Helen Kennedy, August 15, 2002, *The Daily News,* "Anthrax Doc Denies Being at Mail Site," URL: http://www.nydailynews.com/archives/news/2002/08/15/2002-08-15__anthrax_doc_denies_being_at.html accessed on 11/12/2007.

FirearmsID, URL: http://firearmsid.com accessed on 12/21/2008.

Finley, Bruce, December 2, 2001, *The Denver Post,* Soviets Leave Anthrax Legacy," URL:

http://brucefinley.com/pakistan-afghanistan-borderlands/soviets-leave-anthrax-legacy/ accessed on 3/23/2010.

Fleischer, Ari, "Press Briefing, October 4, 2001," URL: http://www.presidency.ucsb.edu/ws/index.php?pid=47575#axzz1Xaa42jlI accessed on 1/18/2009.

Foster, Don. "The Message in the Anthrax," *Vanity Fair*, October 2003. URL: http://www.ph.ucla.edu/epi/bioter/messageanthrax.html accessed on 10/6/2008.

FrederickNewsPost, "Ivins alone responsible for attacks, feds claim," http://www.fredericknewspost.com/sections/archives/display_detail.htm?StoryID=85740 accessed on 11/12/2008.

Gellman, Barton and Jo Beecker, "A Different Understanding with the President," URL: http://blog.washingtonpost.com/cheney/chapters/chapter_1/ accessed 2/5/2009.

Gellman, Barton and Jo Beecker, "Pushing the Envelope," URL: http://blog.washingtonpost.com/cheney/chapters/pushing_the_envelope_on_presi/ accessed 2/5/2009.

George Washington University, "FOIA Basics," URL: http://www.gwu.edu/~nsarchiv/nsa/foia/guide.html accessed on 12/16/2008.

Georgia Tech Research News, "Protecting Sensitve Data: Researchers Develop Fail-Safe Techniques for Erasing Magnetic Media," URL: http://www.gtresearchnews.gatech.edu/newsrelease/erase.htm accessed on 2/12/2009.

GlobalSecurity.org, Weapons of Mass Destruction, "Stepnogorsk," URL: http://www.globalsecurity.org/wmd/world/russia/stepnogorsk.htm accessed on 1/29/2009.

Goldstein, Harry, "Who Killed the Virtual Case File?" URF:

http://spectrum.ieee.org/computing/software/who-killed-the-virtual-case-file accessed on 10/16/2008.

Government Accounting Office, "Allegations That Certain Audits at Three Locations Did Not Meet Professional Standards Were Substantiated," URL: http://www.gao.gov/new.items/d08857.pdf accessed on 2/13/2008.

Government Printing Office, "Appendix: Moussaoui-Related FBI Field Agent Notes and Field Office/Headquarters E-Mails," URL: http://www.gpoaccess.gov/serialset/creports/pdf/appendices3.pdf accessed on 11/27/2007.

Greenwald, Glenn, "The FBI's selective release of documents in the anthrax case," URL: http://www.salon.com/news/opinion/glenn_greenwald/2008/08/06/fbi_documents/print.html accessed on 11/15/2008.

Gugliotta, Guy and Gary Matsumoto, *The Washington Post*, October 28, 2002, "FBI's Theory on Anthrax is Doubted," URL: http://www.ph.ucla.edu/epi/bioter/fbitheorydoubted.html accessed on 11/28/2008.

Gurney, Ian, "The Very Mysterious Deaths of Five Microbiologists," URL: http://www.rense.com/general18/five.htm accessed on 10/14/2008.

Guterl, Fred and Eve Conant, February 25, 2002, *Newsweek International,* "Huge Stocks of BioWeapons In the Former Soviet Union," URL: http://www.rense.com/general20/hugestocksAL.htm accessed 8/12/2008.

Halliburton Watch, "Cheney/Halliburton Chronology," URL: http://www.halliburtonwatch.org/about_hal/chronology.html, accessed on 2/27/2010.

Higgins, Sherry, "Virtual Case File-Congressional Testimony," URL:

http://www2.fbi.gov/congress/congress02/higgins071602.htm accessed on 10/26/2008.

History Commons, "Profile Behrooz Sashar," URL: http://www.historycommons.org/entity.jsp?entity=behrooz_sarshar accessed on 11/24/2008.

History Commons, "Scientist Confirmes Deadly Anthrax is Ames Strain," October 5, 2001. URL: http://www.historycommons.org/context.jsp?item=a100501amesidentified&scale=0#a100501amesidentified accessed on 2/5/2009.

History Commons, "Spring 1998 and After: US Army Secretly Produced Powdered Anthrax Similar to Anthrax Used in 2001 Attacks," URL: http://www.historycommons.org/searchResults.jsp?searchtext=anthrax+powder+William+Patrick&events=on&entities=on&articles=on&topics=on&timelines=on&projects=on&titles=on&descriptions=on&dosearch=on&search=Go accessed on 11/28/2008.

History Commons, "Spy Plane Crash in China," http://www.gtresearchnews.gatech.edu/newsrelease/erase.htm accessed on 2/12/2009.

Horowitz, Leonard George, Tetrahedron, LLC, August 30, 2002, "Investigators Conclude Russian Defector is Lead Suspect in Anthrax Mailings," URL: http://www.tetrahedron.org/news/NR020830.html accessed 11/29/2008.

International Atomic Energy Agency, "The Semipalatinsk Test Site, Kazakhstan," URL: http://www-ns.iaea.org/appraisals/semipalatinsk.asp accessed on 9/15/2008.

Iraq Watch, "Iraq's Biological Weapon Program," URL: http://www.iraqwatch.org/profiles/biological.html accessed on 11/28/2008.

Ivins, Molly, "Cheney's Mess Worth a Closer Look," URL: http://www.moveon.org/moveonbulletin/bulletin1.html accessed 8/5/2008.

Johnston, Lauren, "FBI Whistleblower Claims Confirmed," URL: http://www.cbsnews.com/stories/2004/07/29/evening news/main632983.shtml accessed on 11/24/2008.

Johnston, William Robert, "Review of Fall 2001 Anthrax Attacks," URL: http://www.johnstonsarchive.net/terrorism/anthrax.html accessed on 7/8/2008.

Judis, John B and Spencer Ackerman, "The Selling of the Iraq War: The First Casualty," URL: http://www.globalpolicy.org/component/content/article/168/37699.html accessed on 11/20/2008.

Kelley, Matt, March 30,2004, Associate Press, "Iraq: Halliburton Continues to Profit," URL: http://www.corpwatch.org/article.php?id=11240 accessed on 1/11/2009.

Kerchieval, Jeff, "Standards Employed to Determine the Time of Death," URL: http://www.arrakis.es/~jacoello/date.pdf accessed on 3/27/2010.

Kestenbaum, David, August 8, 2008, NPR, "FBI Details Science Tying Ivins to Anthrax Mailings," URL: http://www.npr.org/templates/story/story.php?storyId=93728829 accessed on 9/18/2008.

Kestenbaum, David, "New Angles Emerge in Anthrax Attacks of 2001," URL: http://www.npr.org/templates/story/story.php?storyId=6140863 accessed on 9/21/2008.

Ketcham, Christopher, *The American Conservative*, August 25, 2008, "The Anhtrax Files," URL: http://www.theamericanconservative.com/article/2008/aug/25/00012/ accessed on 12/1/2008.

Kristof, Nicholas, "Case of the Missing Anthrax," URL: http://www.nytimes.com/2002/07/19/opinion/case-of-the-missing-anthrax.html accessed on 12/6/2008.

Kumagi, Jean, "Mission Impossible," URL: http://spectrum.ieee.org/computing/software/mission-impossible accessed on 10/26/2008.

Lake, Ed, "Analysing the Anthrax Attacks," URL: http://www.anthraxinvestigation.com accessed on multiple dates November-December, 2008.

Laurich, V., "DNA Forensics," URL: http://www.wsu.edu/laurich/bios/102-2003/lecturenotes/lecture%2016-2008/forensics%20genetics.pdf accessed on 11/22/2008.

Lautenberg, Frank, "Congratulations Halliburton and Vice President Cheney," URL: http://lautenberg.senate.gov/newsroom/record.cfm?id=254548 accessed 2/24/2010.

Lazaroff, Tovah, "Leaders mourn immigrant air crash victims," URL: http://www.ncsj.org/AuxPages/100501crash.shtml accessed 10/15/2008.

Leahy, Patrick, "Summary of the USA Patriot Act," URL: http://leahy.senate.gov/press/press_releases/release/?id=6b5e5685-73db-4707-85b0-122eadf8fd23 accessed on 11/15/2008.

Lee, Jeanyoung, "Korean-Chinese Migration into the Russian Far East: A Human Security Perspective," URL: http://src-h.slav.hokudai.ac.jp/coe21/publish/no6_1_ses/chapter5_lee.pdf accessed on 1/25/2009.

Lengel, Allan and Joby Warrick, "FBI Is Casting A Wider Net in Anthrax Attacks," URL: http://www.washingtonpost.com/wp-dyn/content/article/2006/09/24/AR2006092401014.html accessed on 9/20/2008.

Levy, Adrian and Cathy Scott Clark, "The man who knew too much," URL:

http://www.guardian.co.uk/world/2007/oct/13/usa.pakistan accessedon 10/13/2009.

Lewis, Dana, October 20, 1999, NBC News, "Legacy of Soviet germ war lives on," URL: http://www.phaster.com/news_articles/germ_factory/ accessed on 8/11/2008.

Lincoln Memorial, URL: http://www.nps.gov/nr/travel/wash/dc71.htm accessed on 12-13-2008.

Lunn, Helen, "Slowly Across the Steppe- Kazakhstan," URL: http://www.bootsnall.com/articles/05-10/slowly-across-the-steppe-kazakhstan.html accessed on 9/19/2008.

MacKenzie, Deborah, "The Anthrax in Florida is North American," The New Scientist, October 11, 2001. URL: http://www.newscientist.com/article/dn1418-anthrax-in-florida-attack-is-north-american.html accessed on 2/05/2009.

MacLeod, Scott, "Cheney of Arabia," URL: http://mideast.blogs.time.com/2007/05/17/cheney_of_arabia/ accessed 8/5/2008.

Majidi, Vahid, "Science Briefing on Anthrax Investigation," URL: http://www.fbi.gov/about-us/history/famous-cases/anthrax-amerithrax/science-briefing accessed on 11/22/2008.

Marquis, Christopher, *The New York Times*, April 3, 2004, "Powell Blames CIA for Error on Iraq Mobile Labs," URL: http://www.nytimes.com/2004/04/03/world/powell-blames-cia-for-error-on-iraq-mobile-labs.html accessed on 3/23/2010.

Matsumoto, Gary, "Anthrax Powder: State of the Art?" *Science Magazine* URL: http://www.sciencemag.org/content/302/5650/1492.summary accessed on 11/12/2008.

Mayrakov, Ivan, "How to Find the Sender's Original IP Address Using Email Message Headers," URL:

http://www.johnru.com/active-whois/trace-email.html accessed on 8/4/2008.

McNamara, Melissa, "Anthrax Investigation A 'Cold Case?'" URL: http://www.cbsnews.com/stories/2006/09/18/evening news/main2019769.shtml accessed on 9/20/2008.

Meek, James Gordon, "FBI was told to blame Anthrax scare on Al Qaeda by White House officials," URL: http://www.nydailynews.com/news/national/2008/08/02/2008-08-02_fbi_was_told_to_blame_anthrax_scare_on_a.html accessed 1/18/2009.

Melanson, Donald, "Military-grade 'Guard Dog' hard drive degausser," URL: http://www.engadget.com/2006/06/30/military-grade-guard-dog-hard-drive-degausser/ accessed on 2/12/2009.

Mid-East Realities, "Dick Cheney's Ascent to Power," URL: http://www.middleeast.org/cheney.htm accessed 8/5/2008.

Miller, Judith, June 2, 1999, *The New York Times,* "Cold war leaves a deadly anthrax legacy," URL: http://www.phaster.com/unpretentious/uzbekistan_anthrax.html accessed on 3/30/2008.

Miller, Judith, June 2, 1999, *The New York Times,* "Poison Island: a special report; At bleak Asian site killer germs survive," URL: http://www.nytimes.com/1999/06/02/world/poison-island-a-special-report-at-bleak-asian-site-killer-germs-survive.html accessed on 9/19/2008.

Miller, Judith, June 20, 2000, *The New York Times,* "in a gamble, US Supports Russian Germ Warfare Scientists," URL: http://www.nytimes.com/2000/06/20/science/in-a-gamble-us-supports-russian-germ-warfare-scientists.html accessed on 8/11/2008.

Miller, Judith, Stephen Engelberg and William J. Broad, *The New York Times*, September 4, 2001, "US Germ Warfare Research Pushes Treaty Limits," URL: http://www.nytimes.com/2001/09/04/world/us-germ-warfare-research-pushes-treaty-limits.html accessed on 9/1/2009.

Mitchell, Alanna, Simon Cooper and Carolyn Abraham, "Scientist's deaths are under the microscope," URL:http://www.chemtrailcentral.com/ubb/Forum6/HTML/000623.html accessed on 10/15/2008.

National Academy of Public Administration, "Transforming the FBI: Progress and Challenges,"
URL:http://ceg.files.cmsplus.com/PruneJobsRelevantNAPAPublications/TransformingTheFBI(%2365).pdf accessed on 11/24/2008.

Nordland, Rod and Michael Hirsh, November 3, 2003, *Newsweek,* "The $ 87 Billion Money Pit," URL: http://www.thedailybeast.com/newsweek/2003/11/02/the-87-billion-money-pit.html accessed on 2/13/2010.

Myers, Steven Lee, October 13, 2006, *The New York Times,* "Kazakhstan's Futursitic Capital, Comlpete with Pyramid," URL: http://www.nytimes.com/2006/10/13/world/asia/13astana.html accessed on 9/14/2008.

New York Architcture, "Columbus Circle Fountain," URL: http://nyc-architecture.com/CP/cp021.htm accessed on 3/17/2010.

New York Architcture, "The Flat Iron Building," URL: http://nyc-architecture.com/GRP/GRP024.htm accessed on 3/17/2010.

NOVA, November 13, 2001, "Bioterror," URL: http://www.pbs.org/wgbh/nova/transcripts/2815bioterror.html accessed on 6/7/2010.

NOVA, November 2001, "Interviews with Biowarriors: Bill Patrick," URL: http://www.pbs.org/wgbh/nova/bioterror/biow_patrick.html accessed on 11/28/2008.

Nuclear Threat Initiative, "Kazakhstan Profile," URL: http://www.nti.org/e_research/profiles/Kazakhstan/ accessed on 9/15/2008.

Nuclear Threat Initiative, November 20, 2002, "Kazakhstan: Vozrozhdeniye Anthrax Burial Sites Destroyed," URL: http://www.nti.org/d_newswire/issues/2002/11/20/10p.html accessed on 8/15/2008.

O'Neill, Jennifer, "American Media Inc.," URL: http://www.ibiblio.org/slanews/nln/nln02/winter/index.htm accessed on 10/27/2008.

Pala, Christopher, March 24, 2003, *The San Franciso Gate*, "Hunting down tons of anthrax on a remote island," URL: http://sfgate.com/cgi-bin/article.cgi?f=/c/a/2003/03/24/MN148620.DTL accessed on 8/12/2008.

Pariser, Eli, "Who is Dick Cheney?" URL: http://www.moveon.org/moveonbulletin/bulletin1.html accessed on 8/3/2008.

Pentagon Library, "About the Library," http://www.whs.mil/library/about.htm accessed on 9/14/2008.

Pike, John,"Mossad," URL: http://www.fas.org/irp/world/israel/mossad/ accessed on 12/12/2008.

Public Broadcast Service, "Bioterror," URL: www.pbs.org/wghb/nova/transcripts/2815bioterror60.htm accessed on 9/18/2008.

Purdum, Todd S, October 25, 2001, *The New York Times,* "A Nation Challenged: The Disease; More Checked for Anthrax; US Officials Acknowledge Underestimating Mail Risks," URL: http://www.nytimes.com/2001/10/25/us/nation-challenged-disease-more-checked-for-anthrax-us-officials-acknowledge.html accessed on 2/13/2008.

Reid, Harry, June 27, 2005, Democratic Policy Meeting Hearing, "Opening Statement," URL:

http://dpc.senate.gov/hearings/hearing22/reid.pdf accessed on 2/13/2010.

Rennie, Gabriele, "Decoding the Origin of a Bioagent," *Science and Technology Review*, September 15, 2006. URL: https://www.llnl.gov/str/Sep06/Velsko.html accessed on 11/22/2008.

Risen, James, "Use of Iraq Contractors Costs Billions, Report Says," URL: http://www.nytimes.com/2008/08/12/washington/12contractors.html?ref=jamesrisen Accessed 2/13/2008.

Roffey, Roger, Wilhelm Unge, Jenny Clevström and Kristina S. Westerdahl, "Support to Threat Reduction of the Russian Biological Weapons Legacy - Conversion, Biodefence and the Role of Biopreparat," URL: http://www.foi.se/upload/english/reports/foi-russian-bio-weapons-legacy.pdf accessed on 3/19/2008.

Rowley, Colleen, "Memo to FBI Director Robert Mueller," URL: http://www.apfn.org/apfn/wtc_whistleblower1.htm accessed on 11/23/2008.

Scheer, Christopher, "Ten Appalling Lies We Were Told About Iraq," URL: http://www.alternet.org/story/16274 accessed on 11/19/2008.

Schwartz, Moshe, December 14, 2009, Congressional Research Service,"Department of Defense Contractors in Iraq and Afghanistan: Background and Analysis," URL: http://fpc.state.gov/documents/organization/130803.pdf accessed on 2/13/2010.

Secret Service Codenames, "Locations/Groups/Organizations," URL: http://www.2600.com/secret/more/codes.html accessed 2/5/2009.

Security and Safety Supply. URL: http://www.securityandsafetysupply.com/ accessed on 12/21/2008.

Seisenbayev, Rollan, May-August 2005, University of Oklahoma WLT Kids, "The Day the World Collapsed," URL: http://www.ou.edu/wltkids/Pdf_files_Kazakh/WLTKids_May-Aug05-3Story.pdf accessed on 1/31/2009.

Shane, Scott, "Army Suspends Germ Research at Maryland Lab," URL: "http://www.nytimes.com/2009/02/10/washington/10germs.html accessed 2/11/2009.

Shoham, Dany and Stuart M. Jacobsen, *International Journal of Intelligence and Counterintelligence,* "Technical Intelligence in Retrospect: The 2001 Anthrax Powder, URL: http://newsdetails.blogspot.com/2007/05/technical-intelligence-in-retrospect.html accesed on 3/19/2008.

Simons, Lewis M., "Weapons of Mass Destruction," URL: http://ngm.nationalgeographic.com/ngm/0211/feature1/ accessed on 1/29/2009.

Simons, Lewis M., Online Extra, "Weapons of Mass Destruction," URL: http://ngm.nationalgeographic.com/ngm/0211/feature1/fulltext.html accessed on 1/29/2009.

Simpich, Bill, "Anthrax Case Reopens: Why Did FBI Let Fort Detrich Scientists Investigate Themselves?" URL: http://www.indybay.org/newsitems/2008/09/30/18542046.php accessed 11/15/2008.

Sloan, Sam, "Grand Jury Secrecy Rules," URL: http://www.anusha.com/rule6e.htm accessed 11/26/2008.

Smith, Richard M., "The Anthrax Investigation," URL: http://www.computerbytesman.com/anthrax/princeton.htm accessed on 11/27/2008.

"Status of Pentagon Librarian," http://lists.webjunction.org/wjlists/web4lib/2001-September/004293 accessed on 9/14/2008.

Stegnar, Peter and Tony Wrixon, "Semipalatinsk Revisited: Radiological Evaluation of the Former Nuclear Test Site," URL: http://www.iaea.org/Publications/Magazines/Bulletin/Bull404/article2.pdf aceessed 1/31/2009.

Tell, David, *The Weekly Standard Web*, September 16, 2002, URL: http://www.weeklystandard.com/Content/Public/Articles/000/000/001/623rbipi.asp?ZoomFont=YES accesses on 12/1/2008.

Terhune, Chad, "Canadian Officials Did Research on Anthrax Before US Attacks," *The Wall Street Journal.* December 12, 2001.URL: http://www.ph.ucla.edu/epi/bioter/canadianresearchanthrax.html accessed on 1/2/2010.

The 9-11 Commission Report, URL: http://www.gpoaccess.gov/911/index.html accessed on 9/21/2008.

The Cold War Museum, "Fall of the Soviet Union," URL: http://www.coldwar.org/articles/90s/fall_of_the_soviet_union.asp accessed on 10/20/2008.

The Military Librarian, "Pentagon Library News," http://units.sla.org/division/dmil/Fall01.pdf accessed on 9/14/2008.

"The mysterious deaths of top microbiologists." URL:http://whatreallyhappened.com/WRHARTICLES/deadbiologists.html accessed on 10/15/2008.

The National Security Archive, "Volume V: Anthrax at Sverdlovsk, 1979," URL: http://www.gwu.edu/~nsarchiv/NSAEBB/NSAEBB61/ accessed on 9/18/2008.

ThinkQuest, "Time Since Death." URL: http://library.thinkquest.org/04oct/00206/text_ta_time_since_death.htm accessed 12/21/2008.

Tucker, Jonathan B. and Raymond A. Zilinskas, eds., Center for Nonproliferation Studies, Monterey Institute of International Studies, Occasional Paper No. 9, "The 1971 Smallpox Epidemic in Aralsk, Kazakhstan, and the Soviet Biological Warfare Program, URL: http://cns.miis.edu/opapers/op1/op1.pdf accessed on 9/19/2008.

Tucker, Jonathan B., November 6, 1998, "Biological Weapons in the Former Soviet Union: An Interview with Dr. Kenneth Alibek," URL: http://cns.miis.edu/npr/pdfs/alibek63.pdf accessed on 11/30/2008.

Tucker, Jonathan B., *Arms Control Today*, October 2004, "Biological Threat Assessment: Is the Cure Worse than the Disease?" URL: http://www.armscontrol.org/act/2004_10/Tucker accessed on 9/19/2009.

United States Courts, "Amendments to the Federal Rules of Criminal Procedure, URL: http://www.uscourts.gov/uscourts/RulesAndPolicies/rules/supct1105/CR_Clean.pdf accessed on 11/26/2008.

United States Department of State, "Background Note: Kazakhstan," URL: http://www.state.gov/r/pa/ei/bgn/5487.htm accessed on 9/18/2008.

United States District Court for the Eastern District of Virginia, "Indictment against Robert Philip Hanssen," URL: http://www.fas.org/irp/ops/ci/hanssen_indict.html accessed on 10/14/2008.

United States Marine Corps, "Marine Corps Base Quantico," URL: http://www.quantico.usmc.mil/ accessed on 10/12/2008.

University of California Los Angeles School of Public Health, Department of Epidemiology, "American Anthrax Outbreak of 2001," URL: http://www.ph.ucla.edu/epi/bioter/detect/antdetect_intro.html accessed on multiple occasions 10/4/2008 - 1/11/2010.

University of Dundee, "Department of Forensic Medicine, Lecture Notes: Time of Death," URL: http://www.dundee.ac.uk/forensicmedicine/notes/timedeath.pdf accessed on 12/21/2008.

United States Army, "About Dugway Proving Grounds," URL: http://www.dugway.army.mil/index.php/index/content/id/6 accessed on 3/22/2010.

United States Department of State, "Chapter 6—Terrorist Organizations," URL: http://www.state.gov/s/ct/rls/crt/2007/103714.htm accessed on 11/30/2008.

United States House of Representatives, December 5, 2001, Committee on International Relations, "Russia, Iraq, and Other Potential Sources of Anthrax, Smallpox and Other Bioterrorist Weapons," URL: http://www.house.gov/international—relations accessed on 1/30/2008.

Velsko, S.P., February 15, 2005, Lawrence Livermore National Laboratory, "Physical and Chemical Analytical Analysis: A key to Bioforensics," URL: https://e-reports-ext.llnl.gov/pdf/316652.pdf accessed on 11/6/2007.

Vulliamy, Ed, and Ed Hellmore, "So who is terrorising America with anthrax?" URL: http://www.guardian.co.uk/world/2001/oct/21/terrorism.anthrax?INTCMP=SRCH accessed on 9/16/2008.

Waggoner, Kim and Kathryn H. Suchma, editors, "FBI Handbook of Forensic Services,"URL: https://www.ncjrs.gov/app/publications/Abstract.aspx?id=250140 accessed on 1/24/2010.

Warrick, Joby, *Washington Post,* June 17, 2002, "Security Lacking at Facilities Used for Soviet Bioweapons Research," URL: http://www.ph.ucla.edu/epi/bioter/ruspoorguardedpast.html accessed on 10/21/2008.

Warrick, Joby, April 12, 2006, *The Washington Post,* "Lacking Biolabs, Trailers Carried Case for War," URL: http://www.washingtonpost.com/wp-dyn/content/article/2006/04/11/AR2006041101888_pf.html accessed on 3/23/2010.

Washington University,"Lecture Highlights 3/4/20; Forensic Genetics," URL: http://public.wsu.edu/~earthsch/data/lec_34.pdf accessed on 3/3/2010.

Weiss, Rick and Joby Warrick, December 13, 2001, *The Washington Post,* "Army Working on Weapons-Grade Anthrax," URL: http://www.ph.ucla.edu/epi/bioter/armyweaponsgradeanthrax.html accessed on 3/22/2010.

Weiss, Rick, December 14, 2001."Army's Anthrax Material Surprises Some Experts," *The Washington Post,"* URL: http://www.washingtonpost.com/ac2/wp-dyn?pagename=article&contentId=A40896-2001Dec13 accessed on 3/22/2010.

Wikipedia, "First Chechen War," URL: http://en.wikipedia.org/wiki/First_Chechen_War accessed on 2/12/2009.

Wikipedia, "Second Chechen War," URL: http://en.wikipedia.org/wiki/Second_Chechen_War accessed on 2/12/2009.

Wikipedia, "Secret Service Codename," URL: http://en.wikipedia.org/wiki/Secret_Service_codename accessed 2/5/2009.

Wilson, Joseph C., July 6, 2003, *The New York Times, "What I Didn't Find in Africa,"* URL: http://www.nytimes.com/2003/07/06/opinion/what-i-didn-t-find-in-africa.html accessed on 8/5/2008.

Woellert, Lorraine, Richard S. Dunham, and Diwata Fonte, "Tom Daschle hits the ground running," URL: http://www.businessweek.com/magazine/content/01_29/b3741054.htm accessed on 11/15/2008.

York, Anthony, "Why Daschle and Leahy?" URL: http://dir.salon.com/politics/feature/2001/11/21/anthrax/index.html accessed on 11/15/2008.

Zahn, Paula, CNN American Morning with Paula Zahn, August 8, 2002, "Interview with Stan Bedlington, CIA Counter-Terrorism Expert," URL: http://transcripts.cnn.com/TRANSCRIPTS/0208/08/ltm.17.html accessed on 11/30/2008.

Zahra, Peter, "DNA- Analysis and Probability," URL: http://www.lawlink.nsw.gov.au/lawlink/pdo/ll_pdo.nsf/pages/PDO_dnaanalysis accessed on 11/22/2008.

ZFacts, "Reasons for Iraq War: Bush or Cheney?" URL: http://zfacts.com/p/775.html accessed 2/24/2010.

Acknowledgments

This was not my first attempt at writing a novel and while I have never climbed Mount Everest, I liken the process to that feat of endurance. You start your journey looking at a blank page on a computer screen much in the way that climbers must view the distant summit. You ask yourself, how will I ever get there? With head down, you plod ahead, one step at a time, until you reach base camp, the first draft. Several drafts and numerous edits later you've made it to through camps I, II and III and have reached High Camp number IV at an altitude of 26,000 feet. You feel dizzy, the atmosphere is impossibly thin, and the mind can easily lose its grip. What stands between you and success is negotiating the world of publishing, which may be more difficult than the Cornice Traverse or Hillary Step.

The idea for *Mailaise* came out of research for a non-fiction chapter that appears in Mark Dworkin's book, *Cases in Field Epidemiology: A Global Perspective.* I thank Marci Layton for her support and understanding and for being too busy to write of our experiences during the 2001 anthrax investigation herself. Writing the chapter helped me find the discipline missing in previous attempts at completing a novel.

I wish to thank some of the many people I've met along the way who provided support, encouragement and inspiration: Lindsay Moore, Steve Morse, Joan Curtis, Joel Ackelsberg, Nancy Perry, Marilyn Campbell, Vasudha Reddy, Catherine Dentinger, Farah Parvez, Bonnie Um, Sekai Chideya, Jeff Ojemann, Karen Selboe, Sangeeta Hingorani, Lisa Cregan, Laurie Slotnick, Ira Levine, Nel Yomtov and Louise Quesada.

Many thanks to Gaywyn Moore whose kind but insightful comments on a very early draft kept this project from ending up in the unfinished works folder on my MacBook Pro. To Marvin Cohen, author and octagenarian first baseman, who critiqued a draft and provided cheery encouragement. To Sharon Balter, poet, friend and colleague whose gentle prodding kept me moving forward. To Matthew Pitt and Celina DeLeon for their help in shaping the manuscript and Bill Vernick whose knack with words helped sharpened my own. And warm thanks to Suki Tsui, proofreader and HTML whiz, who endured innumerable hours of silence and solitude while I secluded myself in a world inhabited only by my characters. And finally to all my real-world disease detective colleagues whose real-life escapades far outdo my imagination in suspense and humor.

September 21, 2011

About the Author

Don Weiss was born in the Bronx and composed his first story at the age of six while sitting on the stoop of his Inwood apartment building. It was an illustrated story about the misadventures of a neighborhood boy named Andy. He attended a small liberal arts college in Pennsylvania and embarked on a career as a chemist before switching to medicine. He practiced urban pediatrics in New York City and the Midwest for seven years and then entered the field of public health. He was one of the epidemiologists who investigated the 2001 anthrax letter attack and resides in New York City.

Website: http://thedetectologist.blogspot.com/
Twitter: @detectologist

Made in the USA
Charleston, SC
13 November 2011